ROBERT A. SIGAFOOS

Wave the Bloody Shirt

The Life and Times
of
General Nathan Bedford Forrest, CSA

A CIVIL WAR NOVEL

ARC Press of Cane Hill

© 2000   Robert A. Sigafoos
All Rights Reserved

ISBN: 0-938041-48-7

No part of this book may be reproduced or transmitted in any form or by any means, electronic or mechanical, including photocopying, recording or by any informational storage or retrieval system except by a reviewer who may quote brief passages in a review to be printed in a magazine or newspaper, without permission in writing from the publisher or author.

Special Thanks:

Front cover drawing of the Battle of Fort Pillow is from *Harper's Weekly*, April 30, 1864. The Thomas Nast caricature, "This is a White Man's Government" is from *Harper's Weekly*, September 5, 1868.

The author gives special thanks for the use of their resources to the Library of Congress, The National Archives, Walter Reed Hospital, the University of Arkansas, Duke University, the University of Memphis, the University of North Carolina, Tulane University, the Memphis and Shelby County Public Library, the Tennessee State Library, the Chickamauga and Chattanooga National Military Park, the Pea Ridge National Military Park, and the Shiloh National Military Park.

Typography/Design: Barbara Shumaker Meeker

ARC Press of Cane Hill
13581 Tyree Mountain Road
P.O. Box 188
Cane Hill, Arkansas 72717
501-824-3821

Printed in the United States of America

Table of Contents

Foreword v

Chapter

  1. The Reporter 7

  2. Slave Trader 24

  3. Recruiter 49

  4. Basic Training 67

  5. First Combat 85

  6. Panic 101

  7. Furlough 109

  8. Shiloh 112

  9. General Wheeler 134

10. The Chase 146

11. The Last Supper 153

12. Lieutenant Gould 169

13. Chickamauga 176

14. General Bragg 192

15. Reunion 197

16. Jefferson Davis 208

17. Winter Camp 216

18. Fort Pillow 228

19. Uproar 240

20. The Execution	249
21. Brice's Cross Roads	262
22. The Days After	272
23. The Planning Session	288
24. Discipline	303
25. Franklin and Nashville	316
26. Surrender	331
27. Reconstruction	351
28. New York	361
29. Radical Republicans	380
30. The Convert	383
31. Funeral	396
Appendix • Final Roll Call	410
About the Author	415

FOREWORD

General Nathan Bedford Forrest was the most controversial military figure of the Civil War, and even today his reputation lingers on as one of history's greatest and most brutal leaders. This book dwells on the reasons why in the latter 19th century he generated such emotion in both the North and the South. Forrest takes his place with Robert E. Lee, Ulysses S. Grant, William Tecumseh Sherman, Abraham Lincoln, and Jefferson Davis as leading Civil War figures.

Forrest was unique — an original. His strong, vitriolic personality, his boldness, and his lack of formal education and military training in the conventional style of the 19th century caused him to be an outcast among his peers. Readers of this book will either admire him, pity him, or hate him. His life exemplified the best and worst in people of his time.

An effort has been made to be accurate in describing locales where events unfold. The dates and places where major events occur are true to the record. The major characters were real. Many of the minor characters are fictitious.

Lafcadio Hearn, correspondent for the *Cincinnati Commercial* writing under the pseudonym, Ozias Midwinter, covered General Forrest's funeral. His extensive notes written on November 1, 1877 appear in the *Commercial*'s edition of November 6, 1877.

This is an historical novel. Liberties have been taken in developing the conversations between General Forrest and many of the supporting characters. From the evidence I gathered in researching General Forrest, other war and postwar personalities, and events of the day, the topics discussed in the give-and-take among them were based on relevant themes in their private, military, or business lives.

R.A.S.
Fayetteville, Arkansas

1 • The Reporter

Memphis, Tennessee, Tuesday, October 30, 1877

The paddle wheeler A.C. Donnelly from Cincinnati arrived at 7:30 a.m. at the levee in front of Memphis. The one-year old packet carried passengers, general cargo and mail on its scheduled run to New Orleans. On board was 27-year old Lafcadio Hearn, a part-time correspondent for the *Cincinnati Commercial*. Hearn was on his way to Louisiana to do a special report on political corruption in that state.

Hearn, curious to see the colorful panorama of a dozen steamboats tied up one behind the other along the one-half mile long levee, stood in the pilot house next to Captain Henry V. Hart, the A.C. Donnelly's master.

"Isn't that a circus down there, Mr. Hearn? Look at all those roustabouts loading and unloading cotton bales. And look at all the draymen and mules moving along like busy ants up there on Front Street."

"Mr. Hearn, I've seen as many as 30,000 bales of cotton out there on the levee. You're probably looking at 10,000 today. Memphis is the largest interior depot of cotton in America. Look up there on Front Street — all those cotton factors: J.R. Godwin & Co.; J.T. Fargason & Co.; Hill, Fontaine & Co.; Porter, Taylor & Co. They buy and sell all this cotton. Memphis lives on cotton. A lot of fortunes are being made here."

"Captain, I've never seen anything quite like this. Look at all the black smoke against the bluffs. Are steamboats causing that?"

"Some of it, Mr. Hearn. But much of it comes from Memphis. It's a dirty city and it also smells bad. The people burn soft coal which throws a black cloud over the city. Mixed with the smell of garbage they throw into open drainage ditches a few blocks from here, this isn't a healthy place to be. It's a disease-ridden city. Four years ago both yellow fever and cholera struck here. Some 7,000 cases, and about 2,300 deaths."

On the levee in front of the A.C. Donnelly a group of passengers who were waiting to board crowded around a newsboy who had an armful of newspapers.

"Read about General Forrest...the General is dead...the great General died last night," the boy kept yelling even as he passed out copies and made change.

Hearn asked Captain Hart, "Is that General Forrest the noted Civil War cavalry raider? The Fort Pillow massacre fellow?"

"Yes, but let's find out." The Captain then yelled down, "Hey, boy!...Hey, boy! Bring some papers on board. I'll take ten copies."

"Yes, sir, Captain. Give me a few minutes."

Within five minutes, Captain Hart handed Hearn a copy. The latter's eyes caught the headline: "A Great Man Has Fallen: The Death of General Forrest." Quickly Hearn scanned the two-columned article. Fascinated with the account, Hearn turned to Hart and said, "Captain, I'm going to get off here at Memphis. This is a real story. Forrest was no ordinary soldier, was he?"

"No indeed, Mr. Hearn. If you were to ask in Memphis or almost any other Southern city who were the three most important people of all time they would probably say, Jesus, Robert E. Lee and Nathan Bedford Forrest. At least most would say that. Not everybody was fond of Forrest.

"If I were you, Mr. Hearn, I'd get over to the Peabody House right away. Most of the influential businessmen and politicians will be there discussing Forrest. You can probably interview several who were close to him.

"Write a good story for me. We'll talk about it the next

time we meet on the river. And Hearn, one word of warning. Order only bottled water at the hotels and restaurants. The private wells are all contaminated. The citizens here drink their own liquefied excrement."

"Thank you, Captain Hart."

Hearn gathered his belongings, and disembarked the A.C. Donnelly. He asked a policeman stationed on the levee directions to the Peabody House. "It's a short walk across the levee to Jefferson Street. Go about a city block, then turn right on Main Street. It's about three blocks down Main at the northwest corner of Main and Adams. Get one of those niggers sitting over there on the wagons to help you with your valise.

Lafcadio Hearn

"What do you think about General Forrest dying, sir?"

"It's a big story around here, isn't it?" said Hearn.

"Yes, sir, he was one of us. No goddamn Scotch-Irish blueblood! Worked his way up the hard way, I'll tell you, he's a hero among us Irish."

Hearn acknowledged what the affable officer told him with a nod, and proceeded across the cobblestone levee. On Jefferson Street in front of almost every business were small groups of men discussing the only major topic on anyone's mind in Memphis that day — the death of General Forrest.

The same was true around the corner on Main Street. Standing alone in front of the large retail store, "B. Lowenstein & Bros." at Main and Jefferson Streets, was an elderly man who asked Hearn as he passed, "Sir, when is the funeral? Do you know? I don't want to miss it. No, sir!"

Hearn responded politely, "I don't know. I've just arrived in Memphis."

Then the man said, "Old Forrest was some fighting machine, yes, sir."

Just before 9:00 a.m. Hearn arrived at the five-story Peabody House. The lobby was crowded with men. A thick haze of cigar smoke hung just below the ceiling. The conversations were about the death of General Forrest. Some small groups talked quietly showing respect for the Civil War leader. Others were more animated as if some in the conversation were arguing perhaps negatively about Forrest. Hearn approached the front desk, and asked to see the hotel's manager.

"I'm Seth Appleby, assistant manager, sir. The manager is indisposed right now. How may I help you?"

"I'm with the *Cincinnati Commercial*, assigned to cover General Forrest's funeral," said Hearn in an authoritative voice. "I would like to interview some of the General's friends and associates. Would you be able to introduce me to some of these people, sir?"

"You just missed Jefferson Davis. He was here for about one hour, but left 15 minutes ago to visit his wife and daughter. They still live here in Memphis. I'm certain he'll stay for the funeral, sir. President Davis will undoubtedly be a pallbearer," replied Appleby.

"Is there anyone else in the lobby or dining room right now who knew the General intimately?"

"Yes, Dr. James Cowan and Major Gilbert Rambaut, both of whom served with Forrest throughout the war, are in the dining room. Come with me. I'll introduce you. What's your name?"

"Lafcadio Hearn."

"This way, Mr. Hearn."

"Gentlemen, this is Mr. Hearn, a reporter from Cincinnati. He'd like a word with you concerning General Forrest," said Appleby.

"Please join us, Mr. Hearn." said the gracious Dr. Cowan. "Are you here to cover the funeral?"

"Yes, I am. I also hope to prepare a lengthy profile on

General Forrest. Mr. Appleby mentioned that both you and Major Rambaut were close to him."

"Well, I'd say so," said Dr. Cowan. "I first met the General in 1844 or 1845. He married my cousin, Mary; and I attended the wedding. So I guess I was his oldest friend other than his brothers and Mary."

Major Gilbert Rambaut, the 41-year old former Chief of Commissary in Forrest's Cavalry kept looking at Hearn and smiling injudiciously. Hearn was odd looking. He had a dark olive colored face with a sharp nose and an enlarged, protruding right eye. And he was slight of build, weighing no more than 130 pounds.

"You speak with a distinct Irish accent, Mr. Hearn," interjected Rambaut in his slow drawl. "Do you come from Ireland?"

"Yes, I grew up in Ireland, but I was born in Greece. My mother was Greek; my father, a soldier in the British Army. But I went to school in Dublin, Ireland, and emigrated to the United States eight years ago."

"Then you weren't here for the war?" asked Rambaut.

"No, but as a boy I read about the war."

"What did you read about General Forrest?"

"Only that he was a daring Confederate cavalry leader, and that he was widely acclaimed here in the South," replied Hearn.

"Well, Mr. Hearn, I think Dr. Cowan would agree with me that General Forrest had a lot of arrows in his quiver. As well as being a great military leader, he was an energetic businessman throughout his whole life. But I guess your main interest would be his military career."

"That would be my first interest, of course," said Hearn.

"I was with Forrest almost the whole war," said Rambaut. "I was a prisoner of war for three months in 1863. That was the only gap. He had a keen, trenchant military perception of everything going on around him. He had those fierce-looking eyes on a twisted face shouting wildly first to the right then to the left, 'Forward boys and give 'em hell,' or 'Rally boys, rally!' He had that strange, shrill voice that could be heard above the roar of gunfire. He was totally without caution. It was difficult not to be aware of his presence. He was at the center of every fight screaming orders of encouragement. Why he wasn't killed is a mystery."

Then Dr. Cowan added, "Undeniably Forrest had intuitive powers. In addition, he had one real advantage over his enemy. He knew almost every square mile of terrain in Tennessee, North Mississippi and Alabama from his pre-war business travels and his boyhood days. He knew hundreds of people by name and they knew him. So during the war he had an effective intelligence system using friendly citizens."

Then Rambaut continued, "Some of the Confederate high command in Richmond considered Forrest the most undisciplined of all ranking officers. General Bragg, who President Davis brought to Richmond after the debacle at Chickamauga and Chattanooga, disliked Forrest. He felt Forrest was not only an untrained officer, but also an insubordinate one. He poisoned Jefferson Davis' mind about Forrest. That assessment I would not agree with. Forrest, unlike many of the West Point-trained officers, realized the advantages of boldness at critical moments in the fighting. He wasn't in the habit of consulting a military handbook or manual before making a decision. It wasn't as if he didn't have a logical plan to implement. He understood quickly what was happening around him and reacted spontaneously. Federal commanders were bewildered by his nonconformity. And Forrest was relentless."

Hearn asked, "I remember reading that General

Forrest had no formal education. How did he function so successfully?"

"I'll answer that briefly," said Dr. Cowan. "He learned all of what he knew from experience and using his inquisitive mind. He spent a lifetime learning by observing and asking questions of others. It's true he knew nothing of English grammar. He could express himself well verbally, but not in writing. Without the help of Major Anderson and Major Strange, and editor Matt Gallaway, to put his ideas and orders into writing, he could not have functioned. The General would tell them what he wished to say, then they would prepare a draft copy for his review."

"Do you fault the General for anything?" Hearn asked.

Rambaut looked at Dr. Cowan first, then said apologetically, "General Forrest had a wicked temper. Some would say a violent temper. But wicked is how I would describe it. He had it back in his slave trading days when I first met him, and he still had it up until a few years ago. He took offense easily, and often reacted by assaulting his adversary. He had a primitive, backwoodsman sense of justice. Those of us who knew him well understood his temperament, and knew when to back away."

Dr. Cowan added, "Oh, he had his idiosyncrasies and a mean streak, but what I most fault him for was his failure to seek promotions for some of his outstanding officers. Take for example Major John Strange and Major Charles Anderson. Fairness dictated that each should have been at least a full colonel. No two fellows on Forrest's staff worked harder and showed more leadership and courage. I believe Forrest regarded them highly. But still he didn't send forward recommendations for promotion. He just didn't do anything about it despite my

13

occasional suggestions."

Hearn looked at Rambaut, and asked, "What about you?" Did you feel you should have been promoted to the rank of colonel?"

"Well, Mr. Hearn, I was just a lowly innkeeper in 1861, and rising to the rank of major was a high honor for me. I was proud to be on the General's staff. He liked me even though he thought I was more interested in being mischievous than fighting. I used to upset him, I think. He always thought I spent too much time horsing around. He'd holler, 'Rambaut...Rambaut...get in here. Stop acting like a jackass.' I'd go in his tent, and he'd say, 'Rambaut, what are you up to?' And I would answer, 'Just telling some jokes, sir.' Then he would say, 'Some of those salesmen's jokes you heard when you worked at the Worsham House in Memphis?' I'd answer, 'No, but would you like to hear the one I just told?' He would look at me and say, 'Save it until after the war. I don't have time to waste.'"

"Mr. Hearn,...Major Rambaut and I must go," said Dr. Cowan who was still smiling after listening to Rambaut's discourse on Forrest. "We're meeting with Mrs. Forrest and her son, William, this morning."

"May I ask one more favor, please?" said Hearn. "Would you suggest some others I should interview?"

Dr. Cowan answered, "Yes, you must talk with Colonel Minor Meriwether and with Matt Gallaway, editor of the *Memphis Daily Appeal*. They were closely associated with the General throughout his adult life. Meriwether lives over on Union Street; and Gallaway will be in his office at the *Appeal* at 282 Second Street."

"Thank you very much, gentlemen. You have been most kind," said Hearn.

Hearn, back in the lobby, was greeted by Seth Appleby. "Did your meeting go well?"

"Yes, they were quite candid, thank you."

"Mr. Hearn, I don't know what type article you are preparing, but it occurred to me that you might want to talk with Solomon Featherstone, our shoeshine boy over there in our billiard parlor. He was a slave sold out of Forrest's Mart about 20 years ago. Solomon can tell you some interesting stories, I'm sure."

"Thank you again. I shall do that," said the grateful Hearn.

Approaching the shoeshine stand, Hearn asked, "Are you Solomon Featherstone?"

"Yas, suh, I am."

"I'm in Memphis covering the funeral of General Forrest. I understand you were one of the slaves sold by him when he had his slave mart."

"Yas, suh, that was in 1857. I was 18 years old, and brought here from Virginia by the Forrest brothers. The ol' Gen-ril bought and sold us like hogs. The Gen-ril and his brothers all worked there. They wuz debbils foh sure. Mean critters. Used bullwhips on all us if we didn't move fast enough. But de Gen-ril treated his brothers jest like us niggers. When he came in de pen, we'd all start shakin'.

"Ol' John, de cripple, he'd git drunk and holler at us somethin' awful. I kinda felt sorry for him. He always say, 'If you don't mind, it will be hard times when my brothers git here.'

"I wuz bought by Colonel Carroll, along with Sevilla and Flora to be house servants on Lauderdale Street. After de war, I started doin' odd jobs. Came to de hotel here last year."

Hearn asked, "Did you ever speak with General Forrest when he came into the hotel?"

"I'd always say, 'Good morning or good afternoon.' I don't think he knew that I had been sold out of his pen.

How would he remember me? I wuz jest one of hundreds and hundreds of niggers he sold. But, I'll tell you this, mister. He made me nervous when he wuz in here. I'd start fidgetin'."

Hearn left the Peabody at 10:30 a.m. to try to find Colonel Meriwether, the 50-year old civil engineer who resided a few blocks from the hotel. Fortunately, Meriwether was home recovering from a cold and invited Hearn to come in. Hearn explain his mission, and Colonel Meriwether said he would be pleased to answer any questions.

"How long did you know the General?"

"Well, it was sometime in the mid 1850s he came to see me. I was chief engineer for the construction of the Memphis & Grenada Railroad. Forrest was interested in plantation land speculation at the time. Specifically, he was probing for business opportunities such a railroad might create down in Mississippi. He had also been to see Colonel Sam Tate, president of the Memphis & Charleston Railroad, asking somewhat the same questions. Tate's railroad went east out of Memphis over to Stevenson in northern Alabama.

"From time-to-time he'd visit me to ask additional questions about railroads. I enjoyed these meetings. He was so curious and so energetic. Of course, my wife Elizabeth and I were never pleased that our new friend made his living dealing in slaves. I told him he should engage in less unsavory pursuits. Maybe it was our influence that got him to close his slave mart a year or two before the war."

"Colonel Meriwether, you say you knew General Forrest almost from the time he moved to Memphis from Mississippi. Sir, can you describe what he was like in those days?"

"Before I met Forrest, I had heard of his reputation in

those days?"

"Before I met Forrest, I had heard of his reputation as a ruffian and violent man. Supposedly, he had killed several people down in Mississippi. He lived his early life as a primitive frontiersman. Unless you were landed gentry in northern Mississippi in those days, you lived a survival existence at best among some desperate people. That life molded his rough hewn character. Although he became a man of affairs later in life, he still bore the traces of violence in his personality. He couldn't brook a personal affront back in the 1850s and he still couldn't come to terms with such a circumstance right up until the time he got sick."

"What did you most admire in the General?"

"I guess it was his industriousness a few years after the war in trying to construct a profitable railroad between here and Selma, Alabama. He was tenacious in his dedication. It totally consumed his energies for five years."

"Didn't his railroad venture cause some difficulties between you two?"

"If you are referring to the temporary severance of our friendship, you are correct — sad to say. Forrest was at a breaking point physically and financially with this failed railroad. It sucked up money like a sponge. There was never enough to keep construction on schedule. So when I refused to certify the completion of certain portions of the rail line when in fact they had not been completed, he was outraged and he verbally threatened me. You see...he needed certification in order for bond funds to be released for the railroad's use.

"Fortunately, two years later Matt Gallaway — our mutual friend — reunited us at the Confederate ceremony at Elmwood Cemetery in 1875. We remained friends to his death.

"Colonel Meriwether, what were General Forrest's outstanding strengths or qualities?"

"Mr. Hearn, Forrest had great natural intellect. He was a good judge of human nature. In the postwar years he was keenly interested in the major political and business issues of the times. He could penetrate the maze and get to the heart of issues.

"I was always impressed with his uncanny ability to organize things whether it was in the military or in his private business ventures. He could sift through the details then act swiftly. Constant preparedness was his principal strength, I believe."

"What about his faults?"

"Well, Mr. Hearn, we all have faults. Forrest's? His lack of formal education was a handicap. It caused him to be classified as a social misfit among the Confederate aristocratic leadership. His brutishness caused many to avoid him and to fear him. There is probably some truth that he may have enjoyed killing or intimidating some people. Or perhaps more correctly I should say that it didn't appear to bother him that he killed someone or thrashed someone unmercifully. As far as I can remember, he never expressed regret. He wasn't a compassionate person."

"Colonel Meriwether, you seem so different from the General in education, social breeding, and temperament. What did you two have in common?"

Laughing cautiously he replied, "To be truthful, not much. I suppose it was his energy and resourcefulness. I admired his ability to create successful businesses before the war. And after the war, despite all the obstacles of Reconstruction and a destroyed South, he remained optimistic that somehow or other he could succeed. Only when his railroad collapsed in 1874 did he seem discouraged. He never got over that failure. It affected him far more than the surrender of the Confederate army in 1865."

"I've been looking at you carefully since we started talking trying to figure out whom you remind me of, Colonel. Now I know! With your profile and well-trimmed graying beard, you look like General Robert E. Lee," said Hearn in a serious tone.

Laughing heartily, Colonel Meriwether said, "Mr. Hearn, how do you know that? General Lee was dead at the time you came here from Ireland. Or are you saying I look like the dead Robert E. Lee?"

Hearn, slightly embarrassed answered, "Sir, I saw a portrait of General Lee in his prime."

Both laughed as Meriwether led Hearn to the door. As they shook hands, Meriwether asked, "Are you planning to visit editor Gallaway?"

"Yes, sir, I hope to see him this afternoon."

"Good, Gallaway was with Forrest throughout the war. They had been close friends for over 20 years. Gallaway is a man of principle. He's a strong-willed person who never budges an inch if he thinks principle is involved. He should be a fine source for you."

"Thank you, Colonel Meriwether."

Hearn walked to the *Memphis Daily Appeal* office on Second Street to make an appointment to see Colonel Gallaway. "He'll be here at 3:00 p.m. if you want to see him," said a clerk.

As Hearn returned to Main Street near the Peabody House, he noticed he was missing a button on his coat. He was directed to a nearby tailor shop run by Emanuel Zoeller, a German immigrant who had come to Memphis in 1850. As Hearn entered the shop, he was greeted by Zoeller, a wiry, bespectacled, 50-year old master tailor wearing a tape measure around his neck.

"Do you have a button for this coat?" inquired Hearn.

"Yes, of course. I can sew it on in two minutes, then you can be on your way," said Zoeller in his thick German accent.

"I am with the *Cincinnati Commercial* newspaper, Mr. Zoeller. May I ask your feelings about the death of General Forrest?"

"Sir, I will give you my opinion. Justice required that he should have met with a violent death. Forrest was a hypocrite. He had no deep philosophical convictions about the Confederacy. He was a vicious brute with blood all over his hands. He went to war for two reasons only — so he could keep his niggers and his friends, theirs; and he could kill people legally.

"Old Bedford wasn't the hero folks think he was. He was a bully of the worst kind. From the day he came to Memphis until last night, he was a mean, no-good, sonafabich. If you don't believe me, just walk up and down Main Street and ask some of the shopkeepers about their dealings with Forrest. He always got his way. If he didn't threaten you verbally, he'd stare at you with those fierce eyes as if he'd kill you just as soon as look at you any longer. I'd breathe a sigh of relief when he left. No, sir, I can't say that I'm sorry he's dead.

"I heard at the end he pissed more than he drank. He suffered from constant thirst and a nagging fever. Isn't that something! Here we have this menacing Captain Blackbeard laid low by disease, and not shot in the back.

"Now go ask some other shopkeepers about Forrest. I'd be surprised if they told you anything different from what I've said."

Promptly at 3:00 p.m. Hearn entered Matt Gallaway's small disheveled office. The 57-year old, heavily bearded Gallaway was leaning over from his scratched wooden chair trying to spit into a tarnished brass cuspidor. The floor around the metal cylinder was heavily stained, undoubtedly the result of Gallaway's failure to hit it on frequent occasions. The room had an odor of stale cigar smoke.

"Does the *Cincinnati Commercial*'s office look like this, Hearn?" growled Gallaway looking up just briefly to acknowledge Hearn's presence.

"Of course, sir. All newspaper offices look like this. That's the nature of the business, I guess."

"What do you get paid in Cincinnati, Hearn?"

"Right now, I get $22.50 a week if I contribute acceptable essays. If the editor doesn't like what I submit, he doesn't pay me anything."

"Sounds like you should be looking for a different line of work. Is your paper in financial trouble?"

"Yes, of course. That's why the pay is uncertain."

"What in-the-hell kind of a name is Lafcadio? Doesn't sound Irish to me."

"Sir, I was born in Greece on the island of Leucadia, one of the Ionian islands. I'm Irish-Greek. My father was Irish serving with the British Army Medical Service in Greece. My mother is Greek."

"Well, I've heard everything now. I've got an undersized Irish-Greek sitting here with a pencil and pad to ask me about a fallen, great Confederate military leader. Why did they send you?"

"They don't even know I'm here, Colonel Gallaway. I'm supposed to be on the river bound for New Orleans. When the A.C. Donnelly docked this morning, I heard the news. It looked like a great opportunity to get a big story."

"So now they'll give you $25 a week, Hearn?" said Gallaway, who was now smiling.

"Hearn, this is a terrible day for me. General Forrest and I were like brothers. Despite the fact that I saw him dying slowly over the past two years, his death last night shocks me. You cannot possibly imagine what a vibrant force this man had been for the past 20 years."

"Well, Colonel Gallaway, people in Memphis have told me today that you too have been a vibrant force. You are referred to as the 'fiery editor,' and Forrest's chief political advisor for 20 years or more. Is that so?"

Gallaway took his huge hand and placed it initially on his partially bald head, then moved it down across his long nose which extended almost to his upper lip, grunted, then said, "I admit it. The banner line of my old newspaper, the *Avalanche*, was: 'The Pen is Mightier Than The Sword.' I have tried to raise the level of consciousness of the citizens of this city. I have presented a spirited defense of the South both before and after the war. General Forrest may have been my first convert. He gave me the impression that he understood I was fighting hypocrisy. And he hated hypocrisy!

"But don't misunderstand me. It was a two-way street. Forrest taught me a lot about courage, resilience and resourcefulness when pushed into a corner. Believe me, we fed on each other's brain."

"How did you two become friends?"

"Forrest was one of the first men I met when I sold my little newspaper in Alabama and moved to Memphis in 1857. Shortly after I started the *Avalanche* he came to my office over on Madison Street to place an advertisement for his slave mart. I needed all the business I could get so I invited him into my office. We talked for an hour or so about the cotton market and general affairs in Memphis. It was a pleasant meeting.

"A month or so later I wrote a provocative editorial questioning the ethics of a certain local politician. Needless to say, that despicable rascal challenged me to a duel. The rules of dueling called for each party to have a 'second,' and often a surgeon to stand by on the dueling field. I had few, if any, friends at the time. Suddenly I remembered Bedford Forrest. So I paid him a visit at his place on Adams Street. He graciously accepted to act as my 'second.' That's how our friendship developed."

"Did the duel take place?"

"No," said Gallaway laughing. "That cowardly rascal feigned illness and the whole thing was forgotten. Frankly, I was disappointed. It had the makings of a great newspaper story — assuming I was successful, of course."

"I'm curious, Colonel Gallaway. What approach did General Forrest take in postwar politics? Wasn't he an outspoken critic of Reconstruction policies introduced by the Federal government right after the war?"

"Forrest like most ex-Confederates opposed vigorously those punitive policies. He was particularly incensed at the policies implemented in Tennessee by the Radical Republicans, particularly by that scoundrel, Governor Brownlow. Those oppressive policies directed at ex-Confederates, like denying us the right to vote, were the root cause of the Ku Klux Klan with which the General may have been nominally involved."

"Nominally, Colonel Gallaway?"

"Yes, Forrest knew about the movement, and he was involved, at least philosophically, in the early organization. But once Governor Brownlow and his Reconstructionists lost control in Tennessee in 1869 and 1870, Forrest urged its disbanding."

"It's been widely reported that General Forrest helped organize the Klan along with General John Gordon of Georgia, General Wade Hampton of South Carolina, and General Albert Pike who lived here in Memphis. And apparently his participation was more than nominal. He held the title of Grand Dragon, or whatever they called the chief. He was more than a sympathizer on the sidelines, Colonel Gallaway."

"Hearn, Congressional hearings were held a few years ago, and the Committee seemed satisfied that Forrest wasn't a Ku Kluxer, or whatever they called themselves.

"Forrest was a convenient whipping boy for many Northerners. They drag that Fort Pillow thing all over the place, and then they added the Ku Klux Klan label.

"Most great men are controversial. Don't you agree? There is always some one or some group trying to pull them down. Believe me, history will be very kind to Forrest. He'll be universally acclaimed as a genuine American hero some day.

"Mr. Hearn, come walk with me over to the Planters Insurance Building on Madison Street. We can continue talking along the way. I'm on the Committee making the arrangements for the funeral tomorrow. It's good to talk with you Hearn about General Forrest. I'll tell you this — I'm going to miss him. He was one of a kind. Forrest proved to the world that it's not always the army with the most men on the battlefield that wins the fight. He was born a military genius just as some men are born poets."

2 • Slave Trader

Memphis, Tennessee, April 1852

At age 32 Nathan Bedford Forrest sold his livery stable in Hernando, a small town in North Mississippi. With his wife, Mary, and his eight-year old son, Willie, they moved 20 miles north to Memphis. Forrest had done business in Memphis since he was 22. He had watched the city grow into an active Mississippi River port handling much of the South's annual cotton crop. So in 1852, using his savings from ten years dealing in horses in Mississippi, he opened stables in Memphis.

Mary influenced Forrest to leave Hernando. "I want Willie to have proper schooling," she said. "Memphis has several private academies. He's a bright boy and deserves an opportunity not available here." Mary was also concerned about her husband's reputation as a violent man with many enemies. "You frighten many people here, Bedford. I worry about what might happen to you."

The river was Memphis' lifeline in the 1850s. The city attracted rugged frontiersmen and German and Irish immigrants — all seeking to carve out a living. Since its origin in 1819 it had a reputation as a haven of toughs and brawlers. It was strategically positioned on the eastern edge of the American frontier. Saloons, card rooms and houses of prostitution catered to the newcomers and transients moving up and down the Mississippi. Street fights, open drunkenness and petty thievery were commonplace. Among the upper class the frequent duels fought by so-called "gentlemen of the city," were held on dueling grounds across the river in Arkansas, or over the Tennessee state line in Mississippi.

The business leaders were from the pioneer Scotch-Irish families that had crossed the Appalachians from Virginia and North Carolina in the 1830s and 1840s. From their offices and warehouses on Front Row — the city's commercial street bordering the Mississippi River — they controlled the region's cotton business, the wholesale grocery and dry goods businesses and the financial institutions.

At the time of Forrest's arrival a new merchant class of Germans was emerging in the city's daily business life. And, unlike the Irish immigrants, the Germans gained social respectability among the established pioneer families.

Forrest opened his livery stable on Adams Street in the heart of the principal slave mart district. Slave traders there — DeLap & Witherspoon; Hill, Boyd & Son; and Nevill & Cunningham — became his friends and mentors. Forrest's raw energy and his brutishness in dealing with people who he felt had wronged him impressed them. He settled his differences with his fists in the middle of Adams Street. His brother, Bill, a six-foot, ruggedly-built, swarthy man was often at his side in these brawls.

Josiah Maples, a local businessman, suggested a partnership with Forrest dealing in slaves. Forrest accepted. In the two previous years on Adams Street he watched with envy those making money in slave trading. In January 1855 "Forrest & Maples" opened for business. "Now it's my turn to make money," Forrest told his competitors with assurance.

Within months Forrest bought Maples' interest in the firm. Immediately he brought all five of his brothers into the business. Bill, his 30-year old brother, was made second-in-command. He worked part-time at a branch mart in Vicksburg, Mississippi. His eldest brother, John — a cripple from wounds suffered in the Mexican War [1846-1848] — supervised the day-to-day management of slaves held in the Mart's pen. Brothers Jesse, Aaron and Jeffrey transported slave cargo to and from New Orleans, Nashville, St. Louis and from rural towns and plantations throughout Tennessee, Arkansas, Mississippi, Kentucky and occasionally, Virginia. On sale days at the Mart all of the Forrests helped out.

Forrest's Slave Mart was centered around a four-story brick building at 87 Adams Street. The adjacent four-story building next door at 89 Adams Street served as the Forrest family home. Behind the Mart, Forrest built a 12-foot wall to enclose an area for a slave yard. His sales room had a 20-foot ceiling and was spacious, light and well-ventilated. Slaves were quartered on the upper floors of the main building. All windows had bars; and all doors had heavy locks and bolts.

Forrest advertised heavily in Memphis and in surrounding towns. A typical ad read:

> *We operate the cleanest and best nigger mart in the South. We have fine Virginia and Carolina-born slaves for sale--field hands, house servants, mechanics and factory workers. Merchandise guaranteed.*

Forrest was adept at organization. These same skills of handling details and people were later used to his advantage in the Confederate army. He painstakingly planned what he wanted to accomplish, then concentrated on the details to work his plan. He made all the decisions. His brothers willingly accepted his autocratic style.

On June 9, 1856 Forrest held his bi-weekly meeting with his brothers to assign tasks. "Jesse, I want you to go to New Orleans next week with Aaron and Jeffrey to pick up those niggers I bought at auction at the St. Charles Hotel last month. They are being held for me at Teale's slave pen on Chartres Street. I've made arrangements with Captain Isaac Diamond to transport them up river to Greenville, Mississippi. There, you'll deliver them to the Marberry Plantation in Washington County."

"Can we spend a week or so in New Orleans, Bedford? We'd like to visit some of those places you've been telling us about, and maybe do some gambling."

"No, no, no, goddamnit! You'll get in trouble and forget why I sent you there. Those filthy, hag whores in those barrooms will rob you of everything including your pants. We've got to move quick. Colonel Marberry wants them for this year's cotton harvest. He'll give us $50 a piece extra if he has a good crop.

And make sure you clean the niggers up good before you haul them out to the plantation. The Colonel paid top price. And for Cris' sakes, be polite. No rough talk, and no drinking. Colonel Marberry is a church deacon, and I gave him the impression we're all God-fearing Baptists. Heh-heh-heh!"

Bill Forrest added in jest, "You fellows keep your hands off the Colonel's daughter, too."

Forrest, ignoring the remark, continued, "Bill and I are going to East Tennessee in two weeks to meet with a broker coming over from Roanoke. He's driving about 150 niggers to Knoxville for an auction on July 1st. He wrote me that he's got a good stock of boys, ages 14 to 17, and plenty of young nigger girls. He expects the going price will average between $700 and $800 for field hands, and a little more for carpenters, factory workers, and house servants.

"With a markup of 20 percent, we can make a good profit at those prices. Virginia's got a surplus of slaves. They breed like flies over there."

Bill Forrest interjected, "How will we get the niggers to Memphis?"

"Hell, I don't know, Bill. We'll either chain them together and walk them, or hire some wagons. We'll get them here one way or another. We may need some help to keep them from running away. There's plenty of time to figure that out."

Bill Forrest added, "We'll show them the cat-o-nine-tails, then pick one out that's acting up and put on a demonstration for the rest of them. I haven't lost one yet where we've used the whip for a little show."

"All right then, it's settled. If all goes smoothly, we'll make some money. John! You watch the Mart while we're gone. I'll set the prices for any niggers we've got in the pen. You know how to handle things.

"Everyone keep your eyes open for more inventory. Ask around to find out if anyone in Memphis or out-in-the-country has slaves for sale. We'll buy them, or sell them on a commission basis. If any agents approach you, you tell them our going rate to agents who bring us niggers is one-fourth of the profits from the sale.

"By late October I want our pens full. That's when planters start getting money for their cotton. That's when they're in the best position to pay cash.

"Now let's get ready for Friday's sale. I've placed notices in all the newspapers and passed out handbills across the river in Arkansas and down in Mississippi in Hernando, Holly Springs, Oxford, Clarksdale and places like that. We want to sell out Friday if possible. If we have some left over, we'll get rid of them on Saturday."

Jesse Forrest asked, "How many niggers we got?"

John Forrest, the Mart's custodian, answered, "There are 38 for sale, and we've got three more we're holding for Bedford's friend, Robert Balch."

"Good — I expect a profitable sale then. Everyone helps out. Mix among the crowd to answer questions and to talk up the quality of our stock", snapped Bedford Forrest to his brothers.

Jeremiah, Forrest's 6-foot-2, 24-year old body servant was assigned the responsibility of getting the slaves cleaned and dressed for sale. He took care of the details of making the proper clothing selections for both the male and female slaves. The Mart carried a large inventory of hats, shirts, coats, trousers and shoes for the males; and calico dresses, shoes, and red, blue and yellow bandannas for the females. Clothing was brought from the storeroom the day before. Jeremiah would make the proper choices.

John Forrest, in his menacing voice, gave his standard instructions to the slaves being offered for sale.

"You niggers look lively. Smile! Move quickly when you are called to the platform. If any of you act up, this is what you'll get." Then to make an impression on the already frightened slaves, he swung around several times a cat-o-nine-tails, then struck a nearby pole with it.

Friday morning at dawn — the first day of the sale — Jeremiah and two of Bedford Forrest's house servants, Lizzie and Emma Jane, washed each slave thoroughly. Gray hairs were plucked. Talcum powder was applied to faces and necks. When these tasks were finished, they dressed each slave and conducted a final inspection. Crying was commonplace. Not knowing their fate, most had the look of terror. Slaves chattered nervously among themselves expressing their fears of being sold to a cruel master. Jeremiah, Lizzie, and Emma Jane — slaves themselves — dared not offer any sympathy for fear of retribution from Bedford or John Forrest. They went about their business showing no outward signs of concern for the welfare of their fellow human cargo.

John Forrest's job the day of the sale was to sanitize the slave pen and the sales room. In the pen he spread a coat of lime on the dirt floor to kill the odors. But despite his best efforts during the hot summer days of Memphis, it was impossible to completely eradicate the pungent stench of urine, sweat and mildew.

At 10:00 a.m., the posted sale time, Forrest and all his brothers except Bill greeted a crowd of about 50 potential customers. They mingled freely, talking and joking with old friends. "How are things down in Mississippi, Mr. Kelton," inquired Forrest. "Hope you find what you're looking for today. We'll try to provide you with what you need."

"Just looking today, Forrest. You don't mind do you? If I see the right boy, maybe I'll reach for my money bag. I've got a little headache this morning. Too much whiskey last night and some bad company up at Schwoob's Bar Room."

"I know the feeling, Mr. Kelton. I've had that happen to me on occasion. Heh-heh-heh!"

Forrest scanned the crowd intently to spot unfamiliar faces. He always made it a point to greet personally new prospective buyers. He was extremely gregarious, and enjoyed the excitement of sale day.

John Forrest signaled his brothers that the slaves were in the holding pens, and all was in order. Forrest then leaped onto the platform. He donned his black silk stovepipe hat, and cocked it on the back of his head. At six feet in height and a trim 180 pounds, Forrest was an imposing figure with his white ruffled shirt, black string tie, baggy gray trousers and jauntily positioned silk hat.

"Gentlemen," he announced in a loud voice. "Today we've got for sale some fine Arkansas, Virginia and Tennessee-born niggers. One lot of six over there belong to my friend, Colonel Richardson, who operates a plantation across the river. Two of them are houseworkers, one is a mechanic and carpenter, one is a drayman, and two are field hands. I'd like to see them sold all together if possible. They've been together for 12 years.

"Then we've got several field hands who are off a cotton plantation over in Lee County, Arkansas. I'll sell them individually. They are exceptionally find merchandise. The young ones will be good for years and years of productive labor. The older ones are experienced hands, and can give you quick results if you're thinking about a banner crop.

"John, bring them up here!"

Seven neatly dressed slaves — five males and two females — shuffled slowly onto the platform and formed a line behind Forrest. Several appeared to be staring far beyond the crowd as if oblivious to the proceedings and despite the stern warning beforehand to look happy and anxious to be purchased. Their fear could not be disguised. They were far more concerned about being sold to a cruel master than they were of John Forrest's whip.

Forrest asked John to announce the name and age of the first male slave offered for sale.

In his shrill voice John said, "This is Christian. He's 18 years old, and he was born in Lee County, Arkansas."

"Look at this profitable investment," exclaimed Forrest, feigning excitement. "He's young and strong as a bull, and capable of servicing many of your nigresses. Heh-heh-heh! You can see that he's a good nigger. No strap marks on his back. I invite you to inspect him. He'll give you a good day's work.

"All right, who'll offer $1200? Come on now, this here nigger will return you a profit of a thousand percent! How about you, John Goodloe? You can sure use a strong boy like this on your place in Collierville. Don't you want a good cotton crop this year?"

Goodloe shook his head, no, and responded, "He's worth no more than $900 to me, Forrest. I need a blacksmith, not a field hand."

Forrest nodded. "Who'll give me $1100? I'll tell you what. If this boy doesn't give you a good days work, I'll take him back and refund your money. That's generous, isn't it? Come up here on the platform and feel his shoulders and chest. This nigger is a genuine bull."

Two bystanders took up Forrest's offer, and jumped up on the platform. One burly prospective buyer took Christian's arm and started circling it like a pinwheel. The other one — a tall, trim, distinguished-looking gentleman — waited his turn; then he pried open the mouth of the frightened young slave to examine his teeth. Satisfied, the latter told Forrest, "I'll give you $1000."

Forrest turned to the other fellow, and said, "What will you give?" In a gruff voice he snapped, "No more than $1050 if you guarantee him." Forrest anxious to move on with the sale, nodded. "He's yours. Pay my brother Jesse over there. He'll fill out the papers."

The next six slaves were sold by 10:45 a.m. Prices averaged about $1000 a piece for the field hands. One customer bought three, two males and a female. Another customer bought the other three in that consignment.

Forrest then announced, "The sale will now begin for our featured merchandise today. Gentlemen, I have the pleasure of offering for sale, Sarah. Bring her out, John! This nigress is an outstanding cook and kitchen worker. For the past 18 years prior to the death of Miss Bessie Claypool, head of the prominent Claypool family of Memphis, Sarah served her mistress efficiently and faithfully. We are offering her today to that discriminating family who desires the finest in domestic service. Sarah is 34 years old, very light skinned as you can see, and exceptionally clean in her personal habits. She comes highly recommended by Miss Claypool's distinguished attorney, Mr. Hugh Snowden, Esquire.

"This is a prime nigress. We are offering her for $1500 cash. This is our outstanding buy today. Come up and examine her. You'll find a fine specimen — light skin, no gray hairs, full breasts and sturdy thighs. And she has all her teeth. She is the picture of good health."

When Forrest finished describing Sarah, Colonel Sam Tate, President of the Memphis & Charleston Railroad, signaled him from the crowd. Tate then came forward to talk privately with Forrest. After a three minute discussion, with both Tate and Forrest nodding in agreement, the latter announced, "The nigress is now the property of Colonel Tate."

Forrest paused for a few moments to whisper instructions to his brother John. Then he announced, "Gentlemen, the sale will continue in ten minutes. You are welcome to come back to the slave pen and examine those niggers that have not yet been sold. Feel free to examine them closely. Remember, our merchandise is guaranteed."

Forrest — the Planter

Forrest's slave trade prospered. Each year in the latter 1850s sales volume exceeded 1000 slaves. Forrest's Mart was the leader in the Tennessee, Arkansas, and Mississippi region. Profits mounted. Bedford Forrest netted almost $50,000 each year in 1858 and 1859. His brothers, as employees, earned somewhat less.

But despite his financial success, Forrest made few friends within the old-line established business community of Memphis. Matt Gallaway was perhaps his first true friend from the "right side" of the city's social caste system. He also was befriended by Colonel Robert V. Richardson, a Memphis attorney and a successful cotton plantation operator across the river in Arkansas. And there was also Minor Meriwether, a prominent citizen and engineer by profession. Forrest often solicited advice on business matters from these three.

Forrest was pleased with his success dealing in slaves. But, being a keen observer of business affairs in Memphis, he watched with envy fortunes being made in the cotton market. In the late 1850s over 400,000 bales of cotton, selling on the open market at $5.00 per bale, moved through Memphis each year. The export market in cotton flourished. The mills in New England and in Europe, particularly England, had an insatiable demand for cotton fiber.

With a personal net worth exceeding $100,000 Forrest concluded that he was now in a financial position to become a planter. Gaining control of productive Mississippi agricultural land became a primary goal in 1858. One day in October of that year he saw his friend Robert Richardson sitting by himself in the dining room of the Gayoso House.

"Bob, do you mind if I join you? I need your advice on a cotton venture I am considering."

"Of course, Bedford, it's good to see you. After the wonderful crop I've had this year, I'm delighted to talk cotton. And I'm honored that you ask for my opinion. Please sit down."

Richardson, 37, a tall, gaunt individual with deep penetrating eyes and a balding head had been the Inspector General of the Tennessee Volunteers in the Mexican War. While practicing law in Memphis in the 1850s he had found time to acquire over 100,000 acres of prime cotton land in eastern Arkansas.

Richardson said, "You know Forrest that 'Cotton is King', so the saying goes. Prices are high even with the bumper crops we're having. England is buying every pound it can get its hands on. Everybody is making money — the growers, the cotton factors down on Front Street, the steamboats hauling the bales, the New England and England textile mills — everybody!"

"Bob, I've made some money trading niggers and probably will continue to do so, but I'm thinking of cultivating some fertile, uncleared land I own down in Coahoma County, Mississippi, about 65 miles south of here. What do you think of the idea?"

"Bedford, the key to success is getting enough slaves at the right price. If you pay more than $1050 or $1100 for a healthy 20-year old male, for example, you put tremendous downward pressure on profits. You know far better than me about what's happening with the price of slave labor. I hear slaves are selling anywhere from a low of $1200 to $1800 in New Orleans, and also in newly-opened cotton areas in East Texas. I know I can't make any money if I have to pay over $1100 per head for field hands.

"There's a movement here in the South to pressure Congress into reopening the slave trade with West Africa. There is such high demand coming from the Border states that in a few years we may have to close down. We can't pay the prices. Our traditional market of Virginia niggers is going to vanish."

Forrest then interjected, "Bob, I have close to 100 niggers now, and they're good field hands. They're working some leased land for me east of Memphis. I'm all right for awhile.

"I don't know whether you've been approached by a Charles Lamar, a businessman in Savannah, Georgia. His agent came to see me last week to ask if I'd be interested in committing to buy 20 or so of what he called 'Simon-pure Congo niggers' at a price of $600 to $700 each. The final price will depend on how many survive the trip from West Africa. If the ship eludes the authorities, it's expected to arrive on the Georgia coast next month."

"Bedford, that's a dangerous game. You could be arrested and jailed for dealing in a smuggling operation. I've heard of Mr. Lamar, and he is a marked man. He organizes these syndicates with the promise of huge profits if the ships reach the East Coast undetected. Personally I wouldn't risk it if I were you. If you are caught, you could be destroyed financially and imprisoned.

"There's a lot of clamoring in states like Louisiana, Mississippi and Texas to reopen the slave trade with Africa. An argument is being made that if it is permissible to buy Virginia slaves and ship them to New Orleans, why shouldn't it be permissible to buy them in Africa or Brazil and ship them here. If Congress is concerned about agriculture in the South, it should repeal the laws prohibiting the African slave trade."

Forrest replied, "Bob, I'm not too concerned about getting caught buying smuggled niggers. I'll deny I knew anything about the scheme. Frankly, I'll be surprised if the ship makes it to Georgia."

"Well, Bedford, you seemed to have answered your own questions about getting deeper into cotton planting. Market conditions look good for the next few years. If you can get to planting soon in Mississippi, you'll probably do quite well. I hope I've been helpful."

"Yes, you have. If I can control expenses, it should work out very well. Thank you, Bob."

In 1859 Forrest closed his slave mart on Adams Street to devote full time to his plantation enterprises in Mississippi. Cotton prices were high, and prospects appeared bright for a good first year's crop.

On Wednesday, November 2nd Forrest stepped into the Wharfmaster's Office near the Jefferson Street Wharf and inquired about some cargo he was expecting from New Orleans. There, seated in the outer office, was his friend, Minor Meriwether.

"Bedford, it's good to see you. How are you? How are things going in Mississippi? Did you get a good crop? And how is Mary?"

"Whoa! Hold on Minor, you ask too many questions. Are you now a reporter for Matt Gallaway at the *Avalanche*?"

"No, I'm just pleased to see you. It has been six months. Elizabeth and I were talking about Mary and you last month. We miss our favorite alderman here in Memphis."

"That's a joke, isn't it Minor? I reluctantly served one

year — not even long enough to stick my hands in the tax receipts box. Heh-heh-heh! I'm too opinionated to be a politician. When someone attacks my suggestions, I want to thrash them. Only because those rowdies in the Third Ward voted for one of their own kind did I get elected. You know that."

"You added some spice to municipal government. And you were probably the only honest man in the bunch. Mayor Baugh points to you when he defends himself from charges he presides over a corrupt government."

"Do you mean he blames me?"

"No, Bedford, you are his cloak of virtue."

"What are you doing in the Wharfmaster's Office, Minor?"

"I'm waiting for Elizabeth to return from St. Louis. She went to a women's suffrage convention. You know Elizabeth. She says women are born slaves under the Anglo-Saxon legal system. You know how she feels. She has told you on more than one occasion that women are no better off than the poor wretches you sold at your slave mart."

"Oh yes, I'm well aware of that firebrand wife of yours. She's certainly full of fight. Didn't she make you free your body servant, Old Henry, last year?"

"Yes, not only Henry, but all the slaves I inherited from my father. But I was happy to do it And besides, Henry is still with us. Now he is a contented employee."

"Well, Minor, that's all right, I suppose. I just hope the emancipation disease doesn't spread beyond your house. Hell, the whole world around us will come tumbling down. Look at all that activity down there on the levee. Do you think it would be like that if the niggers were all free? It's good to have friends like Elizabeth and you. It shows people how broadminded I am. Heh-heh-heh!"

"Bedford, you will soon be a wealthy planter — a prominent Mississippi nabob — a high muck-a-muck. You'll be rich enough to be called 'Mister'."

"No, I don't think so. I wasn't too popular when I left Hernando seven years ago. But maybe that old Chinese saying, 'Money makes bastards legitimate' is correct. I still despise those privileged sonafabiches. Those selfish, useless upper classes have never gotten a callous on their hands in their whole life. They know how I feel about them.

"Minor, I must go now. I've got to browbeat some of those cotton merchants on Front Row. I need at least $5.00 a bale for my cotton. Then, I must attend a meeting of the Memphis Jockey Club. Did you know I was elected vice president?"

"No, I didn't. That's a surprise. But I know how much you enjoy horseracing and betting. Watch your pocketbook, Bedford! There are some scoundrels in that covey."

"I shall indeed, Minor."

While Bedford Forrest was plunging headlong into developing his Mississippi plantation, politics continued to command the public's attention in both the North and the South. States' rights was the principal Southern issue. The abolition of slavery, long advocated by segments of the Northern religious and political community, moved into the forefront of concern. Southern newspaper editors reflecting the viewpoints of the white upper classes flailed away day after day on the theme: "We're not fighting solely for slavery; we're fighting for the rights of Southern states." Alabama-born Matt Gallaway, editor of the *Memphis Avalanche*, was among the most vocal.

The traditionally strong national Democratic Party was split apart on the issue of slavery. The Dred Scott decision of 1857 in which the U.S. Supreme Court denied Scott, a slave, the right to be free even though he had lived as a free man in Illinois before returning to Missouri — a slave state — brought protests from Northerners and the leadership of the emerging Republican Party.

In the 1860 presidential election the Northern Democrats supported Senator Stephen A. Douglas of Illinois. He was a strong advocate of preserving the integrity of the Union and the idea of secession rankled him. Democrats in the South opted for the Vice President of the United States, Kentuckian John C. Breckinridge. The latter was personally opposed to slavery, but he strongly defended the Southern position on states' rights.

The Democratic Party's divisional split enabled Republican candidate Abraham Lincoln to win the 1860 presidential election decisively in electoral votes. Lincoln won in 17 states for 180 electoral votes; Breckinridge won 11 states and 72 electoral votes; John Bell of Tennessee, the Constitutional Union Party candidate, 3 states and 39 electoral votes; and Douglas, 2 states and 12 electoral votes.

Douglas won narrowly the popular vote in Memphis. Bell won statewide in Tennessee. Lincoln was not on the ballot in Tennessee.

The *Memphis Daily Appeal* in an editorial on November 10, 1860 urged the public to give Lincoln a chance to dispense equal justice to the South. Four weeks later its editor changed his stance. He declared a virtual end of the Union. "Reconciliation", he said, "wasn't possible".

Reaction was swift in the South following Lincoln's victory. In the minds of many Southern leaders secession was the answer. Forty-five days after Lincoln's election, on December 20, 1860, South Carolina seceded, followed quickly in the next month and a half by Mississippi,

Presidential Election of 1860

Abraham Lincoln
Republican Party

Stephen A. Douglas
Democratic Party

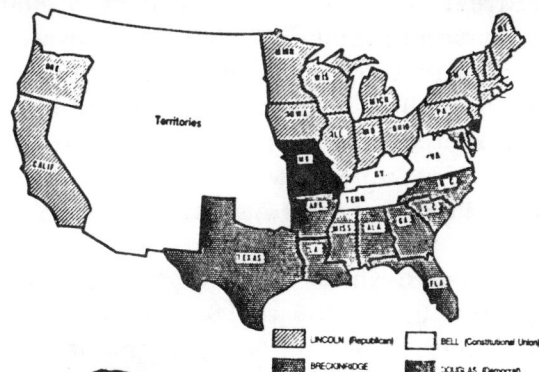

John Breckinridge
Southern Democratic Party

John Bell
Constitutional Union Party

Florida, Alabama, Georgia, Louisiana and Texas.

On Tuesday night, January 22, 1861, Southern sympathizers celebrated the secessions with a giant torchlight parade through the streets of downtown Memphis. The procession extended many blocks with floats, bands, and mounted horses and open carriages. Torchlights were carried in front of signs calling for "Southern Rights," "Secession Now," and "No More Compromise." A huge bonfire was lit at the intersection of Adams and Second Streets to climax the parade.

On February 6th Union supporters held their own torchlight parade. Advocates of secession for Tennessee countered with an even larger parade the following night. One Main Street store built a giant arch of gaslights across its front with the motto, "The South Forever."

On February 9, 1861, in Montgomery, Alabama, the seven states that had already seceded joined forces. There they adopted a constitution and established a provisional government with Jefferson Davis of Mississippi as President, and Alexander H. Stephens of Georgia as Vice President. Davis, 52, a veteran of the Mexican War had been a United States senator, and Secretary of War from 1853 to 1857 in the cabinet of President Franklin Pierce. Davis was a graduate of West Point, class of 1828. Stephens, 51, was a Georgia lawyer and politician.

An attempt to resolve the issues at a peace conference assembled in Washington in late February 1861 failed. This was an omen of impending disaster. On April 12th, Fort Sumter in Charleston, South Carolina, was fired on by Confederate forces under the command of General Pierre G. T. Beauregard. After a siege of 36 hours, the Fort, located in Charleston's harbor, surrendered. On April 15th President Lincoln requested those loyal states to contribute 75,000 militia to quell the uprising.

Tennessee — a state that up to that point had not formally considered the secession question — refused Lincoln's request for troops. In the last week of April, Governor Isham Harris called a special session of the State Legislature to consider secession. Matt Gallaway, who had advocated secession for months in his editorials in the *Memphis Avalanche*, reacted violently when the Legislature meeting at the State Capitol in Nashville did not act on the question immediately. "How long will Tennessee remain in Abe Lincoln's Union," he wrote. "Our people are getting impatient. The legislature has been in session nearly a week, and the *Ordinance of Secession* has not passed! To see Tennessee out of the Union is now the acme of our ambition." Over the vigorous protests of pro-Union members from East Tennessee, the Legislature approved a statewide referendum on the question of secession on June 8th. At the same session, Governor Harris, an outspoken secessionist, used his influence to push through a military bill calling for 55,000 state troops and a $2 million unconditional and a $3 million conditional appropriation to be used to equip this Tennessee army.

On May 20th Richmond replaced Montgomery as the Confederate capital. In May 1861 three more states — Arkansas, North Carolina and Virginia — formally seceded. Kentucky opted to stay neutral.

Acting on the certainty that Tennessee would approve secession when the vote came on June 8th, Governor Harris sent Forrest's friend, engineer Minor Meriwether, and a construction team to a location a few miles up the Mississippi River from Memphis to build the first of a series of earthen forts to protect the city from the North.

The unfurling of a huge Confederate flag over the front entrance of the Gayoso House in Memphis was just one of many visual displays of Confederate sympathy in the city.

Proprietor Colonel Cockrill, a native of South Carolina, was a strong secession advocate.

The drama on how Tennessee would vote ended on Saturday, June 8th. The final count was 104,913 for secession, and 47,237 against. In West Tennessee the vote was 29,127 for and 6,117 against. But in pro-Union East Tennessee it was 14,780 for and 32,923 against. Slavery had never been widely accepted in East Tennessee.

Memphis chose separation despite a highly vocal pro-Union minority, and a citizenry that generally opposed slavery. Fear of freed slaves was a factor in the decision of many voters, particularly the city's large population of Irish immigrants. The Irish feared possible competition in the labor marketplace from freed slaves seeking the same jobs.

Andrew Johnson, Tennessee's United States Senator, refused to break with the Union. He was the only Southern senator to retain his seat in the Senate.

In his first two years as a planter Forrest was successful. But like everyone associated with the cotton economy in 1861, he was nervous. Secession worried him. "What impact would separation have on market conditions?" he and others were asking. "And how would the Federal blockades of such major shipping ports as New Orleans and Mobile affect the exporting of cotton to Europe?"

On June 8th Forrest came to Memphis from Mississippi to vote. He was still legally a resident of Memphis. Nervous over the election results which overwhelmingly endorsed secession, he called on Matt Gallaway at the *Avalanche* office on Monday morning, June 10th to discuss his concerns with his friend.

"Bedford, come on in. What did you think of the vote? Wonderful isn't it? Now we can tie this Confederacy together. I see big things. No more yoke of oppression. The citizens certainly spoke out on Saturday, didn't they? As frightening as it may sound, now is the time for muskets and bayonets!"

"I agree, Matt. The vote was convincing. But I must tell you in all honesty, I'm sad the Union broke up. I voted for Douglas last year. I believed he wanted the Union left intact and would have agreed to compromise on Southern rights. He appeared to be a reasonable fellow.

"But with Lincoln and the Republicans trying to get rid of slavery, I guess secession is for the best. Most of my money is in plantation land, Matt. How will any of us get a crop planted and harvested without the niggers? Free labor, if you could find it, would drive up labor costs. If I lose my niggers, I stand to lose everything."

"Well, Bedford, emancipation would lead to mutiny and armed black men running wild. We have to take steps to see that there are no revolts of the slaves."

"Matt, what about our chances if an all-out war occurs?"

"Bedford, I agree that the numbers may not seem promising now. But our resolves to protect our land and people, and a good military organization with Jefferson Davis and all those other West Point-trained Southerners, we've got a chance to hold them off."

"Are you aware of anything going on in West Tennessee to get ready? I hear there are several local military drill companies in Memphis, but what else?"

"Haven't you heard? No, I guess you haven't. You've been down in Mississippi for the past month. Well, Governor Harris has called for volunteers to serve in a provincial army of Tennessee and he's got plans to fortify the state.

"Harris has lawyer Gideon Pillow, an old veteran of the Mexican War, running the military show right now; and he's got Minor Meriwether supervising the engineering for the fortifications on the river bluffs to protect the city. Harris himself is a whirlwind. He's already contracting to buy arms and equipment for the troops.

"Have either Harris or Pillow contacted you?"

"No, Matt. I just returned to Memphis Saturday."

"Bedford, I have no doubt one or the other will try to talk with you."

"How do you know that?"

"Hell, Bedford, I told them you are the best damn organizer in the Mississippi Valley. You are tailor-made for Harris' army."

"I have to sort all this out in my mind, Matt. I've got a lot at stake. I'll do what I think is right."

Forrest left the *Avalanche* office on Madison Street and walked around the corner to Front Street. This was the center of the cotton factoring business in Memphis. He then spent two hours soliciting opinions from several of his business contacts on the future prospects for the cotton business considering there might be war. Opinions were mixed. Some thought the war would force prices up, and there would be substantial profits to be made. Others worried about the threat of blockades.

Next Forrest visited his bankers on Madison. "Forrest, we have been considering your loan request for the past month. Due to the political uncertainty, we are temporally shutting off all loans," he was told. "If there is war, we won't be extending credit to planters."

Armed with this information he spent the next three days evaluating what he should do given the uncertainty of the cotton economy in the South. He discussed his options with his wife, Mary, and also with his youngest brother, Jeffrey. Then he made his decision. "I shall enlist in one of the local military companies," he told his family. "I shall fight to protect the South. If I don't fight and we lose, I'll have no one to blame but myself."

Forrest's son, Willie, who had eavesdropped on all the discussions, begged his father to let him join too. Willie was only 15 years old. Forrest, after considering it for several hours, decided it might help his son mature more quickly and agreed. Mary, who had not been asked her opinion, remained silent.

At 1:00 p.m. Friday, June 14, 1861 Nathan Bedford Forrest, just one month short of his 40th birthday, his son, Willie, and his brother Jeffrey walked up to Court Square, a public park in the center of Memphis, to enlist in Captain Josiah White's recently organized company of Tennessee Mounted Rifles.

Captain White was a 33-year old local citizen from a prominent Memphis family who had been asked by Governor Harris to raise a company of citizen soldiers. White sat behind a long table draped in red, white and blue bunting. His back was to a 30-inch bust of Andrew Jackson which sat on top of a six-foot pedestal. The Captain, in his immaculate light gray uniform with shiny gold buttons, looked impressive. Surrounding him were at least a dozen young boys making believe they were soldiers. White seemed amused by the spirited lads' antics.

Captain White stood up erectly when the Forrests approached the table. Smiling broadly he said, "I hope some of you have come to enlist in Company D of the Tennessee Mounted Rifles. We still have a few positions to fill before we reach our quota."

Forrest extended his hand to White replying, "All three of us have come to volunteer if that is acceptable to you."

"Well, two of you are qualified. How old is the boy?" asked White.

"He's 15, but look at him, he is as big as an 18-year old. He's my son, William. He'll make a good soldier, I guarantee you."

Captain White was silent for a moment. Then he said, "I'm not supposed to enlist anyone under 18. Look at those kids hanging around over there. Every one of them has begged me to take him. But as you can see, they're just little boys with big imaginations."

Forrest, agitated at White's remarks, snapped in an angry voice, "Is this six foot, broad-shouldered lad acceptable or not? Don't beat around the bush. We all came to Court Square to volunteer. Take all three, or none at all!"

"All right, all right, Mr. Forrest. William is accepted."

"Good. Now let's get on with it," said Forrest with impatience.

With that brief exchange, the conversation ended. Captain White reached for his copy of the *Confederate Oath of Allegiance*. Forrest interrupted him. "Captain White, if it's all right with you, don't read the *Oath*. We know what it says. Give us that quill on your table, and all of us will sign individual copies, then we'll be done with it."

White, well aware of Bedford Forrest's reputation for getting his own way and his wicked temper, hurriedly dispensed the forms for the three to sign. In less than one minute all had signed and handed the forms to Captain White. "Congratulations, gentlemen," said White, "you are fine additions to the Mounted Rifles."

"Now what happens?" asked Forrest.

"The Company is leaving for training at Camp Randolph tomorrow morning early," replied White.

"Well, if it's acceptable to you, we'll be there Sunday. It will take us a day to get ready. Is that acceptable?"

"Of course it is. I am pleased to have you part of the unit."

With their business concluded, the three Forrests

strode off toward Main Street. Captain White overheard Bedford Forrest say, "Come on you two. I'm going to buy us all some good military felt hats, and then let's head over to Steinkuhl's Empire Saloon and Lunch House to brag about our enlisting."

3 • The Recruiter

At 7:00 a.m. the three Forrests saddled up for the 35-mile horseback ride up river from Memphis to the makeshift Camp Randolph. A tearful Mary Forrest, and Jesse Forrest, were there to see them off. At their arrival at 1:00 p.m. Captain White and Sergeant Timothy Van Atta, now their military superiors, were there to welcome them at White's headquarters' tent.

Both Bedford and Jeffrey Forrest recognized many of the other recruits, and smiled broadly acknowledging some friendly shouts. "Now we've got the war won," yelled Andrew Petty, one of Jeffrey's friends. "The Forrests will scare Hell out of those Yankees," Ralph Permar shouted, "That's right, it's all over." Others said, "That's right, that's exactly right."

After some handshaking with Captain White and a brief conversation about the camp's facilities and the tent arrangements, White instructed Sergeant Van Atta, 22, a pleasant young blond-haired soldier who just one week before had been a Memphis fireman, to lead the Forrests to their new temporary home — a double-sized white canvass tent midway in a long double row of tents extending at least one city block. A corporal standing nearby was assigned to take the Forrests' horses to a nearby corral where a patch quilt of bays, black, gray and a few Arabian horses belonging to their fellow recruits were grazing peacefully on a warm June afternoon.

The Forrests settled into their tent and waited to be called for a late afternoon general formation of Company D, then evening mess.

Monday, the Forrest's first full day in camp was devoted in the morning to close order drill and marching, and in the afternoon to lectures by Captain White on military discipline, the care of firearms and horses, and camp and personal sanitation.

Captain White, addressing the subject of personal hygiene, said with emphasis, "All soldiers are required to bathe once a week. Your feet shall be washed twice a week. Your hair shall be kept short and beards neatly trimmed." Since the Forrests were all personally fastidious in their grooming and cleanliness, these requirements seemed quite appropriate. But to many in Company D these orders caused most of the grumbling that night as the men gathered around their campfires.

"Cris' sakes," said one grizzled, long-bearded recruit. "I joined up to fight, not spend my time fancying up."

"You bet, Abner, I agree," replied his young, overweight, blotch-faced friend. Others either nodded or grunted in agreement.

Training and the routine camp life went easily for the Forrests, even Willie. Being away from home, sleeping on the ground, walking around dusty or muddy fields, riding horses hours on end, and cleaning their clothes and equipment had been an integral part of their lives in slave trading or on working cotton plantations. A few others in Company D also took the training in stride. But the majority of the recruits wondered, "What earthly purpose does this daily drudgery serve?"

One disgruntled private summed up his philosophy of soldiering: "War is loading our pistols and shotguns, saddling up horses, then charging forward pell-mell killing those Yankee sonafabiches."

"You're right, Hundley. The idea is to kill them before they kill you. No more, no less," chimed in a skinny baby-faced boy who was probably no more than 17. Others embellished Private Hundley's interpretation of how the war should be fought. This typical nightly discussion ended only when the camp bugler sounded *Taps* at 10:00 p.m.

Private Bedford Forrest listened curiously and said little to anyone except Jeffrey. "Those kids have plenty of spirit, don't they? But have any of them ever been in a fight where their lives were at stake? Hell no! I can't blame them for not liking the training, but we've all got to learn not to panic when the fighting starts. That's what Captain White and his officers need to be concerned with, Jeffrey. If I ever get my own command, I will consider the possibility of panic foremost in my planning."

Week two at Camp Randolph was a complete disaster. Attempts to maintain discipline during daily training were disrupted by the intrusion of swarms of yellow jackets, horse flies, ticks and chiggers. Late June in Tennessee saw the emergence of aggressive yellow jackets. These members of the insect world took exception to having their fields disrupted. The buzzing and frequent stings caused hysteria in Company D during afternoon drills. An even greater menace was the silent unseen enemy in the tall grass — chiggers. These microscopic mites called by some red bugs, lurked by the millions in the fields and woods. Strangely enough, they did serve one useful purpose. Any soldier homesick had no time to feel sorry for himself when he had to devote full time to scratching his ankles and legs or around his waist where chiggers liked to burrow under the skin. Chiggers attacked areas where clothing was tight and in the dark, moist areas of the body.

Bedford Forrest, familiar with chiggers, commented to

Captain White, "Chiggers don't seem to spread disease, but spread about ten days of misery. The itching is terrible. I've yet to find anyone who can resist scratching. We ought to send a bunch of them up North. Heh-heh-heh!"

On July 10th, after 24 days at Camp Randolph, Forrest was summoned to Memphis by Governor Harris. Captain White was ordered to discharge Private N. B. Forrest effective immediately.

Governor Harris and Forrest met at the Gayoso House in Memphis the next morning. Harris greeted Forrest warmly. Then he said, "Forrest ... Matt Gallaway, Sam Tate of the Memphis & Charleston Railroad, and attorney Robert Richardson have all spoken highly of you. They feel you should occupy an officer's position in my Provisional Army. But before we discuss a field command, I would like you to recruit your own battalion of mounted soldiers. Forrest, you are widely known in Memphis and down in Mississippi. That will help attract recruits. As you may know, I'm committed as Provisional Commander of all Tennessee troops to recruit 100,000 men in the next two or three months. If you could sign up 500 to 1,000 recruits by the end of August, you will be contributing greatly to the Confederate cause. Are you interested? If you are, I shall commission you 'Lieutenant Colonel' right here today."

"Of course I am, sir. It's an honor to be recommended by my close friends. But are you sure I'm the right person? Lots of folks don't like me for one reason or another. In slave trading you make a lot of enemies. Some ugly rumors circulate about me and my brothers."

"Forrest, we're fighting a war. We need able people. We need men like you who know how to organize things. You have had wide experience dealing with all kinds of people."

"Well, Governor, I do know men reasonably well. And in the three weeks I was at Camp Randolph, I got a good idea of what kind of soldiers we need to recruit."

"All right Forrest, if you are agreeable, it's settled. I shall prepare a formal notice of your appointment immediately.

"There is one thing I should point out. The State of Tennessee cannot supply you with the funds to support your recruitment effort. Every dollar we have is being spent on guns, ammunition and supplies. Is that acceptable?"

"Of course, Governor Harris. I am prepared to spend my own funds."

"Forrest, or should I say, Colonel Forrest, the Tennessee Provisional Army is proud to have your services."

Forrest wasted no time getting started. Heavy recruiting had been well underway by others since mid-June. Hundreds of the city's young men had already enlisted and left for training camp in West Tennessee. To recruit a battalion — a unit of at least three companies — he needed publicity to attract recruits.

Colonel Cockrill, the firebrand, pro-Confederate proprietor of the Gayoso House, enthusiastically agreed to Forrest's request for free space in the hotel's lobby. The Gayoso was the premier hotel in Memphis. Architecturally, it was an imposing four-storied building done in Greek temple style with six tall limestone columns supporting an angled roof over the front portico. The hotel had 250 guest rooms, several ornate public rooms and a huge chandeliered lobby.

To assist, Colonel Cockrill at his own expense hung colorful red and blue bunting and Confederate flags in the lobby, and prepared recruitment posters with Forrest's name boldly emblazoned on them. These were placed on easels located in front of an alcove set aside for Forrest's office. Posters were also placed outside the entrance to the hotel on Front Street.

The Gayoso House was then the center of the city's commercial and social life. With the war's outbreak, the hotel became the Confederacy's unofficial headquarters in West Tennessee. It was an ideal location for Forrest's recruiting office.

Beginning Wednesday July 17th, Colonel Forrest, wearing his immaculate new officer's uniform, spent eight to ten hours each day either in his office or circulating in the lobby, recruiting directly or asking for referrals from hotel patrons. During the first week he signed up 24 volunteers. Most were 18 and 19-year olds from local Irish families. Those in the Memphis Irish community were enthusiastic supporters of the Confederacy. Parents came to the Gayoso House with their sons to meet Colonel Forrest and to witness the administering of the Confederate *Oath of Allegiance*.

Other recruits that week were several local retail clerks who felt pressured by their friends — mostly girl friends — to sign up. Only one or two of these initial recruits were from socially prominent Memphis families. Many in Memphis considered Forrest a rogue — an uncouth barbarian whose associates were society's dregs. In their minds, he was hardly the type of commander they envisioned leading their heroic sons into battle.

Some who came to enlist were too young. Others, Forrest considered too puny. They wouldn't hold up well to the rigors of military life in the field. A few were rejected outright because of their total unfamiliarity with horses.

Recruitment the second week got off to an amusing start. On July 23rd, as Forrest entered the Gayoso, he was suddenly surrounded by four young men. From their dress Forrest assumed they were farm boys. They were unruly in an enthusiastic way as they tugged at Forrest's coat.

"Are you Colonel Forrest -- the Colonel who's organizing a group of horse fighters?" inquired an excited tall, lean lad who seemed to have appointed himself spokesman for the group.

"Yes, I am seeking volunteers for a mounted battalion of soldiers. Are you fellows here to join up? Come on in, we'll talk a bit."

The four would-be warriors shuffled nervously into Forrest's small office and sat down. "Now who are you lads and where do you come from? Tell me something about yourselves," said Forrest.

They looked at each other for a moment, then one said, "Well, sir, I'm Walter X. Jester. Next to me is Lewis Flippen, and next to him is Amos Snow. Across the table there is Abraham Story, Jr. We're from Lauderdale County, Alabama near Florence. Me, Amos and Lewis are from No Bottom Creek. And Abraham is from Caesar's Head, down the road three miles."

Forrest obviously amused said, "Gee...zus, they sound like big towns."

Jester giggled, "Oh, those places are barely spots on the road. No Bottom Creek has 12 families. Caesar's Head is even smaller. We're just poor farm boys. Our whole world is only about five miles wide."

"What kind of farming?"

Lewis Flippen answered, "I raise a few milk cows and some work animals. My daddy and I growed some sweet potatoes, corn, melons and a lot of greens. We've got some piney woods rooters too."

"You mean razorback hogs?"

"Yes, sir, I guess we all do about the same thing. We're niggerless whites. My daddy says we're beans and taters folks. A big celebration for us is when we have possum, turnip greens and Alabama wedding cake."

"Alabama wedding cake? What's that?"

"Oh, that's cornbread," answered Flippen matter of factly.

Abraham Story, Jr. interjected, "Colonel Forrest, we're all about the same. We all live in places with dirt floors and dirt chimneys and squat outside in the woods. We are barefoot boys whose only fun has been gigging frogs. If we join up with your army, it'll probably be the best we've ever had it."

Forrest, curious about his prospective rural Alabama recruits, asked, "Why did you come to Memphis? You could have gone to Montgomery or Nashville, or lots of other places to join up."

Amos Snow, an 18-year old with a thatch of copper-colored hair and freckles everywhere answered, "We wanted to see the Mississippi River and all the steamboats and cotton bales."

Jester added, "And we heard you could have a good time in Memphis." The others nodded in agreement.

"All right," said Forrest. "As long as you fellows know what your committing to, I believe you will make good soldiers."

All four of the young men looked at each other and smiled in unison.

Forrest then leaned back in his chair and put his feet up on the desk totally relaxing. He began talking slowly and softly.

"Boys, my early life almost duplicated yours. I wasn't born at No Bottom Creek, Alabama. It was a place probably just like it in Bedford County, Tennessee. And my daddy's place was a mud hut too, and located near the Duck River. Maybe the Duck River is a little wider than No Bottom Creek, but that may be about the only difference.

"My father was a blacksmith and a general jack of all trades. Like the other pioneers, he was trying to survive and protect his family. We had our little patch, too; and any free time we had was spent fishing or pig sticking. We didn't know anything about the outside world.

"At 13 we moved to Mississippi to occupy some land just recently vacated by the Chickasaws. And when my daddy died in 1837, I took over leadership in the family. I had my mother and five younger brothers to look after. You fellows all understand how hard a life many poor whites out in the country have had. That's why I think you young men will make good soldiers. You know what sacrifice is.

"And when you told me why you came to Memphis that reminded me of my own sense of adventure when I was 20. I was living in Hernando, Mississippi in 1841 when I decided to volunteer my services to the Republic of Texas. Sam Houston and his people were still fighting the Mexicans. Believe me, the Texas-Mexican frontier was one dangerous place. Volunteers raced there from all over the South to help Texas. I wanted badly to get into it so I made my way to Texas by way of New Orleans. But my luck ran out. When I got to Houston the Texans told me they had too many volunteers. I cannot tell you how disappointed I was. And I had a terrible time getting home to Mississippi. I had no money."

Forrest's remarks made a deep impression on the four young adventurers seated in front of him. They listened in awe.

Then Forrest asked, "What kind of weapons do you fellows have?"

Lewis Flippen answered, "We each have a flintlock. Amos also has a Mississippi Rifle he got from his daddy. And we all have Bowie knives. And I think we can get two or three shotguns."

"How about horses?"

"Don't worry about our mounts. We've got some of the best animals within 50 miles of Florence, Alabama. Yes, sir, our horses brought us to Memphis without breaking stride. When we told our folks we were going off to join up, they made sure we left with good animals. They're proud people. They don't want anyone making fun of us because of our mounts, no, sir!"

After a minute or so passed with Forrest in deep thought, he stood up and said, "I'd be proud to have you volunteer for service in my unit. What do you say? There are no fancy uniforms for you. We are a citizens' army. There isn't enough money to dress you up like George Washington. A fancy uniform is not going to make you a better fighter. We're going to win this fight because we Southerners have more stamina; we can shoot better; and we can ride better than those Northern boys."

No one hesitated. All four agreed to enlist immediately.

"All right," said Forrest, "Who's first?"

The six foot tall, erect Walter X. Jester raised his hand.

"Good," added Forrest. "But first I've got to ask you what the 'X' stands for."

"Xerxes, sir. My daddy says he was the king of Persia."

"Where's Persia?"

"I don't know, sir. I do know it must be some place grand like Heaven. Daddy is real religious, and he probably saw that name in his *Bible*."

"I'll accept that Jester. Now raise your right hand. The others of you will serves as witnesses."

Five minutes later all four had been sworn into the Tennessee Provisional Army. The young men slapped each other on the back and giggled with joy. Abraham

Story, Jr., who was average size, 5-foot-7, had a strangely wide oval-shaped face and a long pointed nose, grabbed Forrest's hand and grinning broadly said, "My friends call me 'The Hawk.' I can't figure out where they came up with that name." Everyone laughed, including the amused Forrest.

After Colonel Forrest gave them instructions on reporting for training at the Memphis Fairgrounds, the four new privates quickly exited to the lobby and left the Gayoso House presumably to look for that good time they expected to find in Memphis.

Forrest walked out into the lobby smiling and shaking his head. Colonel Cockrill who had observed from a distance the proceedings in Forrest's office said to his friend, "Colonel, even the smallest fish have their place in the ocean." Forrest nodded in agreement. "I hope I can find more recruits like those boys.

That evening news reached Memphis by telegraph that a massive battle had taken place the past Sunday in Virginia near Washington, D.C. The latest bulletins were being posted outside of the offices of Memphis newspapers giving sketchy details of what had happened. Forrest raced over to the *Memphis Avalanche* on Madison Street to join a large crowd already gathered there.

The bulletins were brief. Details were promised on Wednesday, July 24th. The most recent bulletin posted at 8:00 p.m. by Matt Gallaway stated that on Sunday, July 21st, Confederate forces led by General Joseph E. Johnston and General Pierre G.T. Beauregard met and defeated an equally large force of Federal troops under the command of General Irvin McDowell. The bulletin stated further, "After several hours of bitter fighting, Confederate forces routed the enemy and won the field. By nightfall the Federal Army was in full retreat back to Washington."

The assembled crowd was joyous. All anticipated

more good news to come. Forrest joined in the enthusiastic ceremony of self-congratulations. He told his friend, Colonel Sam Tate, standing nearby, "Recruitment should be wonderful tomorrow."

Forrest arrived at the Gayoso Hotel at 8:00 a.m. the next day. The lobby was jammed with local citizens and hotel guests— all discussing the news from Virginia.

Waiting for Forrest was local businessman John P. Strange, a 38-year old native of Virginia who had lived in Memphis for many years. Forrest extended his hand. "Do I know you? You look familiar. Do you live in Memphis?"

"I'm John Strange, Colonel. We've never met, but you have probably seen me on Main Street where I work. I'm a partner of sorts at Snead, Donoho and Strange, a dry goods store. I've been there about ten years."

"Oh yes, I recall seeing you there. Well, Strange, what can I do for you?"

"Colonel Forrest, I've decided to enlist, and I want to talk with you about your battalion. I can no longer stand by and do nothing while the city's younger men take up arms. I've preached secession for months. I've been a marshall in several of those torchlight parades promoting secession. Now I want to back it up."

"How old are you, Strange?"

"I'm 38."

"Are you married?"

"No, sir, I'm a widower. My wife died four years ago."

"And how's your health? Do you have full use of your arms and legs? And how about your eyesight and hearing? Have you got any tumors?"

Laughing timidly, Strange, a tall, thin man graying at the temples, answered, "Do I look sickly, Colonel?"

"No, of course not. These questions are required to be answered by older recruits. Governor Harris' instructions are to recruit able-bodied men."

"I realize that at 38 I'm a lot older than most of the volunteers. But I know I can withstand the same rigors they'll probably face."

"Well, Strange, if I can do it at age 40, you can do it. I need to ask you a few more things. What work experience do you have that might be helpful in a military unit like I'm putting together?"

"Colonel, I've been a bookkeeper, inventory clerk, assistant manager, and a salesman. I can handle correspondence and I've hired and trained new employees. If I had enough savings, I'd open my own commission house."

"Strange, that experience could be valuable to me. I need an aide to help me write the paperwork and to contact supply houses for firearms, equipment, horses, and a lot of other things. You could be my sergeant-major. What do you say to that?"

"That's a much different role than I envisioned I'd be playing when I walked down Main Street an hour ago. I kept thinking about the cavalry charges in the Crimean War. I recently read Tennyson's poem, *The Charge of the Light Brigade*, and wondered if I had the courage of those British soldiers in that wild charge into the Valley of Death."

"Well, I don't know anything about that. My belief is that we will all have our moments of ordeal and have our courage tested. You will have all the excitement you can handle if you join my unit.

"Do you want to go home and think about it? Or can I swear you in today? I can go out in the lobby and get some witnesses, and administer the *Oath* right now."

"May I have one hour? My partners need to know what I intend to do. They probably anticipated I might volunteer. They have already lost two young clerks. Both Snead and Donoho have been kind to me and deserve to

61

know my intentions. It's the honorable thing to do."

"That's fine, Strange. Come back with your answer this morning. I must fill that sergeant-major's position soon. In the next several weeks I shall be out in the countryside recruiting. I need an aide to sit here to sign up volunteers in my absence."

Within an hour Strange reappeared in Forrest's office. He stood at attention in front of Forrest. "I am here to take the *Oath of Allegiance*, sir."

Quickly Forrest pulled into his office two elderly men who had been loitering in the lobby. "You fellows make yourselves useful," barked Forrest. "I'm appointing you witnesses for this gentleman."

After taking the *Oath*, Strange shook hands with Forrest and the two captive witnesses. Forrest then told Strange, "I'm going to announce your enlistment and new rank in the *Memphis Appeal* and the *Avalanche*. It will be good publicity for my recruitment drive. Maybe it will convince some of your dry goods store friends to join you. Now, goddamnit, go out and enjoy your last day of freedom. Report here tomorrow morning at 8:00 a.m. in uniform. You can buy one over on Main Street at one of those military supply stores."

Just after 12:00 noon Forrest's friend, Attorney Robert Richardson, came into the Gayoso House to talk with Forrest. "What brings you here, Bob?" said Forrest. "Have you come to join my battalion?"

"No, Bedford," laughed the swarthy, dapper Richardson. "I just want to draw on your recruiting experience. Governor Harris has also prevailed on me to recruit a battalion of cavalry. How is it going so far?"

"Well, it's mostly country boys and clerks. It's a hodge-podge of swamp rats, dirt eaters and some skinny town boys. There's not a born killer among them. But at least some are quite comical. I asked one sorry-looking volunteer why he wanted to join up. He answered me, 'Cris' sakes, I'm a secessionist. But to tell you the truth, I think it was bad whiskey that made a secesh man out of me. But no matter, I'm here to put my 'X' on your papers.'

"Then I said to him, 'Do you know you could be killed or captured by the Yankees? Are you prepared for that?' Then he said to me in no uncertain terms, 'If I'm captured I'd tell them: Go to Hell, you lowdown devils, and kiss my rosy red ass you sonafabiches!' "

Richardson and Forrest laughed heartily. Forrest then became serious. "Bob, these last few days I haven't recruited too many. There's too much competition in Memphis for the limited number of young men that haven't yet made a commitment. I hadn't realized it before the extent of pro-Union sympathy in the city. I may be giving away my secrets by telling you I'm going up to Kentucky real soon, then over to North Alabama after that to recruit. I'm probably going to contact my old slave dealing friends there to help me out. That's how I intend to fill up my battalion. Most of those boys out in the country are great horsemen and are looking for some excitement. And they'll fight when the time comes."

Richardson shook his head in agreement. "When are you leaving, Bedford?"

"Probably Saturday morning if I can break in quickly John Strange to take over this office. He's my sergeant-major now."

Forrest and Richardson talked briefly about the cotton market, and the effect the war might have on their plantations. Richardson said he wasn't optimistic, and that he might have to shut his enterprises down. Forrest was pensive as he listened to Richardson's assessment. Richardson then wished Forrest good luck and left.

On Saturday, July 27th, Forrest went down to the

Auction Street Depot and boarded the Memphis & Ohio Railroad passenger train bound for the Kentucky border area north of Clarksville, Tennessee. There he hoped to make contact with agents who would help him purchase and smuggle out of Kentucky equipment and supplies he needed for his battalion. He planned to purchase at least 500 Colt Navy .36 caliber pistols, 100 or more saddles, bridles and miscellaneous other supplies.

With the assistance of Confederate sympathizers, Forrest, operating from a farmhouse near Louisville, quickly assembled his inventory from several smugglers operating clandestinely in that city occupied by Federal troops. Louisville was a center for smuggling, and there was real personal danger to Forrest if he carried out his plan. Fortunately for Forrest, at that time Federal authorities were concentrating most of their efforts in trying to shut down illegal shipments of goods moving south to Nashville on the Louisville & Nashville Railroad.

This distraction helped Forrest and his small, four wagon supply train elude Federal troops by using the back roads of central and western Kentucky to make his way safely to the Tennessee border.

Forrest's supply sortie into Kentucky was not his only success. While there he also recruited several local military companies in Meade County near Louisville and from the Harrodsburg area, southwest of Lexington. Returning with him to Memphis were 150 soldiers for his new battalion who were sympathetic to the Confederate cause.

When asked by Matt Gallaway upon his arrival home, "How did things go?" Forrest answered, "Matt, I was discouraged before I left for Kentucky, but now I'm on top of the world. Recruiting a full battalion now seems realistic. Give me a day to rest up, then by God I'm going out to raise a couple of hundred more soldiers."

Gallaway then said, "Bedford, I heard that you brought back four wagons of guns and saddles. Is that true?"

"Yes, that's right."

"Well, who supplied the funds for all those Navy Colts and the saddles?"

"I did. Did you really think I could have squeezed $16,000 out of Governor Harris or Pillow? Not on your life, Matt. Hell would have frozen over and elephants would have wings before I got a penny from them."

"What are you trying to do Bedford, finance the whole war?" asked the startled Gallaway.

"No, goddamnit, I promised Harris I'd raise and equip a battalion. Why start something if you don't finish it!"

August 29, 1861

At 10:00 a.m., when Forrest arrived at his office in the Gayoso House, Sergeant Strange was out on an errand. While waiting for his return, Forrest sat down to read the morning's edition of the *Avalanche*. He had placed a recruiting announcement in that issue in the hopes of attracting more recruits.

Outside his office door he heard someone ask, "Is that Colonel Forrest in there?" Someone answered, "Yes, that's him — all six feet and then some of him. Go on in. He appears to be in good humor today."

David C. Kelley, a tall, sallow-faced, lofty-browed man, walked in, and extended his hand to Forrest. "Sir, I'm Parson David Kelley. I have just arrived in Memphis from Huntsville, Alabama with 90 volunteers. They elected me Captain — at least I'm Captain for the moment."

"Parson Kelley, you say! Are you one of those primitive Baptist preachers?"

"You might put it hardshell if you choose, not primitive," answered Kelley. "And by the way, sir, I'm a Methodist preacher."

"That doesn't matter. I'm glad you came. What kind of firearms did you bring with you?"

"We have single and double-barreled shotguns, squirrel rifles, flintlocks and old pistols. And every man has his own horse and saddle. Some of the horses are jumpers. I hope that is satisfactory, sir."

"Praise the Lord, Parson...or should I say, Captain Kelley. You are indeed the second coming if you know what I mean."

"I get your meaning Colonel Forrest and I thank you."

"Well Parson, are you and your men ready to make war on those rascally Yankees?"

Characteristically when Kelley listened intently he craned his neck and head forward. This he was doing when Forrest asked that question.

"I sincerely believe my Alabamians will give a good account of themselves. We are dedicated to the new Confederacy, yes, sir."

"Let me notify Governor Harris of your request to join my battalion. That's just a courtesy to him. There will be no problem."

"Where are you camped?"

"Out on the edge of town along the Wolf River, sir."

"Well, Captain Kelley, move them to the Fairgrounds. We are starting training on Monday morning, September 2nd. Bring the tents you have. If you need more, I'll get them quickly. My headquarters are there. Lieutenant Schuyler is my acting Adjutant. He'll get you settled in," concluded Forrest.

With the 28-year old Parson Kelley's Alabamians, Forrest's quest for a full battalion now was in reach. He was elated.

As he left the Gayoso House, Forrest hollered at Colonel Cockrill, the proprietor, "I've succeeded." Cockrill didn't have time to ask, "Succeeded at what?" Forrest had already bounded out of the hotel onto Front Street on his way to Matt Gallaway's office to report the good news

4 • Basic Training

Memphis Fairgrounds, Thursday, September 19, 1861

New companies of mounted volunteers from Alabama, Kentucky and Texas kept arriving at the Memphis Fairgrounds during September. Colonel Forrest ordered Lieutenant C.A. Schuyler, acting Adjutant, to prepare detailed personnel records. "I want to know everything about them — their name, age, occupation, home area, and name of next of kin," directed Forrest. "And I want you and Sergeant Major Strange to prepare an inventory of all equipment and weapons brought by each volunteer, including a description of the horse they brought, if they brought one. Governor Harris wants this inventory too. The Confederate government has promised some reimbursements for these recruits.

"And Schuyler," continued Forrest speaking firmly and rapidly, "tell Strange I want a copy of this inventory tomorrow, first thing. Do you understand?" Schuyler nodded his head in agreement. "Do you know why I need this report, Schuyler?" questioned Forrest.

"Yes, sir, Colonel."

"All right then. This list will tell me how many pistols and shotguns we need. And how many horses, saddles and other items we need to put our soldiers in the field. On Saturday, Governor Harris will be here for inspection, and I want to present him with an accurate list of our needs. Do you now understand the urgency, Schuyler?"

"Yes, sir, Colonel."

"Good, now get moving," snapped Forrest.

Friday, September 20, 1861

Promptly at 8:00 a.m. Sergeant Major Strange came to Forrest's tent. He was nervous as he started to talk. Strange was well aware of Forrest's attention to detail and accuracy. When he operated his slave mart in Memphis, he had a reputation for being well organized and a stickler for detail. And Strange was aware of Forrest's violent temper when things weren't done correctly. Stammering slightly as he started his report, Strange said, "Colonel, about half the men are reasonably well equipped. Most brought a horse and saddle, so we are all right there. It's with weapons where we have problems. As you expected, most came to Memphis with only hunting rifles and Model 1816 muskets. Not much was brought to camp that you would call useful military weapons."

"Are there many Navy Colts? Or short-barreled shotguns?"

"No, not many. I'd say we're woefully short."

"Well, Strange, I'll look into it quickly. I don't know when we'll be called to the field, but let's assume it will be a matter of a few weeks...maybe sooner. Let me check around the city and see what I can purchase, or get some citizens to donate."

Surgeon S. M. Van Wick came in with his report at 9:30 a.m. "Colonel Forrest, we have a reasonably healthy group of young volunteers. I recommend that we reject those on this list. You will see my notes behind each soldier's name. There are 19 of them."

"Let me see that list! I am curious about what you found, Dr. Van Wick," said Forrest. "I see that several are marked, 'chest too retracted.' What does that mean?"

"It means Colonel that these men don't have the strength to withstand long riding or any other vigorous exercise. And the first cold weather they experience, they are almost certain to get sick."

"All right then, what about these two? You've written 'atrophied arm.' You haven't noted which arm — right or left.

"Doctor, if he can hold onto the reins of his horse and fire his weapon when dismounted with his good arm, wouldn't these two qualify?"

"Maybe, sir, but having only one serviceable arm is a handicap."

"Do you know, Van Wick, if these two are anxious to serve?"

"I'm certain they are, otherwise they wouldn't have volunteered."

"All right then, I am going to cross them off your list and mark them available for duty," concluded Forrest.

Then Forrest examined the list again. "I agree with you on these three you've marked 'syphilis.' Send them home tomorrow. If it is one thing we don't need, it's syphilis in the ranks. Gee...zus! How did their commanding officer not know that when he recruited them?

"I don't know, sir."

"Dr. Van Wick, you are obviously a qualified doctor. I'll accept your recommendations for the rest of the list. Thank you for your good work. I know it's painstaking to examine 600 or so men in just two days. But we are all under pressure to get our little army ready for action."

Just before Dr. Van Wick got up to leave, Private Hiram McNally entered Forrest's headquarters tent and slipped the Colonel a note. "Well, Dr. Van Wick, this is my lucky day. The note says that Mr. H. R. Wade, a book dealer on Main Street, is here to donate some training manuals. I don't know what he's got, but it is a nice gesture. Show him in, McNally!"

"Colonel Forrest, so nice to see you. I haven't seen

you since you closed your mart and moved to Mississippi. I know you are busy, so I won't take much time. It may seem presumptuous of me to bring you some military training manuals, but perhaps some of these items will be useful to your junior officers."

"Presumptuous Hell, Wade! I appreciate your kindness. I see you've brought copies of both Volume One and Volume Two of General William Hardee's *Tactics*. The book, I understand, is the standard textbook on rifle and infantry tactics. Old Hardee was regular Federal army until Georgia seceded, wasn't he?" asked Forrest.

"Yes, that's true," replied Wade. Then he added, "I've also brought out a dozen copies each of *Manual for Light Dragoons and Mounted Riflemen*, and *Manual for Colt's Pistols*. If you need more copies, let me know."

"Thank you, they'll be put to good use. We rely on the patriotism and generosity of local citizens. The support we are receiving is overwhelming. Please visit me again. Tomorrow afternoon we are planning a formal inspection. Bring Mrs. Wade with you and your children. We are planning to have a military band, too."

"I shall be here, Colonel Forrest. You can count on it," replied Wade as he got up to leave.

Forrest summoned Lieutenant Schuyler to his tent. "Schuyler, formal training is suspended for tomorrow morning. The men need a break from the routine, and I need the time to cement goodwill with the community. As you know, new recruits have been arriving here steadily since September 1st. If we are to get any kind of fighting machine, we need to start training right away. Pressure!...Pressure!...Pressure! That's what is needed. If I relax training one day, we'll not achieve our goal. If I make it hard on them now, the battlefield will look easier to them when we get there.

"Tomorrow is not a day off. It's just different. I need

to take care of some politics, and I need your assistance. I've been hounded by local merchants and commission agents to have a Merchants' Fair. These fellows want to bring some of their military goods out here for display and sale. I understand they plan to sell gray flannels and belts. Some will bring fancy dress items like gold cords and tassels, lace and feathers. Miller & Dunn's agents tell me they've got a stock of 10,000 hats of various colors. And they say some have plumes on them. Isn't that something!

"Now, Schuyler, if I catch any of my boys with a plumed cap, they'll get 30 days of guard duty. The same goes for lace and feathers. How would you like to serve with a bunch of sissies? Heh-heh-heh!

"Those peddlers will set up promptly at 9:00 a.m. I want them out of here by 12 noon. I want you to be in charge. Keep your eyes open for any overcharging. If you catch any of them doing that, have them pack up and leave. If they complain, send them over to me. If they so much as open their mouths, they'll find a fist in it.

"Now, I want you to understand that the only reason I'm permitting those Main Street shopkeepers to come out here is to turn the tables on them. They're going to be real surprised when I ask them for donations next week. I want to see the expressions on some of their faces, particularly those who are Union sympathizers. And I know for a fact that several of them are trying to arrange contracts with Union forces up around Cairo, Illinois."

Then Schuyler, who had found it hard to get a word in, asked Forrest, "Should I warn the men about buying some of the goods? A lot of the fancy stuff will be of little or no use to them when we are called up."

"That's a good idea, Schuyler. Get all the Company commanders together and tell them to spread the word to be careful with their money and not buy any 'dog do.'

"Now, Schuyler, it's 1:00 p.m. and time for camp inspection. Come with me with your notebook. I want you to write down my comments. If I find trash in front of tents, put down exactly where those tents are. Find out the names of the soldiers occupying those tents and their Company commander's name. And if I find a lame horse in a Company's corral, I want the name of the soldier assigned to that animal. You understand?"

"Yes, sir," replied Schuyler.

"I will not have a filthy camp. And for any soldier who does not take care of his mount, there will be Hell to pay," concluded Forrest as he got up to leave for inspection.

Saturday, September 21, 1861, 2:00 p.m.

Promptly at 2:00 p.m. Governor Harris, General Pillow and their aides arrived at the Fairgrounds. Harris was in Memphis primarily to discuss troop needs with Pillow. The latter had just arrived in Memphis after a scouting trip to Kentucky. They were welcomed by Forrest and escorted to his tent where Forrest's staff were waiting to be introduced to the distinguished visitors.

After introductions by Forrest, Governor Harris asked permission to ask a few questions. "Of course," replied Forrest, "I want you to have a clear picture of what we're doing here."

Both Harris and Pillow asked several questions about morale and about the adequacy of equipment and supplies. On the latter subject Forrest interjected, "To be truthful we are lacking much."

General Pillow, the 55-year old veteran of the Mexican War and former Memphis attorney, laughed. "Where have I heard that before? It's a problem we are trying our best to solve, Colonel Forrest. We started with no resources in June, but now we're making progress. I'm optimistic we'll have you fully equipped before you receive your orders to move up north of here."

Governor Harris than added, "Colonel Forrest, I am well aware that you have spent a substantial amount of your own funds to equip your battalion. That has been a patriotic gesture."

General Pillow then asked permission to tour the campgrounds and greet some of the soldiers. "Yes indeed, General. We want you to see the Camp," replied Forrest. "Feel free to talk with any of the recruits."

Pillow's conversations were mostly in the form of light-hearted banter. Harris, on the other hand, was much more the politician. He kept saying over and over to the soldiers he greeted, "We're proud of you young men," as he put his arm around their shoulders. "We know you will give a good account of yourselves when the time comes. This war won't last too long. You'll be back home soon."

Just before 3:00 p.m. Lieutenant Schuyler reminded Forrest and his visitors that it was time for the military review ceremony. Harris, Pillow, their aides, and Forrest and his staff walked a short distance to a temporary reviewing stand that had been built that morning.

Carriages and wagons of Fairground visitors were parked haphazardly encircling the parade ground. A crowd of 1200 people had come out for the review on this hot, early Autumn afternoon. Children darted around the field. Several small boys were dressed as soldiers. Most of the guests carried small Confederate flags which they waved frequently throughout the afternoon.

Major David Kelley, second in command to Forrest, was the officer in charge of the review.

At 3:00 p.m. all eight companies in Forrest's cavalry were in formation off to the side of the parade ground. On the reviewing stand with Governor Harris, General Pillow and Forrest were Mayor Richard Baugh and the city's aldermen; Sam Tate, the railroad entrepreneur; Matt Gallaway, editor of the *Avalanche*, and their wives.

Major Kelley strode briskly to the center of the parade ground, faced the reviewing stand, then saluted smartly. Then he turned facing the mounted troops who by that time had been positioned in formation on the opposite side of the field.

"Orders of the day," he barked in a high shrill voice. He then proceeded to read the following from a scroll:

Soldiers! By order of Colonel Nathan B. Forrest, Commanding. We are here to honor our distinguished Governor, Isham G. Harris, General Gideon J. Pillow, the honorable Mayor Baugh and city aldermen, special guests on the reviewing stand, and the citizens of Memphis assembled here today.
We promise you and the citizens of this great State of Tennessee faithful service to our noble cause fighting for freedom from oppression. Our review today is the culmination of several weeks of rigorous training. We are proud to have you witness the results of this effort.

Kelley paused for a few seconds, saluted again, then announced: "The Memphis Fire Department Band under the direction of Captain Jewell Moriarty will now perform. This will be followed by a parade of all eight companies in our battalion."

The band, resplendent in their white uniforms with gold buttons and red caps, marched sprightly from one end of the parade ground to the other and back, playing first *The Girl I Left Behind Me*, then *The Last Rose of Summer*, and followed by a rousing rendition of *Dixie*. Band leader, Captain Moriarty, reacting to the cheering crowd, halted the band. Then he had the band face the crowd, and played *Dixie* again. The popular band marched off the field with the crowd pleading, "Play *Dixie* one more time. Please, one more time!"

Major Kelley reappeared in the center of the parade ground, paused, then shouted for all to hear, "Troopers, pass in review!"

The sudden movement of hundreds of horses created a loud rumble and clouds of dust. Company commanders barked out orders to their troopers in staccato fashion. Then, one company after the other moved slowly from the west end of the rectangular field to the east end, wheeled around in a broad, semi-circular sweep, and headed back passing in full view of Governor Harris, General Pillow and the other dignitaries on the reviewing stand, and the citizens spread out along the sidelines.

Company C led by Captain May was first in line. May's unit received this honor because the entire company were Memphis volunteers. Their families and friends represented a substantial part of the crowd.

The dust stirred up by the horses, combined with the 85° temperature should have lessened the enthusiasm of the spectators. But they seemed oblivious to the discomfort. They were enjoying the patriotic military show.

Governor Harris and General Pillow were ecstatic. Each complimented the other as if they were personally responsible for the well-organized review. Forrest pulled Major Kelley aside and whispered, "Major, look at those two slapping each other on the back. So far they haven't said a word to me. But that's all right. Now that our little show is almost over, it's time to twist their arms for more equipment and supplies. Next week it will be too late. What they've seen here today will be far from their minds. Let me see what I can do."

Forrest unfortunately never got the opportunity. Both

Harris and Pillow had other engagements in Memphis that afternoon. They quickly excused themselves, entered a nearby carriage, and departed the Fairgrounds.

Monday, September 23, 1861

The day began like all previous days at the Fairground. Reveille was at 5:30 a.m., breakfast from 6:15 a.m. to 6:45 a.m., and camp cleanup at 7:00 a.m. Promptly at 7:30 a.m. there was general formation of all companies on the drill field. Here the troops would hear the "Orders of the Day" and special announcements by Major Kelley.

That particular day, Company A under Captain Overton, was ordered to report at 8:00 a.m. to the grandstand area for its first sanitation lecture of the week. Dr. Van Wick, the battalion's surgeon, was assigned by Colonel Forrest to spend one hour with each company going over the rules of camp sanitation. "I expect nothing less than total compliance with these regulations I've prepared," Forrest told Van Wick. "The appearance of these soldiers and our campgrounds shall be spotless. I've just notified all officers and noncoms that inspections shall be held twice each day. Any violations of regulations shall be reported to me. Understand?"

"Yes, sir," said the apprehensive battalion surgeon. Van Wick, realizing that Colonel Forrest would be carefully scrutinizing his performance, spent one whole week preparing his lecture. He requested two meetings with Forrest to clarify certain points. Van Wick told Major Kelley resignedly, "My teaching skills on the subject of camp sanitation are of far more concern to Colonel Forrest that my surgical skills."

Kelley, smiling, answered, "Dr. Van Wick, I think you are learning very well the Colonel's idiosyncrasies and his zealousness for details."

Each regulation was carefully explained to Captain Overton's troops assembled in the grandstand after which Dr. Van Wick solicited questions. Not too many bothered to ask. Most seemed bored by the detail, or disturbed by what many considered their loss of personal freedom to dress or cleanse themselves as they pleased. The only break in the tedious explanation of the rules and regulations was when Dr. Van Wick said, "Soldiers, there shall be no defecating behind your tents or in the open field over there."

Finally, a hand went up. "Yes," said Van Wick.

"Sir, what is dee...fee...ca...ting?"

"Soldier, that is squatting down to relieve yourself," replied Van Wick good-naturedly.

"Oh, I understand. You mean shitting."

Pandemonium reigned. The grandstand rocked with uncontrollable laughter. When order was restored, Dr. Van Wick regained his composure long enough to say, "Centrally located pits will be dug and that's where we expect you to urinate and squat. Do you all know what urinate means?" he said grinning broadly. Several soldiers hollered out, "It's pissing...it's pissing."

When Dr. Van Wick finished going over his list, Company A was dismissed. Captain Overton yelled, "Men, our next training exercise today is over at the pistol range."

Dr. Van Wick prepared to meet his next group, Company B, at 10:15 a.m. for the same lecture. He tapped his assistant, Sergeant Lawrence Prehn on the shoulder and said, "When I get to Regulation 18, slip me a note which says, 'squat, not defecating.'" Both laughed. Then Dr. Van Wick added, "I don't think Colonel Forrest would ever use the word defecation, do you?" Sergeant Prehn shook his head, "It's not likely, sir."

Throughout the Fairgrounds that morning the eight

companies met the carefully crafted training schedule set by Colonel Forrest. Some companies did close order drill. Others were given instructions in horsemanship and on the grooming and personal care of their mounts, and others received weapons training. In some instances, a particular training exercise didn't go smoothly for the obvious reason that many of the officers had no prior experience in military procedures. This was understandable. Just a few weeks before most had been civilians.

Tuesday, October 1, 1861

Forrest scheduled an officers' meeting at 7:30 a.m. to discuss several subjects. "I am worried about the distribution among the troops of the equipment and supplies we're getting. Governor Harris has kept his word. He has released enough funds to help us get on the field, but goddamnit, we've got a circus going on around here. Many of you are grabbing more goods than you need. We've ended up with some companies undersupplied. I want that stopped. Do you hear me?

"Now here's what's going to happen. Do some of you know Gilbert Rambaut, the innkeeper at the Worsham House? Well, he joined up and has been transferred over to me. He's going to serve as temporary Quartermaster and Chief of Commissary under my personal supervision. Now cooperate with him, goddamnit! If he tells me some of you company commanders are not playing straight, you're going back in the ranks as privates. Is that understood?

"All right, now the next subject is the matter of readiness for full action. Unless I hear a convincing objection, I'm alerting Governor Harris that Forrest's Cavalry Battalion is ready for assignment. I'll tell him if we're called upon, we'll fight like hell.

"The final subject this morning is election of officers. Governor Harris wants an up to date list right away. Now because Parson Kelley is my right hand man in the field command, I am proposing the Parson for Major. Do you all agree? I know this will be popular with the soldiers."

There is a short silence, then the staff applauded enthusiastically. "Good," said Forrest. "Now my next recommendations are that Sergeant Major Strange and Private Rambaut be elected Captains. I want Strange as my assistant Adjutant and Aide, and Rambaut as Chief of Commissary. These are two crucial staff positions. Do you agree?"

Before waiting for any reaction, Forrest continued on rapidly, "Here is my list of other recommendations. I am proposing to the soldiers that all the rest of you keep your present rank.

"Hold the election tonight after mess. Report the results to Captain Strange by 9:00 p.m. I said, 'Captain Strange,' didn't I? As far as I'm concerned, it's now Captain Strange. Heh-heh-heh!

"This meeting is adjourned."

Friday, October 11, 1861

At noon Colonel Forrest returned to his headquarters tent. The newly elected Captain Strange handed him a message. "Sir, this communication is from Major General Polk's headquarters in Columbus, Kentucky. It came by special courier fifteen minutes ago."

"General Polk?...the Bishop?...the Commander of Department No. 2?" questioned the surprised Forrest. "What does he want from me? Let me read it before I die of curiosity."

Then Forrest read it aloud slowly.

Lieutenant Colonel N. B. Forrest...You are to make preparations to phase out your battalion's training schedule immediately.
This is to alert you that you will be receiving orders in the very near future to undertake a full assignment from this command.
By order of Major General Leonidas Polk, Commanding, Department No. 2, Columbus, Kentucky, October 9, 1861

"At last, Strange, at last! I've been marking time since the middle of June to get into the fighting. Hallelujah! Get Major Kelley over here quick. Now, Strange, don't say anything to anybody, understand? I want to hold this under my hat as long as I can. When we get the formal orders I expect in a few days, we'll call an assembly of the battalion and surprise the men.

"I'll tell only Major Kelley, and maybe Mary. That's all! Strange, I'll sleep well tonight. It won't be long now.

"Are you as excited as I am, Strange?"

"Of course I am, sir. I'll be on pins and needles until General Polk issues the orders."

As Captain Strange left the tent to find Major Kelley, he glanced back at the Colonel. Forrest had a look of elation, and nervously clapped his hands. Strange told Major Kelley a few moments later, "He's probably fighting a battle in his mind right now. All he sees are Yankees in front of him waiting to be slaughtered."

For the next thirteen days Forrest awaited nervously for the arrival of his orders from General Polk. Each successive day he became more agitated. He yelled at his staff frequently and seemed to find fault with everyone for their actions in administering the day to day routine of camp life. Captain Strange was hesitant to ask Forrest anything for fear of being called an "idiot" or a "stupid clerk." But Strange and Major Kelley understood the reasons for his irritable disposition and outbursts of temper. They stood their distance.

Finally, late Friday afternoon, October 25th, the orders came. "Call a full assembly of all soldiers tomorrow morning at 8:00 a.m.," he shouted at Strange. "I've got an announcement to make."

"Do you mean the official orders have arrived?" asked the excited assistant adjutant.

"Yes, yes, yes, they are right here in my hand. You will hear them tomorrow morning with everyone else. Don't tell anyone why the assembly is being called, Strange. If anyone asks, you tell them it's the Saturday morning battalion inspection being held early because I am canceling training for tomorrow afternoon."

Saturday, October 26, 1861

All commanders had their companies in formation promptly at the scheduled hour — 8:00 a.m. Forrest's staff, except for Major Kelley, was positioned at the far left of the parade ground. Kelley escorted Colonel Forrest to the center of the field.

"Battalion...Atten...shun," yelled Major Kelley authoritatively. "Company commanders report!"

Beginning with Captain Overton of Company A, each commander through Captain Miller of Company H reported, "All present and accounted for, sir."

Major Kelley turned and saluted Forrest, then stepped backward several steps, giving Forrest sole possession of the center of the field.

"Soldiers!" Forrest said firmly. "At last our time has come. Orders have been received for the battalion to move north to the Tennessee-Kentucky state line. The Federals are moving into western Kentucky and apparently into Missouri across the Mississippi River.

"Two companies, A and G, will be detached temporarily from the battalion and will be transported by packet to Columbus, Kentucky. Captain Overton will be in command of these units when they leave Memphis on Monday morning.

"The six other companies, under my leadership, will depart on Monday for Fort Henry on the Tennessee River near the Kentucky line. Specific orders as to the nature of our mission will be given to us by Colonel Adolphus Heiman, Commander of the Tenth Tennessee (Irish) Brigade."

A loud roar of approval went up from the troops. "Yahoo!" "Let's go!" "Hurray for the Confederacy!" "Tell Jeff Davis we are coming!" Enlisted men were slapping each other playfully, and congratulating themselves for their good fortune.

When the company commanders restored order, Forrest continued: "You all know what I expect of you. You will always face forward to the enemy and display courage." He paused for a few seconds, then continued, "Now, let's have a heap of fun and kill some Yankees, too!"

Again, a rousing cheer went up. Like Forrest, his soldiers were ready to go into action immediately.

Forrest, obviously pleased by the reaction, then said, "Every soldier will remain in camp tomorrow. Church services and *Bible* reading will be scheduled in the morning. Tomorrow afternoon you will clean your weapons and check your mounts. See that your mount is shod properly. I want no lame horses on the ride north to Fort Henry. Severe punishment will be handed out to anyone who abuses his mount.

"Now finally soldiers, I am pleased to announce that the Paymaster's tent will be open at 9:30 a.m. Each private shall receive the $12.00 authorized monthly pay.

Noncommissioned officers and officers will be paid this afternoon.

"That's all! Major Kelley, dismiss the troops!"

In unison, a mass yell went up before Major Kelley could give the command. Seeing the commotion, he didn't bother. Colonel Forrest and Major Kelley quickly strode off the field. It was time to start breaking camp.

Monday, October 28, 1861

By dawn the Fairgrounds training camp was barren except for the 650 mounted cavalry soldiers of Forrest's battalion in company formation, and a long line of 30 wagons and their teams of draft horses and teamsters. Many of the latter were Forrest's slaves he had brought into the Confederate service with him. Tents had been taken down and packed, the temporary wooden platforms dismantled, and targets removed from the rifle ranges. And in keeping with Forrest's reputation for cleanliness, the Fairgrounds was left spotless.

Forrest summoned Captain Strange to get the latter's assurance that the Fairgrounds was in better shape now than when the battalion first occupied it in late August. "If I hear any criticism from the Mayor, I'm going to be hard on you, Strange," said Forrest sternly.

"Sir, it's in good shape."

"All right then, send Rambaut over here. I want to check with him about the wagon train."

One by one the various staff members were questioned about the state of readiness. In frustration Rambaut said to Strange, "Well, I'll be happy when it's 8:00 a.m. and we move out. Colonel Forrest is driving us all crazy with his interference in every facet of our duties. My ears are drooping like a wet mule."

"I know that feeling, Gilbert," answered Strange.

"That's just the way he is. You cannot get away with anything. He pokes around everywhere."

Rambaut laughed. "Do you think battle action will get his mind off small details?"

"I seriously doubt it," said Strange slapping his friend on the rear end.

At 8:00 a.m. the order came, "Let's move out!" Captain Overton's small force of two companies mounted and headed to the Memphis levee to board a transport to move them upriver to Columbus, Kentucky to join a large Confederate force assembled by General Polk to counter a threatened move south by Union forces operating out of Cairo, Illinois.

Colonel Forrest signaled his main force to ride out of the Fairgrounds. Several hundred citizens stood outside to wave goodbye, Forrest's commanders shouted orders to their troops: "Wheel right, Company B"; "Stay in formation, Company C"; "Hold your heads up, troopers"; and "Speed it up!"

The enlisted volunteers wore no single, standard uniform. Most had short gray jackets, but their baggy wool trousers were a rainbow of tans, blacks, maroons and grays. All wore soft felt, slouch hats and the standard issue leather brogans, fitting high on the ankle. Truly it was a citizens' army, devoid of traditional military frills, leaving Memphis to go to war.

5 • First Combat

Captain Overton's detachment was delayed in moving up the Mississippi River by seasonally low waters. It arrived at Columbus, Kentucky, located on the east bank of the river, on November 9, 1861. Two days earlier, Confederate troops based at Columbus crossed the river to Missouri to stop a probing movement by a force of 3500 Union soldiers commanded by the 39-year old Brigadier General Ulysses S. Grant (West Point, 1843). The Confederates were led by Major General Leonidas Polk

(West Point, 1827), 55, an Episcopalian bishop who had joined the Confederate service just a few months earlier.

After a brief, spirited fight of just a few hours which left 120 Union and 105 Confederate soldiers dead, Grant called off the fight, and ordered his troops to reload on their transports for the return trip up river to their base in Cairo, Illinois.

Militarily, neither side gained anything. Polk, however, claimed victory, and so notified his superiors.

When Overton's troops arrived, Polk no longer needed them. They were ordered to march overland some 100 miles to Fort Henry, Tennessee, then to proceed to Hopkinsville, Kentucky, a town just north of the Tennessee state line, to reunite with Forrest's battalion.

Forrest's main force of some 500 soldiers and 30 wagons loaded with ammunition, tents, commissary supplies, grain for the horses and water arrived at Fort Henry — a distance of 160 miles from Memphis — on November 14th. Here, Forrest received from the Fort's commandant, Colonel Adolphus Heiman, orders to move the battalion to Hopkinsville.

"Forrest, your assignment is to scout the rural areas of west-central Kentucky for signs of Federal military activity. Your group is part of our defensive position against the enemy which we expect will be coming down from Illinois," said Colonel Heiman. "General Albert Sidney Johnston, who commands the Confederate Western Department, has designed a defense line from Columbus, Kentucky on the extreme west, southeast to here at Fort Henry and nearby Fort Donelson, then northeast to Bowling Green, Kentucky. Our job is to hold this line until we can get our forces up to full strength. Any signs of enemy movements we want to know immediately."

General Johnston's Confederate troops faced a potential force of 200,000. One-half of these troops were commanded by General Don Carlos Buell (West Point, 1841); and the other half by General Henry W. Halleck (West Point, 1839). This disparity of numbers was of great concern to General Johnston and the Confederate military leadership in Richmond.

Defense of the Tennessee River and the Cumberland River transportation routes was a major part of the Confederate strategy in the first year of the war. Both rivers, which empty into the Ohio River east of Paducah, Kentucky, were navigable routes into the heart of Tennessee. And protection of the Confederate supply depot at Nashville was imperative to the success of Western Theater operations.

From mid-November 1861 through January 1862 Forrest's Cavalry scouted Union troop movements operating from its base at Hopkinsville. Scouting parties moved deftly through the region. Occasionally, there were minor skirmishes. With one notable exception, casualties were few. Dr. Van Wick, battalion surgeon and valued staff aide, was murdered by a Northern sympathizer in an unrelated military action in Kentucky.

Van Wick's loss was critical. Forrest needed a qualified replacement quickly. He thought immediately of his wife Mary's cousin, Dr. James B. Cowan. But at the time Dr. Cowan was already serving with Colonel James R. Chalmers' 9th Mississippi Regiment at Pensacola, Florida. Forrest sent word to Colonel Heiman requesting that he get General Polk's permission to have Cowan transferred. Polk approved the transfer.

Dr. Cowan, 30, was a graduate of the University Medical College of New York in 1855. He had had six years of experience as a surgeon before entering the service. At 6-foot-1 and weighing 190 pounds, the barrel-chested Cowan seemed perfectly suited for the rigors of military life in the field. He reported for duty on December 1, 1861.

On December 28, 1861, while scouting near the small village of Sacramento, Kentucky, Forrest and 160 of his troops caught by surprise a Federal cavalry force of similar size. Without hesitating to coordinate his plan of attack with his junior officers, the excited Forrest screamed, "Charge...Go after them...Let's give 'em hell." And charge they did with a vengeance with Forrest out in front of the assault firing his two Navy Colt pistols at the startled enemy force who were quickly routed by the wild charging Confederates.

Major Kelley, Forrest's second-in-command, wrote of that day's events, "Colonel Forrest showed reckless disregard for his own life at Sacramento as he unleashed a personal assault on several of the enemy who challenged him. He was yelling in his high shrill voice like a wild Indian. Right then and there I knew he loved fighting and killing." Kelley continued, "His boldness and recklessness surprised and routed the enemy not prepared for Forrest's style of slashing attacks. That day at Sacramento I was personally concerned we were about to lose our commander."

On a historian's list of Civil War events of significance Sacramento is hardly a speck. But it was a violent baptism of fire for Forrest, Kelley and 158 others of Forrest's Cavalry.

Notification came on January 31, 1862 that Forrest's unit had been upgraded to regimental status. The following week Forrest received orders to move his forces to Fort Donelson, located on the west side of the Cumberland River, just one-half mile north of the small town of Dover, Tennessee. Fort Donelson had been constructed just four months earlier. Its purpose was to deny access of Union gunboats and transports to a river route leading to the well-stocked warehouses holding food and military equipment at Nashville. Physical structures, except gun emplacements, were few. The fort's defensive works were earthen embankments constructed in a broad semi-circle around the artillery batteries containing a total of 11 guns. These weapons were aimed toward the adjacent Cumberland River.

On Tuesday February 11, 1862 General Gideon Pillow, who just five months earlier had reviewed Forrest's raw recruits in Memphis at the Fairgrounds, ordered Forrest to lead a force of 300 cavalrymen westward out of Fort Donelson toward Fort Henry, which was 12 miles west on the Tennessee River. Their assignment was to reconnoiter and to report any movement of Union troops toward Fort Donelson. Pillow had just assumed command on February 9th after being absent from Confederate service for over two months. He had a bitter dispute with General Polk over his conduct in the fight against Grant's Union troops at Belmont, Missouri. Pillow, angry at Polk's accusations, resigned the army. President Jefferson Davis, a long-time friend of Pillow's, coaxed the latter to change his mind and return to service. Fort Donelson was his first assignment upon return.

Fort Henry, a Confederate fort constructed to protect the Tennessee River from access by Federal troops moving down from Illinois by boats, fell to General Grant's forces on February 6th. Some 15,000 of Grant's troops disembarked at Fort Henry to join other Federal units. Grant's plan was to move across the 12-mile, narrow neck of heavily-wooded land between the two navigable rivers and attack Fort Donelson. Grant waited at Fort Henry for the harsh winter weather to abate.

On Wednesday, February 12th Forrest was again assigned to reconnoiter the area west of Fort Donelson. It rained heavily that day, and Forrest reported no Federal activity.

General Pillow and General Simon Bolivar Buckner, a principal Confederate commander at Fort Donelson, waited for Grant's impending attack. By nightfall, they were puzzled as to why Grant hadn't made a move.

Early that evening after officers' mess Forrest decided to visit with his enlisted men. Most were huddled around campfires, wrapped in blankets, seeking protection from the bitter winds. "When do you think we'll fight, Colonel?" was the question asked by most.

"Soon, men, very soon! Are you all prepared?"

"Yes, sir," they answered in unison. "We're ready to kill some Yankees, yes, sir. This is what we've been waiting for since we left Memphis."

"Are your mounts in good condition? I'm going to be hard on anyone who rides out on a lame horse. See the blacksmith tonight if you need to have your mount shod."

Forrest then hurried over to Dr. Cowan's hospital tent with Captain Strange, his Assistant Adjutant.

The harsh winter had taken its toll physically on some of his men. Common colds and sore throats were the principal ailments; and Dr. Cowan and his assistants had been busy early that evening treating dozens of soldiers. Forrest wanted Cowan's report on the physical readiness of his troops for the battle he expected the next day, February 13th.

As he entered the main tent Forrest asked, "Dr. Cowan, how are the men? Do we have any serious problems I should know about? How big is the puny list?"

Dr. Cowan motioned Forrest to step outside.

"Colonel, do you see that sorry-looking fellow sitting in there on a keg? He says he's deaf and can't hear a thing. I don't think he is telling the truth. What should I do?"

"All right, let's find out," said Forrest.

Back in the tent Dr. Cowan approached the patient claiming deafness. "What's your name and unit, private?"

There was no response. The soldier just stared ahead with no expression. Meanwhile, Colonel Forrest had quietly moved behind the private, pulled out his Colt revolver,, and fired one shot beside the soldier's left ear.

"Goddamnit, James, look at him jump," yelled the gleeful Forrest.

Everyone in the tent started laughing — even the startled victim of Forrest's dramatic prank.

"Strange, make certain he's on the lead horse tomorrow morning. I want this coward to see all the action up front when we move out on patrol.

Then, looking around Dr. Cowan's tent Forrest spotted another possible malingerer.

"What's the matter with him?"

"Private Hudnut has a case of what they call down on the plantation, 'dyasthesia aethiopis'."

"What's that?"

"In slaveowners' terms, it's known as rascality."

Again, much laughter among those in the tent.

"Well, Captain Strange, mark Private Hudnut for duty, and make certain he's out front tomorrow too," ordered Forrest.

"Now, Colonel, did you have a specific reason for coming to see me?" asked Dr. Cowan.

"Well, yes I did. I'm suffering something awful from festering boils. A Yankee musket ball would be welcome if it opened one of those damn boils."

"Colonel, the best medicine I know for boils is to thank the Lord it isn't rheumatism."

"Now, that's not funny, Cowan. I need some help."

"What we need is a conjure man to perform a little witchcraft — some black magic."

"Oh you mean some hocus-pocus?" grunted Forrest half-heartedly.

"Exactly," replied Dr. Cowan. "But the problem is that

no self-respecting conjure man would come out on a cold night like tonight.

"Let me tell you a story I heard in Memphis a few months ago. A patient came in to see his doctor and said, 'I've got a bad case of rheumatism, a painful buzzing in my ear, a sprained ankle, a dislocated thumb and spots before my eyes.'

"The doctor looks at him in amazement, then says, 'My, my... you must be awfully healthy to stand all that pain'."

Dr. Cowan laughed as he finished telling his story, and Forrest, not amused, said, "Goddamnit, James, I wish to God I was a doctor. A doctor can cut and slash at will and not have to answer for it. He can even get away telling a story like that to somebody suffering from goddamn boils. Now, dammit, lance this one on my hip before I pass out."

Suspecting Forrest was in no mood for his light-hearted humor, Dr. Cowan proceeded to administer treatment to the Colonel's boils. When finished Cowan told Forrest, "Bedford . . . I mean Colonel, you have got to stay off your horse for a few days if you want to clear up those boils. Constant riding just irritates them."

"I can't do that! I expect the next several days to be hell. The Federals have a huge army at Fort Henry. They're going to head this way in force -- maybe tomorrow. I'm going to a commanders' meeting now at General Pillow's headquarters to get the latest intelligence reports. The Federals already have advance scouting parties just two or three miles from here. I'm going to be doing some hard riding, so I guess I won't be back to see you soon."

Gen. Pillow's Headquarters, Wed., February 12, 1862, 9:00 p.m.

When Forrest arrived, the meeting had already begun.

General Pillow was announcing that he would be replaced the next day by Brigadier General John B. Floyd, and that he, Pillow, would be second in command. The assembled commanders were surprised at the change, and were talking rapidly among themselves until Pillow said, "Gentlemen, this should be no surprise. As you know I just returned to Confederate service four days ago. I was asked by President Davis to take command of Fort Donelson on a temporary basis until General Floyd arrived.

"Now, gentlemen, were it not for the fact that attack may come at any hour now, we would postpone this meeting until after General Floyd settles in here tomorrow, and is thoroughly briefed on the situation. He may be bringing special instructions from General A. S. Johnston or from the War Department in Richmond. I don't know. I am still in command. General Buckner has discussed with me in some detail his recommendations as to our defensive strategy. We've discussed the circumstances under which we should counterattack. It's a good plan. He will now present it."

General Pillow then yielded to General Buckner.

Buckner (West Point, 1844), a one-time Federal army officer, had volunteered his service to the Confederacy in September 1861. Buckner opposed slavery, and originally opposed secession. But he deeply resented the intrusion of Federal forces into neutral Kentucky, his home state. His first assignment as a Confederate officer was to command all units operating in Kentucky. At Fort Donelson, Buckner was one of only a handful of Confederate senior officers who had had any prior military experience.

In a slow, halting voice barely audible Buckner outlined the general field assignments for the various infantry and cavalry commands at Fort Donelson. "A perimeter defensive line circling Fort Donelson and the village of Dover has been developed. It will be from assigned locations where our units will either move forward against the enemy, or defend against enemy penetration." Buckner continued explaining the details over the next 15 minutes. Then Buckner asked, "Any questions?"

After several moments of silence, Forrest, one of the lowest ranking officers present, asked, "Why don't we move out and strike them before they get here? Wouldn't catching them by surprise throw them into panic, and perhaps force them to retreat? The weather is so bad with all the rain and snow they may think it's not worth chasing us out of Fort Donelson."

"What's your name, officer?" asked the stonefaced Buckner.

"It's Lieutenant Colonel Forrest, sir. I command a cavalry unit."

"Well, Forrest, your suggestion is unorthodox to say the least. Frankly, we don't have the manpower to take the offensive. Our plan, as I mentioned, is to await Grant's arrival, determine his weaknesses, then strike hard where we think we can break through."

"Are there any other questions?" asked Buckner.

There were none, and General Pillow moved forward again and said, "All units should be on the ready. I anticipate a hard fight. Good night and good luck, gentlemen."

Thursday, February 13, 1862

General Grant's plan was to surround the west side of Fort Donelson's defenses. Then he would wait for the Federal gunboats to fire on the Fort's artillery batteries from a position on the Cumberland River just to the north of the Fort. He reasoned this attack plan would block all escape routes, and the Confederates would be forced to surrender.

Grant's army had 24 infantry regiments, seven batteries of artillery and cavalry. They moved in force to the front of the Confederate defenses. One Union division was commanded by General John A. McClernand, an irascible 49-year-old officer who before volunteering had been a lawyer and a member of Congress from Illinois. Grant assigned him to the right of the Union line. The other combat division, operating on the left, was led by career army officer, the 54-year-old Major General Charles F. Smith (West Point, 1825).

General Floyd arrived at Fort Donelson on schedule. With him were reinforcements for the Confederate Army. The 54-year-old Floyd, like McClernand, was a pre-war politician. The three-term governor of Virginia had also served as President James Buchanan's Secretary of War in the late 1850s.

The Confederate forces assembled for Floyd had 27 regiments of infantry, Forrest's Cavalry, and an artillery section. The combined force was about 15,000 soldiers. The Federals had fewer regiments but a far greater number of troops.

Grant's army was poised for attack by dark. That evening at General Floyd's headquarters his principal commanders, Pillow, Buckner and Bushrod Johnson all agreed they were ready for the attack. Forrest and his troops in their camp behind the lines were restless and anxious awaiting their first major fight of the war. Late in the evening Forrest had his officers checking and re-checking ammunition and equipment.

Friday, February 14, 1862

The day began with the arrival on the field of additional Union troops. The combined force of Grant's army had now reached 27,000, almost double the size of Floyd's army.

At 3:00 p.m. four Union ironclads and several gunboats began a heavy bombardment of Fort Donelson. The Confederate batteries countered with equally heavy fire from their gun emplacements on the river's bluffs. At 4:30 p.m., the Union fleet, badly damaged in the intense exchange, retreated back up the river toward the Kentucky border. As the fleet moved off, the Confederates at the Fort celebrated what they considered a great victory.

Frontal attacks by Grant's infantry against the Confederates dug in behind earthworks were minimal, mostly of a probing nature.

Friday night General Floyd gathered his key commanders to plan a strategy for dealing with Grant.

"Federal gunboats will be back tomorrow on the Cumberland," said Floyd. "I don't think we can hold the Fort." Several nodded in agreement. "We should evacuate the inner Fort tonight," he continued. "We're better off strengthening our outer works on the left of our line in front of Dover."

"But, General, it's snowing. The weather's terrible," interjected Buckner.

"All the better," replied Floyd. "We can probably move the bulk of our forces without detection. The Federals are pretty well bedded down tonight because of the horrible weather."

Pillow supported Floyd.

"All right," decided Floyd. "Begin the move within the next hour. By dawn we can probably shift a large portion of our troops to the left and center of our defense line."

Floyd's decision proved to be a good one. Overnight the entire Confederate force was repositioned without any difficulty.

Saturday, February 15, 1862

Forrest ordered his cavalry mounted at 7:00 a.m. He waited for orders to move forward. As they waited, Major Kelley, the Methodist preacher and now full-time soldier, moved from unit to unit saying short prayers to the shivering men. Almost yelling to be heard, he asked for bowed heads, then would say:

We are on the side of righteousness. Please God, show us the way to victory. Protect each and every one of us as we undertake this bold mission.
From the Book of Proverbs, Chapter 24, Verse 10, 'If thou faint in the day of adversity, thy strength is small.'
God bless all of you!

At 7:30 a.m. the Confederates struck swiftly the Union army's right line. The impetuous, high strung General Pillow was out in front of the attack on the right side of the Union line. General Buckner, positioned in the center, also attacked the right side of the Union line. Forrest's Cavalry came out from Dover to join Pillow's soldiers. Bitter fighting broke out immediately as both large armies clashed head-on.

Late that morning Grant's forces became disorganized. His troops ran low on ammunition. Pillow and his commanders urged their troops forward to put maximum pressure on the Federals. At this point in the fighting the Confederate army had successfully escaped its entrapment at Fort Donelson. It was in a position to withdraw intact, and safely make its way toward Nashville without serious challenge from Grant's army.

But General Pillow, sensing victory and perhaps dreaming of plaudits from Richmond's high command, continued forcing the action. Reacting to the chaos within the Union forces operating against Pillow, General Grant ordered the veteran General Charles Smith, leader of the Union's 3rd Division, to counterattack against Pillow on the Confederate left. At 2:00 p.m. the Federals charged forward successfully, and within one hour forced the Confederate army back to their original defensive positions it held early that morning.

Observers concluded in the critique of the fight at Fort Donelson that General Pillow, at the start of the Federal counterattack, had lost his nerve. He decided not to meet the advancing Federals head-on. Instead, he ordered a retreat; and in so doing, lost the opportunity for the possible destruction of Grant's army.

By 3:00 p.m. all hope of an orderly escape from Fort Donelson by Confederate forces had vanished.

When darkness came just after 5:00 p.m., rifle and cannon fire subsided and a quiet prevailed as each army gathered up its wounded. Forrest met with his officers, and calmly ordered them to report on the condition of the men and their horses. He was told that some of the men were scattered among other units and probably wouldn't return until Sunday morning. Casualties among Forrest's Cavalry appeared to be light.

Sunday, February 16, 1862, 12:30 a.m.

At Pillow's headquarters, Floyd, Buckner and Pillow met to consider their options. A message had been received earlier in the evening that Grant was being reinforced.

General Floyd in an anguished voice, said, "Our position appears hopeless if we try to continue the fight. We'll be crushed or starved into submission. We should try to evacuate before daylight."

"No, I disagree, sir," replied Buckner. "Grant has overwhelming superiority in troops. Our soldiers are exhausted after today's fighting. We can't make it out of here without heavy losses."

The consensus of the three key commanders was that it was useless to fight on.

Outside around an open fire were Forrest and several other officers waiting for their orders from General Floyd. When informed that the decision had been to surrender, Forrest, visibly upset, rushed into the headquarters yelling, "I shall not surrender. It serves no purpose. What makes you think a large number of us cannot escape? My scouts tell me they have found a route that is clear. If we act now, most of us can be gone by daylight."

"Forrest, ordinarily I would resent your impertinence," answered Pillow. "You are not the commanding officer here. But I do agree with you. I too will not accept surrender."

General Floyd then nodded in agreement. "Colonel, you are free to take your regiment out of here. I don't relish prison camp. I may go out too."

Then Floyd turned to Buckner and asked, "What's your decision, General?"

Buckner, extremely depressed at the hopelessness, answered, "I shall stay and surrender to Grant in the morning."

"All right, Buckner," snapped Floyd. "You're in command as of now. Good luck to you. I hope I shall have the honor of serving with you again if this war continues much longer."

Forrest didn't waste a minute exiting Pillow's headquarters. Within 15 minutes he had called his staff and the commanders together, and announced his decision.

Captain Strange, standing next to Forrest, grinned when he heard the decision.

"Strange, you better grin because there isn't a damn

thing you can do about it," announced the determined Forrest.

By 2:00 a.m. on that bitter cold February night and with snow on the ground Forrest's Cavalry cut its way across rain swollen Lick Creek and along the flooded Cumberland River road east of Dover, and headed toward Nashville.

Floyd, Pillow and Bushrod Johnson also escaped Fort Donelson taking with them some 2000 troops. They boarded transports and headed toward Nashville.

Left behind at Fort Donelson were about 13,000 Confederates to be surrendered to General Grant by General Buckner.

Before dawn on Sunday morning Buckner ordered white sheets draped over all Confederate fortifications. Grant, informed of Buckner's actions, sent a communication to the latter demanding "unconditional surrender." Grant emphasized in his message: "No terms can be accepted."

Immediately, Grant's victory at Fort Donelson was hailed throughout the North. *The New York Times'* headlines of February 18, 1862 proclaimed: "Glorious Victory," "Floyd Denounced by Rebels as a Black Hearted Traitor and Coward," "Immense Amount of War Material Captured," "Heavy Losses in Killed and Wounded on Both Sides." The *Times* printed word-for-word Grant's demand for unconditional surrender and also General Buckner's acquiescence to the Federal ultimatum.

As he distanced himself from Fort Donelson in the early hours of Sunday morning, February 16th, Forrest was agitated and discouraged. "I've learned something valuable to my future career in this army," he told Dr. Cowan.

"What's that, Colonel?"

"Simply put, James, I learned from my superiors the

lessons of how not to conduct a military operation."

6 • Panic

"Good God, Kelley! Are we too late?" said a startled Forrest as they approached the outskirts of Nashville in mid-afternoon, Monday, February 17th. "Look at the blackened sky ahead. See it? It's all around the turret top of the State Capitol Building up on Campbell's Hill. What do you think is happening?"

"I have no idea, Colonel Forrest. Could it be that the Federals have already taken Nashville? I didn't know that Buell's army was anywhere near the city."

"Well, it looks like there are a number of fires there. That dark sky isn't from burning coal. Memphis never looked that dark on a cold winter day. Let's step up the pace and get there soon. The messenger that came out from General Johnston's headquarters brought me a note stating that I am to meet him and Governor Harris at the State Capitol as soon as possible. It's 3:00 p.m. now. Do you think we can get there by 4:30 p.m.?"

"The horses are exhausted, Colonel; but let's go. I'll send the order back through the ranks for double-quick."

As Forrest's Cavalry proceeded forward, the road became crowded with wagons and carriages exiting the city. Men, women and children, and furniture were packed in tightly. The people had the look of urgency and panic.

Captain Strange rode up to Forrest and said excitedly, "These people are evacuating Nashville. They say that the Federals are heading that way, and the City is defenseless. Many are bitter about General Johnston and General Floyd. They blame the surrender of Fort Donelson on them, and say they have lost confidence in all of us to defend them and their property."

"I told you there would be Hell to pay for surrendering. It opens up all of Tennessee to the enemy," replied Forrest. "Nashville will probably fall soon. I'm anxious to find out what General Johnston and Governor Harris intend to do."

One evacuee yelled from his wagon," Nashville is being looted by ruffians from Slabtown and Smokey Row, those terrible neighborhoods down near the Cumberland River. They're robbing the government warehouses, stores and citizens on the street. And they're setting buildings on fire to create total chaos. There's no law in Nashville. There are no police. Be careful! Protect yourselves, soldiers!"

Evidence of the total collapse of law and order soon became visually apparent to Forrest's troops as they entered this war-swollen city of over 30,000. Looters were in full view carrying goods out of stores and yelling obscenities to protesting, helpless merchants. Angry mobs were setting buildings on fire, oblivious of Forrest and his troops riding by.

"This is a sickening sight," said Forrest to Major Kelley. "I'd like to charge them all out, Kelley. It would be good target practice."

An aide from General Johnston's headquarters, Major Kent Crow, rode out to greet Forrest near the State Capitol Building. "General Johnston is expecting you, Colonel Forrest. He asked me to escort you to Governor Harris' office. The General has provided quarters for your mess, Colonel Forrest. Sergeant James Collier will guide them there. Your soldiers will be provided food and lodging, and stables for your horses and wagons."

"Thank you, sir," responded Forrest. "But first, let me speak to my Major before I go up the steps to the Capitol."

Turning to Kelley, Forrest said in a stern tone, "Kelley,

I shall report our assignment to you as soon as the meeting is over. It may be several hours though. I want you to keep the men confined to quarters. No one is permitted out. I know damn well half of them would dash to that riverfront district known as 'the Jungle.' That's a rough place — saloons, brothels, gambling dens, pickpockets, and low-class Irish criminals. Remember the three 'Bs.' Stay away from barrooms, brothels and betting parlors. You stand a better chance of getting killed there than on the battlefield."

Kelley laughed good-naturedly at Forrest's admonishments. "Are you also including me in that confinement to quarters?" asked Kelley.

"Major, preachers are the worst of the lot."

Forrest entered the foyer of the Governor's office just inside the main entrance to the Capitol Building.

"Colonel Forrest, I'm Colonel Charles Ray Wilson, General Johnston's Adjutant. Welcome to Nashville. We're all delighted you were able to withdraw from Fort Donelson. Please come with me to Governor Harris' inner office."

"Has the meeting been going on for awhile, Colonel?" asked Forrest.

"Yes, it started about 2:00 p.m."

As Forrest entered the office, Governor Harris stood and extended his hand. "Colonel, it's a pleasure to see you safe and sound. Have you met General Albert Sidney Johnston before?"

"No, sir, I have not. General, I am honored."

"Thank you, Forrest," replied General Johnston. "I have been getting complimentary reports on you from our mutual friend, Colonel Sam Tate. I am proud to have you in this army."

Harris continued, "You know General Floyd, of course."

"Yes, sir, I think I've seen him somewhere before. Maybe as recently as two days ago," Forrest said with a wry smile on his face.

"And, Colonel, have you met Nashville's mayor, Richard Cheatham?" asked Harris.

"No, sir, I have not," as he shook the Mayor's hand.

Governor Harris briefed Forrest on the discussions that had already taken place at the meeting. He told Forrest that due to the imminent danger of Federal attack on Nashville he was ordering the seat of State government to Memphis. "Most of the records have been crated and sent to Memphis. When I leave tomorrow I'll take as many cabinet members and state legislators as I can to Memphis. This measure, I hope, will be temporary.

"We've been discussing the question of whether we should try to defend Nashville. The consensus is that we cannot. We've only got limited troops here now, and the city's home guard would be of little help.

"Our scouts have sighted advanced parties of General Buell's Union army just north of the state line in Kentucky. We think Buell's arrival here with a large force is imminent. We cannot stop him other than some limited harassment. We'll destroy the two bridges across the Cumberland River here in Nashville. Things of that sort. General Johnston has made these decisions; and I am in accord with them as are General Floyd and Mayor Cheatham.

"Just before your arrival we discussed how you and your regiment can be of maximum assistance. No doubt, Colonel, you have witnessed the complete mayhem out there in the city. I'll ask your superior, General Johnston, to outline our request."

"Thank you, Governor Harris," responded the tall, square-jawed Johnston. "Forrest, I want you to assist General Floyd first thing tomorrow morning in restoring law and order. I want your troops to join Floyd's small group of Missouri infantrymen and a few Kentucky cavalrymen in controlling the mobs running loose. But after tomorrow, you're on your own. General Floyd and his troops are ordered to withdraw to Murfreesboro, Tennessee. I'm leaving too.

"Forrest, I hate to impose this order on you, particularly after your hard ordeal at Fort Donelson and your long march here. As I understand it your troops have been on the move constantly since February 1st. But I am sure you understand that we have an extreme emergency on our hands. There aren't enough other troops to protect our military warehouses from looting, and to get our equipment and supplies loaded and sent south.

"I am certain Mayor Cheatham's police will do their duty in helping you protect citizens and their property from these thieves."

Mayor Cheatham shook his head negatively. "No, sir, we don't have a police force now. Most have fled the city. They are frightened to death about what might happen to them if the Federals catch them."

General Johnston interrupted the Mayor. "Forrest, you are our only hope. What do you say to that?"

"Give me the authority and I will try to settle things down long enough so we can evacuate the city in an orderly fashion," answered Forrest. "What is your schedule?"

"Forrest, I wish I could say one week, but reports coming into my headquarters say that General Buell is moving quickly down from Louisville, and we also have reports that Grant is assembling his river transports on the Cumberland to send to Nashville in four or five days. I am asking the impossible. Can you do it in two days...three at the most?"

"General Johnston, if I can commandeer every wagon in town, and every boxcar and engine from the Louisville & Nashville, Nashville & Chattanooga, and the Tennessee & Alabama yards, maybe I can do it. You will have to order the yardmasters and their superintendents to cooperate. If there are any Union sympathizers amongst them, I want your authority to deal with them harshly."

Governor Harris interjected at this point, "Of course, you have the authority, doesn't he, General Johnston?"

"Yes, you do. I shall send my Assistant Adjutant, Major Boatright, to accompany you. He will send dispatches to Murfreesboro apprising me of your progress.

"Colonel Forrest," continued Johnston looking at him with his piercing eyes that displayed anguish, "my command has been savagely criticized for surrendering Fort Donelson and my reputation apparently has been tarnished. General Pillow, who must have thought he was almighty Caesar himself, sent me misleading reports from Fort Donelson. Now the citizens in Nashville and the high command in Richmond are crucifying me. So this exit of our supplies must go well.

"I have implicit faith in you. Your friends say you have unique organizational skills. And that's what we need to get these military stores on their way south. If we are to survive this precarious military situation, we will need every pound of that inventory."

"Yes, sir, General Johnston. We'll do it!"

The meeting adjourned at 6:00 p.m. Forrest returned immediately to his command. He summoned Major Kelley and his staff and company commanders to discuss his orders.

"Major Kelley, as of now I am imposing curfew. No one leaves camp tonight for any reason," declared Forrest.

"Don't worry, Colonel, there isn't a man awake right now. We'll be lucky to rouse them in the morning. They are exhausted," answered Kelley again smiling about Forrest's orders for a curfew.

"All right then, let's talk about tomorrow. We need two 12-hour shifts to both guard the warehouses and to help load supplies on wagons. Schuyler, I want Strange and you to handle these details. Each of you will be in charge of a shift. We'll operate 12 hours on and 12 hours off for each shift until we get everything loaded...that is, if Buell and the Federals don't get here first. We need a couple of days.

"Your men are ordered 'shoot-to-kill' if any unauthorized person tries to take anything. Understood?"

Kelley then interjected, "Colonel Forrest, the men will grumble about the curfew. They haven't seen civilization since we left Memphis."

"Tell them we may be granted furloughs after we relocate. General Johnston discussed this possibility with me. He realizes we are about wore out."

"Good, very good," responded Kelley.

"And another thing, Major. There shall be no drinking in quarters or on guard duty. I want the names of anyone caught drinking. Understood?"

"Yes, sir!"

By daybreak Forrest had worked out a plan. He assembled all commanders to give them their instructions.

"I want all civilian-owned wagons commandeered and brought to a center I've designated on Front Street. There, we'll assign the wagons," ordered Forrest. "I want a party assigned to prepare accurate accounts of all boxcars and flatcars at the railroad yards. And I want marshals posted at the rail yards to prevent any trains from leaving Nashville unless cleared by me."

Throughout Wednesday, February 19th and Thursday, February 20th, Forrest's soldiers worked furiously getting wagons loaded, hauled to the railroad yards, and reloaded into box cars and on flatbeds. Heated disagreements broke out among Forrest's men and civilians over cooperation. Forrest was in a foul mood, and he was displaying his wicked temper.

"Goddamnit! Arrest the superintendent over at the Louisville & Nashville if he doesn't release two more engines," roared Forrest. We'll ship him to Murfreesboro and let Johnston deal with these Yankee sympathizing sonafabiches."

When one of his own enlisted men was caught selling a large slab of bacon to a civilian, Forrest ordered him arrested and put in irons. "If anyone else tries that, hang 'em!" Forrest told Captain Rambaut who was standing nearby transcribing messages.

There were still additional supplies to be loaded on Friday. Orders came from General Johnston to evacuate as soon as possible. Since Buell's forces still had not reached Nashville, Forrest and some of his troops stayed until Sunday, February 23rd. The assignment proved more difficult than initially outlined by General Johnston. The fact that Johnston's own quartermasters and their staffs abandoned Nashville immediately after news reached Nashville of the surrender of Fort Donelson made the task much more difficult.

Sunday afternoon when Forrest and his soldiers left Nashville bound for Decatur, Alabama via Murfreesboro, they had completed a herculean task. Regretfully for Forrest's Cavalry, no one in authority was left in Nashville to say, "Thank you" except the beleaguered Mayor Cheatham who felt it his duty to stay on.

Buell's Union army arrived in force in Nashville on Monday, February 24th. Mayor Cheatham formally surrendered the city. The Federals had captured the largest southern city to that date. To the Confederacy the loss of Nashville was serious. It had been one of its leading river, rail and turnpike transportation centers and the heart of a large, productive agricultural region.

7 • The Furlough

General Albert Sidney Johnston kept his promise. Forrest and his Cavalry were granted leave until March 10, 1862.

On Wednesday morning, February 26th, Forrest, his son Willie, Dr. Cowan, Strange, and Rambaut and most of the soldiers from Memphis boarded the Memphis & Charleston Railroad in Decatur bound for home. Major Kelley and his Alabamians left on leave for Huntsville and surrounding Alabama towns. Left behind were Forrest's troops from Kentucky and Texas.

Captain Strange, now Colonel Forrest's key staff aide, was invited to sit with his commander for the first leg of the journey to Corinth, Mississippi. Thinking that Forrest intended to dictate some correspondence, Strange pulled out his notebook.

"Put that away, Strange," said Forrest laughing. "I'm going to be easy on you today. Mind you, this won't happen too often, but today let's forget about the war."

"That's fine with me, Colonel," responded Strange.

"Look at this advertisement in the *Memphis Daily Appeal* I picked up from the conductor," said Forrest. "You know old George Crook, don't you? He sells insurance in Memphis. Look what it says:

A $50 reward will be paid to anyone who can prove the Valley Insurance Company of Virginia failed to pay any claim quickly without quibbling.
Signed: George W. L. Crook, Memphis Agent

"Isn't that funny? A fellow named Crook is advertising 'honesty.' Do you know that Crook wouldn't sell me or my brothers a policy? He thought we were desperadoes, and probably wouldn't live too long. Heh-heh-heh!"

Then Strange asked, "How do you plan to spend your leave, sir?"

"Well, Strange, I'm going to give my devilish boils a rest. That's one thing. Then I want to check my investments. I haven't been notified by my overseers about what's happening on my places in Mississippi. They've probably gone to Hell!

"Then, I want to spend some time with Mary. She'll want to know all about Willie and his welfare. You know... Is he getting enough to eat? Is he safe? All that kind of thing.

"Of course, Mary and I will visit with Matt Gallaway and his wife, Fannie. Old Matt will want to know everything about the war. I'll have to be careful what I tell him for fear he'll print something that will get me court-martialed. But he is as well-informed about political matters as anyone in Tennessee. He's full of fight. I'd like to get him on our staff.

"About a month ago my brother, Jesse, sent me a letter telling me he was recruiting a company of cavalry. Maybe I can persuade him to join up with us when we return from leave. You know that we lost about 150 at Fort Donelson — about 100 or so of them surrendered.

"I may do some recruiting too while in Memphis. I'll place an announcement in the *Avalanche* and the *Appeal* for volunteers. After our defeat at Donelson, recruiting may get harder. I don't know.

"What will you do on your leave, Strange?"

"Well, sir, I'll visit the store and my partners. I'll see if they've survived without me. Then I'll visit my wife's grave at Elmwood Cemetery and talk with her."

"Talk with her?"

"Yes, I will kneel beside her grave and tell her all that has happened to me since last October," said Strange in a subdued voice. "Colonel, I miss her. She was only 27 when she died of fever. The war has helped take my mind off her death."

Forrest just stared straight ahead and remained silent for the next 25 miles. Then, shortly before the train approached Corinth, Forrest looked over to Strange and noticed he was reading a book.

"Captain, I am curious about the book you're reading. What is it?"

"Sir, believe it or not, it is a book written in Latin. It's a collection of Cicero's political and philosophical writings."

"Can you actually read Latin? Where did you learn?"

"Well, the basic grammar I learned in school in Virginia. Did you ever hear of the textbook, *Jones' Latin Lessons,* Colonel?"

"No, I can't say that I have," said Forrest with a twinkle in his eye.

"Well, sir, for the past 20 years I've practiced by reading a great number of books in Latin — the four books of Caesar, orations of Cicero, Virgil's *Aeneid,* and other things."

"Of what use is it to you, Strange?"

"I guess you could say 'none.' But at least I can read inscriptions on public buildings," replied Strange laughing.

"Captain, I'd say you certainly live up to your surname." Then Forrest who was intrigued by his unusually learned aide asked, "Well, who was Cicero? What made him famous enough to have his writings in book form?"

"Colonel, Cicero was a leading Roman statesman,

scholar and writer back before *Christ* was born. He was a contemporary of Caesar."

Forrest interrupted and said, "I've heard of Caesar. Wasn't he a Roman warrior?"

"Yes, and also a statesman — the same as Cicero. But they were different. Cicero pleaded for the rights of citizens. Caesar, on the other hand, was autocratic. He didn't support democratic rule. The odd thing is that both were assassinated within a year of each other."

"Strange, that's interesting! Just a week ago I heard General Johnston telling Governor Harris that General Pillow thinks he is another Caesar. Promise me that when we are next in camp, you will tell me more about Caesar and the Romans. I'd like to know how their armies operated.

Strange, looking directly into Forrest's eyes to determine if he were serious, nodded his assent.

8 • Shiloh

"Welcome to Burnsville, Colonel," shouted General Breckinridge smiling broadly. "Did you enjoy your leave; and are you rested and ready to go?"

"Yes, sir, it was an enjoyable change. Not only did I get to visit my wife, Mary, and some close friends, but also I have returned with two companies of recruits. One of them is commanded by my brother, Jesse."

"That's wonderful, Forrest. If Jesse is anything like you, those Federal boys better watch out. Now there are two Forrests to contend with."

"Oh no, sir, there are now six of us. There's Willie, my 15-year-old son, and my other brothers, Bill, Aaron and Jeffrey. And I have two half-brothers serving. I guess you can say we are for the Confederacy, General."

"Yes indeed, there's no disputing that."

"Forrest, what's it like in Memphis now? How do the citizens feel about our cause?"

"It depends on who you talk with, sir. My close friends are doing all they can to assist us — contributing money, supplies, and clothing. But Memphis is full of collaborators selling cotton for gold. I wish I could say that all of this is the work of Northern speculators and Federal Treasury purchasing agents. But the truth is that a certain lowdown class of Memphis citizens and merchants are involved in these cotton rings. They are reaping huge profits. It's sickening. These vermin don't give a damn who wins the war.

"Another surprise to me is the success the Yankees are having recruiting in Memphis. Hundreds of young men have taken the *Oath of Allegiance* with the Union and left the city to fight. I had always thought of Memphis as a southern town. I'm disappointed about what is happening there."

"That is disheartening, Forrest," interjected Breckinridge. "We need Memphis under Confederate control to keep the Mississippi River closed to Federal military traffic. If the city falls, the whole lower Mississippi Valley is vulnerable.

"Now, Forrest, I know you need some time to get your regiment reorganized. That Fort Donelson disaster disrupted all of our units lucky enough to escape. And the surrender of 13,000 of our soldiers creates an enormous gap that we must try to fill. There's not much time.

"Do you know why we're here in Burnsville, Mississippi?" asked General Breckinridge. "I'm sure you do. The Federals are moving south. The dike broke when we lost Fort Donelson.

"General Johnston and General Beauregard have just

drawn up a defense line to replace the one we had across Kentucky prior to Fort Donelson. This new line extends east and west along the Mississippi and Tennessee state line from Memphis to Chattanooga. It generally parallels the tracks of the Memphis & Charleston Railroad. We're trying to protect Mississippi, Alabama, Georgia and Florida from occupation by the Federals. Our main military strength is centered around Corinth, Mississippi. General Polk and General Hardee and their Corps are based in Corinth. General Bragg's Corps is just a few miles outside, and we're over here in Burnsville about 20 miles away. If we're called to join forces with the others, we can easily assemble within a day.

"Forrest, I have no idea when an attack may come. The rumor is that General Halleck, commander of the Union's Department of Mississippi, has ordered Grant and Buell to combine their armies just north of here in Tennessee. The Federals, as you know, now control the Tennessee River as far south as a place called Pittsburg Landing. That's just 30 miles or so from here.

"Since you've been on leave, General Johnston has issued orders to gather up every isolated Confederate unit south of here. They've all been moved to the Corinth area.

"Your cavalry regiment must be prepared to fight at the earliest moment. You have a reputation for getting results. General Johnston and I were both impressed with your gallant escape from Fort Donelson. And Johnston is still raving about your success in getting our military supplies out of Nashville. Without your help Johnston says Buell could have helped himself to several millions of dollars worth of food and equipment."

"General Breckinridge, give me a week or two. As soon as we settle in, we'll elect our officers and establish the proper discipline of the troops. I can tell you truthfully the men are in good spirits. The furlough did wonders for them. They are itching to get into a good fight."

"Good, Forrest. Keep me informed of your progress."

On March 16th the Regiment's soldiers unanimously elected Forrest, colonel; Kelley, lieutenant colonel; and Robert Balch, an old business associate of Forrest, major. Most of the other officers were re-elected to their previous ranks.

Detailed accounts of the Confederate loss at Pea Ridge, Arkansas, reached Burnsville that same day. General Van Dorn's Confederates had been defeated in a two-day battle at this remote site in northwest Arkansas just south of the Missouri state line. Dr. Cowan, commenting on the implications of that defeat, said, "That Union victory prevents Missouri from joining the Confederacy." Forrest didn't say anything for a minute, then reacted, "Goddamnit, we've got to start winning, or all is lost. Cris'sakes, our luck's got to turn! I hope those West Point boys of ours know what they're doing."

General Grant established headquarters at Savannah, Tennessee on March 17th. This town on the east bank of the Tennessee River was just 40 miles north of Corinth. Reports of a large military build-up reached General Johnston. Worried about an all-out Union attack, he consulted daily with his leading commanders: Pierre G. T. Beauregard, Bishop Polk, Braxton Bragg and William J. Hardee.

The initial Confederate scouting reports were that Grant's main force of his Army of the Tennessee was near Pittsburg Landing, a minor river freight depot on the west bank of the Tennessee River. His soldiers were camped around a small, rough-hewn log church called the Shiloh Meeting House on the Corinth Road near its intersection with the Purdy-Hamburg Road. Johnston was relieved to learn that Grant's soldiers had made no effort up to that point to construct entrenchments.

But on April 1st a much more disturbing report was received. Scouts reported that General Buell had left Nashville with his Army of the Ohio, and that they were marching overland on their way to Savannah, Tennessee. It was now decision time for General Johnston. He chose to attack Grant before Buell's army would arrive.

One hour later Johnston issued orders to prepare for an attack on Grant's army. All Confederate forces under Johnston's command were ordered to assemble at one location. The march north to Pittsburg Landing would commence on the morning of Thursday, April 3rd. General Breckinridge's Corps, and Forrest's Cavalry, located in Burnsville, were ordered to rendezvous with the other Confederate Corps near the village of Monterey, Tennessee — a point just 10 miles from Shiloh Church and 13 from Pittsburg Landing.

The Confederate march north was delayed until mid-afternoon.

Rains of the two previous days had turned roads into muddy quagmires. Progress was painfully slow that afternoon. A similar result the next day — the long train of artillery with their limbers and caissons, ammunition wagons, portable forges, cook and ambulance wagons, forage wagons and other vehicles bogged down on the road. Valuable time was lost pulling deeply-immersed wheels from the thick mud.

Johnston's original plan was to attack early Saturday morning, April 5th. But heavy rain again Friday night made travel conditions even worse, forcing Johnston to change plans. Saturday was a day of waiting for the roads to dry out. That night Johnston called a council of war with his key commanders. He announced, "Gentlemen, time is running out. We can wait no longer. We must attack. We left Corinth with only four days' rations. We have 50,000 troops ready to fight. If we wait until Buell's army arrives, we will probably lose any opportunity for victory."

Beauregard argued forcibly for caution. "Grant knows where we are. He's probably concluded we will attack him. He has watched our every move."

"I disagree, General," responded Johnston instantly. "Our scouts report no specific preparations for fighting have been made by Grant. Camplife over there is quite relaxed say our observers."

Bragg, Breckinridge, Hardee and Polk supported Johnston's position that it was time to attack.

Johnston then announced, "We'll attack at daybreak tomorrow morning. We shall use General Beauregard's battle plan." Four corps of Confederates were readied for action. At dawn the attack began.

The 1st Corps was led by General Polk. He was four days shy of his 56th birthday. Although he had fought briefly at Belmont, Missouri in November 1861, Shiloh was his first major action. Soon after graduating from West Point, he chose to enter the Episcopal clergy, and for nearly 30 years had been far removed from military life.

Major General Braxton Bragg (West Point, 1837), 45, led the 2nd Corps. Bragg, a native of North Carolina, was a veteran of both the Mexican War and the Seminole War. Immediately prior to the Civil War he was a planter in Louisiana.

Johnston's 3rd Corps was commanded by Georgia-born Major General William J. Hardee [West Point, 1838], 46. Hardee was called "Old Reliable" by his peers. The one-time commandant of West Point [the United States Military Academy] was also a veteran of the Mexican War. He resigned the regular army in early 1861 to accept a Confederate commission.

The 4th Corps, designated by Johnston as the reserve

unit, was led by Kentuckian John C. Breckinridge, 46. He was a lawyer and a pre-war political leader serving in Congress, and as Vice President of the United States under President Buchanan.

Commander-in-Chief, General Albert Sidney Johnston (West Point, 1826), 59, was a Kentuckian. A veteran of the Mexican War, Johnston earlier fought with Sam Houston in the Army of the Republic of Texas. Like Hardee, he had served in the regular army until 1861 when he resigned to join the Confederacy.

Johnston's second-in-command was General Pierre Gustave Toutant Beauregard (West Point, 1838), 43. The native of New Orleans served in the Mexican War. Just prior to the Civil War he had been appointed superintendent of West Point, but at war's outbreak he resigned to join the Confederacy. Beauregard was the first Confederate leader to gain military recognition in the South. He had commanded Confederate troops at the bombardment of Fort Sumter on April 12, 1861. And in July 1861 he received additional praise for the role he played in the Confederates' stunning victory in the First Battle of Bull Run in Virginia.

Opposing the Confederates that Sunday morning near Shiloh Church were five Union divisions.

Brigadier General John A. McClernand, 44, headed Grant's 1st Division. He fought at Fort Donelson just two months earlier. Before the war he practiced law and also served in Congress.

Heading the 2nd Division was Illinois native Brigadier General W. H. L. Wallace, 40. He was a veteran of the Mexican War, and a pre-war practicing attorney.

Brigadier General Stephen A. Hurlbut, 40, led the 4th Division. He had been a prominent Republican politician in Illinois.

The 5th Division was commanded by Brigadier General William Tecumseh Sherman (West Point, 1840), 42, an Ohio native. He had been a career army officer until 1853 when he resigned to become a banker. Later he practiced law before accepting the superintendent's position at a new military academy in Louisiana [this institution was the predecessor to Louisiana State University]. When Louisiana seceded from the Union, Sherman rejoined the regular army. His first Civil War action was at Bull Run in July 1861.

Brigadier General Benjamin M. Prentiss, 42, headed the 6th Division. The Illinois pre-war politician was also a veteran of the Mexican War.

Sunday, April 6, 1862

When fighting began on April 6th, the 3rd Division commanded by Brigadier General Lew Wallace was camped several miles away from Shiloh. Wallace, 34, didn't arrive until after fighting ended that first day. The Indiana native was a lawyer and a published author.

Similarly, Buell's Army of the Ohio had not arrived in time to make a contribution that first day. Brigadier General Don Carlos Buell (West Point, 1841), 44, was a veteran of both the Seminole War and the Mexican War.

The Confederates formed along three parallel lines — the front, center and rear lines. Each line had a center point and two flanks. General Hardee's forces were in the front line. Bragg's Corps was in the center line behind Hardee's Corp. The artillery was positioned with Bragg. General Polk's Corps formed the rear line. General Johnston and General Beauregard were positioned behind Polk's forces with Breckinridge's reserve forces. Forrest's Cavalry was part of this reserve.

Colonel Forrest, after being informed of the plan of attack, called his staff together to explain it to them and to let them know too how Forrest's Cavalry was to be deployed. When he finished, he asked Captain Strange to communicate his instructions to his company commanders. When Forrest completed dictating his brief orders, he looked over at Strange. "Captain, you look like you want to tell me something. What is it?"

"Oh, sir, it's about that discussion of Julius Caesar we had on the train to Memphis a few weeks ago. You said you'd like to hear more."

"Well, not at this time unless it's damn important."

"Sir, General Beauregard's plan of three attack waves straight at the enemy is as old as Caesar himself. He believed in the shock effect of the initial charge. The very best cohorts in his legions were positioned in front. The first line threw their javelins in several volleys, then the swordsmen charged. If this failed to rout the enemy, Caesar called the second line forward to move in front of the first, and so forth. Even on the defensive Caesar demanded that his soldiers attack."

"Strange, I'm pleased to know that. I'd tell Caesar if he were around here today that he ought to consider flank attacks in his plan."

The Battle of Shiloh opened with heavy artillery fire aimed at the Union front. Infantry units moved forward quickly to achieve an element of surprise. Grant's forces positioned along a defensive line were slow to adjust to the sudden Confederate rush at General Prentiss' Division in the center of the Union line. A major charge, about 8:30 a.m., overran four enemy batteries.

Forrest had moved his cavalry across Lick Creek when he received orders from General Breckinridge to move to the front. This stream, which emptied into the nearby Tennessee River two miles south of Pittsburg Landing, was on the extreme right of the Confederate line.

Colonel Kelley noted later, "I observed his excitement

and his agitation waiting to get into the thick of the action. He kept asking me questions which I thought were a little odd. For instance, he asked, 'What kind of a church is that Shiloh Meeting House?' I said it's my denomination — Southern Methodist. Then he asked, 'Is Shiloh some kind of an Indian name?' And I said, 'No, it's a place in Palestine. Back around the 13th Century B.C. it was a place north of Jerusalem where the Israelites had an important temple established by Joshua after he conquered Canaan. You know, General — *Joshua in the Battle of Jericho.* Then Forrest's face brightened and he said, 'Well, Parson, if we defeat the Yankees here, Jefferson Davis may have to build a large temple here.' And then I said, 'Maybe so, sir; maybe so'."

The principal fighting was concentrated in the middle of the wide battle line — a zone the Confederates quickly named "the Hornets' Nest" because of the bloody, indecisive nature of the intense combat and the staggering number of casualties hour after hour.

Hundreds of Confederate and Union soldiers were killed in the blazing crossfire as the former attacked across the cleared field called "the Peach Orchard" attempting to dislodge thousands of Union troops from entrenched positions behind picket fences stretched along an old wagon trail called "the Sunken Road." Commanders of infantry and dismounted cavalry troops urged their soldiers forward, or to reposition themselves. But the noise of rifle and artillery fire made it impossible for many to hear the orders. The screaming of hundreds of wounded men lying exposed in the open field, or in the nearby thickets, was muffled by the roar. Many Confederate units lost their bearings in the confusion and often were found out of position. Field commanders had difficulty measuring their success.

The temperature had risen to near 75° at midday. The

humidity, smoke and dust were taking their toll among the combatants, adding to the massive battlefield chaos.

The Confederates attempted to encircle the center of the Union line. They gained momentum about noon. The principal Confederate pressure was exerted on Federal units led by generals McClernand, W. H. L. Wallace, Prentiss and Hurlbut. Union forces gave ground on their flanks. Both Bragg's Corps and Breckinridge's Corps enlarged the circle around Prentiss's and Hurlbut's forces.

General Albert Sidney Johnston, overseeing the action, positioned himself near the fiercely-contested "Hornets' Nest." Every few minutes messengers dispatched by their field commanders would bring the General messages. Johnston, in turn, would send back instructions. His role was to coordinate the often disparate Confederate units caught up in the confusion of the ebb and flow of the fighting on the broad attack line.

Unfortunately, Johnston did not live to witness the conclusion of events that Sunday afternoon. At approximately 2:15 p.m., Johnston while seated on his spirited horse, Fire-eater, was struck in his right leg by a minié ball — a cone-shaped bullet capable of massive internal injury. The popliteal artery behind his right kneecap was severed. Unfortunately, there were no surgeons or medical aid men nearby. Aides attending the wounded Johnston knew nothing of the techniques of first aid. Had they known, they could have stopped the bleeding by placing a tourniquet above the wound to cut off circulation long enough to get the general to a field hospital. Instead, they hovered around the stricken Johnston trying to comfort him as he bled to death. Johnston died at 2:30 p.m.

Bragg received the news immediately. But Beauregard, Johnston's second-in-command, wasn't notified until 3:00 p.m. Immediately Beauregard named

Bragg his second-in-command, then issued an order to all field commanders to keep the news of General Johnston's death quiet.

Bragg's and Breckinridge's corps were ordered to intensify the pressure on the seemingly beleaguered Union commanders, Prentiss, Wallace and Hurlbut and their units in the "Hornets' Nest."

Forrest's Cavalry, under General Breckinridge, was ordered to strike hard. In that same action were two additional Confederate officers destined to play a role in Forrest's subsequent military career — Colonel Joseph Wheeler (West Point, 1859), a 26-year old brigade commander of Alabama infantrymen; and Brigadier General James R. Chalmers, 31, a brigade commander of Mississippi infantrymen.

For their heroic action at the "Hornets' Nest" that Sunday afternoon at Shiloh, both received praise from their superiors. Wheeler earned the nickname "Fightin' Joe" for his aggressiveness in helping capture General Prentiss' Division.

By 4:00 p.m. the Union army was in full retreat toward the west bank of the Tennessee River. The Confederates were in close pursuit, leading to the capture of several thousand Union prisoners and wholesale quantities of weapons and supplies. During this retreat Union General W. H. L. Wallace was killed.

The entire Union line had collapsed in the final hour before darkness. Escaping Union soldiers found refuge on the river bank under the protection of Federal gunboats out on the Tennessee River. Many boarded transports. By dark Union commanders had been able to establish the semblance of a perimeter defense line less than one mile from Pittsburg Landing and the river.

Advance elements of General Buell's Army of the Ohio had reached the battlefield at 5:30 p.m. to reinforce General Grant.

At 6:00 p.m. it was dark. Fighting all but ceased except for isolated skirmishes. But at 7:00 p.m. it was quiet. Confederate troops returned to their camps exhausted after nearly 14 hours of fighting.

Forrest's Cavalry assembled in a wooded area on the right flank of the Confederate line. They were camped less than two miles from Pittsburg Landing. Still excited from the day's events, Forrest ordered Captain Strange to gather his staff for an 8:00 p.m. meeting in his tent. Colonel Kelley was the only aide not available. He was part of the Confederate party escorting the captured General Prentiss and his troops to the rear.

Colonel Forrest opened the meeting saying, "It's a goddamn shame about General Johnston. That poor devil had a black cloud hanging over him. Ever since Fort Donelson fell, President Davis in Richmond had been under pressure to relieve him of command. Well, he won't have to answer to the sonafabiches now.

"When I met him in Nashville after Fort Donelson he seemed humbled...like his whole career as a soldier was on the brink of ruin, and there wasn't a goddamn thing he could do about it. And now this. I'm sick about it. He was truly a soldier's soldier. He was head and shoulders above those pitiful commanders that failed him at Fort Donelson."

While Forrest talked about Johnston, Captain Strange had been waiting patiently to read him a message delivered by a courier a few minutes earlier.

"Colonel, I have in my hand a message from General Breckinridge. He's asking for 50 volunteers from our unit to go out on the field tonight to help gather up the wounded. He says there are hundreds out there who are still alive. He desperately needs litter bearers to get the wounded to the field hospitals. Many will die overnight if left out there."

"Goddamnit, Strange, our boys are all wore out," said Forrest angrily. "Aren't there any reserves to send out there? I thought this army was supposed to have litter bearers."

Strange, who was sympathetic to Breckinridge's request, hesitated for a moment, then said softly, "Every able-bodied man was on the field today. Some of those laying out there are our boys. I'll volunteer."

"No, Strange, I need you here. But if any of our soldiers want to go out there tonight, they can go. I'm not ordering anyone. Understood?"

"Yes, sir," said Strange as he quickly exited the tent to contact company commanders asking for volunteers.

Colonel Kelley arrived back about 8:30 p.m., and reported to Forrest on the disposition of the Union prisoners. Forrest nodded and said,"Good work, Parson." Then he continued, "If we would have had just one more hour of daylight, we would have pushed them into the river. Tonight we would be celebrating. But now we've got to face them again tomorrow with a much weaker army.

"I'm certain General Grant is being heavily reinforced tonight. We saw troops arriving across the river just before dark. I would like to find out if the main part of Buell's army has arrived. They were reported up at Savannah late this afternoon. They've probably been loaded on river transports and on their way down river."

Kelley responded, "Colonel, there's only one way to find out. Let's scout the area tonight. It's dark. And besides, both armies are either tending to their wounded tonight or sleeping. I doubt if the Federals got much of a guard around their encampments tonight."

"You're probably right, Parson. Handpick a small squad of our best scouts to move through the lines to take a look. It's less than two miles to the river. Put them in those Yankee coats we collected today so they won't be challenged by any of the Federal guards."

Despite lightning, thunder and a drenching rain just before midnight, Forrest sent out the first of two scouting parties to observe Union activity at Pittsburg Landing. And again at about 2:00 a.m. he sent out the second group. Each party reported much the same thing — that a massive force of Union troops was being ferried across the Tennessee River at Pittsburg Landing.

Forrest, alarmed by the reports of the reinforcements, told Kelley, "Beauregard has got to order an attack tonight. It may be too late in the morning. I'm going to visit General Breckinridge and General Hardee and alert them of what's going on down at the river."

Breckinridge and Hardee were both headquartered nearby. When Forrest reported his information to them, neither took it seriously but suggested that he take his information to General Beauregard at Shiloh Church, or to General Bragg. When Forrest arrived at the Church, he found that it had been converted into a field hospital.

"Where is General Beauregard and where is General Bragg?" asked the excited Forrest.

"We don't know, sir. No one has seen them for the past two hours."

At 3:00 a.m. Forrest returned to Hardee's headquarters to notify the General of his failure to find either Bragg or Beauregard. Hardee offered no solution. "Keep me posted, Forrest. We'll find General Bragg and General Beauregard first thing in the morning."

Forrest, who hadn't slept in 22 hours, was frustrated his Confederate superiors had failed to grasp the opportunity to take the offensive with a middle-of-the-night attack. In disgust he told Kelley, "These are gentlemen soldiers. West Point told them it was ungentlemanly to fight after the sun goes down."

"I believe you are right, Colonel Forrest. They probably think we are frontier buffoons, and ignorant of the rules of modern warfare."

"All right, Parson, let's get a couple hours of sleep."

Monday, April 7, 1862

At 6:30 a.m. Grant ordered his army to attack. Fresh with reinforcements he was ready to move forward. General Lew Wallace's 3rd Division of 7000 troops had arrived shortly after 7:00 p.m. on Sunday night. And during the night Buell's Army of the Ohio, numbering some 15,000 troops, had arrived. Now Grant's combined force was 30,000 effectives.

The Confederate Army was not reinforced overnight. That morning General Beauregard could muster only 20,000 troops to put on the field. Sunday's losses in killed, wounded and missing had seriously crippled Confederate fighting strength.

Buell's army pushed forward on the left flank of the Union line. Grant's army was in the middle, and Lew Wallace's 3rd Division was on the right pointed toward Shiloh Meeting House. Early in the attack the Union army enjoyed success in reclaiming ground given up on Sunday afternoon. But the first serious resistance encountered was at the "Hornets' Nest." Here Bragg's Corps and Hardee's Corps stood their ground. Heavy fighting also broke out near Shiloh Church about one mile to the west.

One army attacked, then the other counterattacked several times over a period of seven hours. Once again the dead and the wounded were strewn all over the landscape. The carnage was a grotesque sight for even the most hardened and cynical veteran soldiers. The screaming of the wounded pleading for help made many wish they could plug up their ears. Cries of: "I'm blind. I can't see," and "Water — water — please give me water," and "Oh, *Jesus*, save me!" were heard everywhere.

After 1:00 p.m. the Union's superiority in numbers of soldiers began to overpower Beauregard's army. The Confederates had retreated over two miles back from near Pittsburg Landing where fighting began that morning. They were now back where they started the original attack early Sunday morning.

Beauregard assessed the deteriorating position. He saw major cracks in the Confederate defenses. At 3:30 p.m. he concluded that a victory at Shiloh was no longer possible and ordered a general retreat back to Corinth, Mississippi. To paint the best picture possible, he informed his commanders, "This withdrawal is merely a move back to our original defensive line along the Memphis & Charleston Railroad tracks. It's not a defeat; it's a standoff."

Tuesday, April 8, 1862

The following day most of the Confederate army was still in full retreat on the road back to Corinth. General Breckinridge was ordered to protect the rear of the column. Forrest's Cavalry was given this assignment by his superior, Breckinridge. That afternoon Forrest and 350 of his cavalry were attacked by two regiments of Federal infantry and one of cavalry led by General Sherman at a place called Fallen Timbers near Monterey, Tennessee. Forrest turned his troops around to face the enemy and led a wild, reckless charge into the middle of the Federals. It was a frantic scene of close, slashing combat of a smaller Confederate force against a much larger Federal force.

In the skirmish Forrest was shot in the hip by a rifleman just a few feet away. At first Forrest didn't think his wound was serious. The most he anticipated was some minor first aid when he returned to Corinth, then he would be back to active duty within a few days.

Wednesday, April 9, 1862

When Forrest was examined by Dr. Cowan on his return to Corinth, it was determined that his wound was serious. A bullet was lodged near Forrest's spine.

"Colonel, I could excise the minié ball now, but I seriously doubt you can withstand the shock of the operation. Your body has been weakened by the loss of blood. I strongly recommend you take a two-month leave to regain your strength."

"I hate to leave now. My Cavalry has had heavy losses, and I've got to rebuild it soon," responded the agitated Forrest.

"Well, I'm telling you, Colonel, you're not fit for service right now. You've got Colonel Kelley to take charge."

"Yes, I know that. Kelley is a capable soldier. But I can probably get more out of General Beauregard than Kelley in terms of men, horses and firearms. Kelley's too polite. I'm such an irritation, they have to give in to me."

"Take my advice! If not for me, for Mary's sake. She may be your wife, but she's also my cousin. You don't want to leave a widow, do you?"

"All right, James. I'll go on leave to Memphis."

Within three weeks Forrest interrupted his leave despite persistent pain and returned to Tupelo, Mississippi where his cavalrymen were camped.

Dr. Cowan immediately examined Forrest. "I've got to operate, Colonel. That bullet's in a dangerous location near your spinal cord. But I guess it's your decision. There's something you should know before you decide. We've got no anesthetics, so this surgery is going to be painful."

"Goddamnit, Cowan, it couldn't be any more painful than what I'm going through now. Let's get the damn thing over with!"

Miraculously, Forrest not only survived this dangerous operation but recovered within a few weeks. He spent his rehabilitation period recruiting. As a result of his recruitment notices in the Memphis newspapers during late April and early May, 1862, Forrest or one of his agents enlisted several hundred recruits. When he returned, he met daily with his staff, painstakingly going over every detail as if the fate of the war depended on his decisions.

While Forrest was headquartered in Tupelo, Mississippi, about 50 miles south of Corinth, General Beauregard sent him a message wishing him a speedy recovery, and added, "I look forward to meeting with you upon your complete recovery." Seizing the initiative, the assertive Forrest — weeks away from a possible full recovery — boarded the Mobile & Ohio Railroad for the ride north to Corinth to visit General Beauregard at his headquarters at the Curlee House.

Corinth, located in the far northeast corner of Mississippi, had a pre-war population of 1200. It served as a railroad center for the region. But overnight in early 1862 it became a major Confederate military compound with thousands of soldiers camped in and around the town. Immediately after Shiloh it became by necessity a hospital center. The prominent Tishomingo Hotel and the Corinth House, as well as most public buildings and churches, were converted to hospitals. Many of the recovering wounded were placed in private residences

The sight of seriously wounded Confederate and Union soldiers shocked the normally imperturbable Forrest. In the excitement of battle, encircled by dead and wounded, Forrest could dismiss the bloodshed from his mind. "When trying to achieve victory," he said, "there was no time for pity." But now on the streets of Corinth, with his own wounds still bothering him and the sight of limbless, blind and seriously burned men sitting on benches outside the Tishomingo Hotel, he grasped war's damage completely.

General Beauregard, surprised to see Forrest, greeted him warmly. The ever-courteous, impeccably dressed General instantly inquired about Forrest's health and news of his family. He listened intently as Forrest described the events leading up to being shot at Fallen Timbers, and the ordeal of his subsequent period of recovery. It was obvious from Beauregard's intense interest that he admired soldiers like Forrest.

Forrest concluded, "I'm recovering, General, but it bothers me that I am unable to move about as I'd like to. But I guess I'm one of the lucky ones."

"Yes you are, Forrest. I have just reviewed the casualty figures, and they are shocking. At last count we had 1700 killed; and the enemy, about 1700 too. Each side had over 5000 wounded. It's unimaginable, Forrest — nearly 15,000 casualties in a two-day fight. The northern newspapers have headlines calling Shiloh "a glorious victory." Isn't that ironic? Nothing changed as a result of the battle. What's glorious about all of that bloodshed?"

"General, after arriving in Corinth today and looking around, I agree with your assessment. It's horrible."

"Forrest, the Confederate War Department and President Davis in Richmond still don't understand the enormity of Shiloh. But they will when Grant rebuilds his army and starts to move this way. General Halleck, Grant's superior, came down from St. Louis soon after Shiloh to plan their next action against us. And, in all honesty, I don't know how we are going to hold on here.

I'm considering ordering our forces south to Tupelo. I think we'll be safe from enemy attack there."

Beauregard paused for a few seconds to change subjects. Then the short-statured, dark-complected, mustachioed General told Forrest,"I've had good reports on your leadership. General Breckinridge says you are a great soldier."

"I appreciate hearing that, General."

"Forrest, I have a larger role in mind for you. We've experienced a breakdown in discipline in three cavalry regiments operating in Middle Tennessee from their base in Chattanooga.

"Do you know colonels Adams, Wharton and Scott?"

"No, sir, I do not."

"Well, Forrest, with your approval, I'm placing you in command of these three cavalry regiments. You'll be assigned to operate in North Alabama and Middle Tennessee. I know you can whip these units into an effective force. And I shall also submit a request to Richmond that you be promoted to brigadier general. So what do you say to that, Forrest?"

"Sir, I'm probably not qualified," Forrest replied modestly. "And also, sir, I haven't completely recovered from my wounds."

"Of course you're qualified. I have complete confidence in you. You have that unique quality I admire — initiative!"

"Just one thing, sir. I hate to leave my regiment behind. I recruited and trained all those men."

"Forrest, as soon as these men can be spared from the Army of the Mississippi, they'll be sent back to you."

"In that case, General, I accept with deepest thanks. But I need to get my surgeon's approval before leaving for Chattanooga."

Shiloh — the Hornets' Nest

Railway station and Tishomingo Hotel, Corinth, Mississippi

9 • General Wheeler

Forrest, in high spirits as a result of the recognition received from General Beauregard, returned immediately to Tupelo to confer with Dr. Cowan about his new assignment.

"James, am I in good enough condition to travel to Chattanooga? General Beauregard has assigned me to a new command, and he wants me to take over as soon as possible. What do you think?" added Forrest nervously looking at Dr. Cowan.

"Colonel, how soon is Beauregard's 'earliest moment?' Is that immediately? Or is it when you are completely healed?"

"Hell, I don't know James. But I think he means in a week or two."

"Doesn't General Beauregard know how seriously you were wounded? Doesn't he know that a bullet wound near the spinal column is no minor thing? I'd say you need at least a month. And if you are going to do any extensive riding, I'd suggest at least two more months. Do you want to end up a permanent cripple, Colonel?"

"What if I were to tell you James that I'd like to leave in three weeks or less?"

"Only on one condition, Colonel."

"What's that?"

"You must take the train east to Chattanooga. Absolutely no horseback riding! And I want another surgeon to accompany us in case of an emergency. And when we get to Chattanooga, you must remain inactive for a few weeks."

"Cris' sakes, James, you're trying to scare the hell out of me, aren't you?"

"No, Colonel, I'm telling you what any responsible physician would. You may think you're Hercules, but you aren't right now."

Fearing a Union attack on Corinth, General Beauregard moved his headquarters south to Tupelo within days of his meeting with Forrest. Then suddenly, complaining of ill health, he left Tupelo on leave.

But the real reason for Beauregard's departure was that President Davis had dismissed him from command of the Army of Tennessee. Davis, who had previously called Beauregard a cocky, bantam of a man, and who had long disliked him because of his flamboyance and arrogance, totally rebuked the proud Louisianian. "I no longer have confidence in Beauregard," Davis told his Secretary of War, J. A. Seddon. "I realize he has a good grasp of military planning, but he doesn't understand organization or cooperation. He's an irritating man."

Davis took the opportunity to humiliate Beauregard further by assigning him to the Department of South Carolina when the latter came off three months recuperative leave. He was given responsibility for defending the Southern coastline, and specifically the defense of Charleston and Savannah.

Davis replaced Beauregard with General Bragg as commander as commander of the Army of Tennessee.

General Bragg approved Beauregard's choice of Forrest to command the three cavalry regiments then based in Chattanooga. He also approved Beauregard's recommendation that Forrest be promoted to brigadier general.

Forrest waited three weeks; then he boarded the train to Chattanooga with Dr. Cowan and the rest of his staff. He arrived in that small city on June 19, 1862. Bragg in the meantime had transferred the bulk of the Army of Tennessee to Chattanooga. This was to be Bragg's base camp for a planned invasion of Middle Tennessee.

On July 9th, Forrest's new Cavalry was assigned to operate against Union forces in the vicinity of Murfreesboro, Tennessee, a small town 100 miles northwest of Chattanooga, and 35 miles southeast of Nashville.

On July 13, 1862, in a surprise slashing attack on several larger and better equipped Federal forces, Forrest's new Cavalry unit captured Murfreesboro, taking many prisoners and a large store of equipment and supplies. This victory was followed eight days later by the news of his promotion to brigadier general.

In September, Forrest's Cavalry, as part of General Bragg's Army of Tennessee, accompanied the latter on a military strike into south-central Kentucky. Forrest was with Bragg's army when Union forces surrendered on September 17th at Munfordville. But unexpectedly on September 25th, for reasons not clear to Forrest, Bragg relieved him of command, and ordered him back to Murfreesboro with instructions to raise a new cavalry brigade. So at the time of Bragg's failure to win at Perryville, Kentucky on October 8th, Forrest was more than 100 miles away recruiting a new command.

Forrest's new recruits saw their first major action near Nashville in early November. But their first extensive campaign came in mid-December 1862. Bragg ordered Forrest's Cavalry to destroy or disrupt General Grant's supply line into Mississippi. Grant was using the Mobile & Ohio Railroad line which extended from Columbus, Kentucky on the Mississippi River, south across West Tennessee to Jackson, then by the Mississippi Central Railroad to Holly Springs and Oxford, Mississippi where he was marshalling materiel for a planned drive to Vicksburg. Forrest complained to Bragg before starting that his force was ill-equipped for the expedition, but Bragg ignored his complaint.

With a small force of 1500, Forrest crossed the swift moving, icy Tennessee River in mid-December. Then for the next 17 days ending on New Year's Day, 1863, his

Cavalry tore up railroad tracks and equipment and captured and burned 20 Union stockades. When Forrest recrossed the Tennessee River, his Cavalry returned with a hugh cache of arms and supplies. To Forrest's dismay Bragg commandeered most of this booty for disbursement to his other forces. Forrest and his troops returned to Columbia, Tennessee on January 6, 1863 to await a new assignment.

Palmyra, Tennessee, January 30, 1863

Forrest's Cavalry camped overnight at this tiny village on the Cumberland River in north central Tennessee. It was enroute to Dover, Tennessee as part of General Joseph Wheeler's force that had been ordered by Bragg to destroy the Federal garrison located there.

Neither Forrest nor any of his key staff could comprehend the wisdom of attacking Dover. They could see no strategic gain by a Confederate victory. Dover was a remote Federal outpost long since bypassed by Grant's army after the latter's victory at Fort Donelson one year earlier. So here they were in the middle of the winter, quartered in an open pasture waiting for instructions from General Wheeler on his plan of attack.

Seated at officers' mess that evening in General Forrest's tent were Captain Matt Gallaway, Dr. James Cowan, Captain Charles A. Anderson and Captain John W. Morton, Jr. Forrest was in excellent spirits even after a hard day's ride in bitter cold wind from Charlotte, Tennessee. He was eager to talk.

"Matt, how long have you been with me?"

"Well, General, to tell you the truth, it seems like ten years. But actually it's been almost seven months. So much has happened since the Federals ran me out of Memphis. I've almost forgotten about being editor of the

Avalanche and Postmaster of Memphis."

Forrest shook his head, "Yes, we've been a lot of places and seen plenty of action. You will have much to write about when this war ends. Old Bragg has kept us on the move since we beat the Yankees at Murfreesboro back in July. I hope you are keeping a good diary."

"Yes, we've been in Kentucky in September; then back to Columbia for a while; then off to fight all those skirmishes in West Tennessee. I've only got a few complaints though."

"What are they Matt?"

"First of all, it's been so goddamn cold. Then if you want another, how about missing Fannie's cooking. But that's insignificant stuff. I am still seething at what Bragg did to you right before the Battle of Perryville last October. Why did he relieve you of command and send you back to Middle Tennessee? Was he worried you would outshine his hand-picked protege, 'Fightin' Joe Wheeler? Is that the reason Bragg tried to humiliate you?"

"Matt, I don't know and maybe I don't care. Those West Point boys stick together. You know, military gentlemen and tradition, and all that. Bragg and Wheeler have a lot in common. Both love drilling and parade ground ceremonies, and quoting out of those Army manuals by the hour."

Captain Anderson interjected, "General, did you know that Wheeler has just had a training manual published? I think it's called *Cavalry Tactics*. That may have been why he recently was promoted to major-general."

"I don't know if that's the reason," said Forrest. "The mere fact is that he can do no wrong in Bragg's eye. That's the real reason."

"But Hell, if he is as good as Bragg thinks he is, that's fine with me. I give him credit for bravery. He really proved that at Shiloh."

Then Forrest turned to the 36-year old Captain Anderson and said, "Anderson, how do you like your position as Acting Adjutant?"

"I like it fine, General, but it doesn't feel right with Captain Strange gone. He's a prisoner in Alton Prison in Illinois, I understand. We won that fight at Parker's Crossroads a few weeks ago, but losing John threw a cloud over the whole affair."

"I agree," said Forrest nodding his head. "We all miss him.

"Tell me, Anderson, what did you do before you joined up? We've never had much of a chance to talk about our lives before the war."

"I operated several steamboats on the Cumberland River out of Nashville. I even had mail packets operating between Nashville and Memphis. In more recent years I was a general freight agent."

"Then you know all about the Cumberland River?"

"Yes, sir, every foot of it from Nashville to the Ohio River."

"We could have used you at Fort Donelson last year, Anderson."

"Well sir, I was in Chattanooga. I joined you after Shiloh."

"Are you married, Anderson?"

"Yes, sir, my wife's name is Mattie. We were married in 1852, just over ten years ago. I've got four children now. We're all good Baptists."

Dr. Cowan interjected, "My Lucy and I have three children. James is four, Mary Lou is three, and little Otey Clements is just a year and a half."

"Gee...zus, James--bang! bang! bang! You don't waste any time do you?" shouted Forrest gleefully.

"Yes, General...and just coming off leave, maybe number four is on its way. I'll tell you what. The next one's middle name will be Forrest in your honor."

"Well, I'll be damned. That would be an honor."

Then Forrest, realizing that his 19-year old chief of artillery, Captain Morton, seemed shy about expressing himself to his four comrades who were 42, 41, 37, and 31, said, "John, is military life in the Confederate Army agreeing with you?"

"Yes, sir, I like it better now that I am out of a Federal military prison."

"I guess anyone would," said Forrest. "What were the circumstances that got you into a Union prison?"

"Sir, I was with an artillery battery recruited in Nashville. We were shot up pretty well at Fort Donelson last year, and forced to surrender. The Federals sent a whole bunch of us to Johnson's Island on Lake Erie. I'll never forget that cold wind coming off Lake Erie in March. The weather around here is balmy compared to that place. The wind came right through those crude wooden huts they kept us in.

"Then after seven months, I was shipped to Vicksburg to be exchanged. I wanted active artillery service, and that's how I happened to be sent to you in Columbia, Tennessee."

"I remember that day well," said Forrest. "Somebody told me a soldier wanted to see me. I looked over your shoulder, and said, 'Where?' Now I know that wasn't funny to you, but I couldn't believe you were older than my son, Willie, who was 16 at the time.

"I must say, it was the furthest thought in my mind to put a boy so young in charge of my artillery battery."

"How old were you then?"

"A couple days short of 19," replied the embarrassed Morton. Forrest, Gallaway, Dr. Cowan and Anderson all grinned broadly, and then Morton broke into a grin hoping it would end the agony of being teased about his schoolboyish appearance.

After fifteen minutes, Matt Gallaway asked, "General, what are our orders? When will we attack Dover? The weather is bitter cold and it could snow anytime."

"I'm waiting to hear from General Wheeler, Matt."

"Could it be tomorrow or the next day?"

"I hope so. We are in short supply of everything — ammunition, rations, overcoats, blankets, horseshoes — everything. I told Wheeler, and even wrote to Bragg before we left Columbia that we were ill-equipped to make this attack. Bragg took most of the equipment and supplies we captured in West Tennessee last month for his own use, and left us very little useful equipment.

"Goddamnit, Matt, can you believe it? We've got only 20 rounds of ammunition per man for our rifles and pistols. Hell, that won't last long. Maybe fifteen minutes if we get into it. Morton, how many rounds do you have for your Rodmans?"

"Sir, there are only 50 for our entire artillery battery."

"Those idiots! We should have refused to go. It's like fighting with sticks and stones," complained Forrest who was then flushed with anger.

"But Wheeler, who wouldn't for one second dare to protest to his friend, Bragg, just ignored my complaint. His only response was, 'Our scouts report that the Dover garrison has only 700 or 800 men at most, and we've got 3000' "

"We could get slaughtered in front of Dover. The Federals are probably dug in behind those rifle pits we built last year to protect Fort Donelson. And I have no doubt they've got one or two of those 32-pounder cannons we had protecting the Cumberland River. They could blow us to Hell and back.

"If something should happen to me, I want all of you to file charges against Wheeler. Is that understood?

"I hate to scare you, but those are the facts. We don't

have any advantage over the Federals. We cannot surprise them. Hell, they know we're nearby. Our 2000 or 3000 against their 800 doesn't mean a damn thing."

No one said much for the next few minutes. Then Forrest announced he was going to bed. His body servant, Jeremiah, had prepared his bed, and laid out his master's uniform to be worn the next morning. The subdued guests left the tent to retire for the night.

Early February 2nd, General Wheeler summoned Brigadier General John A. Wharton, the 34-year old commander of the 8th Texas Cavalry and Forrest to his temporary headquarters. "We're moving to within eight miles of Dover today. Weather permitting, we'll strike Dover tomorrow afternoon. Make your inspections of men and horses today. Anyone sick or disabled should be kept in the rear of your columns," said Wheeler.

On February 3rd, the day of the attack, advanced units of Wheeler's forces skirmished briefly with a company of Federals stationed a few miles east of Dover. Any opportunity for a surprise attack vanished as word reached Colonel A. C. Harding, Commander of the 83rd Illinois Infantry, whose troops occupied Dover. Harding immediately notified his superiors at Fort Henry, 12 miles west of Dover, requesting reinforcements.

General Wheeler and his two cavalry units—one led by General Forrest and the other by General Wharton — arrived in front of Dover at 1:00 p.m. The weather was partly cloudy and the temperature was 25°. Unlike the year before, there was no snow or ice.

Forrest's Cavalry was assigned the right side of the Confederate attack line which extended from near the Cumberland River bank on the east side of Dover to the south side of the town in a semi-circle. It faced the

Federal rifle pits 1500 feet in front. Wharton's Texans were positioned to the left of the Forrest's troops, and faced Federal entrenchments on the west side of town.

Wheeler promptly sent an ultimatum to Colonel Harding to surrender. Harding refused. He told his staff, "Why should we! We have 600 effectives behind the earthen entrenchments with plenty of ammunition, and we have our 32-pounder cannon which we can rotate against the Confederate positions."

Wheeler ordered a simultaneous attach by Wharton and Forrest at 2:30 p.m. sharp. Ten minutes before the planned 2:30 p.m. signal to charge, Forrest believed Union soldiers in front of his position were trying to escape. He ordered his troops to charge. Wharton, not informed of Forrest's decision, stood fixed in position.

Despite artillery support from Captain Morton's battery, Forrest's lead soldiers suffered heavy casualties from gunfire of the 83rd Illinois Infantry. Forrest ordered his troops to dismount for a second frontal charge. Again, Forrest's troops were repulsed.

At the other end of the Confederate line, General Wharton's forces managed to push Harding's soldiers back into Dover. But at the peak of Wharton's success, his troops ran out of ammunition, forcing them to withdraw under heavy Union fire.

Fighting ebbed and flowed until near dark. At 5:00 p.m. Wheeler, Forrest and Wharton met to discuss whether to continue the fight or withdraw. They agreed there wasn't any choice. There was no ammunition left, and Union reinforcements were on their way to Dover from Fort Henry. Both Wharton and Forrest said to Wheeler simultaneously, "We're whipped! The slaughter will only get worse." Wheeler agreed, and ordered a retreat. The 600 Federal troops in action that day had successfully held Dover against a force of 2000 Confederates.

That night, Forrest was in an emotional frenzy. Meeting in an abandoned house east of Dover with Wheeler and Wharton, Forrest's pent up animosity toward Bragg and Wheeler could no longer be contained. It started when Wheeler questioned Forrest about his premature attack before the scheduled 2:30 p.m. plan. "Impulsive suicidal attacks are illogical Forrest, and more often than not lead to disaster," remarked Wheeler in his deep voice. "Why didn't you wait until 2:30 p.m.?"

"Well, goddamnit General, to tell you the truth, there is no good way to charge dug in soldiers with a battery firing at you," Forrest replied angrily as he jumped off his chair and pointed his finger at Wheeler.

"Forrest, it is absolutely necessary to bring a uniformity to all cavalry units. Just mounting a horse and charging forward pell-mell doesn't make a cavalry regiment. Discipline and a standard way of doing things are critical."

"General, you are only 26 years old, but you're like an old woman. You're a book soldier — a stickler for all those West Point manuals. I say, 'West Point, be damned!' Your perfection is ridiculous."

Wheeler, showing no emotion whatsoever, looked at Forrest and asked, "General, have you ever read any of those books?"

"Hell, yes. I read Hardee's *Tactics* — at least part of it. I put it away after a few pages. That drilling and procedures stuff isn't useful in the type of war I'm fighting. The Southern boys I know are natural born fighters. They lose their spirit with all that restrictive nonsense.

"Wheeler, I never rubbed my back against a college, and I don't know anything about tactics except what I learned by fighting. With a little more military genius in this army, we'll confuse the Yankees and everybody else.

I prefer pistols and rifles and mixin' it up. Flashing sabres and 'wheel right' and 'wheel left' and waving *the Stars and Bars* are for dress parades in Richmond."

General Wharton sat there with an astonished look on his face. He had obviously never seen such a display of temper.

Forrest wasn't finished. "I warned you and Bragg about the foolishness of this expedition. You sent us here unprepared.

"General Wheeler, you have some explaining to do to the parents and wives and sisters of those brave boys who died today. They didn't have a chance with one hand tied behind their backs. It was a doomed venture. It's a damn disgrace.

"You have my resignation. You may think I'm insubordinate and disrespectful of my ranking officers, but I'm telling you here and now in front of Wharton, I will go to my grave before I will fight under you again. And you can put that in your report to General Braxton Bragg," he snorted in disgust.

"Forrest, may I say a word?" said the embarrassed Wheeler in a calm voice. "I accept the blame for what happened today. I thought our 2000 effectives and those behind the lines could offset our shortages of ammunition. I underestimated the fight in Colonel Harding's men. I feel worse than you can imagine.

"As far as resignation, I will not accept it. The Confederate Army needs you, Forrest. You're a brave soldier. You have expressed yourself candidly and I hold no animosity toward you.

"We need to move south at dawn, and put in a hard ride tomorrow to clear out of this area. We don't need to get ourselves captured, do we?"

On Wednesday, February 4, 1863, Forrest was in the lead of his retreating cavalry. Riding along side was his confidant, Captain Matt Gallaway. Forrest was still agitated.

"Matt, that Wheeler knows nothing about fighting except what he's read in a book. He looks at that goddamn manual of his before making a decision about anything. If he were in my cavalry, I'd make him a clerk.

"How did he expect to win without ammunition, Matt?"

"General," replied Gallaway, "Adam and Eve had nothing — no horse, no clothes, nothing — just an apple. And they thought they were in paradise. Hell, they must have been in Wheeler's Cavalry."

"Matt, Wheeler's perfection is unbelievable. He and those other West Pointers remind me of the habit of rats. I heard that a string of as many as a half-dozen rats will hold each other up by the tail to enable the lowest one to steal an egg from the bottom of the barrel.

"But maybe I shouldn't be too hard on Wheeler. He's Braxton Bragg's dog. If old Bragg tells him to bite someone, he bites 'em."

10 • The Chase

"Matt, it's 'out of the frying pan into the fire.' Have you read the order from Bragg transferring us to General Earl Van Dorn?" Forrest said in an exasperated voice. "Wheeler got to Bragg when we returned from Dover, and there is no telling what he reported. No doubt he put some of the blame for the Dover disaster on me. And he probably is going to bring charges of insubordination."

"You're a pariah, General. Here we are one day back and all beat up by that retreat over rough country, and now this," commented Gallaway in a tone of frustration.

"Bragg is aware of the friction between Wheeler and

me, but he did me no favor by assigning me to Van Dorn. Cris' sakes, Matt, Van Dorn is a much greater outcast than me. He was damn lucky to get out of that court-martial for his own disaster in Corinth last October. As I hear it, Van Dorn should have easily beaten General Rosecrans' Union boys. But he was disorganized, and ended up retreating.

"Van Dorn's an egotistical, arrogant man with a notorious reputation with the ladies. I understand he combs his blond hair every chance he gets. And his body servant stands by him constantly brushing his uniform as if he were about to go to a cotillion. He is a real jack-a-dandy.

"I know he resents being assigned to the backwater of the war. Now he's trying everything possible to impress Jefferson Davis and Bragg.

"Well, I'll cooperate with him as long as he doesn't try to use us exclusively to feather his nest.

"Did you see what Van Dorn gave me today, Matt? He suggested I might want to give the same speech to my troops before our next battle action. Look at it! Read it out loud!"

Gallaway took the piece of paper from Forrest, gazed at it for a minute, then slowly read it out loud:

Soldiers, behold your leader. He comes to show you the way to glory and immortal renown. He comes to hurl back the minions of the despots of Washington, whose ignorance, licentiousness, and brutality are equalled only by their craven natures. They come to free your slaves, lay waste your plantations, burn your villages, and abuse your loving wives and beautiful daughters.

"That's enough, Matt. Cris' sakes, he's a lunatic, isn't he?"

"General, how can anyone take him seriously? He

must write to impress himself with that pompous, theatrical, meaningless language. You can wonder what those farm boys and clerks that make up our army think when they hear that nonsense coming from their commander."

"He's a real horse's ass for sure, Matt," concluded Forrest, shaking his head in wonderment.

The 42-year old Van Dorn, native of Port Gibson, Mississippi, was a distant relative of Andrew Jackson's wife, and a member of a socially-prominent Southern family. Van Dorn, a classmate of his recent Union army opponent, General Rosecrans, graduated from West Point in 1842. He then spent the next 19 years in the regular army, including fighting in the Mexican War, Seminole War, and in actions against the Comanches in 1856. And like many of his West Point colleagues from the South, he resigned in 1861 to join the Confederate army.

The week following his return from Dover Forrest spent working with his somewhat depleted staff assessing his losses at Dover in both personnel and equipment, and making plans to rebuild his cavalry unit.

Forrest paid special tribute to Captain Gilbert Rambaut, his Chief of Commissary. "Gilbert was captured a few days ago just a few miles before we arrived here in Columbia, Tennessee," said Forrest. "He'll be missed around here. He's a good officer and has been our chief joke teller and prankster. Let's hope he gets exchanged and returns soon.

"Now Captain Anderson, how do we stand with the enlisted ranks?"

"Sir, we had about 100 killed at Dover and we left a lot of wounded on the field there. And there are many missing."

"All right, I want to discuss our shortages with General Van Dorn, and decide how we can rebuild. We may want to send a recruiting party into West Tennessee.

"We're short of everything. We need horses, rifles, ammunition, wagons, medical supplies, blankets and much more.

"Anderson, get together with Captain Severson and Dr. Cowan, and prepare an inventory. Do that right away. Understood?"

"Yes, sir, we'll take care of it," replied Anderson.

Van Dorn's precise mission in Middle Tennessee was unclear. There were Union detachments operating in the region around Nashville. Van Dorn was ordered to seek out and defeat them. In the first weeks of March 1863, Forrest's Cavalry operated either jointly with Van Dorn's Cavalry, or on its own. They were victorious in several lesser skirmishes with Union troops.

Relations between Van Dorn and Forrest were cold and distant. Headquarters were moved from Columbia to the village of Spring Hill, Tennessee, just a few miles away. Heated arguments were frequent. Van Dorn accused Forrest of commandeering much of the captured equipment and supplies. Forrest argued he was entitled to them. "This material is to go to General Bragg, Forrest!" shouted Van Dorn.

"No, sir, my need is more urgent that Bragg's. How do you expect me to rebuild my cavalry? I've requested supplies from you, but so far your quartermaster hasn't sent us anything. You have forced me to take matters into my own hands."

On March 5th, the combined forces of Van Dorn and Forrest defeated handily a Union unit at Thompsons Station, a place just north of Spring Hill. A few weeks later the *Chattanooga Daily Rebel* published an article praising Forrest for his skillful fighting in that encounter which had resulted in capturing 1200 Union troops.

Van Dorn seethed in anger when he saw the article.

"Forrest, you have deliberately sought publicity for yourself, and you have gone over my head. I will not tolerate it!"

Forrest, furious at this accusation, fired back, "General, I knew nothing about that article. I did not, nor did any of my staff or line officers, talk with any news correspondents. You have falsely accused me, and I resent it deeply."

Bystanders to this highly vocal, heated exchange thought they heard Forrest challenge Van Dorn to a duel to decide their many differences. But if such a "demand for satisfaction" were made by Forrest, no duel took place. When tempers cooled each realized that nothing would be gained for the Confederacy if one of them were lying mortally wounded on a dueling field. Both recognized that their relationship was tenuous at best, and decided to ignore one another.

On April 23rd orders came from General Bragg in Shelbyville, Tennessee for Forrest's Cavalry to join forces with Brigadier General Philip Roddey's Cavalry near Tuscumbia, Alabama, a small town in the northwest corner of the state. Bragg feared that Union General Glenville Dodge's army was planning a drive eastward across north Alabama from its base in Corinth, Mississippi with the objective of disrupting the Confederate supply line between Atlanta and Chattanooga.

Bragg was unaware at the time that a force of 1700 Union troops under the command of Colonel Abel B. Streight had arrived by river transports at Eastport, Mississippi — a town 25 miles east of Corinth on the south bank of the Tennessee River near the Alabama state line. Streight's force had left Nashville two weeks earlier under orders from General William S. Rosecrans, Commander of the Army of the Cumberland, and had moved by circuitous route to Eastport.

Forrest became aware of this new Federal force that was independent of Dodge's Union forces on Sunday, April 26th. He reviewed reports that a force of mostly infantry had left Tuscumbia, and was headed south. Two days later, Forrest learned that this army of about 1700 had now turned eastward and was moving across north Alabama using mules as the principal means of transportation.

Confederate intelligence confirmed that Colonel Streight's primary objective was to disrupt communications and supplies moving between Atlanta and Chattanooga on the Western & Atlantic Railroad. Enroute Streight was ordered to destroy warehouses, factories and bridges.

Forrest and Roddey conferred on the course of action. Getting approval from Bragg, Forrest set out in pursuit of Streight to prevent the latter's force from reaching the rail line in western Georgia.

Quickly organized, Forrest's Cavalry of 600 men and Captain John Morton's horse drawn artillery battery began the chase. Roddey, a native Alabamian familiar with the regional terrain told Forrest, "I think you can catch up with them near Day's Gap and Sand Mountain. You are 12 hours behind them, but you're on horses and they're on mules. They can't be moving too fast. My forces will stay behind and keep General Dodge from pursuing you."

Skirmishing broke out as Forrest's Cavalry approached Day's Gap. It continued on in a running battle to nearby Sand Mountain as Forrest's troops pursued the enemy relentlessly. Streight's army offered stiff rear guard resistance as his main force moved steadily eastward across Alabama.

Forrest gathered his commanders together after the

first day's fighting to consider a strategy and tactics. "Streight's got the advantage of having 1700 soldiers versus our 600," said Forrest. "We must bluff them into thinking we've got three times our actual strength. Make a lot of noise with those kettles we've got. Let them hear our yelling. Pressure...pressure...pressure--that's what I want. Don't let up for a minute, men! Act like a king snake. When a king snake seizes another snake, it wraps its body firmly around the victim and chokes it. All right then, let's scare 'em half to death."

Colonel Biffle, Commander of the 9th Tennessee; Colonel Dibrell, the 8th Tennessee; Major McLemore of Starnes Regiment; and Captain Morton then agreed on the plan to exert maximum pressure on Streight's forces.

The chase continued eastward — across the Black Warrior River and on to Gadsden, Alabama. On the night of May 2nd it was apparent that Streight was reeling under the pressure. To try to distance his troops from Forrest's Cavalry, he ordered a night march. But his troops were near the point of exhaustion, and barely crawled forward on that overnight march. By morning they were only a few miles farther east and totally worn out.

Forrest, on the other hand, had rested his troops overnight. On the morning of May 3rd, his small army of 600 traversed in less than four hours the same ground that Streight's army had covered overnight.

At midday Streight who was now convinced that Forrest's Cavalry exceeded his own force in size decided he had no chance. He agreed to surrender his surviving force of 1466 at Lawrence, Alabama — a place just 20 miles short of his original target, the Western & Atlantic Railroad at Rome, Georgia.

Later that day, after surrender, Streight appeared to be in a state of shock when informed by Forrest's staff of the actual strength of the victors.

Forrest was jubilant. "Captain Anderson, organize a celebration for tomorrow. The men are too worn out today," shouted Forrest for all to hear.

11 • The Last Supper

Lawrence Plantation, Alabama, May 4, 1863

Promptly at 7:30 a.m., Monday morning Forrest called a staff meeting to critique the results of the five day running battle with Streight's Union forces, and to plan for the transportation of prisoners to the rail depot in nearby Rome, Georgia.

"Captain Anderson, can you give me a summary report on how many soldiers we lost,and also information on our equipment and supplies?"

"No, sir, I hope to finish the inventory today. Darkness yesterday prevented my team from getting reports from our field officers."

"Well, get on it Captain as quickly as you can. I want to move the prisoners tomorrow morning and deliver them to the Provost Marshall in Rome, then get back quickly to Tennessee.

"Let me ask you, Captain Morton, did we lose any more of our artillery?"

"General, we lost those in Lieutenant Gould's battery as you know. But other than those, no additional losses."

"Yes, Morton, that loss of Gould's battery should not have happened. I want to deal with that matter after we return to Columbia. That's a serious matter.

"Now, men, I want you to know how pleased I am with this mission. Tonight, at 5:00 p.m. we will celebrate. I've ordered a canopy set up where we shall hold officers' mess. And as a courtesy I am inviting Colonel Streight and his staff to join us."

Matt Gallaway interjected, "It won't be their celebration, General, will it?"

"Not exactly, but let's make every effort to be hospitable. Hell, where they're going, this may be their last decent meal."

"Do you know where they'll be sent, General?" asked Gallaway.

"Yes, at least I know where the officers will go. Libby Prison in Richmond."

"Libby Prison, General? I hear that's a horrible place."

"Well, Matt, it's not meant to be a health spa."

Promptly at 5:00 p.m., under minimal escort, Colonel Streight and his party arrived at General Forrest's quarters. Forrest, his staff, and his principal field commanders, colonels Biffle and Dibrell, Major McLemore and Captain Morton were there to greet their guests.

Colonel Abel Streight, 34, partially bald, pleasant-looking former book publisher from Indianapolis, saluted General Forrest who, in turn, responded with a precise return salute. The two foes shook hands, then spoke privately with one another for two minutes. When asked later the nature of their conversation, Forrest said, "Colonel Streight asked for the normal courtesies extended prisoners of war, that's all!"

Forrest and Streight were a contrasting pair physically. The former was 6-foot-0 tall and weighed 185 pounds. With his intense, deep set eyes and piratic beard, he had a menacing appearance. He towered over the slight, 5-foot-7, 135 pound Streight. The latter had rich green eyes, a neatly trimmed short beard, and a pleasant, relaxed demeanor.

"All right everyone," said Forrest. "Please join me

under the canopy where we have set up the tables. They're arranged in a horseshoe shape so we can all talk with one another more easily." Forrest then guided Colonel Streight to his seat in the center. "Mix up all of you! One of yours next to one of ours, Colonel Streight," said Forrest in a commanding tone.

Momentarily there was silence after all were seated. Then Forrest stood and said, "Colonel Streight and your people, my officers and I extend our greetings. Tonight we gather as fellow human beings, and not as fighting adversaries. If I may, I would like to introduce my staff. Then I would be pleased if you, sir, Colonel Streight, would introduce yourself first, then your staff."

Forrest quickly introduced his staff and field commanders, then he turned to Colonel Streight. Apprehensively Streight stood, maintained a silence for a moment as if contemplating his remarks, then spoke softly, "On September 4, 1861, Governor Oliver P. Morton of Indiana asked me to recruit a regiment of Indiana volunteers. Without any prior military experience on my part, Governor Morton commissioned me a Colonel. By October 1861 I had raised a regiment — the 51st Indiana Infantry Regiment to be exact. When we had our first review, the newspapers referred to my unit as 'The Pride of Indianapolis.' When we passed through the center of the city — down Penn Street — the crowd was yelling, 'Hurray for Lincoln!! Hurrah for Indiana!'

"Believe me, I was one proud Hoosier. With my 51st Infantry I believed the war wouldn't last long once the Confederates saw us in action," said the now smiling Streight. "I was 32 years old and wanted a little adventure. Anything to escape the printing business! And by golly, my wish came true," he said shaking his head. "Today I feel like I'm 82 and a person who in the last five days has had enough adventure to last a lifetime [laughter].

General Forrest's Staff (military rank as of the War's end.)

"Well, gentlemen," he said looking at his own officers, "It wasn't easy, was it? Never did I dream we would have to deal with the likes of General Forrest. It's a sobering experience to get whipped. I thank God I am not a career military officer. To them a defeat is far more devastating to their ego and their careers, I'm sure.

"General Forrest, I thank you for the hospitality. Tonight, for a few hours, let us forget our differences. Thank you."

"Colonel Streight, would you introduce your officers?" Forrest requested once again.

"Of course, General. It will be my pleasure."

Pointing as he introduced each officer, Streight said, "First, this is Colonel Robert Hibbard, 3rd Ohio Regiment. He's been with me from the start. Before the war the Colonel was a schoolmaster.

"Next is Lieutenant Colonel Austin Brown of the 18th Illinois Regiment. I believe he was a shipwright."

General Forrest, thoroughly curious about his guests, exclaimed, "A shipwright in Illinois? Where's the ocean? Heh-heh-heh!"

Responded Colonel Brown, "Sir, in Chicago on Lake Michigan."

"All right, I guess I don't know my geography," said Forrest good-naturedly.

Then continuing, Streight introduced Colonel Raymond Dodge. "Colonel Dodge is my aide-de-camp. Old Dodge is an expatriate from Philadelphia. Before the war, he was practicing law in Indianapolis. As a matter of fact, he was my attorney. Look at the mess you've gotten me in, Dodge!"

Laughter prevailed for a few moments, embarrassing the ruddy-faced Dodge.

"Next over there is our Chaplain, Father Sidney Champion from Ireland. He moved to Michigan as a young man. He's Catholic. Of course, Father Champion was exempt from service as a clergyman, but he volunteered up in Michigan in October 1861."

Two more officers were introduced by Colonel Streight. Both were Indiana businessman prior to the war.

Forrest rose once again. "Thank you, Colonel Streight. Dinner will be served momentarily. But first, would Chaplain Champion honor us with a blessing?"

"I shall be honored, sir," said the tall, distinguished looking Champion.

"Gentlemen of both forces, let us pray please.

"Seek ye the Lord while he may be found. Call ye upon Him while he is near. Be faithful to God. His banner of love is over you. His eye of approval is on you.
"Let us all pray for peace on Earth and goodwill toward man. Amen!"

"Thank you Parson," said Forrest. "I shall ask you to pray for the souls of your hosts tonight. Heh-heh-heh!

"Parson Champion, as a man of peace, how are you adjusting to war?"

"General Forrest, like the Chinese philosopher and teacher Confucius said 2300 years ago, 'As water shapes itself to the vessel that contains it, so a wise person adapts himself to circumstances.'"

"Father, that's a good way of putting it."

Chief of officers' mess, Sergeant Flaxson Berry, approached General Forrest. "Should dinner be served now, General?"

"Yes, Flaxy, but be sure to serve the wine first."

"Of course, sir. My assistants, Uncle Ben and Sweet Henry, are just outside ready to serve you all."

Sergeant Berry snapped his fingers, and instantly Forrest's long-time house servants entered the dining area dressed in mess boys' white cotton jackets. Red wine was served. This was followed shortly by the serving of heaping plates of red beans and rice with ham hocks. Dessert was plantation pecan cake and a choice of chicory or coffee as a hot drink.

Both groups thoroughly enjoyed the unusual meal. Several of Colonel Streight's officers ate like they were half-starved. When all had finished, Colonel Streight asked Forrest if he could thank personally Sergeant Berry for his preparation of such a fine meal.

"Ask Flaxy and his staff to come on in here," Forrest said to Captain Anderson.

"Colonel Streight, this is Sergeant Flaxy Berry. He's in charge of officers' mess. Helping him are my slaves, Uncle Ben, the tall one with the big grin; and Sweet Henry, that skinny fellow. They have been with me for years. They're good boys."

"Sergeant Berry, were you a cook before the war?" asked Colonel Streight.

"Yes, sir, I was assistant head chef for seven years at the St. Charles Hotel in New Orleans."

Forrest interrupted, "Don't believe old Flaxy, Colonel. I never saw him there."

"Well, General, I was there. I never saw you come back to the kitchen."

"Flaxy, you're quite right. Why in the hell would I come back there. I was too busy looking for a card game after dinner when I stayed at the St. Charles. Heh-heh-heh!"

Colonel Streight then added, "Wherever Sergeant Berry learned his trade, he learned it well. My compliments on the fine meal you prepared. It was delicious."

"Thank you, sir. I just hope you and your officers liked the Cajun cooking. Red beans and rice is a delicacy down in Louisiana. The spicier, the better.

"I hope the ham hocks and the spices agree with you. The dash of garlic and Louisiana hot sauce gives it a lot of spark.

"Did you all like the cake? I think what makes it good is the bourbon I put in it."

"That's all right. I know of no teetotalers in our group, Sergeant Berry."

"Well sir, I am pleased you liked the meal. We almost didn't make it here tonight with the cook wagons. That was a mighty fast chase across Alabama. Those old mules were straining to keep up."

Forrest was in high spirits enjoying the temporary comradeship with his guests. He asked them to stay for a while.

Turning to Matt Gallaway, Forrest added, "Captain Gallaway, have you heard any funny stories lately?"

"Yes, General. I've got one for Father Champion.

"A Mississippi Baptist preacher named Scruggs was baptizing one of his flock in a stream. The preacher pushed the poor soul under water again and again. Each time he asked, 'Brother, what do you believe? What do you believe?' At last, soaked and gasping for breath, the poor fellow sputtered, 'Damnit, preacher, I believe you are trying to drown me.'"

Everyone laughed heartily. Forrest then looked at Dr. Cowan. "Do you have a story, James?"

Dr. Cowan said, "Yes, but first let me apologize beforehand to Father Champion."

Father Champion, with a wide grin, said, "That's perfectly all right, Doctor. Please proceed."

"Well, two thoroughly inebriated Irishmen went into the woods to shoot a bear, and by some stroke of luck they killed one. The sorry devils then began to drag the bear back home by the hind legs, but the hind legs broke off. 'What are we going to do now?' one said to the other.

'I don't know,' the other fellow replied. Meanwhile, a third hunter came along, and after he listened to the dilemma facing the two Irishmen, he said, 'Why don't you fellows pull the bear by its head?' The Irishmen looked at him like he was an idiot, and replied, 'because we ain't goin' that way.'"

Again, howls of laughter by all. General Forrest swayed his body back and forth in obvious delight.

Matt Gallaway, not to be outdone by Dr. Cowan, asked Forrest is he could tell the true story about Private Levi Stoltzfus, the Pennsylvania Dutch soldier they had captured near Nashville in March.

Forrest said, "Certainly, that's a good one."

Gallaway then proceeded to tell the story. "We captured this roly-poly, rosy cheeked, comical fellow a few weeks ago. Unfortunately, some of our soldiers were a little rough with him. He was frightened and asked, 'Vat you fellows vant do vit me?' Faking grim looks, we teased him by telling him, 'We're going to take you down to that red oak tree and hang you.' The Dutchman calmed down strangely, and in a voice of hopeless resignation said, 'Vell, fellows, vatever is de rule.' So when we all started laughing hilariously, old Dutchy started laughing too, not really knowing what to make of it all."

Again, laughter. Dr. Cowan whispered in Captain Anderson's ear, "Look at General Forrest! He's having the time of his life. Two days ago if he had met Colonel Streight face to face in a skirmish he would have killed him. Now look at them having a good time."

The conversations then became more serious. Forrest asked several of the Union officers their feelings about the war. Chaplain Champion talked about the moral basis of slavery, and how this concerned him and most Northerners. He pointed out the inconsistency of condemning murder, kidnapping, theft, fornication, adultery, and prostitution, yet supporting human bondage.

The fiery Gallaway, the most outspoken advocate of the institution of slavery among Forrest's staff, answered Chaplain Champion forcefully. He explained at length the slave holding economy of the South and the legal and economic aspects of the issue which led to secession.

Gallaway continued, "Some weeks at the newspaper I'd get two or three bushels of letters from strong-minded women and weak-minded men in the North who didn't know any more about niggers than they did about the man in the moon."

Champion interrupted, "But I really pity them."

"Pity costs nothing, and it's worth nothing.

"Chaplain Champion, you're from Michigan, aren't you?

"Tell me, what percentage of Michigan's population is Negro?"

"Not many," answered Champion with a slight smile on his face.

Determined to make his point, Gallaway persisted.

"Would you guess one percent or less?"

The Chaplain now getting annoyed whispered, "Yes, about that."

"And what about you gentlemen from Indiana, Illinois and Ohio?" continued Gallaway. "Would your states have any more Negroes than Michigan?"

"No, I guess not," said Ohioan, Colonel Lawson.

"Well, you see," continued Gallaway, "General Forrest, Dr. Cowan, Captain Anderson, Captain Morton and I come from Tennessee where we have about 26 percent. It's 55 percent in Mississippi, and about 50 percent in Alabama.

"So you see, gentlemen, my point is that you in the North do not understand the realities of our dependence on Negro labor in our vast agricultural economy. We need the Negroes in our cotton fields, our tobacco fields and our sugar plantations. You Northerners are also the beneficiaries of this source of labor.

"Our churches down here, Chaplain, preach to the White population that slavery conforms to God's will. They believe that critics are servants of the anti-Christ movement.

The bewildered Father Champion wanted the lecture by Gallaway to end, but felt compelled to ask, "Are you saying that the churches support slavery?"

"Yes, indeed."

Then Forrest, spellbound by Gallaway's eloquence on the issue of slavery, told Colonel Streight and his officers that Captain Gallaway is also a strong proponent of dueling. "Captain Gallaway, as you may not know, is the finest example of a true Southern gentleman. He is a man of strong convictions and personal honor."

Colonel Streight asked, "What's the point of dueling? Why can't differences be settled in a civil manner? Dueling to settle matters is barbaric, isn't it? Dueling has all but disappeared in the North."

Gallaway, as if he were writing out of his vitriolic editorials, snapped at Streight, "Sir, it's a matter of personal honor. A strong insult in our culture burns deep within the recipient, and settling the matter on the dueling field is the only true way a gentleman done an injustice can maintain his pride and reputation."

"It seems so barbaric," said Streight shaking his head.

"Sir, it is far less barbaric than the fighting between our two armies. Dueling operates with hard and fast rules and traditions. Each of the participants knows why he is on the dueling field and he knows it involves him personally.

"In this war we fire away at people we often don't see, and, of course, don't know. And we kill people who have wives, children, parents and sweethearts. Now, that is barbaric."

Streight responded, "Both dueling and war are barbaric."

Gallaway, obviously anxious to educate the Northern prisoners, continued, "Over in Mississippi there is a group called 'the Anti-Dueling Society' and they publish a list of known duelists. The General and I are on that list for whatever that's worth. I can't say that I am not pleased to be classified as a gentleman of honor.

"General Sam Houston, Andrew Jackson and Henry Clay all fought duels. That didn't dishonor them in any way."

Forrest, interrupting the emotional Gallaway, then asked Colonel Streight, "Do you play poker?"

"No, sir, the Methodists back in Indiana frown on cards. The preachers rail against the wickedness of gambling."

"Well, Streight, do you think I'm a wicked man for playing cards for money?"

"No, sir, it's your business. Personally, I'd be too frightened I'd lose."

"That rules out any card games tonight unless your officers would enjoy a small stakes game," said the amused Forrest.

"I enjoy cards. Hell, I've played in every cardroom from St. Louis down river to New Orleans. Some of those places were plenty rough, but you had to go there to get into the high stakes games. One of the roughest places was at Natchez-Under-the-Hill. Ever been there, Matt?"

"No, not me," answered Gallaway emphatically.

"Me either," said Dr. Cowan. "Only a big tough fellow like yourself would have dared stick his nose in one of those gambling dens."

"Cardsharps, confidence men and other low-class

folks were shoulder to shoulder in Natchez and New Orleans. Guns and knives were as abundant as cards. I never went into a game without my bowie knife. No, sir.

"They all had rules. Anyone caught with marked cards was taken out back and shot.

"I played a lot of poker on the riverboats. My brothers and I rode the boats hauling slaves when we had our Mart in Memphis. But nobody did any gambling on boats operated by Captain Tom Leathers. Old Leathers was 6-foot-4 and weighed easily 275 pounds. He used to say to us, 'If you want to gamble, y'all get off at Vicksburg or Natchez. If you don't want me to unload you on a sandbar, I better not see any cards.' Heh-heh-heh!"

"Gambling got so bad in Vicksburg, the town passed a law making it mandatory that gamblers who couldn't prove they made an honest living had 24 hours to get out of town."

Colonel Streight, Chaplain Champion and two other Union officers were spellbound by Forrest's exposition on poker playing. None of them had ever met anyone quite like him. And Forrest, with his captive audience that night, relished in telling of his gambling exploits. Even his close friends, Gallaway and Dr. Cowan, hadn't heard Forrest expound on his gambling life before.

"Now, New Orleans, that was some place," Forrest continued. "When the slave auctions ended for the day in the rotunda of the St. Charles Hotel, I generally ate dinner, then walked over to Count Lorenzo Lewis' place. He had all the games — poker, monte, faro, craps and roulette."

Streight asked, "General, you said Count Lorenzo Lewis?"

"Yes, he claimed he was European royalty. But he didn't fool me. He was native born in New Orleans over in the disreputable Second District.

"But the biggest game I was ever in was at the St. Louis Hotel in New Orleans. On one hand I won $47,000."

Gallaway, somewhat in shock, asked, "General, what did you hold?"

"Three kings and two nines — a full house."

Gallaway again, "Did your opponent pay up?"

"Yes, he had to. It was Colonel Marquis Le Blanc, a prominent Louisiana planter. He had his reputation to protect. There were just too many witnesses that watched the play.

"I tell you what — he didn't feel so good.

"That night, my brothers Jesse and Jeffrey guarded me all night. We all wanted to leave New Orleans as fast as possible."

Then Gallaway, curious that Forrest had won all that money on just a full house, asked, "General, can you tell us what Colonel Le Blanc held?"

"I don't know. He stood up, tore up his cards, and threw them on the floor. And I wasn't about to bend over and scrape up the pieces. And I didn't ask him either."

Promptly at 10:00 p.m. Forrest stood, surveyed the assembled officers for a moment with a pleasant smile, then asked Colonel Streight to stand with him.

"Colonel Streight, it has been a pleasant evening. You and your officers are fine men. I wish we all could have met under different circumstances.

"It is unlikely we shall meet again in this war. No one can predict what may happen to any of us. I do hope you will all carry with you the memory of this quiet evening in this turbulent war.

"Please accept my good wishes. Good night, gentlemen."

At 5:30 a.m. Forrest rose, dressed and went immediately to Captain Morton's tent. Morton, with a lantern near his head, was peering in a small mirror with a look of intensity.

"What are you doing Morton," inquired the curious Forrest. "Don't tell me you're trying to find a whisker. Gee..zus, don't be discouraged that you can't grow a mustache. It sometimes happens when a mustache does best, nothing else does so well."

"General, it isn't fair. I'll be twenty my next birthday, and probably will still be beardless.

"Regulations state that when a beard is worn, it must be kept short and neatly trimmed. Unfortunately, that's a problem I don't have to worry about, do I?"

"Look at it this way, Morton, beards are a nuisance."

"Maybe so, sir, but it does make a soldier look older."

"Morton, forget about whiskers. I want you to assist Captain Anderson today in the guard detail moving Streight's soldiers to the rail depot in Rome, Georgia. It's a 20-mile march; and I want to be able to turn over the prisoners to the Provost Marshall's Office no later than 6:00 p.m. We've got to move them quickly. Rumor has it that perhaps the Union troops may be following us across Alabama. We don't want this sweet victory of ours to end up a disaster.

"I will ride ahead with the rest of the staff and some soldiers from my escort company. Dibrell, Biffle, McLemore and the other field officers will stay behind, and prepare for our return journey to Spring Hill, Tennessee."

When the prisoners arrived in Rome, most of the town's citizens had lined the streets leading to the depot to witness the spectacle of some 1400 of the hated enemy getting ready to be sent off to prison. The jeering was raucous: "You Yankee trash! You murderers! You deserve to hang!" many shouted. Some irate citizens stepped into the street and pushed the frightened captives and beat them with sticks. The local women were far more physically militant than the men and boys.

Colonel Streight, when asked by Confederate Major George Hemphill who represented the Provost Marshall's Office in Rome, Georgia, how he felt, answered, "I'm relieved we came through that mob not getting killed."

Streight asked Major Hemphill if General Forrest had arrived in Rome. "I wish to speak to the General about a very serious matter."

"And what might that be?" asked Hemphill.

"Major, serious violations of the rules of warfare have occurred. Since early this morning, General Forrest's soldiers have systematically and deliberately robbed my men of their private property.

"My troops have been strip-searched and robbed of their boots, watches, rings, money, tobacco and personal mementos from their families. Their conduct is barbaric. I want to protest this gross violation of the traditional rules of warfare.

"I've written this statement to him. Would you please see that it is delivered?"

"I'll try sir, but I doubt you will be able to speak with him. My orders are to release the prison train for its journey south to Atlanta by 7:15 p.m. It is now 6:55 p.m. I am sorry, sir."

Later, when word reached Forrest about Colonel Streight's protest, the General shrugged his shoulders, "I seriously doubt he has a valid complaint."

12 • Lieutenant Gould

Black Creek, Gadsden, Alabama, May 8, 1863

At mid-morning Forrest's Cavalry had just crossed Black Creek and was resting for 30 minutes before continuing toward Decatur, Alabama on the journey back to Spring Hill, Tennessee.

General Forrest was drinking coffee. With him were Matt Gallaway; Colonel Biffle; Colonel Dibrell; Captain Morton and Captain Bill Forrest, the general's brother.

Looking directly at them, Forrest said, "Two things I can't stand — a liar and a coward. Losing those two Rodman field guns up on Sand Mountain last week gnaws away at me. To think that I may really have young officers with no courage. Goddamnit, that upsets me. What the hell kind of an example does that set for the men.

"I'm referring to Lieutenant Gould in your artillery unit, Morton. I feel the same way about Gould as I felt about that spineless Floyd and that fool Pillow at Fort Donelson last year. They willingly surrendered our 13,000 or so troops, then scampered out of there to save their own skins.

"If Gould hadn't abandoned his battery when Streight's soldiers attacked, we'd have driven them back. And 20 or so of our men would still be alive today."

Then, looking at his brother Bill, he said, "Bill, you were there. Am I right? Did he run away? Could he have saved our guns?"

Captain Bill Forrest, known for being headstrong and fearless, answered, "Bedford — I mean General — that counterattack was furious. Streight pulled us into a trap. As we moved forward the Federals were hiding in the underbrush and gulleys. Then bang! — they jumped all over us. I got shot near my hip. Some of our boys were killed in the same ambush. I tell you — it was a goddamn mess. I know that some of his men abandoned him or got shot, but Gould was struggling to get his artillery in position. I guess he could have fired a few rounds. I don't want to judge him on what I saw."

"Matt, what do you think about Gould?" the General asked, hoping to get support for his feeling that Lieutenant Gould panicked out of fear.

"General, cowardice is defined as lacking courage in the face of danger or trouble. A coward is shamefully unable to control his fear. Gould may have been on the horns of a dilemma. His choice was an unpleasant one. He could stand his ground with the enemy firing at him directly, and perhaps die a hero; or he could abandon his post and his guns because he felt he could accomplish nothing by staying there."

"Well, Matt, that doesn't help me a damn bit. Talk to some eyewitnesses. Let me know what they say, will you?"

"And Captain Morton, you do the same thing. After all, he's part of your battery. You are in a better position to judge.

"Ask Captain Anderson to bring me a copy of the *Articles of War*. I want to see what it says about cowardice."

Anderson came within minutes with his copy.

"What's it say about cowards, Anderson?"

"It's *Article 52*, sir. Let me read it:

Any officer or soldier who shall misbehave himself before the enemy, run away, or shamefully abandon any fort, post, or guard which he or they may be commanded to defend, or speak words inducing others to do the like, or shall quit his post or colors to plunder and pillage, every such offender, being duly convicted thereof, shall suffer death, or such other punishment as shall be ordered by the sentence of a general court-martial.

Forrest said, "Thank you! That seems to fit this case."

On Sunday, May 10th, Forrest's Cavalry reached Decatur, Alabama. To that point no Union forces had been sighted. Forrest assumed the remainder of the overland march back to Spring Hill, Tennessee would continue without incident.

At 5:00 p.m. Forrest received a dispatch from General Bragg's headquarters in Shelbyville, Tennessee. The message said:

> *Major General Van Dorn killed on May 7th. Report immediately to General Bragg at above location.*
> *Colonel George W. Brent, Adjutant*

"What does it mean, General?" asked Gallaway.

"I don't know, Matt. I wonder what happened. Do you think he may have been killed in action? We've been out of contact for two weeks, and he may have gone into the field."

"What do you think Bragg wants with you, General?"

"Damned if I know. As you know, we aren't the best of friends."

"Isn't that something about Van Dorn?" continued Gallaway in a baffled tone.

"Yes, Matt, I'm shocked. To tell you the truth, I always thought Van Dorn would die from patting himself on the back. He had such a high opinion of himself as you know.

"Call Anderson and Colonel Dibrell in here. I'm going to place Anderson in charge of the staff, and Dibrell, the cavalry. They can take our boys back to Spring Hill.

"You come with me to Shelbyville. We'll leave at daybreak."

Forrest, Gallaway and 12 members of Forrest's Escort Company arrived in Shelbyville Tuesday night, May 12th. An aide from General Bragg's headquarters informed Forrest that Bragg wished to see him at 8:00 a.m. the next morning.

Forrest, excited about the meeting with General Bragg, arrived at the latter's headquarters at 7:30 a.m. He didn't have to wait long. Bragg had just finished reading a pile of dispatches and conferring with several aides.

"Come in, Forrest, I'm pleased you're here," said the haggard-looking, but friendly Bragg as he half rose from his chair to extend his hand to Forrest. "May I offer congratulations for your recent success in Alabama. We needed that victory to impress General Rosecrans in Nashville that we intend to keep his Army of the Cumberland from moving toward Chattanooga.

"Now, let's get down to business, Forrest.

"I want you to take over General Van Dorn's command immediately. As you know, he was killed on May 7th in Spring Hill. It was unfortunate — yes, unfortunate! You will hear the details, no doubt, when you confer later today with my staff.

"You will be in charge of the left wing of the Army of Tennessee. General Wheeler, as you know, commands the right wing. You will report directly to me.

"Now, what do you say, Forrest?"

"General Bragg, I accept. There isn't much to say except I'll fight with every ounce of my energy."

"That's what I expect, Forrest. Good luck!"

"Thank you, sir."

Forrest was then escorted by Captain Steve Farnsworth, an aide, to a nearby house where General Bragg's staff had assembled for the scheduled early morning briefing session. Farnsworth introduced Forrest to the individual staff members, then Forrest joined them for the one-hour briefing.

It was during this meeting that Forrest learned the details of Van Dorn's death.

"General Van Dorn was shot in the left side of his head just above the ear, killing him instantly," said Colonel Brent, General Bragg's adjutant. "It happened about 1:00 p.m. last Thursday over in Spring Hill."

"Who killed him?" asked the curious Forrest.

"It was a Dr. Peters, General."

"Do you mean Jessie Peters' husband?"

"Yes, I believe that's correct."

"Do you know why?"

"Apparently, Dr. Peters believed that General Van Dorn was having an affair with his wife. Peters believed his wife was being pressured by General Van Dorn to enter into this affair, and he demanded that Van Dorn exonerate his wife. Upset that Van Dorn ignored him, and that Van Dorn refused to comply with his request, Peters shot him."

"Isn't that something," exclaimed a wide-eyed Forrest with a half-smile on his face. "Poor Dr. Peters! He probably didn't know that Jessie was having several affairs at the same time. Not with me, of course. Heh-heh-heh!"

"Well, Forrest, those are personal matters, and I make no further comment on them. The reality is that General Van Dorn is dead. Dr. Peters has escaped through Union lines; but we expect to apprehend him."

Forrest mumbled in a low voice, "I hope the poor sonafabich gets away. He did us all a big favor."

Forrest returned immediately to Spring Hill. Three days later he moved his headquarters to Columbia, Tennessee. Although part of his cavalry skirmished with elements of General Rosecrans' Union army operating around Nashville, Forrest himself spent the next several weeks in Columbia reorganizing his command. He established an office in the town's Masonic Lodge building. Here he conferred with his staff and some of the line officers who had served with Van Dorn's command prior to the latter's death.

Lieutenant Gould's conduct at Sand Mountain, Alabama continued to rankle Forrest. He couldn't get his version of the incident out of his mind. Finally, as part of the reorganization, he decided to get rid of Gould by transferring him out of Forrest's Cavalry. Gould, when notified of the transfer, believed Forrest's decision was based solely on the cowardice accusation. He told his friends, "The General is trying to humiliate me publicly, and to make me a scapegoat to frighten his other junior officers. It's unjust."

On Saturday, June 13th, Lieutenant Gould walked quickly down West Market Street in Columbia, and strode into Forrest's office located just inside the front door of the Masonic Hall. Gould was 22 years old and just one year out of college. He was described as a handsome and proud young man from a prominent Nashville family. His military experience was limited.

Bystanders who observed Gould enter the building, noticed he was wearing a long gray linen coat and that he appeared highly distraught.

Approaching Forrest, Gould unleveled a barrage of abusive words on his superior. Then he said, "I'd rather be found lying with my face to the moon that to have you call me a coward. What you say about me is false! You are a great liar, sir! You are the instrument of the Devil himself; and you shall die, by God!"

Persons on the street heard Gould and Forrest yelling at one another, but there were no witnesses to the altercation which occurred in Forrest's office.

Within minutes, Lieutenant Gould ran out of the Masonic Hall clutching the right side of his chest. After running about half a block down Market Street, he darted into a tailor shop.

Forrest emerged from the Masonic building just seconds behind Gould. "That sonafabich shot me in the hip and I'm gonna kill him. He pulled a gun on me and shot, but I got him with a pocket knife."

Bystanders told Forrest that Gould had entered the tailor shop. Forrest headed through the front door in pursuit. When Gould saw him with a pistol in his hand, Gould, bleeding heavily, raced out the back door and ran down an alley. As he reached a patch of weeds nearby, he fell.

"I'm going to kill him! I'm going to kill the sonafabich!" shouted the enraged Forrest.

Within minutes a large crowd had gathered in front of he tailor shop. They were alarmed at Forrest's rage and his uncontrollable swearing. Suddenly, Forrest, with his uniform soaked with blood, halted his pursuit to seek medical assistance.

Gould, in the meantime, was carried to the Nelson House, Columbia's major hotel. He died there two days later on June 15th from pneumonia which occurred as a result of his severe lung wound.

Forrest's wound, despite the intense bleeding, proved to be superficial, and he quickly recovered.

Witnesses later denied a rumor that Forrest in a moment of compassion visited the dying Gould at the Nelson House where it was said each forgave the other for the altercation.

Forrest worried about the repercussions resulting from the incident. He called Captain Anderson to his headquarters one week later to discuss it. "Anderson, what do the *Articles of War* say about the penalty for an officer striking or shooting his superior?"

"Sir, the penalty is death, or such punishment that might be decided by a court-martial. It seems like it depends on the nature of the offense."

"Well, Anderson, I guess I'm in the clear. I appointed myself as the Confederate court-martial body when I stuck my knife in Gould's chest."

"General Bragg's legal counselors may not see it that way. One person court-martial boards aren't exactly legal," replied Anderson in a cautious tone.

"The hell with them, Anderson! Anyway, the Confederate army needs me more than Lieutenant Gould.

"I don't want to talk about it anymore. I know the other officers understand why Gould died. He committed violence against me. He should have been prepared for the consequences. What kind of discipline is it if a junior officer who doesn't like his orders decides to kill his superior?"

Anderson said nothing. The one-sided conversation ended.

13 • Chickamauga

"General Forrest, while you were out on inspection, orders came from General Bragg's headquarters to move our troops to Tullahoma, south of Shelbyville. There we're to join forces with General Wheeler's to protect the rear of Bragg's withdrawal of his infantry south toward Chattanooga. We're to rendezvous with Wheeler the morning of June 30th. That's next Tuesday."

"Captain Anderson, Bragg's decision doesn't surprise me. Rosecrans' Army of the Cumberland in Nashville has been reinforced for what I think will be a big drive south to Chattanooga. He's going to surround us or push us out of the way. Then, I believe he hopes to move into Georgia and tear up our supply lines from Atlanta."

"I wouldn't be surprised if Burnside's Union army up in Kentucky will be brought in too. It could be a double-pronged movement. The Federals would also like to chase us out of Knoxville up in East Tennessee, then drive south to join Rosecrans' army.

"Call a meeting of all commanders for tomorrow at noon. That will give everyone time to get here.

"Start preparations for the move. Have Captain Severson and his staff make a complete inventory of everything this afternoon. And I mean complete! I don't care if it takes them all night. Understand? We are probably leaving here for the last time.

"Now put all soldiers on alert. I want no skulkers. They are to clean their weapons, groom their mounts and get their letters written home. Tell Major Kelley I want a good sermon prepared for Sunday morning right before we leave.

"Don't wander off today, Anderson. I've got a lot of work for you. I need some communications prepared. Tell Captain Gallaway I need him too. All right, Anderson, get busy," concluded the nervous Forrest as he paced quickly from one side of the room to the other in his headquarters.

General William S. Rosecrans (West Point, 1842) had battled Bragg in an inconclusive fight just six months earlier at Stone's River, near Murfreesboro, Tennessee. Now, in late June 1863 the 44-year old, Ohio native had his second chance to try to destroy Bragg's Army of Tennessee. It was the opportunity Rosecrans desperately sought to impress President Lincoln and the Union high command in Washington of his abilities as a commander.

Bragg's slow retreat south to Chattanooga was uneventful. The move south by Rosecrans was equally slow. By mid-August Rosecrans' army was less than half way of the total 133-mile distance from Nashville to Chattanooga.

Forrest's Cavalry arrived west of Chattanooga in early July, and was granted leave. Forrest ordered his soldiers to reassemble on August 9th.

Chattanooga was a riverport on the upper portion of the Tennessee River. It had been since the 1850s a pivotal railroad center in the Southeast. At the outbreak of the war, the city had 5000 residents. Its physical location and features were unique. These special characteristics created for military leaders on both sides problems about either (1) how to attack the city, or (2) how to defend it.

The meandering Tennessee River wrapped around Chattanooga on the city's north and west sides. Nearby, some 1700 feet above the river valley floor, was the pinnacle of the formidable, rocky landmark, Lookout Mountain. On the eastern side of the city was another prominent landmark -- the northern portion of Missionary Ridge. The 25-mile long mountain was divided physically into two distinct sections. The northern portion was primarily in Tennessee; the southern half, across the state line in Georgia.

The south section, located on the western side of the site of the main fighting at the Battle of Chickamauga, rose between 300 and 350 feet above the Chickamauga Creek Valley. McFarland's Gap in the center part of the southern section and Rossville Gap at the northern end were the two major transportation routes from nearby Georgia into Chattanooga.

The city had been for two years a major Confederate garrison and marshalling point for troops and for the warehousing of military supplies.

Bragg's retreating army swelled the city's population to thousands.

Local citizens and the temporary Confederate military personnel alike were all highly excited about the unfolding events. Full details of the Confederate defeats at Gettysburg and Vicksburg had been reported by early August. This news from distant battlefields and fear of the impending attack by Rosecrans' Army of the Cumberland created widespread speculation and fear in the city. The questions most asked by local residents were: "Is this the beginning of the end of the war?"; "What happens if we don't hold off Rosecrans?"; and "Should we evacuate?"

General Bragg was under enormous pressure to not only block Rosecrans' move south, but also to defeat him.

In mid-August 1863 Forrest, now back from furlough, joined with General Wheeler's Cavalry in skirmishing with smaller isolated Union forces operating in northwest Georgia trying to disrupt rail service into Chattanooga on the Western & Atlantic Railroad.

Unexpectedly, one day Captain John Strange, Forrest's former Adjutant, walked into his old commander's tent, and announced proudly, "I'm back, General Forrest."

"Well, I'll be goddamn! This is a surprise. I know you heard Captain Anderson was doing such a good job shuffling papers you got jealous, and skedaddled out of prison to get your old job back. Heh-heh-heh!"

"No, sir, I want a better job than I had before. How about battalion commander?"

"John, what the hell do you know about fighting? You got yourself captured at Parker's Crossroads by not paying attention. Now admit it! Isn't that true?"

"Maybe, I don't know how it happened to tell you the truth."

Spotting Dr. Cowan and Matt Gallaway who were standing outside, Forrest yelled, "Hey, look who's here. He's back from the dead. Come in here to greet our long, lost Adjutant. A month ago Gilbert Rambaut wandered back from a Union prison. Now it's John Strange."

Not only Dr. Cowan and Matt Gallaway entered the tent, but most of Forrest's staff came in to join the backslapping and handshaking. Captain Strange was obviously well-liked.

"What was it like in prison, John?" asked the eager, excited Lieutenant Willie Forrest, the General's son and Aide-de-Camp.

"If you really want to know, Alton Prison in Illinois is a rat-infested Hell hole. There weren't enough beds, so half of us slept out in the open prison yard. Many of our boys died of pneumonia. I don't recommend spending the winter in Illinois.

"And the smell of the place! Even the lime they threw around couldn't kill the stench. The prisoners pissed anywhere they could."

"Couldn't you and the rest of them escape?"

"Not from Alton. The place is a solid stone fortress. Illinois built it before the war to hold its worst criminals."

Then Forrest pulled Strange aside. "John, I'm pleased you rejoined me. As you know, of course, you could have gone back to Memphis and forgotten about the war. But you didn't. You've got more courage than brains. I'm proud to have you back in one piece."

On August 21, 1863 Rosecrans' Army of the Cumberland reached the Tennessee River near Chattanooga. Ten days later his army started crossing the river. By September 4th some 60,000 soldiers, hundreds of supply wagons and ambulances, and artillery were safely across. This army had moved freely without Confederate resistance.

Rosecrans, baffled by this lack of harassment, asked his second-in-command, General George H. Thomas, "Why do you think Bragg chose not to attack us?" Thomas answered, "I can only conclude he's fleeing us."

Operating on this assumption, Rosecrans ordered part of his force to move south of Chattanooga across the Georgia state line to try to contain Bragg's army. "They may be trying to flee to Atlanta," he told Thomas.

Fearing his army might be entrapped in Chattanooga, on September 6th General Bragg ordered his force of 43,000 to relocate to Lafayette, Georgia, a tiny village 25 miles south of Chattanooga. This new base, because of rail service from Atlanta, would make it easier for reinforcements to rendezvous with Bragg's forces at that location.

General Simon B. Buckner's Confederate troops based in Knoxville, Tennessee were ordered on August 28th to join Bragg. And General James Longstreet's army in Virginia which only two months earlier fought at Gettysburg was assigned to Bragg. This trek of Longstreet's proved to be the longest single journey for an army in the Civil War. Longstreet's soldiers travelled 842 miles by a circuitous rail trip to reach Bragg. General Longstreet, who had received much criticism for his cautiousness at Gettysburg, was again to be a principal player in one of the war's great battles.

Friday, September 18, 1863

Forrest's Cavalry skirmished off and on throughout the day with advanced elements of Rosecrans' army just south of the Tennessee state line. Bragg had ordered Forrest and others to cross the Chickamauga Creek near Reed's Bridge to attempt to cut off Rosecrans' forces from Chattanooga. Forrest's first contact was about 7:30 a.m. about one mile east of Reed's Bridge against Union cavalry troops commanded by 32-year old Colonel Robert H. G. Minty, a former British Army soldier. After nearly five hours of skirmishing Forrest's Cavalry drove the Federal troops across the Creek. General Bushrod Johnson's Division of Hood's Corps crossed the Creek in mid-afternoon to join Forrest's soldiers to continue to carry out Bragg's plan to sever the Federal army from its communications and supply lines to Chattanooga. They moved one mile south of Reed's Bridge before dark and camped overnight. The fighting that day had been the unofficial start of the Battle of Chickamauga.

The Chickamauga Creek was the eastern boundary of what would become the next day the battlefield. A three-mile zone lay between Chickamauga Creek and Missionary Ridge on the west.

Part of this valley had been cleared and farmed. There were open fields scattered about in checkerboard fashion. But a large portion of the battlefield was heavily forested with stands of oaks and hickory trees, or covered with thickets of pines and cedars. Limestone outcroppings added to the difficulty of troop movements in this terrain. Much of the heaviest fighting was in these thickets.

Bragg's Army of Tennessee had two major wings. The Right Wing was commanded by Lieutenant General Leonidas Polk; the Left Wing by Lieutenant General James Longstreet (West Point, 1842), 42, a veteran of the Mexican War, and the Civil War battles at Bull Run and Gettysburg, among others. Longstreet didn't reach the field until the second day of the major fighting.

Serving under Polk were: Major General Benjamin Cheatham, 42; Major General John C. Breckinridge, 42; Major General Patrick Cleburne, 35, the Irish-born former British army officer; and Brigadier General St. John Liddell, 48.

Under Longstreet were: Major General Simon B. Buckner, 40, the officer who surrendered the Confederate forces at Fort Donelson to Grant in February 1862; Major General Thomas C. Hindman, 35, a former Congressman from Tennessee; Major General John Bell Hood (West

Point, 1853), 32; and Brigadier General Bushrod R. Johnson (West Point, 1840), 45.

The Confederate cavalry had two corps: Major General Joseph Wheeler's and Brigadier General Forrest's.

Rosecrans' Army of the Cumberland had three corps. The 14th Corps was commanded by Major General George H. Thomas (West Point, 1840), 47. The native-born Virginian had declined a Confederate commission offered him in 1861.

The 20th Corps was led by Major General Alexander McCook (West Point, 1852), 32. In 1861 McCook had been an instructor at West Point.

Rosecrans' 3rd Division was led by Major General Phil Sheridan (West Point, 1853), 32. And his 21st Corps was commanded by Major General Thomas L. Crittendon, 37, an Indiana lawyer and a veteran of the Mexican War.

Saturday, September 19, 1863

The Battle of Chickamauga began formally at 7:30 a.m. Braggs's 66,000 Confederates faced Rosecrans' 60,000 Union soldiers. Hundreds of cannons were positioned in the valley to contribute to the impending destruction.

Bragg's plan of the previous day to drive a wedge between Rosecrans' army and Chattanooga, and to entrap the Federals by drawing them into McLemore's Cove, was still operative. This plan depended on the success of Forrest's Cavalry and Major General W. H. T. Walker's Reserve Corps which included Walker's Division and Brigadier General St. John Liddell's Division striking the northern end — the Union's left flank — with a hard blow.

Forrest's Cavalry had moved north one mile to the Reed's Bridge Road, west of the Chickamauga Creek, from its overnight camp. It faced General George Thomas's Third Division led by Brigadier General John M. Brannan.

Forrest had two able division commanders assigned to

him just one month earlier: Brigadier General John Pegram and Brigadier General Frank C. Armstrong. Pegram (West Point, 1854), 31, resigned his regular army commission in 1861 to join Confederate forces fighting in his native state of Virginia. Armstrong, 27, had served as a captain in the 2nd Cavalry of the Union army at the First Battle of Bull Run in Virginia in July 1861. He resigned his commission on August 13, 1861 to join the Confederate army. Although born and raised near U.S. army forts in Indian Territory (Oklahoma), his sympathies were with the South. Armstrong's Division didn't arrive at Chickamauga until the evening of September 19th — the first day of the major fighting.

Contact by Forrest's Cavalry was made at 7:30 a.m. with Union forces led by General Brannan. The latter's 3rd Division was reconnoitering near Reed's Bridge Road at the north end of the Confederate line. After a heated skirmish Forrest's forces fell back. Quickly, Confederate infantry led by Brigadier General States Rights Gist of Walker's Division struck Brannan's forces and drove them back one mile during that morning's fighting.

In the afternoon Forrest's Cavalry remained near Reed's Bridge Road one-half mile from where Liddell's infantry and Cheatham's infantry were successfully driving Union General Richard Johnson's troops west to the Lafayette Road — a major road running north and south splitting the valley and the battlefield in half.

Counterattacks by Brigadier General Absalon Baird's 1st Division of Thomas' 14th Corps and Brigadier General Richard Johnson's 2nd Division in McCook's 20th Corps pushed Liddell's and Cheatham's forces back in bloody fighting in the woods and thickets. The center of the Confederate line was more successful. Major General A. P. Stewart's Division and Brigadier General Bushrod Johnson's Division fought bitter standoffs with the Union troops back and forth across Lafayette Road.

Fighting ceased at dark after a day of some of the hardest combat of the Civil War.

Several thousand soldiers fell in direct frontal assaults. Others were killed or wounded by the intense artillery fire. Mangled bodies were everywhere. Some were stacked two and three deep on top of one another with their rifles clutched in their hands. The greatest horror were the faceless ones. Some heads were literally blown off. Equally gut-wrenching were sights of dead with their eyes wide open, or grinning as if laughing at a joke when shot.

The dead and wounded were laying in the cedar thickets on both sides of Lafayette Road. The jungle-like terrain had cut off clear vision, making it impossible to know if a target was an enemy soldier or one of their own. There was no doubt that many were killed by rifle or cannon fire from their own comrades who mistakenly thought they were firing at the enemy.

"The scene out there today was reminiscent of Shiloh," Dr. Cowan commented to General Forrest that night. "I just came from one of our field hospitals. You should hear the screaming. Oh God, it is terrible! There's blood everywhere, and grotesque piles of sawed-off arms and legs. I puked when I came out of one tent. I was sick to my stomach from the sight. Don't go anywhere near there, General.

"There are hundreds and hundreds still out there in the woods, and we can't get them yet. It's dark, but you can hear them pleading for help. The litter bearers are able to get some to the ambulance wagons, but the roads are clogged and nothing is moving.

"General, this damn war is a horror."

Forrest nodded sympathetically. Then he turned to Captain Anderson and Captain Strange who were nearby listening intently. "Get me the casualty report for my cavalry. We put 3,500 in the field today. How many did we lose? I know that Pegram's Division is pretty well shot up."

Captain Strange shook his head. "We don't know yet, sir. Some of the wounded are scattered around in several field hospitals and we think there are anywhere from 100 to 200 of our boys lost out there in the woods trying to find camp. Some are probably with other units until morning."

"Did we lose any of my staff?"

"No, sir, but one or two did sustain minor wounds."

"Have the commanders take count tomorrow morning if they have time. Try to get me the casualty reports. We may have to take soldiers from one unit and assign them to others that are short."

"Yes, sir."

At 10:00 p.m. General Bragg conferred with his senior staff to plan an attack on Rosecrans' Army early Sunday morning. The plan Bragg chose was an aggressive one, designed to confuse the enemy. It called for a staggered attack extending along the entire Confederate line. The attack would be at daybreak.

General Breckinridge's Division on the right would strike first; then the adjacent unit would strike; then the third in line, and so forth successively down the long Confederate attack line. Bragg expected Union commanders would be running every which way not knowing where to shore up their defenses.

Sunday, September 20, 1863

Through a tragic mix-up, General Breckinridge claimed he did not receive Bragg's orders until 9:30 a.m. Sunday morning, three hours after the scheduled first assault against the Union army. Bragg's carefully crafted plan was now worthless. Rosecrans, Thomas and other Union commanders were already in position, and prepared for the expected Confederate attack.

Forrest's Cavalry was again assigned the important right end of the Confederate line. From dawn until after 9:30 a.m. he waited nervously for instructions. Finally, when notified, his cavalry, fighting dismounted as infantry, fought a large force of Union reserve troops led by Major General Gordon Granger who had come from Chattanooga. When engaged by Forrest, these troops were on the Lafayette Road trying to move south to join General George Thomas' troops near the center of the battlefield.

After heavy fighting, delaying Granger's advance for two hours, the Union troops drove Forrest back. General Armstrong's Cavalry was dismounted and pressed into infantry service. Pegram's Division — badly undermanned from losses the previous day — was assigned a reserve position.

General Thomas, whose forces faced the aggressive left side of the Confederate line, held tight that morning against intense pressure. At noon, the Confederate leadership discovered an unexpected gaping hole in the right center of the Federal line caused by miscommunication among Union commanders in positioning their units. General Longstreet was ordered to storm this gap with five Confederate divisions.

Longstreet's drive through the middle of the Union line put victory within reach. A rout might have been possible had Longstreet been reinforced by other Confederate units. But Bragg wasn't able to organize the follow-up, decisive blow in the middle to clench victory. General Polk didn't react to General Bragg's plan for a coordinated attack to support Longstreet. And without Polk's support, Longstreet lacked the strength to stage a final massive blow. General Thomas, quickly made aware of the tactical mistake, moved ahead to correct it. Calling up a huge force to plug the gap, Thomas halted Longstreet's drive preventing a possible rout of Rosecrans' army. For his defensive action at Chickamauga, Thomas won instant acclaim; and forever after was referred to in the North as "the Rock of Chickamauga."

At 5:30 p.m., Thomas, aware of huge losses sustained in two days of the raging battle ordered a withdrawal of his forces through McFarland's Gap in Missionary Ridge. This was one of the major routes to the Tennessee line and to Chattanooga. The Confederate army had apparently achieved victory; or at least victory was close at hand if Bragg would have ordered an aggressive pursuit. But Bragg didn't act as if that were the case. He failed to grasp the necessity of a follow-through right then and there. Apparently the reports he was receiving from some of his field commanders that their soldiers were exhausted played a major role in his decision to rest and reorganize his army rather than pursue Thomas in the darkness.

Monday, September 21, 1863

Forrest didn't accept the fact that the Battle of Chickamauga was over. At dawn on Monday on his own initiative he rode to a vantage point on nearby Missionary Ridge where he knew he could observe movement of the Union army retreat toward Chattanooga. What Forrest saw was an army vulnerable to attack before it could reach and cross the Tennessee River to the safety of the city. Shortly after 10:00 a.m. he rode to General Polk's headquarters near the battlefield to report what he had observed. Forrest also told Polk, "I've received information from several captured Union soldiers that General Thomas had ordered pontoons built to get his army across the Tennessee River." Forrest told Polk that this would take time, and that the Union army was vulnerable.

Bragg, now fully aware of the Union army plan to occupy Chattanooga, ordered his Army of Tennessee to surround the city. But he would not order an attack.

Forrest, highly agitated by Bragg's failure to fight, would not accept his superior's decision that attack wasn't feasible. Bragg had notified his commanders, "Our army is exhausted and we have serious shortages of ammunition, equipment and supplies."

"What does Bragg fight battles for?" complained Forrest to his staff. "What kind of a monkey show is Bragg directing? He's like a fox who decides in the morning he will eat an elephant, but by noon he thinks different. He decides he better catch a rabbit."

Wednesday, September 23, 1863

By late Wednesday Union forces had safely crossed the Tennessee River and were encamped in Chattanooga. Bragg's only action was to relocate his headquarters to the northern section of Missionary Ridge, just east of the city. From there he would direct a siege of Rosecrans' army locked up in Chattanooga.

Forrest was still fuming about Bragg's lack of aggression that afternoon when he received orders from Bragg's headquarters to rest his command, and to give the horses time to recuperate.

General Bragg, when informed of Forrest's impertinence in criticizing him publicly, remarked to his adjutant, Colonel George W. Brent, "What we need most in this war are real officers, not mediocre lawyers, clergymen and slave traders trying to play soldier." Bragg's reference was not only to Forrest, whom he considered a petty annoyance, but to Breckinridge, Polk, D. H. Hill and several other senior officers he believed incompetent and for whom he had contempt.

Bragg's plan developed quickly. "A tight siege will starve the Federals into submission," said Bragg. "To achieve this, we must shut off any Federal supply and communication lines into the city."

General Bragg was highly distraught. Preliminary casualty reports stunned him. Over the period from the build-up to the two-day full battle at Chickamauga some 3800 Confederate and Union soldiers had been killed. The preliminary count was 24,000 soldiers wounded and 6200 missing in action. Details of Chickamauga were just beginning to be reported in both Northern and Southern newspapers. Bragg knew there would be repercussions from the Confederate War Department for his failure to win decisively. Several of Bragg's key field commanders were at odds with him over his performance at Chickamauga, and were complaining to Jefferson Davis.

Thursday, September 24, 1863

After less than one day's rest, Forrest was ordered to lead his cavalry northeast of Chattanooga to picket a 40-mile area extending to the Hiwassee River. His precise assignment was to probe for signs of General Ambrose Burnside's Union army reported unofficially to have left Knoxville for Chattanooga to assist the beleaguered Rosecrans in Chattanooga.

Without clearing it with Bragg's headquarters Forrest led his cavalry not only to the Hiwassee River, but some miles beyond toward Knoxville in pursuit of a small Union force.

Bragg was furious at Forrest's contempt for orders. It disrupted Bragg's plan to have Forrest's Cavalry join with Wheeler's Cavalry in an action to move northwest of Chattanooga to cut Rosecrans' communication line in the Sequatchie River Valley located 20 miles from the city. But Forrest's Cavalry was far away near Athens, Tennessee.

By now Forrest had become a major irritation to the already stressed Bragg. When told that Forrest was "out on his own," Bragg said in exasperation to Colonel Brent, his Adjutant, "Though you dress the shepherd in silk, he still smells like a goat. He's nothing but a raider with his own peculiar agenda. The Sequatchie Valley mission is crucial and I need all the cavalry I can muster. Where is Forrest now?"

"Sir, the last report was that Forrest is near Athens."

"All right, Colonel Brent, send this communication immediately:

The Commanding General desires that you will without delay turn over the troops of your command to Major General Wheeler.

Braxton Bragg
Commanding

Gen. Forrest's Commanding Officers (1861 - 1865)

Gen. P.G.T. Beauregard   Gen Joseph Wheeler   Gen. Braxton Bragg

Gen. Leonidas Polk   Gen. Joseph E. Johnston   Gen. John Bell Hood

Gen. Stephen D. Lee   Gen. Richard Taylor   Gen. Earl Van Dorn

Saturday, September 26, 1863

The message reached Forrest on September 26th. A second order followed within hours ordering Forrest to turn over to General Wheeler all of his troops except Colonel Dibrell's Brigade and Captain Morton's Battery.

Forrest's reaction was explosive. "The mission into the Sequatchie Valley is a mistake. Mark my words!" he said to Captain Strange, "It's a disgrace that I have to turn my troops over to Wheeler. Bragg's doing this to break me and to humiliate me. This is not the first time Bragg has done this. But I knew it was coming. I just didn't know when it would happen. I smelled the rat long before it died. Bragg and his yaller-dog staff sit there like a knot on a tree with moss growing down their backs. Why Strange, I'd rather end up in a war hotel [prison] then not fight when we had the advantage.

"Captain Strange, you work with Matt Gallaway on a response to Bragg for me to sign. I want you to put my objections to his orders in the strongest possible language. Don't worry about being polite. What the hell can I lose by attacking him.

"And tell him I shall report in person to his headquarters to confront him face to face about his unwarranted decision to strip me of my command."

Action at Chickamauga

14 • General Bragg

Forrest's Camp, Tuesday, September 29, 1863

"General, a message has just arrived from General Bragg's Headquarters. It says the General will see you at 3:00 p.m. tomorrow afternoon."

"Good ... ask Matt Gallaway and Dr. Cowan to come on in here," said General Forrest to Captain Strange.

Forrest had calmed down somewhat from his highly emotional state earlier that morning. He was in deep thought when Gallaway and Dr. Cowan entered his tent.

"I want you two to go with me tomorrow to see Bragg. If necessary, you can confirm what I'm going to tell him about the shabby treatment I have received over the past 18 months."

"General, are you certain you want to confront General Bragg with all that?" asked Gallaway squirming as he spoke. "Won't that make it worse? You may end up under arrest for insubordination or even get dismissed from service. I know your temper and your tendency to be brutally frank when you are angry. If you go, I'd be cautious. Think about what you are going to say to Bragg before you meet with him."

Forrest looked over at Dr. Cowan. "James, what do you think?"

"Matt's quite right. I think the meeting may result in your signing your own death warrant. Bragg may decide to make you a scapegoat for all his troubles. I know he wants to put the blame for the blunders at Chickamauga on some of his senior field commanders. He may not be able to get to Polk and Breckinridge and the others because they've got political support in Richmond."

"But you know I fought well at Chickamauga," said Forrest.

"Cowan's right, General. You don't have any political support whatsoever to throw against Bragg. He can say any damn thing he wants to say about you in his reports to Richmond."

"Well, gentlemen, I'm going to Missionary Ridge tomorrow. I want you two to put your heads together this afternoon, and help me organize my statements.

"We'll leave at 8:00 a.m. in the morning.

Gen. Bragg's Headquarters, Wed., September 30, 1863

At 2:30 p.m. Forrest, Gallaway and Dr. Cowan arrived at Bragg's command center and were greeted courteously by several of the General's staff.

"How is General Bragg?" inquired Forrest.

"Confidentially, General Forrest, he is completely worn out. I think he's ill. I know he's distraught. That discussion he's been having for the past hour may push him over the brink," answered Colonel Stephenson, an aide, in a cautious tone.

"What's going on in there?" asked the inquisitive Forrest.

"The General is very upset with the newspaper correspondents hovering around our encampment. He is now discussing whether to arrest several of them for what he considers disloyalty to the Confederacy. I heard him call several of them Yankee spies. All I know is that if I were a correspondent I'd get out of the area quick. God only knows what he's going to do. He's paranoid. He sees demons and devils everywhere. He believes they have one objective — to discredit him."

Promptly at 3:00 p.m. Forrest was escorted into General Bragg's office. Dr. Cowan accompanied him. Matt Gallaway persuaded Cowan to go with Forrest. "You're more diplomatic, James," said Gallaway. "I might get more emotional than Bedford if I'm in there."

Forrest looked around furtively at Gallaway who remained in the outer office area. Then he said to Dr. Cowan in a low voice, "Remember what Bragg says, James, so you can tell Matt later."

Bragg was sitting on a dark wooden chair behind a

small camp table. He didn't stand to shake hands. Instead, he motioned with his head for Forrest and Cowan to sit down.

Both noticed how gaunt and jaundiced Bragg looked. He was disheveled. His normally ragged-looking gray beard and wild gray eyebrows were even more out of control, and his uniform was rumpled. It appeared that he had been sleeping in his uniform. And from his general appearance it was questionable whether he had been sleeping at all.

"Forrest, I know why you are here," said the thin-lipped Bragg. "You have 15 minutes only."

"General, I want to know why you have relieved me of command and why you continue to make it difficult for me to be a successful commander?" asked Forrest in a nervous and slightly elevated pitch of his voice. "You robbed me of my command in Kentucky last year before the Perryville Campaign. I had personally armed and equipped and trained that unit. That was after I raised a second command with absolutely no help from you.

"After that campaign you stripped me of my captured supplies and equipment which I badly needed.

"You sent me to Dover with Wheeler without enough ammunition and supplies, and we got whipped bad.

"Now you take away my command that is as good a unit as you have in this whole damn army.

"You have ruined my career. It's spiteful, that's what it is."

Bragg, without flinching or changing his expression whatsoever on his haggard face, looked at Forrest with his stone-gray pupils and said calmly, "Forrest, you know little of cooperation. You disobey orders that don't suit you. Why did you allow yourself to go charging toward Knoxville capturing villages that don't mean a damn thing? Why are you so meddlesome? Just where did you get your military education?"

Forrest then got emotional and shouted, "Blah! blah! blah! General, you have never given me adequate reasons for your decisions. People where I come from just don't do other people that way."

Bragg now had a tight smile, but it failed to mask his uneasiness of having to deal with the unconventional, blunt Forrest.

"Forrest, you should never criticize a person until you've walked a mile in his shoes," said Bragg softly.

Forrest was now worked up. "Why do you favor Wheeler so much?" exploded Forrest with clenched teeth.

"Wheeler is a scientific soldier, and he is as brave and bold as any officer I have. He disagrees with me like you do, Forrest, but he doesn't go running off in tangents. For the good of the Confederate service, we need Wheeler-like commanders."

"Oh Wheeler's all right, I guess. But he's a book soldier. If it's not in the book, he won't do it."

"We're not here to talk about General Wheeler, Forrest!"

"That's right. Wheeler's a better soldier than most of your old fogy officers who keep blowing off about their heroic service in the Mexican War.

"Look what happened at Shiloh! Same damn thing happened last week at Chickamauga! I use my initiative and go out and find valuable intelligence on enemy operations, and pass it on to you — or try to at least. That night at Shiloh when Buell's army crossed the Tennessee at Pittsburg Landing, I tried to inform you, but you didn't tell anybody where you were headquartered. Old General Hardee told me not to worry about it, and to go get some sleep.

"Last week I scouted the Union retreat to Chattanooga and reported back what I saw. But General Polk either didn't tell you, or if he did, you just sat on the information.

"I know you don't like me, General; but we are fighting the same enemy, aren't we? Just because an uneducated businessman and planter brings you information doesn't mean it is worthless, now does it?

"I consider your actions toward me as pure meanness, and I resent it. Go ahead and court-martial me. I dare you. If a fair and square court of inquiry hears what I've got to say, your goose is cooked."

"Forrest, you have not been accurate in your statements that I have persecuted you. You know very well that I have personally written citations commending you and your cavalry for your success in West Tennessee last December, and this past April against Streight's Federal unit over in Alabama.

"All right, Forrest, you've had your say. I'm placing you on leave for ten days. Let my adjutant, Colonel Brent, know where you can be reached. You'll be receiving your new orders in a few days.

"Goodbye, General Forrest. Goodbye, Dr. Cowan."

•

Forrest's visit to Bragg's headquarters, September 30, 1863

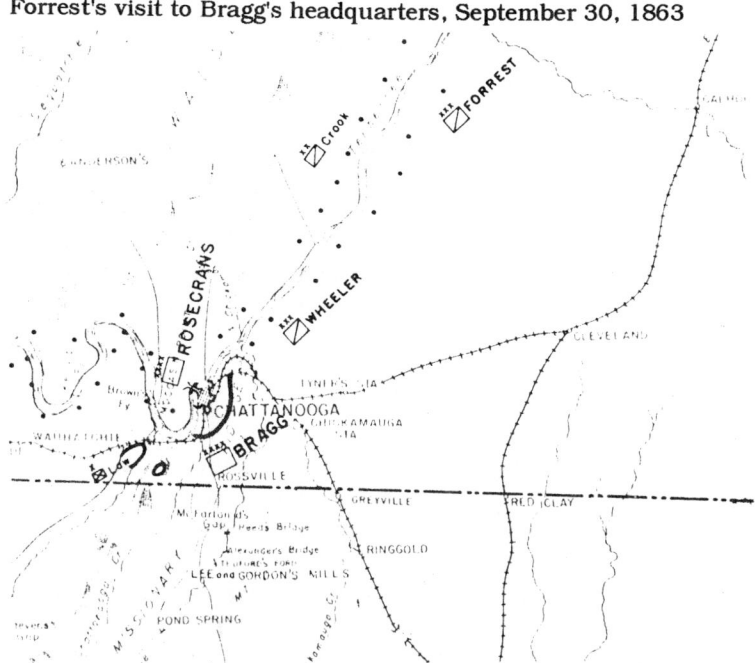

15 • Reunion

La Grange, Georgia, Saturday, October 3, 1863

General Forrest, after leaving Bragg's headquarters, went immediately to the military telegraph office and sent a message to his wife asking her to meet him in La Grange, Georgia as soon as possible. Mary Forrest was in Montgomery, Alabama in the company of Fannie Gallaway, Matt Gallaway's wife. Both had left Oxford, Mississippi the week before to go to Montgomery hoping at some point to visit with their husbands.

Forrest in his message told Mary his leave was only ten days. He suggested that she seek military priority for train seats for Fannie Gallaway and herself.

Matt Gallaway accepted enthusiastically Forrest's invitation to join him. Like Forrest, Gallaway hadn't seen his wife in nearly 18 months.

La Grange, a small town in cotton-rich Troup County, Georgia was halfway between Montgomery and Atlanta on the Atlanta & West Point Railroad line. This peaceful town was the ideal place to spend a short leave.

Waiting for the train to arrive from Montgomery, General Forrest was surrounded at the depot by a large group of young boys and old men. He was shaking hands, laughing and joking, and answering questions about the war. One elderly citizen with a flowing white beard said to Forrest, "General, we're all glad to see you. La Grange is a patriotic town. Have you noticed the absence of young men over 15 years of age?"

"Well, yes, I have. I don't think I've seen any."

"And you won't, General. Every last male from 16 to 45 has gone off to war. All we have here are women, small boys and girls, and old men like me."

"That's a compliment to this great town, sir."

"Yes, sir, and it's also true for the entire county. We're true Confederates in Troup County."

The stationmaster carrying a large megaphone

ascended a baggage wagon and announced, "The noon train from Montgomery is arriving in ten minutes. Please get off the tracks. I repeat...please get off the tracks!" He repeated the announcement several times, but no one moved off the tracks. Finally, he shrugged his shoulders and went back into the station not particularly bothered by the lack of cooperation.

The train was packed with soldiers on their way to Chattanooga to reinforce Bragg's army. Everyone got off while the train took on water and porters unloaded baggage and freight. Mary Forrest and Fannie Gallaway were lost in the mass of humanity around the platform. Finally, the tall Forrest, looking over the crowd, spotted them and rushed forward to greet them.

Forrest when he reached Mary didn't say a word. He picked her up under her arms and held her high in the air.

"Put me down! Put me down, Bedford! You're embarrassing me."

"No," said Forrest smiling broadly, "I want the world to see my pretty wife."

"The whole world can see me standing on my own two feet," she said feigning irritation. Then Forrest turned and hugged Fannie Gallaway before Matt Gallaway was able to reach her.

"Fannie, I've got to tell you. Matt's turned into a noble soldier. He loves this life. He's found a home in the army, so help me! I don't think he'll ever publish another newspaper. Heh-heh-heh!"

Mary was smiling broadly. She hadn't expected her husband to be so good-humored. She had heard the news that he had been relieved of command by General Bragg, and knew full well of his animosity toward Bragg.

"We are all to be guests at Bellevue," Forrest announced to Mary and the Gallaways. "That's the mansion of Colonel Benjamin Hill, the Confederate Senator from Georgia. He's in Richmond now, so we have the whole house for a week. All his servants are at the mansion. Colonel Hill has sent word that we are to be treated like royalty. Isn't that something?"

Bystanders to the Forrests' celebration there at the station were not only impressed with the tall, powerfully-built General, but with the shyness and gentleness of this small-statured woman with unblemished facial skin and brown, expressive eyes. When people saw them together for the first time, they couldn't help but notice the contrasting appearances and personalities.

The expectation, it appeared, was that Mary Forrest would be a well-weathered pioneer woman who showed the effects of a hard life after living for many years with the rough-hewn Forrest.

"We all need refreshments and some rest," said Forrest. "Colonel Hill's carriage is here to take us to Bellevue."

Monday, October 5, 1863, 11:00 a.m.

The Forrests sat on the veranda of Bellevue on this warm, sunny early October day talking about family life, friends and the status of the war.

"Mary, do you realize that we have been married over 18 years? Can you believe that?"

"Yes, I can, Bedford; it seems longer because of all that has happened to us since 1845. Why Willie celebrated his 17th birthday last week, and the two of you have been at war all over the South for 27 months."

"Do you remember when we got married, Mary?"

"Yes, no one seemed to think we were suited for each other. My family — the Montgomerys — were against it. And my uncle, Reverend Samuel Cowan, the pastor of the Cumberland Presbyterian Church, was most emphatically against it."

"I know, Mary. He came to me all excited and said, "Bedford, I cannot consent to this marriage. You cuss and gamble and Mary is a good Christian girl."

"And I said, 'Preacher, I know that, and that's why I

want to marry her!' And one month later the wedding took place."

"Bedford, you thought I was old because I was 18. But I had just finished school at the Nashville Female Academy, and knew nothing about real life.

"I remember my wedding attire. It was a plain, long white dress with muslin petticoat and pantaloons. You were handsome in your black suit and white bow."

"Willie was born the next year; and Fanny, the following year. Poor, beloved Fanny, she only lived a brief few years. That terrible fever! She would be 16 now."

"Mary, Willie has turned out well. You won't recognize him with his mustache. He tried for one year to grow one; and finally about a month ago, he succeeded. And Mary, he has grown tall and has put some meat on those skinny bones. He's no longer a boy."

"Is he in any danger of being killed or injured or captured?"

"Willie isn't always out front, but he is usually close to the skirmishes. He's been a real good soldier; and just because he's my son, he gets no special treatment. To tell you the truth, I'm probably harder on him than the rest of the staff. Willie seems to understand the position I'm in.

"Mary, when Willie joined up with me, he was a mere boy — just 15. But now, at 17, he is a young man any father would be proud of.

"Thank goodness, though, he's not like me. Willie has your gentle qualities and good manners. I've never heard him swear or even lose his temper despite some provocation when the others tease him too much. He loves a good prank played on him if it isn't mean-spirited. And he gives as good as he takes. We've had some rowdy times in camp, and Willie is often in the thick of the mischief. Now, I don't mean drinking whiskey. Willie knows better than that!"

"Bedford, I do worry about Willie and you. I worry about all of you in the Confederate army. Do you think it will end soon? It's so tragic for everyone."

"I can't answer that, Mary. I've been so involved in the war day after day that I haven't determined if we're winning or losing.

"There are so many battles and skirmishes from Pennsylvania to Texas that I doubt if either Lincoln or Davis and their war departments know. I do know, however, we still have the will to fight. I'm optimistic if we can get better leadership. Generals like Bragg worry me a great deal more than the Union boys."

There was a short silence, then Mary asked, "Bedford, are you still gambling?"

"Mary, I have no time for cards and besides I have very little money. That $310 General's pay isn't worth much even if they ever get around to paying me."

"I know swearing is common among officers, but please remember to set a good example. Please try to maintain a Christian bearing among your comrades. Do your men have enough Bibles and religious tracts? Do you have daily prayer?"

"Mary, Bibles are as treasured as enemy rifles or cannons when found on the battlefield after a fight.

Colonel Kelley makes sure we all pray before moving forward against the Federals. There are few nonbelievers in those minutes before an attack.

"The Parson does well in converting lost souls by proclaiming the *Gospel*. Sometimes he gets carried away and scares the wits out of a bunch of them. He gets a distorted frown on his face when he describes the *Devil* tempting us night and day. When he finishes the soldiers are far more frightened of the almighty *Devil* himself than Yankees out in front of them."

"Well, Bedford, what about you? What does that experience do for you? Do you feel close to *God*?"

"Mary, I know you worry that I'm probably a convert to pokeweed religion. You know — getting momentary religious excitement that has no lasting value. And that may be true! But I hope not."

At that moment one of Colonel Hill's house servants

brought the Forrests tea and coffee. In a few moments they continued talking.

"Mary, what do you hear about the Meriwethers?"

"I spoke with Elizabeth some weeks ago in Mississippi. She is still furious at the treatment she received from Union officers when they took command in Memphis last year. They asked her to leave the city in no uncertain terms. I think they thought she was smuggling. She's now is Tuscaloosa, Alabama.

"Minor is a lieutenant colonel in the engineers. The last Elizabeth heard was that after he escaped from Vicksburg, he was assigned to Florida to help plan a railroad."

"That's a good use of Minor's ability. He'd make a rotten field officer. He can't even control Elizabeth. Heh-heh-heh!"

"It must be awful in Memphis. I hear that city is being flooded with Northern Israelites getting into the smuggling business. One of my friends says it's like a plague of locusts. They're dealing in cotton, weapons, food and everything else. And it's going on either under the noses of Union officers who are not paying attention, or perhaps it is with their direct participation. The sad thing is that some of our own people are involved in it too," concluded Mary.

October 5, 1863, 2:00 p.m.

Following lunch with Matt and Fannie Gallaway, the Forrests strolled around the extensive grounds of the Hill mansion still talking about events of the past 18 months.

Oliver, one of Colonel Hill's servants, approached Forrest to tell him a messenger was waiting in front of the mansion with an important communication. Forrest excused himself to accept the message. When he returned, he was in a violent mood. His face was beet-red from anger, and he was yelling, "Matt...Matt...come quickly." Mary was startled by her husband's sudden swing in mood.

"Matt, read what that goddamn Bragg has done to me! Read that message," Forrest said as he handed it to Gallaway.

"He has put you under General Wheeler, and stripped you of the rest of your command. That's outrageous. I know he doesn't like you, but this decision is pure spite. He is indeed trying to humiliate you, General."

"Matt, I'm not accepted by those West Pointers. They think I don't know much about soldiering. They see me as an uneducated backwoodsman who doesn't know what it is to be a gentleman. Oh, they like me as a recruiter; and they're delighted when I turn over captured supplies and medicines to them.

"Bragg is a terrible thorn in my side. That old porcupine-face fool doesn't understand this war and how to get the best results from his officers and their soldiers. He acts like he'd be more comfortable reviewing a fancy dress parade with bands playing and standards being displayed by spit-and-polish cavalrymen. He's a third class general and a first class liar. He doesn't trust anyone and argues with everyone. He's sick in the head. He looks like a goddamn scarecrow. Unfortunately, he is supported by Jefferson Davis.

"So long as Bragg is in the service, I have no future in the Confederate army. My relationship is as bad as it can get. Right now Bragg is probably getting ready to court-martial me for insubordination."

Mary Forrest, who had been silent, finally interjected, "Bedford, that couldn't be true. You have contributed too much for that to happen. General Bragg is under terrible emotional distress. Surely his aides will convince him otherwise."

"When Bragg relieved me and placed Wheeler in charge of my cavalry that was the end of me. Bragg has persecuted me for the last time. As long as he is in command and influential in Richmond with Davis, I have no future in this army.

"Today I shall send a letter of resignation to President

Davis. He will receive it when he arrives October 9th at Bragg's headquarters on Missionary Ridge."

Matt Gallaway asked, "Are you sure you're doing the right thing, General? You will disappoint your men, and all of your friends in Tennessee and Mississippi who admire you so."

"Matt...Matt...I know I'm worn out, and the goddamn boils and dysentery, along with Bragg's persecution, have driven me crazy. But my usefulness as a Confederate officer has ended. I'm convinced of that.

"And who knows...I may become more useful to the South in a civilian capacity. I could easily get into the contraband business in Memphis or raise a lot of cotton in Mississippi."

"General, please sleep on it, will you? I'm asking as your long-time friend," pleaded Gallaway.

"Matt, it's decided. I'll write Davis tomorrow. You may want to put what I say in proper English."

"Of course, if you wish," said Gallaway in a tone of anguish.

October 5, 1863, 4:30 p.m.

"General Forrest, there's a gentleman — a Mister George W. Adair — at the door. He wants to speak with you, sir. Shall I invite him in?" said Ivan, Colonel Hill's head servant.

"No, Ivan, but I'll see him out on the front porch. I know Adair. He's the editor of the *Atlanta Daily Southern Confederacy*. He's a damn journalist. I wonder what in the hell he wants."

Forrest stepped outside to greet Adair.

"Adair, you're a long way from the roar of cannons. What brings you to peaceful La Grange?"

"General Forrest, it is good to see you again. It's been several months since I interviewed you in Rome, Georgia after you rousted Colonel Streight," said Adair, a man with a gentle, expressive face and a distinguished graying beard.

"Are you here to pick at my carcass?" snapped Forrest.

"General Forrest, I was at Bragg's headquarters two days ago and heard a rumor that Bragg was after your hide. And I also heard you had lost your unit to General Wheeler. Can you comment on that?"

"Editor Adair, that's not rumor, that's fact. And in case you haven't heard, I just got demoted. I've been ordered to report to Wheeler when my leave is up."

"General, can you enlighten me on the internal strife within Bragg's command? The way I hear it is that Bragg's desperately seeking a scapegoat for his failure to win at Chickamauga. General Polk appears to be his primary target. But Bragg is also upset with General Daniel Hill who was under Polk and also with General Hindman, part of Longstreet's Division. Rumors are that Bragg wants to court-martial Bishop Polk. Can you tell me anything you've heard?"

"I'm under orders not to discuss troop operations, strategy or personalities. I'm already in deep trouble for expressing my disappointments about recent events around Chattanooga. It wouldn't surprise me if Bragg starts court-martial proceedings against me at the earliest moment.

"If you print any of my statements, I am sure you are well aware of War Department censorship rules. And, of course, I'll deny I ever spoke with you."

"Well, General, we correspondents are well aware of the power of the censors, and the pressure the War Department puts on us to report just favorable news. But, General, you know that citizens sense all is not right. They have ways of finding out. When the casualty lists are posted and food becomes scarce in the markets, they know all is not well.

"Look at what Bragg has tried to do to John Linebaugh. He's got him in jail for treason. Do you know Linebaugh, General? He uses the pseudonym, 'The Shadow', in signing dispatches sent to his newspapers in the South."

"Yes, I know Linebaugh. He contributes to the *Memphis Appeal*. He's a hardworking correspondent. I was outside Bragg's headquarters last week when Bragg was shouting curses at the military correspondents assigned to the Army of Tennessee. He thinks they are spies, and they're out to get him. My aide, Matt Gallaway, a newspaperman himself, uses the word 'paranoid' to describe Bragg. I'm not familiar with that word, but I take it to mean that Bragg's not well in the head. Heh-heh-heh!

"But, Adair, you fellows do stick your nose into things that are none of your business. No offense to you, Adair, but you scribblers are so hard up for news that if I farted right now, you'd send a dispatch without delay. Heh-heh-heh! I never see a pen but what I think of a snake. Heh-heh-heh!

"And when you are lucky enough to get a dispatch through the censors, you take 500 words to tell the readers what you could say in ten."

"General Forrest, I must say you do have a way with words yourself. I promise if you want to fart now, I won't report it.

"I'm on my way back to Atlanta tonight; then in the morning I'm off to Chattanooga to cover President Davis' visit with Bragg and his commanders. I assume you won't be there."

"Your assumption is correct. I am about as far away from the inner circle of this army as it is possible to get."

"I'm sorry you are in hot water, General. You appear to be a useful soldier," said Adair as he got up to leave.

October 6, 1863, 9:00 a.m.

"Matt, read this! It's a letter of resignation to President Davis. Does it sound all right?" said Forrest as he handed a piece of paper to Gallaway.

"Well, General, it's only two sentences long. The

structure is fine. No changes in wording or punctuation are necessary. But are you certain you want to send this? Really certain?"

"Matt, I'm more sure today than I was yesterday afternoon. Would you take it over to the military telegraph operator at the railroad station? Tell him it goes to President Davis, in care of General Bragg's Headquarters."

"All right, General. But I go reluctantly, I guarantee you."

George W. Adair,
Editor and Correspondent
Atlanta Daily Southern Confederacy

16 • Jefferson Davis

On Friday, October 16th, the day before Jefferson Davis ended his visit with General Bragg and other senior officers of the Army of Tennessee at Missionary Ridge, he sent a message to General Forrest who was still in La Grange on leave. Forrest had waited nervously for over a week for an acknowledgement from President Davis that the latter had accepted his resignation.

Forrest cautiously opened this communication, then read it to Mary seated nearby:

Arrange to meet with me in Montgomery, Alabama on either Monday, October 26th, or Tuesday, October 27th at Exchange Hotel. Shall be enroute from Mobile to Atlanta. Plan a one-day stop in Montgomery.
Jefferson Davis, President
Confederate States of
America

"Mary, now I'm really curious," Forrest said almost in a whisper. "I had heard through Adair, that newspaper fellow, that Davis was meeting with Bragg and the others involved in the fight at Chickamauga. Now I'm wondering what happened there. I hope the President has stripped the bark off of Bragg's tree. That old fool doesn't know chalk from cheese.

"If old Bragg is bringing charges against Bishop Polk, sparks will be flying all over the South. Davis and Polk are old West Point friends, and comrades in the Mexican War, according to Matt Gallaway. Well, I'll find out in Montgomery in ten days.

"And Mary, I'll know then whether you and I are going home, or whether it's back to fighting for me. If Bragg gets completely out of my way, I may withdraw my resignation. We'll just see!"

Mary and the Gallaways stayed behind in La Grange when Forrest left for Montgomery at 9:00 a.m. on Sunday,

October 25th.

The train, after a nine hour trip to cover 125 miles, arrived in Montgomery at the Depot on Water Street at 6:00 p.m. No one was at the station to greet him, so he walked alone to the Exchange Hotel just three blocks away at the corner of Commerce and Montgomery Streets.

The Exchange Hotel was an imposing four-story structure with massive columns at its several entrances. There were second story balconies at both the Court Square and the Montgomery Street sides. In pre-war days this hotel was Montgomery's social and commercial center. Now it was the center of local military life.

Forrest was notified at the hotel that President Davis and his party would arrive in Montgomery from Mobile the next night, and that his appointment with the President would be early Tuesday morning.

Monday was a relaxing day for Forrest. He spent the day walking around the city. Pre-war Montgomery had 20,000 citizens. Now because of war activity, it had grown to near 30,000. Forrest was impressed with the excitement in the city that day. Flags lined the wide major streets, and colorful bunting was being draped around the facades of hotels, public buildings and most stores.

As Forrest strolled leisurely around Court Square, a big crowd had gathered in front of the steps of the Montgomery County Courthouse. Captain Avery Stetson's military band was practicing a rousing rendition of *Dixie* Each time the band played it, the crowd roared its approval. Forrest commented to a bystander, "This is exciting. I feel rejuvenated with this positive expression of enthusiasm for the Confederacy."

"It's going to be our day soon, General. The tide is turning in our favor. The Yankees are getting discouraged by the long, drawn out process of fighting us."

"I believe you're right, sir," said Forrest as he turned to continue walking around Court Square. He wanted to see the city's slave block also located on the Square.

Back in 1857 brothers Jesse and Bill and he had purchased a dozen slaves at one of the weekly auctions.

Forrest, curious about the present status of the auction block, asked a policeman standing nearby, "Are weekly auctions still held here, officer?"

"No, sir, they stopped them about two years ago soon after the war started, Oh, they buy and sell them around the city, but not here at the block. I remember those auction days. Planters and slave traders came from all over central Alabama. It was a carnival. Did you ever attend one, sir?"

"Yes, I was one of the slave traders. Came down from Memphis."

"Memphis, you say? Got a brother there — John Leary. Do you know him? He's a policeman like me. Don't you know all the Irishmen are either policemen, or firemen, or saloonkeepers?"

"No, I can't say that I know him. But you're right, all those occupations are held by the Irish."

Forrest then strolled seven blocks east on Washington Street to the Alabama State House, and stood for several minutes on the spot where the Confederacy was born. He made a mental note that he would tell President Davis the next day that he stood proudly at the site of the former's inauguration as Provisional President of the Confederate States of America.

That night in the Exchange Hotel's lobby he met General Polk, and spoke with him briefly. "General Polk, I'm pleased to see you. What brings you to Montgomery, sir?"

"Forrest, I'm meeting with President Davis tomorrow. He invited me to come to Montgomery."

"How about you, Forrest?"

"I'm to see the President too."

"Well then, I shall probably see you again tomorrow. Goodnight, Forrest."

At 8:00 a.m. Tuesday morning Forrest waited in the

lobby just outside the ornate dining room of the Exchange Hotel. Within minutes President Davis, with his small entourage of aides, arrived,

"Forrest, I am pleased to see you. Have we met before?"

"No, sir, Mr. President, but I did see you once at the St. Charles Hotel in New Orleans before the war."

"Oh yes, the St. Charles. Forrest, what I wouldn't give for a few pleasant days there like it used to be."

"Yes, it was a lively place with plenty of interesting fellows."

"General Forrest, may I introduce my two aides? This tall, handsome gentleman is Colonel William Johnston, son of General Albert Sidney Johnston. And this equally handsome officer is Colonel Custis Lee, son of General Robert E. Lee. And my young secretary here is Burton Harrison, All of these gentlemen are indispensable to me."

Forrest replied, "I'm deeply honored to be in all of your company."

"Let's go in and sit down," said President Davis courteously.

President Davis had a wonderful military bearing, although he was dressed in well-tailored, immaculate civilian clothes. He wore a black silk cravat wrapped once around his neck and tied in a bow. His heavily starched white collar was medium width. He wore a dark gray frock coat extending to his knees. It had a single gold button at mid-chest level. His vest and trousers were a lighter gray. The President's aides and Forrest were in uniform.

"Forrest, it's good to get away from that mob in the lobby. Every newspaper correspondent in the South appears to be there clamoring for a statement. But they can wait.

"I understand you have been on leave."

"Yes, sir, over in La Grange, Georgia with my wife, Mary."

"That's wonderful, Forrest. I trust Mrs. Forrest is well?"

"Yes, sir, it was good to see her after 18 months in the field."

"Well, Forrest, my wife Varina never seems to let me out of her sight. She's a lively woman who has kept me jumping for 18 years.

"How about you, Forrest. How long have you been married?"

"Since September 1845. Unlike Mrs. Davis, my wife is a quiet, religious woman who stays well in the background."

"You are a lucky man, Forrest. Varina is into everything. Sometimes I think she believes she's running the Confederacy.

"She was only 19 when we married. I was 37. I had been a widower for many years. Did you know that I was married to Zachary Taylor's daughter, Sarah? You probably didn't. That poor, wonderful young girl died of malaria just three months after we married in 1835. We were down in Louisiana for the summer when struck down by fever. She was a quiet one too."

Forrest observed that President Davis was in a jovial mood. Davis had never been one to talk about his personal life, particularly with strangers. But he seemed relaxed with Forrest and oblivious to his aides who were listening intently to the conversation. As he talked, however, Davis kept focusing on Forrest with his characteristic piercing glance out of his stone gray eyes.

Davis stopped talking for a moment as he looked around the dining room as if suddenly transfixed to some past event. Then he said to Forrest, "General, the Confederacy was born in concept right above us on the third floor of this hotel. Our first administrative offices were hotel sleeping rooms. We had three or four people in each room. God, it was like a rabbit warren up there. The place was filthy and it smelled awful. The place was crawling with politicians, bureaucrats and opportunists of all sorts.

"The night of my inauguration I spoke to a huge crowd from the balcony on the Montgomery Street side. It was quite a sight with all the bands playing and the hundreds of torchlights.

"And to think that was only 32 months ago," concluded Davis looking down at his knees and shaking his head very slowly from one side to the other.

"Mr. President, that was months before Tennessee seceded."

"Yes, Forrest, that was before Virginia, Arkansas and North Carolina, too.

"The Confederate Capital was the Alabama State House down the street until May 1861 when our Congress voted to relocate to Richmond. It seems like a millennium since we had that initial meeting of the Provisional Congress in February 1861."

"I can understand that concept of time, sir. I fought the Federals for the first time in December 1861. But with all those miles on horseback or walking, and all the wounds and the goddamn boils of mine it seems like a lifetime since I started fighting at Sacramento, Kentucky."

"Sacramento, Kentucky, Forrest? Did you know that I was born just 40 miles south of there near Hopkinsville? I hardly remember the area. We moved to Mississippi when I was a child.

"Well, Forrest, it is nice to reminisce, but we've got to move on.

"General Bragg, Colonel Brent and some others at Missionary Ridge apprised me of your status insofar as they're concerned. Now, Forrest, I'm not going to go down every pig path in Georgia trying to sort it all out. Bragg may well be unfairly making you pass under the yoke. Maybe the Inspector-General's office can look into the matter some time. I don't know whether that could straighten it out.

"All I can say to you is that I won't accept your resignation. I've gotten more good reports on you than bad ones. You have made a contribution to our war efforts, and I expect you will continue to do so.

"General Bragg has his good points and his bad points too. We've been close friends since Buena Vista down in Mexico. Looking back to those days there is a certain irony about Bragg's heroic service in the Mexican War. When we were fighting General Santa Ana, General Zachary Taylor ordered two artillery batteries to protect our right flank. One battery was commanded by Braxton Bragg, and the other by George Thomas. Their fire was decisive. It forced Santa Ana to retreat. Now, here we are 17 years later. Bragg and Thomas meet on opposite sides of the battlefield, and Thomas was fortunate enough to prevent the complete annihilation of the Union troops at Chickamauga, robbing General Bragg of perhaps great honors being bestowed on him by a grateful South.

"Bragg, I admit, is peevish and irascible. He's probably a true martinet. He hates anyone who doesn't follow precisely the military rule book. And he expects the impossible, and when a subordinate falters in Bragg's judgment, he dismisses him forever.

"I understand, Forrest, that you think Bragg is persecuting you. Maybe. But you aren't alone. Far from it. I've spent the past two weeks trying to patch things up between Bragg and several of our most senior officers. No one wins in these quarrels. The Confederate cause is the loser.

"Now, my assessment is that Bragg is ill. He suffers from massive headaches, rheumatism, boils and God only knows what else. He should be placed on leave, but we can't spare him right now. He knows the situation around Chattanooga, and I believe he can force the Federals into capitulation. He is an outstanding organizer, and that's what is desperately needed right now."

"Mr. President, I appreciate that appraisal of Bragg. But it's not only Bragg that bothers me. It's the attitude of the West Pointers toward this war. It's like it's their fight alone, and we civilian officers are useless, excess baggage, and just barely tolerated because there's not enough West Pointers to go around.

"Their mentality and training are restricting those natural fighting qualities of Southern men. This war isn't being fought in Prussia. That rigidity and discipline may have been fine 50 years ago, but my quarrel with General Bragg and his kind is that they don't appreciate field commanders who make decisions on the spot to react to opportunities, and that they don't listen to officers of lesser rank who have suggestions about the conduct of the war."

"Forrest, I don't dispute some of what you are telling me. There is a discipline required to be successful. That's certain. We can't have dozens and dozens of field leaders making uncoordinated decisions. That's chaos.

"It's my job, and the War Department's, to make sure that we are all functioning properly in the same war. But, you are correct, we need to adapt to changing circumstances, and define the latitude to be given to commanders like yourself.

"This has been a constructive conversation, Forrest. I must conclude our meeting. I must now go outside and meet my adoring public. Heh-heh-heh!

"Would you accompany me back to Atlanta this afternoon?"

"Yes, of course."

"Good, Mr. Harrison will notify you of our departure time. Thank you, Forrest."

Forrest shook hands first with President Davis, then with Colonels Lee and Johnston and with Mr. Harrison.

At 4:30 p.m. when President Davis' party boarded the train bound for Atlanta both Forrest and General Polk joined the President in his private car.

Forrest was at one end of the car when President Davis was conversing with Bishop Polk. He knew that in the President's mind, the Polk-Bragg conflict was of far greater concern than Forrest's differences with the grating Bragg. Polk was very upset. Forrest observed him waving his arms as he spoke to Davis. But he was out of hearing range of the discussion.

Forrest and President Davis did talk briefly late in the evening. Davis promised Forrest that he would write General Bragg requesting that Forrest's wish for a new assignment in West Tennessee and North Mississippi be granted. And Davis also promised he would request that Forrest take with him his personal staff, his escort company, McDonald's Battalion and Morton's Battery.

On October 29, 1863 President Davis sent his request to General Bragg. Turning to his aide, Colonel Brent, Bragg said sarcastically, "Let Attila the Hun have his wish. God help his next commanding officer."

17 • Winter Camp

Oxford, Mississippi, January 11, 1864

"General, the staff and your field officers are all here in Oxford, and waiting for you to address them," announced Captain Strange.

"Where are they Strange?"

"Sir, they're assembled in the Baptist Church."

"Fine, I'll be there in a few minutes."

Promptly at 10:00 a.m., the announced time of the meeting, General Forrest strode in carrying a sheaf of papers.

"Atten...shun!" shouted Captain Strange, as all officers stood to receive their commander.

"All right, officers. At ease! Sit down!" said Forrest. "Let's not be so formal. We've got work to do."

For the next hour, Forrest explained what he wanted to accomplish in the training program, and asked for individual reports from six of his key commanders. When this was concluded, Forrest announced that Dr. Cowan had asked for a few minutes to address the group.

"Gentlemen, I am not a public speaker, so you will

please excuse me," Dr. Cowan apologized. "There are concerns of public health I wish to address. First, there is the matter of camp sanitation. It is essential that we follow military regulations on latrines. These should be dug at least 100 yards downwind from the tents or the shebangs [crude log-type huts with dirt chimneys].

"Anyone caught not using the designated latrines is to be put on overnight guard duty for one week. We now have a bunch of farm boys from West Tennessee who have never relieved themselves any place other than three feet from where they stood. Well, we can't have that. Now, I know some of them are going to say to you it's too cold to walk to the latrines when you catch them urinating behind their tents. Don't accept that excuse."

Considerable laughing broke out indicating that few believed what Dr. Cowan was explaining was a serious matter. Forrest jumped up and yelled, "Goddamnit, you listen to Dr. Cowan! I want a clean camp. We're not farm animals, you know. Please continue, Dr. Cowan."

"The next matter concerns prostitutes hanging around our camps. It's become a problem. I'm afraid some of them are infected with syphilis and gonorrhea.

"You know what they say, 'Venus for one night and mercury for the rest of your life.' Venereal disease is horrible, and it's debilitating to an army."

Again, Forrest leaped up. "It's an insult to our wives to have those filthy, ugly birds with their faces resembling exactly their asses in our camps. I won't tolerate it. No, sir, I won't!

"Captain Strange, get together with my Provost Marshall, Captain Goodwin, and ship every last one of those hags south toward New Orleans.

"And I swear if any soldier comes down with the pocks or clap, I'll personally shoot him. I guarantee it.

"All right, Dr. Cowan, go on."

"Now, it's not life threatening, but we do have some serious problems with rotting gums and tooth decay. We don't want soldiers on the puny list [sick list] and unavailable for duty because of infection in their mouths.

"I've asked Dr. Benjamin Jeter, a dentist from Holly Springs, to spend several days in each of our camps. Please set aside time for your soldiers to have Dr. Jeter examine them. He can schedule them for fillings, extractions and removal of tartar. Assure those who are frightened of dentists that Dr. Jeter uses laughing gas [nitrous oxide] in extractions.

"That's all I've got to say, gentlemen. If any of you require my services or Dr. Jeter's, please let us know."

General Forrest, once again rose, then announced, "This meeting is over. Return to you commands."

Forrest motioned Dr. Cowan to come with him. "Keep me posted on those problems, James, and also schedule an appointment for me with Dr. Jeter. Next to my goddamn boils, my teeth are like a dark angel hanging over me.

"What's the general status of the health of my troops?"

"General, I'd say it's good. We do have our share of diarrhea."

"Oh, you mean the 'Tennessee Quickstep.'"

"Yes, and we have our usual quota of colds. But so far, not much pneumonia, and no cases of measles and mumps. "I keep my fingers crossed. If any of those things break out among these farm boys, we may want to think about shutting down the war for awhile.

"We can't have that happen. We are probably going to break camp sometime in mid February."

January 25, 1864

"Captain Strange, I want you to visit our encampment and check on the morale of the men. We've been drilling them hard for several weeks now. I'd like to know how they're doing. Take Anderson with you. Report back to me on Thursday."

"Yes, sir, we'll leave before noon today."

January 28, 1864

"General Forrest, Anderson and I have completed the visits you requested. We've put together a report for you."

"Forget the report. Just tell me what you found out."

"All right, sir," said Strange. "Morale is good from the viewpoint of most of the recruits. You may not like some of the things going on, but the soldiers seem to be having a good time."

"Like what, Strange?"

"Well, most evenings, about half are playing cards. Another bunch are staging cockfights. Some are dancing, and a few attending Bible readings."

"Is there much drinking?"

"No, sir, not the recruits. But some of the officers have their nightly whiskey. No one was drunk as far as we could see."

"I'm curious about the cockfights, Strange. What did you and Captain Anderson see?"

"Oh, we think it's harmless. There wasn't any noticeable gambling. It was just some farm boys who have grown up with gamecocks. What we saw was orderly. There wasn't much money changing hands. Of course, it was bloody in the ring, but no different from what we've all seen in the past few years."

"Anderson, what about this dancing Strange mentioned?"

"Sir, it's just a bunch of fellows putting on their version of a cotillion. It was fun watching them. Some of the boys are really lively. A few put on a show of fancy high-stepping. I sort of envied them."

"General, that brings me to something I think you might want to consider for the benefit of the morale."

"What's that, Strange?"

"Do you know Captain Jewell Wilbourne?"

"Hell, yes, old 'Frozen Eye' Wilbourne. What about him?"

"Well sir, he wants to know if you would approve of

the men putting on a minstrel show for all the troops to see. He says the men have been talking about it, and he says there's a lot of talent among the soldiers.

"Sergeant Billy Harrington II used to be with Haverly's Minstrels. He wants to co-direct the show with Captain Wilbourne, and to play the role of Mister Interlocutor."

"Now Strange, I'd give a year's pay to see 'Frozen Eye' Wilbourne in a show. With that wild look of his, and his stuttering, we may all laugh ourselves to death.

"Of course, a minstrel show is a wonderful idea. Can they be ready by Friday, February 12th? I am planning a final parade and inspection of all units here in Oxford at 1:00 p.m. The show could go on immediately following, say 2:30 p.m. — that is, if we don't get rain or snow.

"Can they put together their show in two weeks?"

"I'm sure they can, sir."

"Good, I can't wait to see old 'Frozen Eye' in action. Send a messenger to Wilbourne immediately, and have him and Sergeant Harrington get their talent together. Pull Harrington from regular duty to give him a little extra time"

Friday, February 12, 1864

Promptly at 1:00 p.m. all units of Forrest's New Cavalry were in formation on an open field on the west side of town. Troops had ridden to Oxford from camps in Como and Coldwater to join troops being trained in Oxford.

Bugler Jacob Gaus sounded, "Attention."

Then, led by a flagbearer carrying a large Confederate battle flag, a fifer and two other musicians playing snare drums moved slowly across the length of the field, playing first the lively tune, *Barley Sugar*, then *Bonnie Blue Flag*, *Stonewall Jackson's Way*, and *Queenstown Heights*.

When the musicians finished, General Forrest strode quickly to the middle of the parade ground, accompanied by Colonel Tyree Bell and Adjutant John Strange.

Soldiers, Welcome!
You have finished training and have been certified for active duty. I congratulate you.
I know all of you will conduct yourselves gallantly when called upon to do so. I expect nothing less. Your families...your sweethearts...your friends...expect nothing less.
Be prepared to move out from this encampment at daybreak on Monday. Precise orders as to our mission are expected tomorrow from General Polk's headquarters.
Stand by for inspection!

At 2:00 p.m. the inspection of the various units was finished. Captain Strange made the announcement that the minstrel show would begin at 2:30 p.m. sharp.

At 2:30 p.m on this partly cloudy February day the temperature was 55° — not uncommon in this part of the South for some winter days. It was almost a perfect day.

Near the parade grounds was a natural amphitheater. At the bottom of a long slope a large platform 40 feet long and 26 feet wide had been constructed for the show. A partial backdrop was an 18 foot long canvas painted to represent a grand Southern plantation homestead.

For audience seating some 200 logs had been cut to accommodate part of the 3000 soldiers expected. The others could sit elsewhere on the slope, and enjoy the show. Special seating of canvas camp chairs was arranged near the stage for officers' wives and special guests.

Captain Wilbourne, co-director of the show, was a strange looking man. He was 6-foot-4, but weighed only 140 pounds. He suffered from a neurological disorder which caused his right eye to bulge out, preventing his eye from closing. And his gray-blue eye focused straight ahead, giving him a wild appearance. To add to Captain "Frozen Eye" Wilbourne's physical handicaps, he also stuttered.

Wilbourne was a gentle man who had learned to accept the descriptive name, "Frozen Eye," and the constant teasing. Rather than let it upset him, he turned it to his advantage, Before the war he played comedy roles in amateur stage productions in his home town, Jackson, Mississippi. He was a bookkeeper by profession.

Co-director Sergeant Billy Harrington II, a veteran minstrel show performer, was a tall, handsome Irish-American with jet black hair. He had pronounced rosy cheeks and a broad, infectious smile. His friends called him, "the Smiling Irishman." Harrington was talented. He could sing, dance, play the banjo and tambourine, and serve capably as Mr. Interlocutor — the minstrel show's master-of-ceremonies.

Shortly after General and Mrs. Forrest were seated along with other officers and their wives, and some prominent citizens of Oxford, the show began.

"Frozen Eye" Wilbourne, dressed in a black cutaway coat, white trousers and a black top hat and carrying a white cane said loudly, "Off-off-off-offi-officers, g-g-g-guests and s-s-s-s-soldiers of-of-of For-For-Forrest's ca-ca-cavalry — Welcome!"

A great cheer went up when Captain Wilbourne successfully pronounced one word without stuttering.

"It-it-it is with g-g-g-great pleas-pleas-pleas-pleasure to pre-pre-pre-present this sh-sh-show.

"No boo-boo-boo-booing will be per-per-mitted."

An even louder roar from the audience went up. Wilbourne at first appeared embarrassed. Then good-naturedly, he started laughing too. He took a deep breath, paused briefly, and yelled without stuttering, "On with the show!"

The soldiers yelled again and applauded loudly. In apparent appreciation, "Frozen Eye" in jest took a deep bow. Then the entire ensemble rushed on to the stage in their garish costumes. Most carried musical instruments. In spirited fashion the show opened with the entire cast singing, *Blue Tail Fly*.

The cast peeled off rapidly and formed a semi-circle with the master-of-ceremonies — Mister Interlocutor (Sergeant Billy Harrington, II) in the center, and posted on the outside right and outside left, the "End Men" — Brudder Tambo (Sergeant Finlay Warren) and Brudder Bones (Corporal Theron Sims). The end men were dressed to look and act like slow-witted, happy slaves. But instead of being the butt of jokes by the urbane, sophisticated Mister Interlocutor, they would use him as the perfect foil for their cunning and clever humor.

The singers and dancers were positioned in between the end men; and the banjo players and fiddlers were on the left side of the stage.

Mister Interlocutor, in formal attire with a brilliant red stovepipe hat and a gold-plated walking stick, was the perfect picture of a debonair gentleman of the Old South.

Brudder Tambo and Brudder Bones were in blackface. The black polish had been applied to give each the appearance of large eyes and a gaping mouth with huge lips. Tambo wore a flour sack dress, white gloves and red shoes. He had a tambourine in one hand, and slapped it with his other hand when he thought he had outwitted the haughty, self-important Mister Interlocutor.

Brudder Bones wore a brilliant white robe like an angel which accentuated his black face. His oversized shoes were light blue. He held the "bones" — two flat sticks used as clappers when he too made a fool of Mister Interlocutor.

The show formally began when Mister Interlocutor gave the command, "Gen — tle — men and la — deez be seated!" When the cast sat down, the banter began between Mister Interlocutor and his two audacious end men.

"Mr. Interlocutor, why does a fireman wear red suspenders?"

"Why, I don't know, Brudder Tambo, why?"

"To hold his pants up," answered Brudder Tambo shaking his tambourine and grinning at the audience in an exaggerated fashion.

Then Brudder Bones asked, "Mr. Interlocutor, what's a fortification?"

"I don't know, Brudder Bones. What?"

"Twice a twentification."

Then back and forth between the outrageous end men and Mr. Interlocutor the repartee continued.

"Mr. Interlocutor? Do you have any whiskey?"

"Why, Brudder Tambo, don't you know whiskey has killed more men than bullets?"

"Yas, suh, but wouldn't you rather be filled with whiskey than bullets?"

"Mr. Interlocutor? I heard of one colored brother who indiscreetly asked of another brother, 'What wuz de price o 'dem new britches what you got on?'"

"And what did he say, Brudder Bones?"

"He said, 'How'd I know. De shopkeeper wasn't dar.'"

"Mr. Interlocutor, a judge said to me, 'Brudder Tambo, you have been brought here for drinking whiskey.'"

"And what did you say to that, Brudder Bones?"

"I said, 'Okay, lesh get started.'"

"Brudder Bones," interjected Mr. Interlocutor, "you have been bragging about your incredible exploits. Could you give us one example?"

"Yas, suh, I can indeed.

"My master tied me up like a scarecrow and put me in de woods so de wild animals would tar me up."

"Well, Brudder Bones, how did you survive?"

"Well, I killed a buzzard by blowing on his face; I blinded a panther by scratching out de eyes with my toenails; and I escaped when a weasel gnawing on my leg ate through de ropes."

Howls of laughter erupted from the crowd. Brudder Bones, delighted with himself, snapped his bones in jubilation and took a deep bow.

Mr. Interlocutor, Billy Harrington, II, stepped forward to introduce the first of a series of special entertainment acts by the cast seated in the semi-circle between Brudder

Tambo and Brudder Bones.

"La ... deez ... and gen ... tle ... men, direct from Atlanta, Georgia, and Miss Cornelius' Academy of Music, our featured songstress, Miss Tillie Buttons. She will sing one of your favorites, *The Homespun Dress*. Miss Buttons requests that y'all join in with her for the chorus after each verse."

Miss Tillie, who was Corporal Harry Bozarth dressed in a pink bonnet and a ruffled blouse and a hoop skirt, and carrying a parasol sashayed in an exaggerated style to center stage. A soldier in the crowd yelled, "Honey, can you meet me after the show. I think I'm in love."

Corporal Bozarth [Miss Tillie] turned half-way around to face the direction of the voice and in a concocted high-pitched shrill voice answered, "Why I'd love to, handsome. But it will cost you."

Again, the crowd roared its approval. Miss Tillie, in appreciation, did a curtsy. Then she said, "I'm dedicating this song to that inimitable Southern charmer, Captain John Morton, Jr."

Again laughter. Major Rambaut, self-appointed chief prankster of General Forrest's staff, had put Bozarth up to the kidding of young Captain Morton.

Miss Tillie then began singing:

> *O yes, I am a Southern girl,*
> *And glory in the name,*
> *And boast it with far greater pride*
> *Than glittering wealth or fame.*
> *I envy not the Northern girl*
> *Her robes of beauty rare,*
> *Though diamonds grace her snowy neck*
> *And pearls bedeck her hair.*

Then, most of the audience enthusiastically joined in on the chorus:

> *"Hurrah! Hurrah!*
> *For the Sunny South so dear!*
> *Three cheers for the homespun dress*
> *The Southern ladies wear!*

The applause for Miss Tillie was thunderous, and "she" did another curtsy in appreciation.

"Now, let's have a singing rhyme contest," said Mr. Interlocutor. "Who's first?"

Brudder Tambo jumped up and sang:
> "My mammy was a wolf, my daddy was a tiger.
> I'm what you call de ol' Mississippi nigger;
> Half-fire, half-smoke, a little touch of Thunder
> I'm what dey call de eighth wonder."

Then Brudder Bones, anxious to outdo his rival, took his turn.
> "Went to de river; couldn't get across
> Jumped on a nigger cause I thought he was a hoss
> Got in de river, the nigger couldn't swim
> Hit him in de head with a hickory limb."

"All right you two, that's quite enough," said Mr. Interlocutor in feigned exasperation.

"Now for some real singing from that great Irish balladeer, Lieutenant Thomas Joseph O'Hearne of Colonel Bell's Regiment. He will sing, *Annie Laurie*. And I guarantee you, there will not be a dry eye when he finishes.

"When Lieutenant O'Hearne finishes — probably after three or four encores — we'll have a 15 minute intermission before we begin the Oleo, the second part of our show."

The show continued until just after 4:00 p.m. The Oleo featured many syncopated banjo and fiddler tunes including Stephen Foster's *De Camptown Races* and *Hard Times Come Again No More*; and a spirited performance by the cast of the Virginia reel. The grand finale of the Oleo was the "walkaround." Each performer did his specialty dance or strut while the others stood behind him clapping their hands for encouragement. Again, the crowd roared its approval following each individual's performance.

The show's closing act was Lieutenant O'Hearne singing *Lorena*. No prodding was needed to get the crowd to join in. That happened spontaneously.

The cast assembled in a long line across the stage, and bowed in unison to the wild cheering crowd.

General Forrest invited General Chalmers, Colonel Bell, Colonel Robert McCulloch, Colonel Robert Richardson, Matt Gallaway, Dr. Cowan, and their wives to join Mary and him for refreshments at his headquarters.

In an exhilarated mood Forrest said to his officers, "Gentlemen, well done. I am very pleased with the results of six weeks of training. Of course, we won't know how well we've done until we get into action. But I'm confident they'll fight.

"Captain Strange! Would you bring Captain Wilbourne and Sergeant Harrington here. I want to thank them personally. Those two put on some show, didn't they? My ribs still hurt from laughing so hard.

"Old 'Frozen Eye' is some piece of machinery. And Billy Harrington is a talented entertainer. Make certain neither one gets transferred. Those two are great for morale."

minstrel performers

18 • Fort Pillow

Tuesday, April 12, 1864

"Captain Goodman, call forward the senior commanders," ordered a somewhat disheveled General Chalmers. "I want to go over our plan of attack one more time."

"Yes, sir," replied Chalmers' Adjutant. "Right away."

Chalmers appeared to recover his energy as he drank coffee while bracing his back against a large oak tree. When his officers arrived, he got up; did a few stretching exercises, then began a motivation speech.

"Gentlemen, we are going to take that fort in short order," Chalmers began. "It's infested with Tories and niggers that have no business in Yankee uniforms. They're vermin. If they were real soldiers, do you think General Sherman and General Hurlbut would have assigned them to this worthless outpost? No, of course not.

"We need to stamp out this gross insult to our cause. Pass the word down through the ranks that we aren't fighting brave white boys from Illinois or Ohio. We're fighting cowardly scum from here in West Tennessee and ignorant slaves they've duped into fighting their battles.

"Let's teach them a lesson so every citizen in this region will be aware of the consequences of undermining our cause."

General Chalmers paused for a moment as he read a message handed him.

"Gentlemen, our scouts report a Yankee gunboat on the Mississippi River approaching the fort from the south. We can now expect some shelling from the river as well as from the artillery at the fort.

"Secure good cover for your soldiers. Mr. Shaw, our guide, assures me there are plenty of trees and thick brush between here and the clearing before the fort. And he says that if we can get some soldiers down in the ravines on both sides of the fort, the big guns probably cannot do them much harm.

"Now we've already driven their pickets back toward the fort. Our first objective us to get rid of their sharpshooters on those knolls around the outer fort area. Let's flush them out, then we'll do the sharpshooting.

"Let's strike them hard. Those niggers won't give us any trouble. I can't imagine they've ever faced gunfire before. Once they see one of their own fall, they'll probably cut and run."

"General Chalmers," interrupted Colonel Clark Barteau. "How many niggers are there?"

"Close to 300 says Mr. Shaw. About half of all those at the fort if you don't count the civilians," replied Chalmers.

"Civilians, General?"

"Yes, Barteau. There are some wives and children and some civilian workers living around the fort."

"Well, sir, I hope they have sense enough to get out of there."

"I agree, Barteau. We'll just have to wait and see."

Then General Chalmers continued, "All right men, have your soldiers inspect their rifles and their cartridge boxes. And tell them to make every shot count. Our ammunition supply wagons are somewhere between Brownsville and here. With all that mud, I suspect they won't arrive until sometime in the afternoon. The worst thing that can happen to us is to run out of ammunition while we are attacking.

"General Forrest and his force are a couple of hours away. Let's clear out that fort before he gets here, and give him a surprise.

"Colonel Bell...Colonel McCulloch...send your sharpshooters forward as soon as possible. Then disperse your forces according to our plan. Colonel Bell, your Fourth Brigade will operate on the right and center. Colonel McCulloch, your Second Brigade will take the left and center. I'll be up and down the line to coordinate our attack. The attack begins at 8:00 a.m.

"Good luck, gentlemen!"

Everyone quickly dispersed to begin preparations.

General Chalmers, now showing signs of nervous excitement, called Captain Goodman aside.

"Goodman, pick one or two of your orderlies to take a message to the Bemis Twins and the other blacksmiths. I want all the horses shod. And ask the veterinarian, Lieutenant Hyslip, to pull out all the injured and sick horses."

"General, we've got most of the horses in a pasture about one-half mile from here. The horses are grazing there."

"Make sure, Goodman, that those horseholders remain alert. If for some reason we don't do well, we may have to bring those horses up in a hurry."

At 6:00 a.m. Major Lionel F. Booth, the 25-year old commander of Fort Pillow, and his second in command, Major William F. Bradford, were notified that a Confederate column was approaching from the east. Both Booth and Bradford were without combat experience. The Union command in Memphis, until Forrest's recent raids in West Tennessee, didn't see the urgency of having a seasoned force at this obscure, backwater garrison on the Mississippi River bluffs.

Booth, in addition to his responsibility as post commander, was in charge of the First Battalion, First Alabama Siege Artillery (Colored), with some eight officers and 213 enlisted men. He also headed Company D, Second United States Light Artillery (Colored), with one officer and 41 enlisted men. Prior to joining the regular army, Booth, a native of Philadelphia, Pennsylvania, had been a clerk.

Major Bradford, 32, a lawyer from nearby Dyersburg, Tennessee, commanded the First Battalion, 13th Tennessee Cavalry with ten officers and 285 enlisted men, most white, native Tennesseans. Bradford was well-known to the citizens of adjacent Tennessee counties.

Complaints had reached General Forrest that Bradford and some of his men had systematically robbed them and had assaulted some of the women. "There is no worse Tennessee Tory than Bradford," several citizens had told Forrest.

Fort Pillow's physical design was well-known to the Confederates. The earthen works, forming the inner defense of the fort, were constructed in the summer of 1861 by Forrest's friend, Minor Meriwether, and General Gideon Pillow and their construction crews. The Confederates built the fort to prevent access by the Union to the Mississippi River downstream, and to defend Memphis. When the Union Navy captured Memphis in June 1862 after a battle on the river in front of the city, the Confederates abandoned Fort Pillow.

The fort was sited on a bluff overlooking the river. The natural configuration of the terrain around the inner fort area provided the first line of defense for the Union army on the land side. The river bluff behind the fort protected it from assaults on that side.

The outer line of defense extended almost two miles in a semi-circle extending from a natural depression called Coal Creek ravine at one end to the Mississippi River at the other end. At the center of the outer defense line the distance to the river was 600 yards. There were knolls on this perimeter line where Union sharpshooters had been posted by Major Booth.

The second defense line, closer in toward the river, covered two acres along the crest of a prominent knoll.

The final defensive line was a small, irregular semi-circular earthen wall constructed at the angle of the junction of Coal Creek and the Mississippi River on the edge of the bluff. The dirt parapet was eight feet high and six feet wide. There were six deep cuts serving as gun emplacements. The protective ditch in front was 12 feet wide and eight feet deep.

The artillery at Major Booth's disposal was two six-pounders, two 12-pounder howitzers, and two ten-pounder Parrots. The Confederates brought no artillery. Captain Morton's Battery remained behind in Jackson.

Fort Pillow contained the elements of a small town. On the south side of the inner defensive area were numerous wooden buildings occupied by civilian workers and their families, commissary and quartermaster warehouses, a hospital structure and barracks.

At 8:00 a.m. General Chalmers ordered the attack to begin. Colonel Andrew Wilson's 16th Tennessee Cavalry pushed forward to the Federal's second defense line. Soon thereafter, the Union gunboat, the New Era, from its position on the Mississippi River began a heavy shelling into the areas where Captain James Marshall assumed were Confederate positions. Major Booth's artillery fired simultaneously from its emplacements within the fort.

Confederate sharpshooters quickly gained the high ground outside the fort. From these positions they fired directly into the fort at Union soldiers moving about from position to position.

At about 9:00 a.m., while directing the positioning of his artillery, Major Booth was killed by a sharpshooter. But his death was unknown to General Chalmers or any of his commanders until late that day after the fort had been overrun by Forrest's Cavalry.

Upon notification of Major Booth's death, Major Bradford assumed command of the Union force.

At 10:00 a.m. General Forrest arrived on the field. Shortly thereafter, Chalmers ordered a major assault. Although the attack failed to dislodge the Union forces, there was some success. Colonel Robert "Black Bob" McCulloch's unit operating on the extreme left of the Confederate attack line broke through the Union's second line of defense, and quickly occupied the barracks located only 150 yards from the inner earthen works of the fort.

Forrest was now co-directing his cavalry forces with Chalmers. When Forrest was notified of Colonel McCulloch's position, he sent the latter a message: "Hold in there, and keep firing at anything that moves."

Sporadic fighting continued the remainder of the morning, and into early afternoon. Confederate sharpshooters firing into the fort enjoyed the most success. Near mid-afternoon Forrest yelled, "Get Captain Goodman over here fast." When Goodman arrived Forrest said, "Captain, write this down:

> *Major Booth, as your gallant defense of the fort has entitled you to the treatment of brave men, I now demand an unconditional surrender of your forces, assuring you that at the same time they will be treated as prisoners of war. I have received a fresh supply of ammunition and can easily take your position. Should my demand be refused, I cannot be responsible for the fate of your command.*

"Captain Goodman, take a white truce flag out there. Lieutenant Rogers and my aide, W. H. Rhodes, will go out with you. Now hold the damn flag high and wave it several times before you walk out there. Nothing's to be gained by any of you getting shot."

At the sight of the Confederate's truce flag, Major Bradford, who had been observing the field from his command post yelled, "Captain Young...Lieutenant Leming...you will acknowledge their white flag. Watch out for any trickery. Forrest is well known for trying to take advantage of the flag. Take four mounted soldiers with you as an escort. Find out what this is about. And for God's sake, don't tell them Major Booth is dead!"

At 3:10 p.m. the Confederate and Union truce parties met face to face in an open area between the fort's inner earthwork's defenses and the Union's original second line of defense. Captain Goodman saluted Captain Young, and handed the fort's youthful provost marshall a sealed message. Captain Young accepted the communication, then saluted and returned to the fort to confer with Major Bradford.

Captain Goodman, General Chalmer's aide, and his party remained out in the open area awaiting an anticipated reply from Major Booth who, they assumed, was still in command.

While waiting, Forrest, who had now assumed total control of strategy, surveyed the battlefield's physical surroundings, and considered the tactical plan he would implement should it be necessary to continue the assault. Captain Anderson, who had been assigned temporarily a field command at Fort Pillow, approached Forrest near the left flank of the Confederate line, and said excitedly, "General...General...three Federal gunboats have been spotted steaming upriver. One appears to have troops on it. We think they've come to relieve the New Era. That's not good news."

Forrest reacted instantly, "Somebody get Chalmers over here quick."

Chalmers was nearby conferring with a group of officers and in seconds approached Forrest.

"General, get word to Bell and Barteau to move their soldiers as quickly and quietly as possible into Coal Creek ravine on the north side of the fort. That will put them within 50 yards or so from that ditch protecting their parapets."

"But General Forrest, we're under a flag of truce. Isn't that dishonoring the rules of warfare which say you must hold your positions during truce talks?"

"Goddamnit Chalmers, this is a goddamn war. You win any way you can. Now get it done! Quit arguing with me. If we don't take the fort by sundown, we'll get whipped for sure tomorrow. Do you really think General Hurlbut down in Memphis is not going to do anything? Cris' sakes, he'll be so goddamned embarrassed about what's happened today, you can count on him to retaliate. His military career is on the line."

"Yes, sir," answered the perplexed Chalmers.

Forrest considered that the Federals weakest defensive point was Coal Creek ravine. If he could get troops down in there, they couldn't be hit by enemy fire. And from that close in position, the fort could be stormed in minutes should that be necessary.

Inside the fort Major Bradford, faced with his first major decision as commander, decided he needed time to consult with his officers and with Captain Marshall who was out on the river commanding the gunboat, the New Era. He also realized that if he could stall for 30 minutes or more, this would permit the three Federal gunboats approaching the fort time to get into position.

"Captain Young, take this request asking for one hour to consider the General's demands out to his truce party," ordered Major Bradford.

"Sir, you've signed the communication with Major Booth's name."

"Yes, we don't want them to know the Major is dead. Now, take your time going out there. Every minute counts."

"Is this correct, Major Bradford, that you're requesting one hour?" asked Young in order to be absolutely certain.

"Yes, I want to stall for as long as possible," responded the remarkably composed Bradford who now realized he was making the most important decision of his life.

Captain Young and his party returned to the open area in front of the fort. Without any discussion between Young and Captain Goodman, the former handed over Major Bradford's request to be carried back to General Forrest.

Forrest was furious. "Hell, no. I won't grant them one hour. In that time we will have lost all our advantage. The goddamn fort will be reinforced and those gunboats will be trying to blow us to 'Kingdom Come.' I'll give them 20 minutes, no more!

"Now, Goodman, pick up that white flag. I'm going out there with you. Booth will know we mean business if I show up out there. Come on. Let's go!"

Once again, the Union and Confederate truce parties met in the open area.

Forrest didn't bother to hand Captain Young a written communication. He looked directly at the surprised

Young for a moment to try to intimidate the junior Union officer with his fierce, penetrating eyes. Then he said, "Captain, you've got 20 minutes to surrender. I am General Forrest. If your soldiers are not outside the fort by that time, I shall proceed to assault the fort."

Captain Young, nervous in the presence of the unorthodox Confederate commander, answered that he would take the message to Major Booth. Young saluted General Forrest, performed a formal military about-face, and returned to the fort.

Major Bradford, when told by Captain Young of General Forrest's bold demand, without hesitation asked his provost marshall to prepare this brief message:

I will not surrender.

Young and his party returned again to where Forrest was waiting with Captain Goodman. After saluting once more, Young handed the four-word reply to General Forrest. The General read the reply, and uncharacteristically he said nothing in response. Each party saluted the other, turned around, and quickly walked back to their lines.

Conferring with General Chalmers for just one minute, Forrest yelled to his bugler, the German-born Corporal Gaus, "Sound 'Charge' when I give the signal. We're going to kick hell out of those Tories and niggers. We've just got our fresh supply of ammunition distributed. There's just enough energy left in our boys to run them right into the river.

"Are you ready Chalmers? You're in command of the assault."

"I'm ready, General. I'm going down the middle with Colonel Andy Wilson's 20th Tennessee Regiment."

"Good! Hit the bastards hard, Chalmers!"

General Forrest signaled Corporal Gaus to sound, "Charge." This signal unleashed a wild rush of the Confederates toward the center of the physically compact inner defenses of Fort Pillow. Colonel Clark Barteau's force, positioned in Coal Creek ravine, scrambled up the side of the bluff, crossed the ditch surrounding the inner fort area, and climbed over the earthen embankment to reach the inside.

In less than ten minutes the inner fort's air was flooded with wild Rebel yells and screaming shouts of: "Kill the niggers! — Kill the niggers! — Kill the niggers! — Kill the nigger-stealing homemade Yankees — Kill them before they cut your throat and drink your blood!" Forrest's soldiers whistled, howled and yelled obscenities at the confused, disorganized enemy as the former proceeded forward.

General Chalmers, in command of the attack, was inside the fort shouting encouragement, "Shoot them down! Move quickly! Don't let them reload! Don't let them run off! Kill the officers!" he pleaded over and over to his troops. Nearly 1500 Confederates were in or near the fort attacking the Union enemy they outnumbered three-to-one.

Emotions of Forrest's troops were at a fever pitch. Most were near exhaustion from the long overnight march to Fort Pillow and the seven and one-half hours of fighting off and on that morning and afternoon of April 12th. Many hadn't slept in 36 hours. But, despite their physical condition, the excitement of their mission at Fort Pillow sustained them. They had been reminded time and time again about the infamy of the Federals using Negro slaves to fight their battles. And they had been instilled with hatred toward many of their former neighbors in Tennessee who had sided with the Union.

Major Bradford positioned the black troops behind the center wall of the fort. These troops bore the brunt of the Confederate onslaught. They attempted a defense, but the savage Confederate attack overwhelmed them.

Those black soldiers not killed in the first few minutes of the Confederate attack, and who attempted to escape from inside the fort down to the banks of the Mississippi River, were pursued and shot. In the wild melee there were no apparent attempts to single out calmly those black soldiers still armed from those who had thrown away their rifles before running down the hill to the river. Yells of: "No quarter! No quarter!" rang out unabated during the first half hour of this rout of the Union forces at Fort Pillow.

General Chalmers, even if he thought the ferocious attack within the fort was excessive, did nothing to try to control his troops. With the noise of yelling and rifle fire, it may not have been possible for him to call off the emotionally high-charged Confederates, many of whom were bent on revenge. But Chalmers had to have been aware of the senseless killing of unarmed soldiers and the deliberate shooting of wounded Union soldiers after it was apparent that the Confederates had captured the fort.

The vicious fighting extended to the river's edge. Chalmers was convinced the Federals had a pre-arranged defense plan which included a series of rifle pits near the river's shore and a cache of warehoused weapons at the bottom of the bluff, which, if necessary, would provide for a final stand while troops boarded transports to take them down river. But if this was the plan, it wasn't implemented. Many of those fortunate enough to reach the river without being shot drowned while trying to swim out to the transports.

To complete the assault Chalmers ordered most of the wooden structures at Fort Pillow torched.

At 5:00 p.m. Chalmers left the fort to report to General Forrest who had been observing the assault from a vantage point on a knoll beyond the fort. At the time Forrest was being treated by several medical aid men when Chalmers approached.

"Is it all over, Chalmers?" inquired Forrest in a subdued voice.

"Yes, General, we've wiped Fort Pillow off the face of the Earth. Right now, we're trying to round up some escapees; otherwise, it's over," said the smiling Chalmers who was obviously pleased with his own performance under fire.

"Well done, Chalmers. Please tell the commanders I congratulate them, and their soldiers too."

"What happened to you, General Forrest?"

"I had a horse shot from under me, and that poor beast fell on me, I've got some severe bruises. I hurt all over and I've got to retire to my camp to rest.

"Now, Chalmers, you attend to the prisoners and arrange to remove the artillery, horses and quartermaster supplies from the fort.

"Form a burial detail. Use some of the Union prisoners. Dig the normal two foot wide, two foot deep and fifty feet or so long. Then form another detail to strip the dead Federals of any money, shoes, and anything else we need. Turn the goods over to the Quartermaster and have an inventory prepared for me by tomorrow. We've got to work fast. It will be dark soon. If possible, we want to be gone from here tomorrow."

"Sir," said Chalmers, "here's some interesting information. Major Booth was killed early this morning, and Major Bradford, our Yankee collaborator friend from Dyersburg, had been running things. He's the fellow we've been negotiating with."

"Well, I'll be damned. So it was that Tory traitor, Bradford. Did we capture that white nigger?"

"Yes, sir, we've got him. What should we do with him?"

"Chalmers, I don't give a damn, but let's take him back to Jackson with the other prisoners. We'll let the people of West Tennessee know that we have this miserable traitor. I'll promise those folks that justice will be served. You can count on that!

"Now, Chalmers, I'm hurting too much to continue talking with you. You've got work to do tidying up things.

"Post perimeter guards out about three or four miles tonight, and send some scouts toward Memphis to report any movements by Hurlbut."

"One more thing, General. What should we do with the Federal wounded?"

"Chalmers, somehow or other, get a message to one of those Union gunboats. Let them know we'll permit a transport or two to come pick them up tomorrow.

"Now, Chalmers, no more details. You handle things. I'm exhausted."

19 • Uproar

First reports of events at Fort Pillow were received in Memphis and at Union headquarters in Cairo, Illinois. Then, the reports spread quickly to newspapers in Chicago, New York and Washington, Correspondents raced to Cairo to get firsthand accounts of the battle from wounded Union soldiers who had been transported upriver to area hospitals. Here they hoped to verify that a "massacre" occurred.

When Murat Halstead, the nationally-prominent editor and war correspondent of the *Cincinnati Commercial*, learned that the Confederate forces were led by General Forrest, he asked sarcastically, "Do you mean 'the Prince of Raiders' as both generals Sherman and Bragg call him? Or is it, 'Attila the Hun' or 'Tamerlane,' the Mongolian warrior?" Halstead, who covered military action in the War's Western Theater, concluded, "I suppose any of those names are appropriate. If these reports from Fort Pillow are true, believe me, the North will be in an uproar. All hell will break loose."

The day following Fort Pillow Forrest, now feeling slightly better after a night's rest, first sensed his victory might cause negative reaction even within the Confederate War Department in Richmond. He started framing his response to possible criticisms by preparing a brief account of his capture of Fort Pillow to forward to his Departmental Commander, General Polk in Demopolis, Alabama. Among other details, Forrest wrote:

The enemy force of about 500 Negroes and 200 white soldiers (Tennessee Tories). The river was dyed with

blood of the slaughtered for 200 yards. There were in the fort a large number of citizens who had fled there to avoid the conscript law. Most of these ran into the river and were drowned. The approximate loss was upward to 500 killed, but few of the officers escaping.
It is hoped that these facts will demonstrate to the Northern people that Negro soldiers cannot cope with Southerners.
My loss was about 14 killed and 60 wounded.

A half-hour later, Forrest dictated a long personal letter to President Jefferson Davis. In this letter Forrest described his recent victories in West Tennessee and Kentucky. Forrest asked his friend, William McGee, who at the time was absent from his regiment in Louisiana, to hand deliver the letter to President Davis in Richmond. Forrest didn't want this information transmitted to the President through normal military channels.

Jubilant, although apprehensive about possible public reaction to Fort Pillow, Forrest believed that with his success in West Tennessee against the Federals, Davis and the War Department in Richmond would give him the recognition he felt he deserved.

Later that same day his high spirits of the morning were dashed by another personal tragedy. He received a message from Dresden, Tennessee where General Buford was based, that his brother, Aaron, had died of pneumonia. The young Lieutenant Colonel had just returned with Buford's troops from the fighting in Kentucky. When consoled by Matt Gallaway, Forrest nodded his appreciation. Looking very forlorn, his only response was, "Matt, now with Jeffrey and Aaron gone, we're down to just four of us."

The pro-Union *Memphis Bulletin* published the first accounts of Fort Pillow. Its lead story was captioned in large type: "The Fight of Fort Pillow — No Quarter for Negroes...Rebel Atrocities and Assassinations — Wounded Men Buried Alive."

On April 15th the *Chicago Tribune*'s headline read: "Atrocious Butchery of 400 of Our Black Troops — Fiendish." On the 16th the *New York Times* printed these sensational headlines: "The Black Flag — Horrible Massacre by the Rebels —Four Hundred of the Garrison Brutally Murdered — Wounded and Unarmed Bayoneted and Their Bodies Burned — White and Black Indiscriminately Burned — Devilish Atrocities of the Insatiable Fiends."

Day after day for the next week, *The Chicago Tribune*, *The New York Times* and most other Northern newspapers printed accounts of the events at Fort Pillow with similar sensational captions. One article carried a brief interview with General Chalmers in which the latter said, "...that although it was against the policy of my Government to spare Negro soldiers or their officers, I had done all in my power to stop the carnage. At the same time, I believed it was right."

Reaction in the Union Army was also swift. General Sherman, distressed by recent events in West Tennessee telegraphed General Hurlbut, "You are relieved because there has been marked timidity in the management of affairs since Forrest passed north of Memphis."

General Sherman replaced Hurlbut with General Cadwallader C. Washburn, 46, a former Congressman from Wisconsin who had been serving in the Mississippi River Valley since 1862.

On April 18, 1864 Congress in Washington adopted a resolution instructing the Joint Committee on the Conduct of the War to investigate the Fort Pillow affair. Representing the Senate was the irascible, 63-year old Ohioan, Senator Benjamin Franklin Wade. He was a vocal opponent of President Lincoln and a severe critic of Lincoln's War Department. Wade's counterpart on the Joint Committee was Congressman Daniel W. Gooch, a 44-year old, Massachusetts Republican. Wade and Gooch left Washington on April 19th bound for Cairo, Illinois to conduct their investigation.

Newspapers in the South at first assumed neither a judgmental nor a defensive position about Forrest's actions. But as the furor swept the North these Southern newspapers started defending Forrest. Southern editors railed away at their Northern counterparts for the latters' constant reference to Fort Pillow "as a massacre by Rebel gangs."

Lincoln and his Cabinet debated what to do about Fort Pillow, but opinion was divided as to the appropriate means of retaliation. Lincoln's War Department held steady in its defense of using black soldiers in the Union army. It refused suggestions to remove them from active combat service in either the Eastern or Western war theaters in order to protect them from barbaric treatment if captured. It did, however, warn its black soldiers of the dangers they faced if captured.

At Oxford, Mississippi on April 20th — just eight days after the fight at Fort Pillow — General Chalmers assembled his First Division of Forrest's Cavalry and gave the following address:

> SOLDIERS: *I congratulate you upon your success in the brilliant campaign recently conducted in West Tennessee under the guidance of Major-General Forrest, whose star never shone brighter, and whose restless activity, untiring energy, and courage baffled the calculations and paralyzed the arms of our enemies.*
>
> *In a brief space of time we have killed 4,000 of the enemy, captured over 1,200 prisoners, 800 horses, 5 pieces of artillery, thousands of small arms, and many stand of colors, destroyed millions of dollars' worth of property, and relieved the patriots of West Tennessee from the hourly dread in which they have been accustomed to live. West Tennessee is redeemed, and our friends who have heretofore been compelled to speak with bated breath now boldly proclaim their sentiments.*
>
> *Colonel Neely on the north and Colonel McGuirk on*

the south, by well-executed demonstrations, alarmed the enemy for the safety of Memphis, while the lion-hearted McCulloch, with his "fighting brigade" of Missourians, Texans, and Mississippians, nobly assisted by Colonel Bell, with his gallant brigade of Tennesseeans, from Buford's division, temporarily attached to my command, stormed the works at Fort Pillow, in the face of the incessant fire from two gun-boats and five pieces of artillery from the fort, and taught the mongrel garrison of blacks and renegades a lesson long to be remembered. While we rejoice over our victories, let us not forget the few gallant spirits who yielded up their lives to their country, and fell as brave men love to fall, with their backs to the field and their feet to the foe.

On April 24th Forrest received a congratulatory note from General Polk. It read, "Your brilliant campaign in West Tennessee has given me great satisfaction, and entitles you to the thanks of your countrymen." Forrest felt reassured by Polk's confidence in him.

Forrest and his staff debated the disposition of the 250 Union prisoners taken at Fort Pillow. They were then being held in Okolona, Mississippi where they had been transported under guard by Captain John Goodwin, Provost Marshall, and Goodwin's staff. The decision was made to prepare a list of the individual owners of the 210 black prisoners and their addresses, in preparation for returning them to their legal owners. But Polk had a higher priority for their services. He ordered Forrest to transport these prisoners to Mobile to work as laborers helping to build fortifications around that strategic Confederate city. The Union white soldiers were ordered to be sent to Cahaba Prison, one of the Confederacy's newer prisons, and located just a few miles south of Selma, Alabama.

General Polk soon began to sense trouble on the matter of Forrest's conduct at Fort Pillow. He requested

Forrest to prepare a detailed account of events there. Expressing aggravation, Forrest said to Matt Gallaway and Captain Anderson, "Why is he doing this to me?"

Gallaway replied, "General Polk is trying to protect himself if this Fort Pillow matter gets out of hand. Fellows like Polk have been known to cover their flanks. As you know he has been under a cloud with the Confederate War Department since Chickamauga. They shipped him to our Department to get him out of the way. Watch out for him, General! He's a combination of piety and cunning. He oozes deceptive humility."

"I'll put something together for your review, General," volunteered Anderson. "It won't be any trouble."

"Matt, have you seen this other message from Polk?" inquired Forrest.

"Do you mean the one notifying us that an officer is coming from Richmond to inspect our command?"

"Yes, they want me to be available to him in Tupelo, Mississippi the first week in May," said Forrest in a concerned manner.

"Matt, I think it's that Inspector General Cooper's idea. He's got a burr in his rear end about how I rebuilt my cavalry. And he probably wants to reopen that sore of Chalmers' complaints about me. Frankly, I'm really in no mood to fool with those clerks from Richmond. Just what in the hell do they know about running a war?

"And while I've got Chalmers on my mind, put something in that report to Polk complimentary of Chalmers for his competent and energetic action at Fort Pillow. He did quite well. No one can question his bravery. I know full well that he was trying to show me that he wasn't just another lowly brigadier general. Goddamn! There is no doubt he was a little overzealous inside the fort. Did you observe that, Anderson?"

"Yes, sir, General Chalmers was screaming encouragement to our boys to mix it up, and whirling around in all directions. It's a damn wonder he didn't get shot as exposed as he was."

The Wade Committee arrived in Cairo, Illinois on April 22nd to begin hearings. During the next six days Wade and Gooch took testimony from Union officers, enlisted soldiers and conscripts, and civilians in Cairo; Mound City, Illinois; Columbus, Kentucky; Fort Pillow; and in Memphis. In all some 92 witnesses were interviewed.

Much of the testimony from both black Union soldiers and white was similar. Each witness testified that he either saw in person, or heard from an eyewitness, about the atrocities committed. Many recalled hearing the shouts from the Confederates: "Kill the damn niggers;" "Shoot him down;" "No quarter! No quarter!" "Kill the wench; kill her;" and "The Black Flag for the niggers and their white officers."

The Wade Committee established that 231 Union soldiers, mostly black, had been killed. That contrasted to only 14 dead Confederate soldiers. This disparity in numbers convinced Wade and Gooch that a wholesale slaughter of defenseless black soldiers had indeed occurred.

The Committee heard from one witness that additional black soldiers would have been slaughtered had not General Forrest ordered some spared to help pull the artillery pieces from the fort just before dark the day of the fight. This witness swore that he personally heard General Forrest give the order.

Other witnesses informed the Committee that Forrest's policy of "No Quarter" was announced to the Union commanders at the time of the attacks on Federal garrisons at Union City, Paducah, and at Columbus, Kentucky — just days prior to the Fort Pillow attack.

The visual impact of the bloodshed at Fort Pillow came strikingly to both Senator Wade and Congressman Gooch as they toured the fort soon after their Cairo interviews. It had been two weeks since the attack, yet many of those killed had not been completely buried. Scattered around the fort were shallow graves where it was possible to see arms or legs of the dead sticking out of the ground. "This makes me sick," said the crusty, opinionated Wade with clenched teeth. "They didn't have the decency to give those poor wretches a proper burial. What an example that Forrest and his gang set of inhumanity and savagery."

Wade and Gooch, following a brief visit to Memphis, returned immediately to Washington to prepare their report. They considered most of the testimony valid, considering that most of the black soldiers interviewed were too unsophisticated to lie. There was no evidence that any of the witnesses had been coached.

In record time the Wade Commission's findings were released. On May 6th some 40,000 copies of its report were released for mass distribution throughout the North. And some were sent to the South.

Immediately, in the South, cries of calculated bias arose. A massive, uniform denial was the reaction of Southern editors. "This falsified document has been put together to prop up failing enthusiasm for the war by Northerners" was the principal conclusion of such papers as *The Mobile Advertiser*, *The Richmond Enquirer*, *The Savannah Republican* and others. "How could illiterate niggers speak in such perfect language?" asked Southern leaders and editors after reading all of the individual testimonies. "Words were put in their mouths," was the common reaction.

General Chalmers, who was far closer to the bloody fighting than Forrest, continued to defend himself. "The enemy made no attempt to surrender. No white flag was elevated; nor was the U.S. flag lowered until pulled down by my men. Many of them were killed while fighting, and many more attempting to escape," reported Chalmers in defense of his actions.

Matt Gallaway, who was deeply angered by the *Wade Report*, asked General Forrest point blank his reaction to the Wade Commission findings and also the clamor of the Northern press. "Matt, these people want my head. I'm being called, 'the Son of the Devil.' What do these people really know about the circumstances of war?"

Forrest, at least for ten seconds, hung his head as if feeling sorry for himself. Then he shook it from side to side slowly.

"General, you don't have any regrets, do you?" said Gallaway.

Forrest, darting his head around to stare directly at Gallaway, replied, "No, oh no! People have got to understand that war means killing, and it is not a pleasant thing. In the thick of a fight, it's kill or be killed. And Matt, most of us want to keep on living. I have absolutely no regrets about what happened to that motley herd of niggers, traitors and low-class Yankees."

But the unpleasant notoriety did bother Forrest. He worried that General Polk would abandon him in order to save himself. On May 16th he contacted his immediate superior, and one of his chief defenders, General Stephen Lee, to tell him that he had retained the services of Judge Phineas T. Scruggs of Memphis — a well-known attorney in West Tennessee and North Mississippi — to take testimony from Captain John Young, the Union officer involved in the truce negotiations and several other Union officers at Fort Pillow on April 12th. Their testimony, Forrest believed, would absolve him from the accusation of master-minding a massacre.

Forrest's spirits were lifted considerably when on May 22nd he received a copy of the Joint Resolution of the Confederate Congress thanking him for his brilliant, successful campaign in Mississippi, West Tennessee and Kentucky.

Months later, in August 1864, President Jefferson Davis wrote to his Secretary of War, J. A. Seddon, "Instead of cruelty, General Forrest, it appears exhibited forbearance and clemency far exceeding the usage of war under like circumstances."

Despite these seeming absolutions from the Confederate leadership in Richmond, Forrest was forced to carry the burden of Fort Pillow not only through war's end, but throughout the remainder of his life. Few references to Forrest in the Northern press throughout the latter part of the 19th century failed to include the phrase, "the infamous General Forrest," somewhere within the content of their articles. Fort Pillow, and Andersonville, the Confederate prison in Georgia where hundreds of Union prisoners died of disease or starvation, would be synonymous in Northerners' minds when reflecting on the atrocities in the Civil War attributed to the Confederates.

20 • The Execution

Tupelo, Mississippi, May 9, 1864

"General Forrest, ... Colonel Brent and his party left at daybreak bound for Richmond," announced Captain Strange. "We gave them an escort to the rail station."

"Good riddance, Strange! I hope we've seen the last of them.

"Ask Matt Gallaway to come in. We need to talk."

Within moments Gallaway walked in and saluted.

"Don't do that, Matt! Save that for formal occasions.

"Now, Matt, I don't quite know what to make of those two days Brent spent here. I first thought Brent and those lawyers he had with him were going to investigate my handing of Fort Pillow. There is such a fuss about it up North. People are calling it 'a massacre by that butcher, Forrest.' That's me.

"But Colonel Brent didn't ask me one thing about that. All he seemed interested in was our desertion rate and the way we handle our paperwork.

"Richmond apparently doesn't want to criticize me to my face about Fort Pillow. But I have no doubt old Bragg, Davis's lackey, and that old, squinty-eyed goat Cooper, the Inspector General, want to put me in the soup. They're putting a rope around me. I know they are. You can see that, can't you Matt?"

"General, maybe you're the sacrificial lamb they've chosen to appease Lincoln and the Yankees. Yes, I definitely think Richmond wants to rein you in. Cooper, Bragg and even Davis represent an old, tired, arrogant administration. They've lost sight of what it takes to win the war."

"Well, Matt, to hell with them! I get results. They should be happy we've regained control in West Tennessee and Mississippi. That's got to mean something."

"Oh, I think it does deep down; but General, you and I know we're dealing with enormous egos. Those West Pointers think you're making a fool of them and they don't like it. I think we've got to play their little game for awhile."

"What do you mean by that?"

"Well, Bragg and his friends like spit-and-polish. You could be the worst field commander in history, but if you keep your records in order and account for every horseshoe and nail, they are forgiving.

"May I make a suggestion, General?"

"Of course, Matt, that's why you're here."

"All right...it's this desertion thing that we must work on. First, we've got to put a total stop to it. And second, when we get the opportunity, we should scour the countryside, and round up those cowards and renegades who are out there laughing at us."

"Matt, you're right. I want desertion stopped cold.

"Get together with Strange, and maybe Anderson, and prepare an order to be sent immediately to all commanders putting them on notice that I expect the harshest punishment possible given to soldiers caught deserting. And tell them I expect results, or they may be facing a court-martial.

"Those paper pushers in Richmond are going to find out mighty damn soon that I'm the best damn record keeper and clerk in the Confederate army."

On May 31, 1864, Forrest received the following orders from his superior, General Stephen Lee:

> *You are directed to take your cavalry into Middle Tennessee to cut General Sherman's railroad supply line between Nashville and Sherman's army now located near Dallas, Georgia. The mission's objective is to relieve pressure on General Joseph E. Johnston's Army of Tennessee that is currently retreating back toward Atlanta.*

General Sherman had his own ideas about handling the elusive Forrest. On June 1st, the day following Lee's order to Forrest, Sherman ordered General Samuel D. Sturgis, commander of the 16th Army Corps, Right Wing, to lead a force numbering over 8,000 soldiers from Memphis into northeastern Mississippi. The primary objective — destroy Forrest's Cavalry. Sherman, in stressing the importance of the expedition to Sturgis, told him, "I want Forrest eliminated. Do you remember your *Bible*, Sturgis? What's the saying? — 'When the shepherd is taken away, the flock will scatter.' That's what will happen if we kill Forrest."

Within hours of Sturgis' departure from Memphis, General Stephen Lee was notified this large Federal force was moving east. Not knowing exactly its destination, Lee's scouts continued tracking its movement. On June 3rd, convinced now of Sturgis' real objective, Lee recalled Forrest's Cavalry which was then in Russellville, Alabama preparing to move north into Middle Tennessee.

Forrest returned to northeast Mississippi on June 5th. Not aware of Sturgis' exact route, Forrest deployed parts of his cavalry in Rienzi, Booneville, Baldwyn and Guntown — all hamlets strung out along the north-south route of the Mobile & Ohio Railroad. Forrest established his headquarters at Booneville, and prepared to attack Sturgis. The site and date of this possible attack was unknown. Forrest's commanders were notified to be "on the ready," and to prevent desertions.

Early morning on June 8th scouts of Colonel W. L. Duff's 8th Mississippi Cavalry operating four miles west of Booneville, captured three deserters from Duff's regiment. At noon they were turned over to Captain John Goodwin, Forrest's Provost, who in turn informed General Forrest that he had three deserters to deal with.

"Goodwin, all commanders know the rules about deserters. I want a speedy court-martial here in Booneville."

"Sir, would tomorrow be acceptable?"

"Hell no, Goodwin, I want it to be held in an hour or two. This is serious business."

"Sir, shall I ask your Adjutant to select a military court?"

"Again, no. Go get these officers...Major Anderson; Captain Bill Forrest, my brother; Colonel Kelley; Captain Morton; and Major Warner McFarland of Colonel Duff's staff! Have then conduct the trial over in the stationmaster's office.

"Goodwin...no mistakes! You are in total charge of organizing this court-martial group, and getting those cowards horse-collared.

"Keep me informed of any problems. I'll be here in my quarters all afternoon."

Promptly at 2:00 p.m. the court-martial board appointed by Forrest assembled at the Mobile & Ohio Railroad station. Colonel Kelley, being the ranking officer, was elected president of the Court.

The board members discussed first the trial procedures; then briefly those sections in the Confederate *Articles of War* pertaining to punishments applicable to deserters. They agreed that if any of the accused were found guilty their options were death, flogging, imprisonnment, hard labor, ball-and-chain, forfeiture of pay and allowances, or discharge from service.

Colonel Kelley, after this brief discussion, pointed out that the punishment would be up to General Forrest or possibly a higher command. "Our role is to determine the guilt or innocence of the prisoners," Kelley said. "We will try to ascertain the facts, and to give these soldiers an opportunity to explain why they chose to desert. Do you all agree?"

"Well, Colonel Kelley, desertion is desertion. They all know the penalty," said the blunt, outspoken Captain Bill Forrest. "What difference does it make what their reasons were?"

"No, no, no," said Major McFarland. "Every soldier is entitled to defend himself. Let's be fair and listen to what they've got to say."

All agreed that this was acceptable — even Captain Forrest.

"Captain Goodwin, please bring in the first prisoner," requested Colonel Kelley.

Within a minute, Captain Goodwin and one of his Provost's staff led into the stationmaster's office Private Oliver Tuttle. He was pale and shaking uncontrollably from fear. He had a tangled, weather-beaten face with pronounced pits that apparently were caused by smallpox. The records indicated he was 37 years old, but the stoop shouldered Tuttle looked 57 if one were to guess.

"Sit down, Private Tuttle," requested Colonel Kelley. "We want to ask you a few questions.

"Private, you read the *Oath of Allegiance* before joining the service, didn't you?" asked Kelley.

"No, sir, I didn't read it. It was read to me. I can't read."

"Do you remember what it said about punishment if you violated the oath?"

"No, sir, I do not. When they conscripted me, they read it real fast to a whole bunch of us they had rounded up."

"Private Tuttle," asked Major Anderson, "When were you conscripted and where?"

"January 4, 1864 in Ripley, Mississippi."

"Do you have a family, Tuttle?" continued Anderson.

"Yes, sir, a wife and two boys, 13 and 15."

"Tell us why you deserted your unit."

"I did not want to leave, no, sir, but I needed to help at home. The boys just couldn't handle the Spring planting; and without me around for a few weeks, they'd starve to death. You know how bad things are."

"Then why didn't you ask your superior officers for a furlough," interjected Captain Morton who was listening intently.

"No one was allowed to leave, even for a few days. I don't know why. The officers know that many of us have families near starvation, and need help."

"What were your intentions concerning your military obligations," asked Major McFarland.

"Sir, I would have come back. Yes, sir, I intended to come back. Lots of others have gone home for awhile, then come back without a big fuss being created. I didn't think leaving was a serious offense."

"Well, Tuttle, it sounds to me like you fled in the face of the enemy," said Captain Bill Forrest. "You knew the Federals were moving this way from Memphis, didn't you?"

"No, sir, I didn't know that. I wouldn't have left with Daniel and Floyd if I knew a skirmish was coming up. No, sir, I'd have stayed and fought."

Then Colonel Kelley asked after a short silence, "Do any of you have additional questions of Private Tuttle?"

"Yes, Colonel, I do," said Captain Morton.

"Private, are you a church member?"

"Yes, sir, I'm a Baptist. Belong to the Holiness Baptist Church at Cuyler's Creek. I've always gone to preachin'. I have given myself to God."

Then, Colonel Kelley in a forceful voice asked Private Tuttle, "Are you now willing to give of yourself totally to our military cause, and to see it through to the end?"

"Yes, sir, I feel poorly about the trouble I've caused. If given a chance, I plan to face the enemy with courage."

"Are there any other questions?" asked Kelley. "If not,

Captain Goodwin, please escort Private Tuttle outside, and bring in the next prisoner."

The second deserter was Private Daniel Curbo, a 24-year old conscript from nearby Tippah, Mississippi. Whereas Tuttle was a small, thin man, Curbo was a six feet tall, thick-necked and robust looking soldier with a shock of coal-black hair, a thick mustache and a fleshy nose. He smelled of sweat when he entered the room. He had a nervous smile on his face.

The Curbo interview was similar to Tuttle's. The only difference on personal background was that Curbo had a wife, but no children. At midpoint in the interview, he asked for a drink of water. He appeared to be having a chest seizure as he wrapped his huge arms around his chest for about 15 seconds.

Colonel Kelley asked, "Private, are you all right?"

"Yes, sir, I'm just scared."

The questioning continued for another five minutes; then he too was escorted out by Captain Goodwin.

The third deserter was Private Floyd Flewellen. As he entered the room the members of the court were all astonished to see a young, fair-skinned boy who looked no older than 13 or 14. Colonel Kelley had the most astonished look. He asked, "Has a mistake been made here, Captain Goodwin?"

"No, sir, this fellow is 16. He's a private in Colonel Duff's 8th Mississippi Cavalry."

"Sit down, Private Flewellen," said Kelly. "I'm anxious to hear your story."

Flewellen had long blond hair which hung almost to his shoulders. He was shy, and had difficulty making eye contact with members of the court.

Colonel Kelley again led off in the questioning.

"Private Flewellen, how long have you been in the service?"

"Four months and two weeks."

"Did you enlist or are you a conscript?"

"I enlisted, sir. Me and three of my friends ran away

from home when we heard General Forrest was recruiting in this part of northeast Mississippi. We were afraid the war would end, and we'd miss it."

Then Major McFarland asked, "Now, you've just told us you were anxious to serve; so why did you desert so quickly after you joined up?"

"I don't know, sir. I guess it was because the army wasn't like I thought it would be. And I missed my Ma and my two aunts and my farm animals.

"The older men teased me all the time because I didn't have to shave, and because I told them I hadn't ever had horizontal recreation with a girl. And they were always tying my wet pants legs in knots when I washed them. I don't think they liked me."

"Will you promise to serve out your enlistment now that we've brought you back?" inquired Major Anderson in a sympathetic tone.

"Yes, sir, I hope I'll be given another chance. And I promise I won't let the teasing bother me."

Colonel Kelley then asked, "Do any of you have additional questions to ask this private? All right, hearing none, I shall ask Captain Goodwin to escort Private Flewellen out; then we shall deliberate for awhile on our recommendations to General Forrest."

The court adjourned for five minutes, then Colonel Kelley call it back to order.

"Major McFarland, please tell us your feelings about what you've just heard, and your recommendation," asked Colonel Kelley.

"I'm a line officer, Colonel; and I have explained to my men over and over again the seriousness of desertion. Unless I back it up by making examples out of these soldiers, how can I enforce any discipline? My men won't take me seriously."

"Well, what do you suggest we do with them?" inquired Kelley.

"I'd like to see them in the stockade when we're not fighting. And when we are fighting, I'd like to put them up front."

"I like that suggestion," added Captain Bill Forrest. "If we could flog them too in front of the troops, that would make an impression. I might vote to execute Private Curbo, but not those other two. They are really pitiful creatures."

"Does anyone here vote for execution other than Captain Bill Forrest?" inquired Kelley in a soft voice.

"What do you say, Captain Morton?"

"I'd like to see them confined for a month or so; then put to the hardest work we can find for them. I will not vote for execution, even though it could be justified under the *Articles of War*."

"And Major Anderson?"

"I'll go along with John Morton and Major McFarland. Both of their suggestions are reasonable. And how about you, Colonel Kelley? Which way are you leaning?"

"I recommend clemency and mercy on those three, even though all of you have made some reasonable suggestions. I guess being a man of *God* compels me to be compassionate in these circumstances. It's war...I understand that. The humane thing to do is often dismissed in the name of victory at all costs. That's just the way I feel.

"What I shall do, with your permission, is to present the alternatives to General Forrest. I shall not emphasize my own feelings over any of yours in this matter.

"Is that acceptable, gentlemen?"

All nodded in agreement.

"All right then, this court-martial board is dismissed. Thank you."

It was just after 4:00 p.m. when Colonel Kelley and the others appeared before General Forrest at the latter's headquarters.

Kelley explained the findings of the court to Forrest who sat on the camp stool with a look of amazement on his face. Then, not waiting for Kelley to finish his summary, Forrest jumped up and said in an exasperated tone of voice, "Goddamnit, I want to put a stop to this desertion, and you have not helped a damn bit.

"I want to put on a big show tomorrow morning, and I want every last soldier here and around Booneville assembled to watch the execution of those cowards. I will make an example of them to scare any of the others who may be thinking of deserting us.

"Do you understand my thinking on this? If not, may I point out that one of these days we'll meet the enemy, and we won't have enough men. We'll get whipped like hell!

"Now, pick a firing squad of twelve. Four marksmen for each coward. No coffins. Just shoot them, push them in a hole and cover them up. Simple! Quick! Effective!

"Captain Goodwin, as Provost Marshall, you're in charge. Notify all units they are to assemble promptly at 7:30 a.m. in the morning. Make a formation plan where every soldier can see these cowards shot.

"When it's over, no one breathing out there should have any doubts about what will happen to them if they desert or run from the enemy.

"That's all! Dismissed! I will not listen to any more on this subject."

The three condemned were held in a railroad box car on a siding at the edge of town. Colonel Kelley assigned Sergeant Raymond Stock, an ordained Baptist minister, to pray with the prisoners throughout the night.

Few of the soldiers camped in Booneville slept soundly that night. Periodically in the stillness of night, they could here the sounds of singing coming from the boxcar.

Guards posted outside reported that several times during the night Sergeant Stock led the condemned in singing the old hymn, *Let Us Pass Over the River, and Rest Under the Shade of Trees*. And they heard over and over again the recitation of the *Lord's Prayer*. And occasionally they heard moaning and sobbing, and the consoling voice of Sergeant Stock telling them they were going to a better and more peaceful world.

Corporal David Eacret of the Provost staff commented

to Captain Goodwin, "We were on guard from 8:00 p.m. last night to 7:00 a.m. this morning, some 11 hours. But it seemed like a week. It was so awful. I'm sick to my stomach and can't eat. Those poor devils! They aren't any different than the rest of us. Can't anything be done to help them?"

Goodwin looked down at his shoes, shook his head from side to side and said, "No" in a muffled voice.

The area selected for the execution was a dried up swamp. The weeds had been cut by Goodwin's staff, and the three graves dug at daybreak. The latter were seven feet long, two feet wide and three feet deep. The location of the graves stood out prominently because the earth had been piled up in mounds behind them.

Captain Goodwin, nervous that General Forrest might not like the arrangements, drove his Provost's staff unmercifully to get the field ready. He had them paint with lime two parallel lines exactly 100 yards long and 75 yards apart. He calculated that 375 soldiers, double-file, could line each side of the field, The front line, facing directly the condemned men, was 75 yards across. Here the officers would stand. Goodwin estimated that all of General Forrest's officers could line up single file along this line.

The designated marksmen had been practicing firing since dawn on the other side of Booneville. The volley of fire could be heard clearly throughout the encampment.

Goodwin's plan designated positions to be occupied by each of the units based in Booneville. Monitors were dispatched by Goodwin to direct the various companies and platoons to their assigned positions. Promptly at 7:30 a.m. all units were in formation.

The excitable Goodwin with his squad of handpicked guards marched to the boxcar where the condemned were held with rifles at shoulder arms. Goodwin entered the boxcar apprehensively. He was greeted by Sergeant Stock. The condemned were huddled on the boxcar's floor holding each other's hands. Their eyes were sunken from the hours of crying and anguish while waiting their fate. Goodwin kept his composure despite obvious discomfort from viewing the wretched sight.

Goodwin said quietly, "Soldiers, you will be permitted to keep your personal effects — pictures, newspaper clippings and identification bracelets, Bibles and so forth.

"Do you have any questions?"

Private Curbo said, "Sir, will our families be notified?"

"Yes, they will."

"Thank you, sir."

Within ten minutes Captain Goodwin and his staff arrived at the execution site with the condemned soldiers. With their hands tied behind their backs the three pathetic looking creatures were led to the middle of the field. Each, in turn, was positioned in front of a grave.

The 12 marksmen were at that particular moment stationed off to one side of the field awaiting Captain Goodwin's signal to proceed in single file to the designated firing line drawn exactly 20 yards in front of the condemned.

Private Tuttle, the oldest of the three, was swaying back and forth. It appeared his face was creviced even more than the day before at the court-martial hearing. He stared almost blankly as if he had totally removed himself from his surroundings. His body seemed to quake slightly.

Private Curbo, clad in a torn, gray tunic, started to kneel in prayer, but was pulled to his feet by Captain Goodwin's guards. He fidgeted and moaned, "Dear wife, please do not forget me. We shall be joined together some day in Heaven." He repeated it over and over until the fatal explosion of rifles some five minutes later.

Private Flewellen, the 16-year old, beardless youth, looked far younger. He was just 5-foot-3, and he looked so woeful in his ill-fitting uniform. He was erect and composed, and appeared unaware he was about to die.

Captain Goodwin strode rapidly to the middle of the field. He stopped abruptly, turned toward General

Forrest, and saluted.

"General Forrest would like to say a few words," announced Goodwin in a crisp, loud voice.

Forrest, in full dress uniform, walked 30 yards out in the open field so all troops could see and hear him. Then, he said, "Soldiers, desertion will not be tolerated. You will all do your duty and uphold your allegiance to the Confederacy and maintain your self-respect as men."

Forrest paused briefly and scanned the crowd. Then he said, "Soldiers, because of the extreme youth of Private Flewellen, he shall be spared. Guards! Please escort the Private from the field.

"Captain Goodwin, proceed with the execution of the others."

On General Forrest's command the two condemned were blindfolded. Eight marksmen were selected from the original pool of 12. The other four marched off the field.

Captain Goodwin stood to the left side of his marksmen, prepared to give the signal to fire.

The 800 witnesses to this macabre scene were motionless as they nervously watched for Captain Goodwin's handkerchief to drop.

Within seconds Goodwin dropped the handkerchief. Instantly, a loud, ragged volley of gunfire burst forth; the two condemned deserters fell lifeless next to their graves.

Unceremoniously, members of the grave digging detail dragged the bodies of Private Tuttle and Private Curbo into the graves; picked up their shovels and started throwing dirt over the bodies. Within five minutes the graves were closed. All that remained in view of the stunned, solemn-faced witnesses were two small mounds now just barely visible in this dry prairie swamp.

The troops disbanded silently. They had just seen an example of General Forrest's heavy discipline. If any one there had intentions of deserting before the execution, seeing that horrifying spectacle no doubt erased such design.

21 • Brice's Cross Roads

Booneville, Mississippi, June 9, 1864, 5:00 p.m.

"General Stephen Lee has just arrived by train from Columbus, Mississippi, General Forrest," announced Captain Strange. "He's on his way over."

"Go escort him here. Ask him if he wants a billet for tonight."

"Yes, sir!" replied Strange who quietly headed toward the depot.

Within ten minutes, General Lee entered Forrest's headquarters, and shook hands with Forrest.

"This is a quick visit, General Forrest. Our intelligence reports that Sturgis' army is moving in this direction. It appears that they're going to try to destroy the Mobile & Ohio Railroad. We cannot let that happen. We need that link from Corinth, Mississippi down to the Gulf of Mexico. You know how much we use it to move troops and supplies up and down the length of the Mississippi.

"The enemy was spotted just south of Ripley, Mississippi early this morning. At the pace they're moving, they could be somewhere in this vicinity by early tomorrow.

"Let's look at this map, Forrest. Their present location puts them on the Guntown Road. Now look here! In all probability they'll cross the Pontotoc Road at this place marked Brice's Cross Roads," said Lee pointing at the map with his forefinger.

Forrest said, "That's about 18 or 19 miles from here. Bell's Brigade is up at Rienzi, about 25 miles or so from Brice's; and Colonel Lyons and Colonel Johnson have their troops at Baldwyn. They're the closest to the Cross Roads. Only six miles, more or less. They could get there first if they're prepared to move out at dawn."

"Well, Forrest, your mission is to delay Sturgis as long as you can. I need a day or two to assemble my main force. They're scattered from Columbus to Meridian, Mississippi.

"Harass them all day tomorrow, Forrest. Keep them pinned down and away from the railroad at all costs. I'll be waiting for your reports.

"Now there's no time to spare for either of us. The train is being held for me for the trip back to Columbus. I must go.

"Forrest, good luck."

With that, Lee and his aides left.

Forrest called Captain Strange into his quarters. "Get word to all commanders to be prepared to march at first light tomorrow. Take three days rations. Make certain that everyone realizes we have to beat Sturgis to Brice's Cross Roads. That means double-quick tomorrow morning."

At 8:00 p.m. Forrest received a message that Sturgis' forces were camped at Stubbs Farm, 12 miles east of Ripley on the Guntown Road, and only about nine miles northwest of Brice's Cross Roads.

June 10, 1864

Colonel Rucker's troops at Booneville had reveille at 4:00 a.m. to prepare to leave for Brice's Cross Roads. Captain Morton and Captain Rice also rose at 4:00 a.m. to prepare their artillery batteries to leave,.

At 5:00 a.m. all of Forrest's troops at Booneville were mounted. General Forrest requested Colonel Kelley to give a prayer. Kelley then proceeded down the long column of mounted horsemen, repeating at least four times:

Oh God, be kind to our officers and soldiers. Protect us. Fight for us. Give us your blessing and victory will be ours. Give every soldier the courage to fight for our glorious Confederacy, and to uphold its principles for which we have all pledged allegiance.
Soldiers, God be with you!

At 5:05 a.m. General Forrest signaled, "Forward!"

Bell's Brigade at Rienzi moved out at 4:00 a.m. for its 25-mile march. Colonel Lyon's and Colonel Johnson's troops at Baldwyn, located just six miles from Brice's Cross Roads, left just after 6:00 a.m.

The combined force at Forrest's Cavalry was 3200 soldiers and eight artillery pieces. Within a matter of a few hours they were to engage a combined Union infantry and cavalry army of 7900 men and 23 artillery pieces.

General Sturgis' Union cavalry mounted that morning at 5:30 a.m. and rode out from its camp toward Brice's Cross Roads. His large infantry force didn't march until 7:00 a.m.

Brice's Cross Roads was located in the low, undulating prairie of northeast Mississippi's rich agricultural zone called the "Black Belt." William Brice's house and his store were the only structures at the intersection. His property was surrounded for several miles by dense thickets of scraggly, stunted blackjack oaks and thick underbrush. Similar to the battlefield at Chickamauga, the heavy growth made off-road maneuvering difficult for cavalry movements on horseback and also difficult for soldiers to see their targets.

The Cross Roads was on a slight rise, just 41 feet in elevation above the narrow, meandering Tishomingo Creek which was one-quarter mile northwest of William Brice's house on the road to Ripley, Mississippi. A narrow wooden bridge provided the Creek's crossing point for Sturgis' advancing army.

Sturgis' army had faced nothing but harsh Spring weather since it left Memphis on June 1st. It had rained every day. Roads were almost impassable causing frequent delays. Near Ripley on June 8th Union army wagon trains and artillery caissons and limbers sunk in deep mud. Horses were exhausted and some had died. Sturgis' troops were dispirited.

The Union army's leader, General Samuel D. Sturgis (West Point, 1846), 41, a Pennsylvanian by birth, was a veteran of the Mexican War. His two principal senior officers were: Brigadier General Benjamin H. Grierson, 38, a pre-war Illinois school teacher and merchant who commanded the Union cavalry; and Colonel William L. McMillen, 34, an Ohio physician who led the Union infantry.

The day before the battle at Brice's Cross Roads, the discouraged Sturgis asked his key subordinates: "Shall we turn back?"

Grierson said, "Yes, we've lost the element of surprise. Every Confederate sympathizer in Mississippi has reported our movements to the Rebels. We should abandon the expedition."

"Nonsense," responded the angered McMillen. "To turn back would be a disgrace. I don't want that blemish on my record. The charge of cowardice is bound to stick to us. I am against the idea."

Sturgis considered what these officers advised, then decided to proceed. He realized that his military career as a Union officer had gone absolutely nowhere to date. If he backed away, he reasoned, he would sink even lower in the Union army command structure.

On the morning of June 10th Grierson's Cavalry — mostly soldiers from Illinois, Indiana, Iowa, Missouri, New Jersey and Pennsylvania — reached Brice's Cross Roads first. The time was 9:45 a.m. Colonel George E. Waring's brigade had 1500 soldiers and Colonel Edward F. Winslow's had 1800.

Grierson's forces made their first contact with a small, advance party of Forrest's Cavalry about one mile beyond the Cross Roads. Shortly thereafter, Colonel Harlan B. Lyon's 3rd Brigade of General Buford's all-Kentucky Division, arrived on the scene along with General Forrest's Escort Company. Lyon's troops had ridden from nearby Baldwin. Skirmishing was light. Lyon's mission was to stall the advance of the Union army long enough to give Colonel Tyree Bell's troops and Morton's and Rice's artillery batteries time to reach the Cross Roads.

Forrest's Cavalry, as had been their custom since early in the war, fought largely dismounted as infantry. But Colonel W.L. Duff's Mississippians were kept mounted to protect the left flank of Forrest's forces which by 1:00 p.m. had been deployed in a line extending across the Guntown Road.

The first Confederate battle line, about seven-tenths of a mile east of the Cross Roads, had Colonel Edmund Rucker's 6th Brigade on the left; Colonel Hylan B. Lyon's 3rd Brigade in the center; and Colonel William A. Johnson's Brigade of Alabamians on the right. The line extended one and one-quarter miles across. Forrest's troops were hidden in the black oak thickets masking their actual numbers and movements.

The Union troops were positioned behind fences on the edge of dense thickets at a distance of some 1000 to 1500 feet from the Confederate line. Colonel Winslow's troops were on the Union's right, and Colonel Waring's troops on the left. These cavalry troops had chosen to fight dismounted too.

General Forrest moved up and down the Confederate line barking out commands in preparation for his army's first major attack. After intensive, but ineffective firing, the Union cavalry forces ran low on ammunition.

McMillen's Union infantry was still enroute to Brice's Cross Roads trying desperately to get there to reinforce Grierson's exhausted cavalry. The heat of the early afternoon was intense. The 85° temperature and high humidity were devastating to the advancing Union infantry that had been marched "double quick" for the nine miles distance to reach the battlefield. When McMillen's infantry got to the Tishomingo Creek's bridge they were exhausted. Colonel George Hoge, commander of the 113th Illinois Infantry protested, "My infantry is wilted and suffering from heat stroke. We aren't in the best condition to fight." He was told to keep going.

General Grierson requested permission from General Sturgis to withdraw his cavalry troops from the front lines. "We're low in ammunition," he complained. "Where is the infantry?"

Forrest's forces applied intense pressure as they moved forward. Fighting in the deep underbrush they pushed the Union army to a second battle line just 1000 feet from Brice's Cross Roads. Forrest quickly assessed the physical condition of Sturgis' troops and their apparent ammunition problems. "Give them no chance to rest and regroup," he told his commanders.

Shortly after 2:00 p.m. Forrest rode along the second battle line behind Bell's brigade of Tennesseans, Lyon's Kentuckians and Rucker's Mississippians shouting encouragement. "Forward...forward boys. Give 'em Hell! Come on boys! Aim at their knees! Bullets rise first, then arc downward. We've got them on the run, boys! Charge 'em out! Make it hotter than the blazes of Hell and damnation for them!"

When Forrest spotted Morton's Battery temporarily inactive on the front edge of a clearing, he stopped and dismounted. "What's that awful smell, Morton?" inquired Forrest. "Is that stink weed or wild garlic?"

"It's garlic, I think, General. My father used to say that garlic and sin will likely be with us until this old world goes up in smoke or becomes a frozen ball."

"Well, Morton, let's get this fight over with so you don't have to stand in that stuff."

"You're right, General," said Morton grinning.

"What's happening now, Morton? Your unit isn't firing."

"We're waiting for more ammunition to be brought up, sir. It shouldn't be more than ten minutes."

"Then I'll rest with you a bit, Morton. My damn boils are acting up. It's painful to ride a horse."

"General, I sure hope there aren't any copperheads or rattlesnakes in here. Those slimy devils scare me half to death. If one of them came near me, so help me I'd run out into that open field and take my chances."

"Well, Morton, with all that noise no snakes are about

to show their ugly heads. I'm more worried about chiggers."

"General, are you certain about the snakes?"

"Obviously, you're not a country boy, otherwise you would know something about critters that slither around. Heh-heh-heh!"

Forrest then propped his back against a tree to relax. He closed his eyes for a moment, then said, "Morton, just think, a few miles from here the Chickasaws attacked De Soto's army in 1541. That's 323 years ago. It was a great disaster for De Soto. His whole army was taken by surprise. Those Indians hit De Soto while his men were asleep. They brought in burning wood concealed in clay pots with which they set fire to the huts. Only about a dozen Spaniards were killed, but old De Soto lost 60 horses, most of his hogs and a lot of his provisions. If it hadn't rained that night, the Chickasaws would probably have attacked again.

"Morton, I could have used some Chickasaws in this army. I liked the way they took care of things."

"What happened to the Chickasaws that used to live around here, General?"

"Well, most of the tribes like the Chickasaws that had large landholdings were either bribed or scared off by politicians like Andrew Jackson and his friends who wanted the land for themselves. I remember seeing it when I was a kid. Whole bands of Choctaws, Chickasaws and Creeks were forced to move west. It was a sorry sight."

"I didn't know that, General."

"Yes, Morton, Indians roamed all over these parts. That creek down the slope from Brice's house is called Tishomingo Creek. It was named after the old warrior, Chief Tishomingo. He lived over near the town of Pontotoc until he and the other Chickasaws were forced to migrate west of the Mississippi in 1832."

"You know a lot about this country, General."

"Well, I should. One of the advantages I have over

those Union boys is that I know practically every square foot of North Mississippi and Central and West Tennessee. I lived in a lot of places growing up, and I have also done business with folks in these parts."

Within minutes Colonel Kelley rode up and yelled so he could be heard above the noise, "Are we ready?"

Forrest yelled back, "Almost. We're waiting for Morton's fresh supply of ammunition. We want every unit to move together."

"Good," replied Kelley. "I'm an old firehorse. The hair on the back of my neck stands up when I'm excited."

"Well, Parson, don't shit your pants! It's not as if we haven't been through this before."

"Now, here comes old Abe Buford — all 275 pounds of him. Look at him huff-and-puff! He's sweating like an old sow."

"General, we're ready to go. What are your orders?" said the gruff, but genial Kentuckian.

"Buford, first of all, slow down. I can't afford to lose you."

"Well, thank you, General Forrest, that's the first compliment you ever paid me," said Buford patting himself on the back.

"Now Buford, I want you to order Colonel Bell to outflank the Federal right line when I give the order to charge. If he can get behind their line, he can intercept those Federal infantry and artillery still waiting to cross the Creek."

"Good! That's a good plan," Buford said as he turned, mounted his black stallion and rode off.

Forrest was soon informed that all was ready. "Tell the bugler to sound, Charge!" yelled the excited Forrest.

Colonel Kelley, usually the most thoughtful and composed of the senior officers let loose a primal scream that rose above the battlefield noise. "Eee yow! – eee yow!" came from the mouth of the gaunt, sallow-faced Methodist parson. "Kill them! Send them on their way to Hell! From Judges, Chapter 15, 'And he, Samson, found a fresh jawbone of an ass, and put forth his hand and took it, and smote a thousand men therewith.'"

"Goddamn, Morton, don't you wish we had 3000 more just like him?" said the amused Forrest.

The Confederates bolted forward in a rush toward those Union infantry units now in position in the front lines. Surprisingly few Confederates fell in the explosion of rifle and cannon fire from Sturgis' forces.

The forces of Buford, Lyon, Rucker, Warren, Morton, Rice and most of General Forrest's personal staff moved quickly to the front of the compact second Union battle line close to William Brice's house.

Colonel George Hoge's 2nd Brigade of Illinois soldiers resisted the Confederate pressure for about one hour; then Hoge's line started to sag. At first there was minimal panic among Hoge's troops; then after tremendous rifle fire and artillery fire from Forrest's troops, the panic up and down the Union line was total. Hoge's soldiers began running pell-mell down the long slope in the direction of Tishomingo Creek to escape. But in all the confusion to escape, Hoge's soldiers ran straight into their own reinforcements — some of whom were struggling to get up the slope to Brice's Cross Roads and others trying to cross the narrow wooden bridge across the Creek. Union artillery ordered up to the front line by General Sturgis was stalled on the crowded road approaching the bridge.

Colonel Clark Barteau's 2nd Tennessee Cavalry in Tyree Bell's Brigade successfully circled behind Sturgis' Union forces, creating havoc on the Union's rear columns. Barteau's attack nullified any hopes of Sturgis mounting a major counterattack against the Confederates.

At 6:00 p.m. the Union army, badly disorganized and demoralized, was in full retreat. Troops were running for their lives. Some scrambled through the thick brush; others were in the Creek trying to detour the crowded bridge route. While this panic was occurring, Morton's and Rice's artillery with their eight guns fired round after round toward the road leading to the Creek until nearly dark. Above the artillery fire could be heard the yelling and screaming of the frightened and confused Union army trying to escape.

The panic was not just confined to the retreating white Union soldiers who had been in the front lines of the fighting. Soldiers of the 55th U.S. Colored Infantry of Colonel Edward Bouton's 3rd Brigade had been positioned near the bridge in the late afternoon waiting orders to move up. Witnessing the retreat of their white comrades caused great fear among the black troops. The incident at Fort Pillow was fresh in their minds. General Sturgis in the preceding weeks had encouraged his commanders to create an attitude of revenge among their black troops. But now, believing the worst might happen to them if captured by Forrest, most dropped their weapons and scattered in the thicket to escape.

Forrest's pursuit of the enemy continued unabated until total darkness. Just after 8:00 p.m. he ordered his troops rested. He informed his commanders, "We've done all we can for the moment. Have your soldiers fed, then rested for a few hours. We'll be in the saddle at 1:00 a.m. Then, by God, we're going to run them down."

As ordered, the troops moved out at 1:00 a.m. to continue the pursuit the remainder of that night, and all the following day, Saturday, June 11th. All along the Union retreat route were abandoned wagons, artillery, rifles, medical supplies, food and horses and mules. Forrest's cavalrymen chased and captured many small isolated squads of enemy soldiers as they ran across open fields trying to reach the woods.

By nightfall on June 11th Forrest's troops reached Davis' Mill, just north of the hamlet of Salem. General Forrest had lived in Salem as a young boy after his family abandoned his birthplace in Chapel Hill, Tennessee.

Forrest, after hours in the saddle, dismounted at 8:00 p.m. Within minutes, while giving orders to Colonel Barteau, he collapsed from exhaustion. For the next hour he was unconscious. Aides hovered over him worried that he was quite ill. But to their relief he regained consciousness and rested for another hour to regain his strength. Then he got up, ate a light supper as was his custom; and when finished announced he was retiring for the night. It had been 41 hours since he had led his troops out of Booneville bound for Brice's Cross Roads.

On Sunday morning, June 12th, Forrest ordered part of his cavalry to pursue the remnants of Sturgis' army as far as the Tennessee state line. He rested the remainder of that day, then saddled up to head back to Brice's Cross Roads to savor his victory.

22 • The Days After

Brice's Cross Roads, Saturday, June 11, 1864

At noon Major Charles Anderson summoned those officers of General Forrest's staff who had not joined the pursuit of Sturgis to meet in William Brice's house. Forrest had left Anderson in charge of cleaning the battlefield, and completing the necessary post-battle paperwork to deliver to General Stephen Lee's headquarters in Columbus, Mississippi.

"Gentleman, we've got to work fast. You know General Forrest's penchant for organizational detail. He'll be back here tomorrow night, or Monday. And he'll expect everything tidied up so we can move on from here.

"I won't ask you to stay long, Dr. Cowan. You've got your hands full over at the field hospital. I hear we've got nearly 400 of our own soldiers in your care."

"No, Major Anderson, we've got about 200 right now. This morning we transported about 150 by wagon to Guntown. Most of them were in pretty good shape as far as traveling is concerned. Then, sad to say, about 25 died overnight or this morning. Actually, some of those fellows were dead when the litter bearers brought them in."

"Do you have enough help, Dr. Cowan?"

'No, I don't; but I guess we'll get by. I could use a few more orderlies. But don't send me any boys. Most throw up when the see a stomach with the guts hanging out, or when they witness sawing off an arm or leg. It isn't a pretty sight as you know."

"Well, thank you, Dr. Cowan. I'll check with you later in the afternoon."

Anderson had a check list, and he continued going over the tasks to be accomplished.

"Colonel Bell has agreed to supervise the cleaning off of the battlefield. You know — scouring the thickets for wounded boys still out there; tagging the dead; and collecting the hundreds of rifles, ammunition, horses and mules, wagons and all the other material out there."

"Major Anderson, I have asked Major Rambaut, our Chief of Commissary; Captain Severson, our Quartermaster; and Major Russell, our Chief of Ordnance to assist me. I'll work out the details," said Colonel Bell.

"Now, I've brought along with me, Captain Sylvester Henry, to be in charge of burying the dead. He's outside with his detail ready to start. And Captain Goodwin also has some prisoners available to help dig graves."

"That's good, Colonel Bell, thank you.

"Now, one more thing, Colonel. I'd like Captain Dashiell, our Paymaster, to be in charge of handling the personal effects we find on our dead. Please ask Captain Henry to do a good search of each body. We'll try to get those personal effects distributed to the families when we have time.

"It may surprise all of you how many of our soldiers have given their legal wills to Captain Dashiell for just such an occasion. "

"What about the dead Union boys, Major Anderson?" asked Colonel Bell.

"Colonel, General Forrest's policy has always been to request Union burial details to come forward, and dispose of their own. We can assign some of the prisoners to help bury the dead. One thing you must consider though is that the Federals lost far more than we did. So we can't observe the same burial protocol with their dead we do with ours. Have them dig mass graves; pile the dead in them; and cover them up quickly."

"All right, Major Anderson, I'll take care of it."

"Well, gentlemen, we've got about six hours of daylight left today, and we've got all day Sunday to get the battlefield cleaned up. And I'm organizing a large detail to go out and recover all those wagons and mules and supplies abandoned by the Federals between here and Ripley, Mississippi. There's got to be plenty of good booty for us out there. Keep me informed of any problems."

Captain Sylvester Henry, the 28-year old aide to Colonel Bell and former whiskey salesman from Lynchburg, Tennessee; and his 22-year old assistant, Sergeant Alexander Thurston, a pre-war college student at the University of Alabama, were busy barking out orders to some 50 soldiers assigned to canvass the battlefield for dead and wounded.

"Corporal Tankersley, I want your squad to spread out through that thicket over there and move east about 300 yards. Look carefully under the bushes. We had a lot of men in there yesterday.

"And you, Corporal Morrissy, form a search party down that slope toward Tishomingo Creek. There was some heavy skirmishing there. Blow a whistle if you find someone still alive. We'll rush some medical aid men in there quick.

"When you finish, report back here for another assignment.

"Look around here, Sergeant! Chris' sakes! Look at some of those dead boys they've pulled out of the woods. I sure hope I don't end up like them.

"Look at this one if you can stomach it — a bullet just under his left eye which exited the back of his head. And look over there at that poor devil! Look at his blood-caked face. Gee...zus, it makes me sick if you want God's truth."

"Captain Henry! I've got one over here with a bullet hole right through the bridge of his nose. Perfectly centered! What a shot that was," said Sergeant Thurston as if to say to his superior that he had found a more bizarre fatal wound than Captain Henry.

"Let's get them buried quick. Those miserable horseflies are swarming all over them. And Gee...zus, the smell of burnt flesh. So help me, Thurston, I'm going to throw up," said Henry as he clamped his arms around his stomach as a gesture to make his point.

"Where do you want the graves dug, Captain Henry?" asked Sergeant Thurston nonchalantly.

"I think in that clearing just below Brice's house. It really depends on how many bodies we've got and how hard this goddamn ground is."

"Well, Captain, so far we've got 75 Confederate boys. But I know there are more we haven't found yet. After our squads finish scouring the woods and the creek bottoms, we'll have got a better idea."

"Now, Thurston, that preliminary count is only our boys, isn't it?"

"Yes, sir, the enemy's burial detail is taking the Yank's dead down across the Creek to a clearing about a mile from here. They are stacking them in wagons like cord wood."

In a half-hour Captain Henry had selected the precise location for the Confederate graves. He summoned the 40 spadesmen selected from the Union prisoners, and assigned four of his own soldiers to act as guards and supervisors.

"Have them dig a trench about six feet wide, two and one-half feet deep, and a hundred feet long," ordered Captain Henry.

"Should we dig a separate trench for the 12 dead officers we've got?" asked Sergeant Thurston.

"Yes, I guess so. General Forrest may raise royal hell if we don't give them special treatment."

"That's some special treatment!" whispered Sergeant Thurston to himself.

"Captain Henry...Captain Henry...I've got several bodies over here with their eyes wide open," shouted Private David Hummer of Bell's Brigade. "I tried to close them, but I couldn't. What should I do?"

"After rigor mortis sets in, Hummer, there's not a goddamn thing you can do. I wish I had some coins to set in their sockets. It's frightening to have the dead staring at you. Put them on their sides in the trench when it's ready. I don't want them looking up at us. It sends a goddamn chill down my spine. You know that saying — "But for the grace of God lies me!"'

"Get the shoes off those two over yonder. They've walked as far as they're ever going to walk, those poor sonafabiches. And make damn sure the Quartermaster's boys get those shoes."

Waiting for burial

Captain Henry, as he was surveying the work details, spotted a soldier taking a pocket watch from a body and putting it in his pocket. "Hey you, what in the hell do you think you're doing? You're stealing a goddamn watch. You know the orders! All personal effects are to be turned over to Captain Dashiell. What's your name soldier?"

"Sir, I wasn't stealing anything. I put it in my pocket for safekeeping until we finished."

"Yes, I bet you did. Now what's your name and rank?"

"I'm Private Wilmer Haggard, 4th Alabama Cavalry. Are you going to put me on report just for that, Captain?"

"Only if you don't get your backside moving like lightning the rest of the afternoon," said the irreverent Captain Henry.

The trench for the dead Confederate recruits and conscripts was completed just after 4:30 p.m.

"Captain, the trench is ready to receive the dead bodies," hollered Private Hummer. "How should we place them in the trench?"

"Put them in gently, Hummer, as a sign of respect. Of course, if we throw them in, what the hell difference does it make. But I'd feel guilty if we did that. I only wish it was possible to clean them up a little before we shoveled in the dirt. It's the respectful thing to do.

"Let's get this over with. Have all the bodies been identified? Have their personal effects been gathered up and tagged?"

"Yes, sir, Captain Dashiell's boys picked them up about an hour ago," responded Sergeant Thurston.

"All right then, Thurston, go get the chaplain over here. Make it quick! The goddamn flies are getting on them. And look at those goddamn buzzards and crows circling above the field."

Within ten minutes Chaplain Oliver Maddox arrived at the mass grave. The baby-face, plump 24-year old Maddox had just recently been transferred to Forrest's Cavalry by General Stephen Lee, a Maddox family friend. This was his first funeral ceremony.

"Make it short and sweet, Parson. As you can see, God's little creatures are swooping down on his children," said the cynical Captain Henry.

"Don't be disrespectful, Captain. These soldiers have given their lives for what they felt was a righteous cause."

Then the Chaplain began:

May God pardon them all from the sins of Man and grant them peace. Someday, mercifully, we shall all be together in Heaven and share everlasting rest.

Chaplain Maddox was about to open his Bible to read some scripture when Captain Henry hollered, "Over here Chaplain, we've got some more just brought in. Can you repeat what you just said for those poor devils?"

"You are a callous person, Captain," said the irritated Chaplain.

"No, Parson, it's just that General Forrest likes things tidy and done quickly. No offense is meant."

As he prepared to leave, Chaplain Maddox asked Henry, "Are you going to mark the mass grave with the names of the deceased?"

"No, we don't do that. We've got the names of those fellows in the trench. We'll have to asked General Forrest if he wants us to mark it after he returns. I doubt if it makes any difference to the dead; and it's unlikely any of their kin will ever pass this way."

Chaplain Maddox was shaken by Captain Henry's insensitivity, and just kept staring at him in disbelief.

Captain Henry said in his defense. "Well, Chaplain, that's just the way it is. This is a war we're fighting. No time for formal civility. This isn't some Baptist church here."

"But, Captain, these men were cut down before they could enjoy a full life," responded Chaplain Maddox compassionately.

"Well, Chaplain, I say you'll never miss what you've never had."

Disgusted with these smart aleck remarks, Maddox bolted from the field, and Captain Henry went about his business oblivious to the anguish he had caused the young chaplain.

"Captain Henry! We found some crippled horses wandering through the woods. What should we do with them?"

"Shoot the beasts, what else! But get the saddles."

"Captain Henry," yelled Sergeant Thurston who was at the far end of the clearing, "we've finished digging the officer's graves. Do you want me to get Chaplain Maddox again?"

"No, Thurston, that won't be necessary. It's getting late. I'll just repeat over the graves what the Parson said. Colonel Bell wants us to finish the burials before dark. Let's not worry about ceremony."

"Come on into the main surgical tent, Major Anderson," said Dr. Cowan. I'll give you my report as we tour our little field hospital here. I hope you haven't eaten in the past hour or two. What you're about to see isn't very pretty."

"I think I've got an idea of what to expect," replied Anderson. "I've been looking at bloody scenes like this since Shiloh."

No sooner had they entered the canopied area when Anderson saw his first horrifying sight. A seriously wounded soldier placed on a litter was curled in a ball holding his stomach. He was moaning, *"God, God, God, please help me. God, please...please don't call me back to your flock yet."* His upper pants were soaked with blood. It was obvious he had been shot in the stomach and was close to death.

"Anderson, that poor soul was brought in here about 4:00 p.m. this afternoon. They found him down near the creek. To tell you the truth, I'm amazed he is still alive. He was probably laying out there for 24 hours."

"How could he survive the loss of blood, Dr. Cowan?"

"That's a medical mystery. I have no answer except he must have a supernatural will to live.

"He's next on Dr. Jones' operating table over there."

"My God, Dr. Cowan, look at Dr. Jones, Dr. Bill Summerlin and their assistants. They're covered with blood. It's a frightening sight."

"Well, Anderson, wait till you see what's in back of this tent, and every other surgeon's tent we've got. Come on, I'll show you."

Outside was a grotesque scene of amputated arms and legs thrown haphazardly into a pile.

"There's probably 50 or 60 limbs in that pile, Anderson."

"Why hasn't one of the orderlies hauled them away and buried them?"

"Who has the time, Anderson! The orderlies bring in the wounded and set them on the operating tables; the surgeons do their cutting and stitching; then the surgeons' assistants and orderlies bandage them up and carry them to a recovery tent. They've been at it since yesterday afternoon.

"If we're lucky, we'll finish the amputations sometime today. Then, if those poor devils survive overnight, we'll take another look at them. Those we think can survive a wagon trip to Guntown we'll load up in those crude ambulances we've got outside."

"Do you mean the ones General Forrest's slaves are driving?"

"Yes, they've been of great help to us as teamsters. The General says he couldn't get along without his boys."

"Tell me, how do all of you stand the smell of chloroform and ether in the tent? It's overpowering. I feel like I'm going to faint."

"Thank God for those anesthetics, Anderson. It makes a surgeons' work a lot easier. And besides, it blocks out the awful smell of rotting flesh and gangrene. You'd be vomiting right now if it weren't for the sweet odor of chloroform."

"I can't get over how torn up some of those soldiers are, Dr. Cowan."

"It's those damn minié balls. Most of the amputations

are the result of those cursed bullets. You've seen what they can do. Look around here! When they hit, they burst and shatter the bones. If one hits the intestines, it's almost certain death. Ninety-five percent of those here were wounded by rifle fire. Only a few have shell wounds. And none by bayonet. There's not much bayonet combat in this war."

Dr. Bill Summerlin approached Dr. Cowan and asked if Major Anderson wanted to witness a leg amputation.

"Do you, Major Anderson?" asked Dr. Cowan.

"No, I think I've seen enough for one day."

"Well, our surgeons do good work, Major. They roll back the leg's skin, saw off the bone with a surgeon's special hacksaw; and then tie off the arteries with cat gut or horse hair to stop the bleeding, then wrap the stump with wet bandages."

"I appreciate the explanation, Dr. Cowan. I have just one question, 'What is the survival rate?'"

"Pretty good if we get them early enough. I think three out of four of those we've operated on today will survive. We put morphine powder on the wounds. That seems to help. But we do lose some to shock. Cutting off an arm or a leg is an awful jolt to the body.

"Most of those who have died here today had either head wounds or severe stomach wounds. There wasn't much we could do for those soldiers. They die from severe hemorrhaging."

Major Anderson thanked Dr. Cowan and nodded his appreciation to surgeons Jones and Summerlin who were working on the leg amputation as he left.

Brice's Cross Roads, Monday, June 13, 1864

General Forrest arrived back at 1:00 p.m. amid cheering from soldiers gathered near William Brice's house. He waved his hat several times acknowledging the greetings, then entered the Brice house to meet with his staff.

After shaking hands with Colonel Bell and Major Anderson and engaging in some light banter, Forrest said, "All right men, let's find out the good news and the bad news. We had a fine victory, didn't we? And I thank all of you for your total dedication. We certainly made a mess of Sturgis' army.

"Anderson, give me the good news. How much equipment and supplies did we capture?"

"Sir, a lot of our information is preliminary. We still have work details on the road between here and Salem."

"Yes, I saw some of them this morning. They told me they were gathering up everything of value abandoned by the Federals."

"All right then, General, my statistics are probably pretty accurate," said Anderson.

"Let's take ordnance first. So far it's 16 cannons, 28 limbers, 15 caissons, a huge supply of artillery ammunition, 1500 rifles and pistols, and ammunition.

"And Captain Severson just gave me the list of quartermaster property. It's 161 mules, 23 horses, 168 six-horse wagons, 7 four-horse wagons, 1 two-horse wagon, 16 ambulances and hundreds of harnesses and saddles."

"That's a wonderful haul, Anderson," said Forrest jubilantly. "I'm disappointed we didn't get more horses. Our need for horses never ends.

"How about medical supplies?"

"General, we struck a gold mine. Our estimate is that we captured thousands of dollars worth of medicines, first aid supplies, instruments, operating tables, litters...and so forth."

"Anderson, I promised General Stephen Lee last week that if we captured any medical supplies, we'll take what we need, and ship the rest to him."

"I'll take care of that, General."

"What about prisoners, Anderson?"

"Captain Goodwin, our Provost, is handling that," replied Anderson. "Give us your report, Captain."

"General, so far it's over 2000 Union soldiers. There are more out there, I'm sure. We'll get them here today or tomorrow."

"Goodwin, what arrangements have been made to send them south?"

"Sir, we marched 1500 of them yesterday to Guntown. We're going to hold them there until rail transportation arrives from Meridian to take them south to Cahaba Prison."

"Oh, you mean the place they call 'Castle Morgan,' named after General John Morgan, my cavalry counterpart?"

"Yes, that's where General Lee wants all those captured by any command to be sent.

"We're going to move the rest of them still here in one hour."

"Goodwin, have you done all the paperwork on the prisoners?"

"Yes, sir, we've got names, ranks and units on a master list for your review."

"Good work, Goodwin!

"Now give me the bad news — our casualties. Who has that report? How many were killed?"

"Captain Dashiell has those figures," replied Anderson. "Sir, it's 12 of your officers and 84 non-commissioned officers and privates. Those numbers are as of one-half hour ago. I just checked at the field hospital for any deaths overnight," responded Dashiell.

"Who were the officers killed?"

"The following captains, sir: Hobbitt, Seay, Tate and Wilson. And the following lieutenants: Arnold, Edwards, Govan, Hooper, Neilling, Pope, Revely and Welch."

"Well, that's a goddamn shame. I knew most of them. They were good soldiers. Make sure you get letters prepared for me to send to their families.

"How about wounded, Captain Dashiell?"

"Just about 400, sir — a lot of them seriously."

"Did Dr. Cowan tell you how many of the wounded

may have to be discharged and sent home?"

"No sir, but he's had over 100 amputees. They won't be back."

"Well, keep me posted. We'll need more recruits to cover our losses.

"What about enemy losses, Dashiell?"

"My guess is that they lost one-third of their army-- killed and captured. Our losses were 15 percent of our troops. That's killed and wounded, sir," answered Captain Dashiell.

"I'll be leaving for Guntown early tomorrow. Make arrangements to break camp here no later than Wednesday. Get our wounded over to Guntown until we can find recovery hospitals for them in Tupelo, Columbus, and maybe down to Meridian.

"Major Anderson, my compliments to you and your staff for cleaning up things here.

"Now gentlemen, me and my goddamn boils are going to rest."

Guntown, Mississippi, Tues., June 14, 1864, 2:00 p.m.

"Willie, I want you to join me on a visit to the temporary recovery hospital we've set up here," said General Forrest to his son. "I want you to talk with the younger wounded — those fellows about your age. Give them encouragement. Tell them how much they contributed to our recent victory at the Cross Roads. They won't be afraid to talk with you about how they feel, or if anything is bothering them. I think I frighten them a little.

"Ask them is there is anything we can do, like writing their families. Take down their names and home addresses, and give them to Captain Strange.

"I'll visit some of the older soldiers. Sergeant Boatwright here is in charge of the hospital. Boatwright and Dr. Cowan are going to escort me around. Come see me after while and tell me what the young fellows have to say," concluded Forrest.

"General Forrest, this is Corporal William Pickering. He's lost a leg, but he's going to live," said Dr. Cowan confidently.

"Corporal, the war's over for you. You'll soon be sent home. Where do you live?" asked Forrest, touching Pickering on the left shoulder.

"Memphis, sir."

"We'll try to get you safe escort through the Union lines around Memphis. Good luck to you, Corporal."

Then, out of the corner of his eye, Forrest saw a familiar face.

"Jester, is that you? Is this my old friend, Walter X. Jester? Goddamn, it's been a long time since we joined up, hasn't it?"

"Yes, sir, it was nearly three years ago."

"Well, Jester, why haven't I seen you since? Where have you been?"

"I was captured at Perryville in October 1862 and sent to Alton Prison in Illinois. After they paroled me, I was sent to General Buckner's army. I asked for a transfer to your cavalry just after Fort Pillow."

"How did you get yourself wounded?"

"General, I was running through those scrub oaks and a jagged limb ripped my head open, but I kept on fighting until I fainted about 6:00 o'clock."

"Looks like you'll be all right, Jester."

"Sir, I'll be off this cot in a day or two, and happy as a jackass eatin' sawbriers."

"What has happened to your buddy from Alabama? What's his name?"

"Oh, you probably mean Amos Snow. Old Amos lost his arm at Shiloh. I saw him right before he left Corinth for home, and he was grinnin' like a possum 'cause he said the folks back home would call him a hero.

"I don't know what happened to those other fellows — Lewis Flippin and Abraham Story. They were at Shiloh, too, but after that we all got scattered."

"Well, Jester, I want you mounted in a week or two.

We've got some more fighting to do.

"Tell you what, Jester! In honor of our long friendship, I'm going to give you one of those Spencer rifles we captured at Brice's. What do you say to that?"

"A Spencer Repeating Rifle? One of those new weapons that fires eight shots?"

"Yes, that's what it does."

"Well, yes, sir, General, and I thank you."

"Come see me when you get well, Jester." Sergeant Boatwright directed Forrest's attention to another cot.

"We've got a few Union boys here, General. Would you like to talk with one?"

"Certainly, why not!"

"General, this is Shawn McManus, a private in General Grierson's Cavalry."

"McManus, is that your name, soldier?" asked Forrest. "Are you any relation to John McManus of Memphis, the city drunk? He's in and out of the workhouse continually for drinking, fighting, cussing and generally playing the fool."

"Maybe, sir. A lot of us McManuses came to America 17 years ago during the Irish potato famine. Some went South,"

"What's a self-respecting Irishman doing fighting for the Yankees?"

"I don't know sir. I guess I wanted to get into a good fight. You know us Irish."

"What's the matter with you, McManus? Why are you here?"

"I hate to admit it, sir, but I got shot in the ass."

"Shot in the ass? What were you doing? Running away? Sounds like we've got a coward here."

"No, sir, down there in that creek, Eddie Miller, my friend, was firing every which way when he tried to cross the creek. I was unlucky enough to stoop down to pick up a Confederate officer's hat and put it on for fun, and Eddie shot me before I could turn around."

"Heh-heh-heh! Now I've heard of lying Irishmen. Now

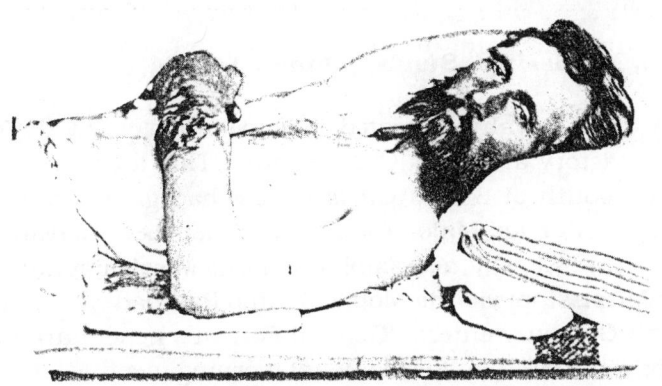

Recovering from battlefield wounds

I'm face to face with one."

"General, I'd rather be found lying with my face to the moon than to have anyone think I'm a coward. And I can think of worse places below the belt where I wouldn't like to get shot."

"Well, McManus, good luck to you. Believe it or not, you've brightened my day."

Forrest made a few more stops to talk with the wounded, then spoke briefly with Dr. Cowan before leaving the hospital.

"James, I admire those lads — both our boys and the Union fellows. They're as brave as can be. Not one of them in there appears to feel sorry for himself."

23 • The Planning Session

Tupelo, Mississippi, Sunday, June 19, 1864

Forrest's Cavalry relocated to Tupelo just a few days after its victory at Brice's Cross Roads. This town, about 20 miles south of Brice's Cross Roads, had grown into a military center for Major General Stephen Lee's cavalry units. It was easily accessible to North Mississippi and South Mississippi via the Mobile & Ohio Railroad.

Matt Gallaway entered General Forrest's headquarters promptly at 7:30 a.m. for his usual morning meeting.

"Have you seen this communique from Richmond, Matt?" asked Forrest as he sipped coffee from his monogrammed tin cup. "It's informing me that the Confederate Congress has spread the conscription age from 17 to 50."

"God, they must be desperate for new soldiers. We've had no trouble getting 17 year olds to sign up, Matt. But getting men up to 50?"

"That's not going to be easy," said Gallaway.

"Well, Matt, Captain Strange informs me we have maybe 100 or so between 45 and 50. They're all volunteers. So far, they have served us well.

"And, Matt, up to this point we haven't been that desperate to horsecollar fellows without teeth and rheumatism."

"General, it won't be too long before the two of us are in that boat."

"No, I guess not. Those damn boils are going to get me.

"But Matt, I've got something that's serious to discuss with you this morning.

"It's that damnable report of Colonel Brent to the Inspector General's office in Richmond. It really makes my blood boil. Maybe Richmond wants my head this time.

"What do they expect of me? I whipped the Federals at Okolona, Union City, Fort Pillow and Brice's Cross Roads — all in the past four months. I wonder how many of their other generals have done as well. From what I hear, not many."

Then smacking his fist into the palm of his hand, Forrest in an anguished voice said, "Hell, Matt, we attack! — attack! — attack! We hit the enemy like lightning. We don't hole up behind barricades and trenches built by military engineers like they're doing in Virginia. And we don't go into slow retreats moving farther and farther south.

"Davis has Bragg advising him in Richmond. Is it any wonder then that the Confederacy is under heavy seige? If they don't start attacking, Lincoln will make certain we starve to death."

"General, you're absolutely right. It's really ironic. On one hand Richmond sends you a compliment. Then, it turns around and hits you with a sledge hammer. And to think Davis and Bragg listen to that fool, Pillow. Why that fellow makes a virtue out of ignorance.

"One of Aesop's fables fits old Pillow, General. It goes like this: 'the fox after futile efforts to reach some grapes, scorns them as being sour.'"

"Well, Matt, I never heard of Aesop, but he told the truth. But Pillow really doesn't bother me too much. I believe the Confederate War Department considers him incompetent. That's some satisfaction to me.

"Now, here's what I want to do. I'm going to beat them at their own game. I am ordering a review of our command. In the next few days I want to know our strengths and weaknesses. Then, I'm going to have a plan. We'll tell Richmond what we need and why we need it; and we'll give them facts. Then let them send their meddlesome clerks down here if they dare.

"Strange, I know you're out there eavesdropping. Get in here!"

"Yes, sir, right away."

"Captain, I want you to prepare a list — or what Matt here calls an agenda — for a meeting tomorrow morning of all staff officers, plus General Buford and General Chalmers. I want a report from each of them about their operations. I want to know where the problems are, and how we can fix 'em.

"No one is excused. We meet at 9:00 a.m. sharp. Understand?"

"Yes, sir," snapped Strange.

"Get on with it, Captain. When those fellows show up from Richmond, they're going to learn a thing or two about an effective military organization."

Monday, June 20, 1864

"Officers, you know why you're here, so let's get started," Forrest began abruptly.

"I'm not interested in recalling our successes or our failures except in those cases where we learned something which will help us in the future.

"Speak freely when called upon. But let's not waste time patting each other on the back. Let's win this damn war, then we can do that!

"There is one matter which shall be last on the list. That's the report from the Inspector-General in Richmond. Some serious and inflammatory charges have been made against this command. I believe them untrue. They were made out of jealousy and spite.

"Captain Strange, who is first on the list?"

"It's Dr. Cowan, sir."

"Good, but before he starts, let me announce my new war against dirt.

"Gentlemen, everywhere I go I see unclean camps, unclean equipment, unclean uniforms and soldiers who never bathe.

"March 'em into the creek and make 'em squat down in the water for an hour or so.

"I hate the goddamn odor of sweating bodies. We're soldiers, not some back fence hogs.

"Let's also get rid of lice, mange and those bloodsucking bed bugs. Cris' sakes, we can't have much of an army if we're up to our britches in filth and head lice.

"All right, Dr. Cowan, I've covered the subject of personal hygiene for you. Let's hear what you've got to say."

"General, I think we are getting more efficient in treating battlefield injuries. The capture of those medical supplies last week puts us in good shape. The Federals have the best drugs and instruments available.

"My concern now is that for every soldier killed, we lose two to some disease other than wounds. Your pointed remarks on sanitation are well taken. That's one problem. There's no doubt of the relationship of the cases of diarrhea and dysentery with cleanliness. Camp diarrhea is a problem in all commands.

"There's some rheumatism among the older soldiers. I've recommended discharges for dozens of fellows since January. We need to see that our soldiers are adequately clothed when the cold weather comes. If your crippled up, you can't ride all day and fight.

"And I regret to report we've had three suicides this year. We had one just the other day. A Private Mathias in the Third Kentucky shot himself near Guntown. His company commander seems to think he just wore out from his aches and pains."

Forrest interrupted Dr. Cowan to say, "Inform all company commanders to watch out for this kind of thing. I assume it's more a problem with the older ones. But to tell you the truth, we're all wore out. A long furlough would help.

"Go on, James."

"All right, General. There are more cases of the DT's than you can imagine."

"Do you mean the shakes, Dr. Cowan?" inquired Captain Morton.

"Yes, there are wholesale numbers of soldiers totally consumed by alcohol, and they are unfit for duty."

"Can we sweat it out of them?" asked the concerned Forrest.

"No, I'd say they are hopelessly incapacitated and unfit for our command. They should be discharged."

"All right, Captain Strange, prepare the papers. Get rid of them.

"What else do you have, Dr. Cowan?"

"I'm almost done. Just a few more things. For instance, I am worried about a possible outbreak of measles and chicken pox among those young farm boys we recruited last winter. So far, so good. But no doubt you've heard how these childhood diseases have shut down some Federal and Confederate units for several weeks while these diseases ran their course."

"What about malingering, Dr. Cowan? Is that a problem?"

"No, not much anymore.

"A less serious problem, General, is excessive masturbation. Some of the boys are wearing themselves out by manipulating their genitals."

"What?" said the astonished Forrest as everyone broke out into laughter.

The mischievous Cowan seized the opportunity to tell a story he made up for just such an occasion. "Gentlemen," he said, "a soldier came in on sick call. His eyes were sunk and he was shaking like he had St. Vitus' dance. It was obvious to me what his problem was. I said to him, 'Private, if you continue masturbating several times a day, you're going to go blind!' He looked at me with a look of desperation, then said, 'Doctor, how much can I do so I'll only go blind in one eye.' Heh-heh-heh!"

"All right, Dr. Cowan, with that bit of comedy you can sit down.

"Now, Captain Dashiell, let's have your report."

"General Forrest, I can tell you that the pay increase from $12 a month to $21 a month for privates has raised morale twofold or more. The change was effective June 9th, but the news just reached camp on Saturday."

"Dashiell, be sure to send our thanks to the Honorable Christopher Gustavus Memminger, our beloved Confederate Secretary of the Treasury. Heh-heh-heh!

"It's a pitiful raise considering what Confederate shucks will buy now. And considering that we've been unpaid for months, what difference does it make anyhow?"

"What you say is true, General Forrest. Confederate paper dollars are now worth about three or four cents in gold, maybe less. One of General Lee's aides told me recently that an item sold in 1861 for $10 now costs $280. Once the Confederate Treasury started printing money with no gold backing, our greenbacks weren't worth the paper they were printed on."

"Now, that's a big problem for us in buying supplies and horses," said Forrest. "If we're going to equip and feed ourselves, we need to make some plans to accomplish it.

"I know from recent experience in West Tennessee

that many purveyors won't sell us anything if we offer Confederate dollars. They want gold or cotton, and maybe sugar and salt. They'll take Federal currency too, even though it's fallen in value."

"But not as much as ours," added Captain Dashiell.

"That's right. Those Federal dollars we confiscated at Union City in late March helped quite a bit.

"Well, then, one of our goals is to confiscate more Yankee dollars in our raids. And if we can get our hands on some cotton, and run it through the blockade, we can trade with it.

"The matter of our commissary is Major Rambaut's area. What about it, Major?"

"General, I've had some of my staff up in West Tennessee trying to secure food supplies. Conditions are bad there. The folks are suffering from shortages. Corn is scarcer than I thought. And much of their livestock has either been stolen by renegades or confiscated by Union troops operating out of Memphis.

"I'm trying to get more variety in our diets. Right now, the soldiers are eating mostly salt pork and corn pone, and very few vegetables. Now that the growing season is here in Mississippi, I hope we'll be able to purchase some local farm vegetables by July.

"Of course, General, if necessary we can use edible weeds to supplement their diets. There's plenty of nutrition in mustard greens, dandelions, wild onions and garlic. There's a lot of blackberries in the fields."

Then the whimsical Dr. Cowan interjected, "Gilbert, recommend wild garlic and onions to anyone who has gout. There's not a better remedy."

Then Rambaut continued, "If the soldiers think the food I'm serving them is bad, they should spend time in a Union prison like I did at Camp Chase in Ohio."

Forrest, totally absorbed in Rambaut's presentation

then said, "Gilbert, I ate some of your food when you were managing the Worsham House in Memphis. Prison food had to be better. Heh-heh-heh!

"I approve the idea of trading cotton for food, Major. The only problem is: 'Where do we find the cotton?' A lot of it has been burned this year in Mississippi to keep it away from the Federals."

Matt Gallaway added, "What we have is a Hobson's Choice. There's probably no alternative except foraging from local farm houses — and that is stealing from our own people."

"Can we get our hands on some salt, Major?" asked Forrest. "That's a good trading commodity."

"I'm looking into that, General. I've got men down in Alabama searching for a supply."

"What we really need to do is raid Memphis," said Forrest. "If we could pull that off, we'd have no more worries. But right now, we're in no condition to try to swallow an elephant.

"Now, gentlemen, another big concern is horses," continued Forrest. "We need 500 or 600 good horses quick; and we need to find where we can get even more over the next two or three months.

"I personally like the Morgans that are widely used in the Federal cavalry. They're powerful, intelligent animals that move fast even at a trot. We can use them to ride, and if necessary, to pull wagons.

"Our best chance to remount adequately is through captured horses. That's one of our major objectives. Take only those animals 15 hands or higher and still serviceable. And by the way pick out a good Morgan or two for me.

"Captain Severson, what's the Quartermaster Department got to say?"

"General, like you say about horses, the news isn't too

good. We didn't capture many horses at Brice's, and the one's we got at Fort Pillow and at Paducah were mostly worn out animals hardly worth feeding."

"What's the present condition of your serviceable mounts? I'm concerned that we might face massive breakdowns when we do some hard riding. Do you have any veterinarians in camp who can give me an accurate report?" said Forrest as he continued interrogating Captain Severson.

"No, sir, but I've got our best farriers and blacksmiths outside. They'll know the situation."

"All right, Captain, call them in here."

Within 30 seconds three ruddy-faced, stocky and powerfully-built soldiers shuffled into the meeting room. Their massive arms were the result of years of hard work blacksmithing.

"Gentlemen," said Captain Severson, "most of you know these fellows. They've been with us for a long time.

"For those of you who don't know him, this sergeant on my left is Bowlegs Teet. What's your given first name, Sergeant?"

"Lionel, sir," he said grinning broadly. "But no one calls me anything other than Bowlegs, Captain Severson."

"Bowlegs, would you introduce the other sergeants?"

"Yes, sir. General Forrest and officers, these are the Bemis twins, Oscar and Jesse. We've blacksmithed together in Corinth, Mississippi for about ten years. I'm married to their sister, Jewell."

"Is she built like the Bemis twins, Bowlegs?" asked the amused Forrest.

"No, sir, she's a real skinny thing, and as pretty as they come."

"Bowlegs, did you know my daddy was a blacksmith?"

"Yes, sir, I did. And that's probably why you know so much about horses, General."

"Do you mind if I ask a few questions, Bowlegs?"

"No, sir, I'll tell you what I know," said the amiable, balding Teet. The Bemis twins will also."

"Tell me truthfully, what is the general condition of our animals?"

"Well, sir, some have bad saddle sores from the hard riding chasing the enemy after we whipped them at Brice's Cross Roads. That's caused by the saddle being on too long.

"And you've got some horses that ought to be plowing a field. They're not cavalry mounts in my judgement. They break down after a couple of hours. Their legs can't stand the fast riding."

"You sound like a veterinarian, Bowlegs."

"Sir, when you see hundreds of horses a week, you learn things."

"What about illnesses?"

"We've got some problems with the rotten hoof."

"Do you mean hoof-and-mouth disease?"

"Yes, sir, it isn't an epidemic yet. It's the young horses most seriously ill. We try to separate them out so a veterinarian can look at them."

"One more question, Bowlegs. How are your supplies of horseshoes and nails?"

"There's a problem, General. We've got just enough to shod the new horses. We need at least 1000 shoes right away. And we should get enough so every trooper can carry one or two extra in his saddle bags."

"Captain Severson, contact General Lee's Quartermaster Department and solve this problem fast. We may even consider raiding Lee's warehouse for some moonlight requisitioning. Heh-heh-heh!

"Do you have any other problems, Bowlegs?" asked Forrest.

"Yes, sir, we do. It's those damn dung flies down in

our corrals. Those bloodsuckers are driving our horses crazy. The animals don't get a bit of rest with those swarms of pests snappin' away at 'em. We're putting up some smoke to try to drive them off."

Forrest thanked Bowlegs Teet and the Bemis twins; and not knowing whether to salute or not, the three robust blacksmiths just grinned, nodded their heads, and left.

"Now the matter of fodder, Captain Severson. Are the animals getting a full ration every day?"

"General, according to regulations a full ration for one horse is supposed to be 26 pounds. We're just exceeding the minimum of 10 pounds of grain per day, plus what the animals get by grazing.

"Oats and hay are expensive if we try to buy these supplies. Of course, we have been getting some by appealing to the patriotism of Mississippi farmers."

"Captain, I guess it's hard for them to be patriotic when they're standing there crying as we haul off their harvest."

"Yes, sir, I agree."

Forrest then turned and looked directly at both General Buford and General Chalmers. "It's up to you two to inform your commanders to stamp out any abuse inflicted by your soldiers on these animals. Nothing less than severe punishment is acceptable for those not grooming their mounts or keeping them properly shod. I will not stand for mistreatment of horses.

"Now Captain Russell, what about ordnance? How are we fixed here?"

"Sir, we're in good shape at the moment. We made a good haul at Brice's. The Federals left several hundred Spencer carbines on the field. Spencers have been in issue in the Union army less than a year, and this particular weapon is popular in their cavalry. We're now servicing a bunch of them for distribution down the line. They're a dandy weapon — only 39 inches long and weighing eight and one quarter pounds. It's a lever action repeater. You can get eight shots off without reloading, and possibly as many as 21 rounds per minute."

"It's a fine weapon indeed, Captain Russell. Are there any drawbacks?"

"Sir, we captured a good supply of ammunition for the Spencers, but getting resupplied may present some problems. So far none is being manufactured here in the South."

"All right then, that's another item we need to strip from the enemy. What else did we get, Russell?"

"Plenty of Springfield Model 1861s. This is the bread-and-butter of the Union infantry."

"Any Henry rifles?"

"No, sir, I don't recall seeing any. As far as I can tell, there aren't too many in existence. It must be a marvelous weapon with that 15-round magazine located under the barrel."

"Well, Russell, I'm satisfied with the Spencers."

Then Forrest looked for Captain Morton to quiz him about the status of his artillery unit.

"Where's Morton, Captain Strange?"

"He stepped out, sir. I think he's got diarrhea bad. When Dr. Cowan kept talking about diarrhea a while ago, Morton turned pale, then bolted out of here when the blacksmiths came in."

"All right, I know the artillery situation. We are in outstanding shape in that department. The Federals gave us some nice gifts of 3-inch ordnance rifles. Rodmans!

"Did you all see Captain Morton and Captain Rice in action at the Cross Roads? That was fine work. I was worried they were almost too far forward when we started our big assault on Sturgis. Old Morton is a little bit of a fellow with a big backbone. Captain Rice is no shrinking violet either."

It was now 10:30 a.m. The temperature outside Forrest's headquarters had risen to 85°. Inside it was 90°. No air was circulating to cool off those in the meeting tent. Forrest was the only one that didn't look wilted. His uniform was still immaculate and he showed no signs of sweating or discomfort.

The others were in varying degrees of distress. The ponderous General Buford had beads of sweat rolling down his face, and his uniform below his armpits was soaked. He was gasping for air and grunting. Matt Gallaway was in similar distress as were several others. But General Forest, if he did notice the discomfort, showed no concern.

"Now, gentlemen," Forrest continued, "there's the matter of Colonel Brent's report to the Inspector-General. It makes a number of ridiculous charges against my command.

"First, the report says we stole soldiers from infantry units in violation of *Article 22* of the Confederate rules. You know that's hogwash!

"Brent says we built our cavalry, not by recruiting or conscripting civilians, but by arm-twisting those already enrolled in other units to jump over to us.

"You know as well as I do that these so-called other units were almost nonexistent. There was no organization whatsoever. The officer who had recruited the soldiers originally had lost all control. Most of them had wandered off and gone home.

"Hell, we did the Confederacy a favor by rounding them up. Some of those fellows hadn't served one real day in the war.

"As I told Matt Gallaway yesterday, Bragg, Pillow and their friends forget we're fighting a war. Their attitude seems to be that if we get licked at least we had accurate records and acted as true Southern gentlemen in our dealings with fellow officers.

"Forrest's Cavalry is winning because we do what is necessary. There is not time to argue everything out through the channels up to Richmond. They sit there with their West Point manuals directing the war or reading false reports from that crybaby Pillow.

"They call us horse thieves. Can you imagine that? Six months ago General Polk ordered us to impress all the horses we could find in Mississippi. The idea was to keep the Yankees from getting them. But, as you know, our farm people raised holy Hell about it and Polk ordered us to stop. And we did stop.

"Now they come along and accuse us of doing things they originally approved. Honestly, they have the brains of a billy goat.

"There is one charge in Brent's report that may have some merit. That's the concern about the competence of some of our officers. Now that's an area where I need your help. If we have problems, let's clean them up.

"I want Major Anderson to get together with General Buford and General Chalmers to conduct a thorough review of their commanders from the top right down to the lowest lieutenant. Look at their performance. Find out how well they conducted themselves under fire. And find out if their soldiers respect them or not. And if they don't respect them, why not? Let's get any bad apples weeded out."

It was now 11:15 a.m. Forrest had gone nonstop in questioning and probing, and explaining his positions, for over two hours. Finally, noticing some uneasiness due to the oppressive heat, he said, "Gentlemen, you all know I expect a great deal from you. If I didn't have such high praise for your recent performances in the field, I wouldn't be so demanding. If this command is to continue being successful, we all must go the limit. There's not one of you here that I don't respect for courage and performance. And I thank you for giving us the great victory at Brice's."

"General, you are the real hero," shouted Major Rambaut.

"No, Gilbert, a hero in this war is a dead general. While you are alive there are just too many varmints out there pulling you down."

Then Forrest said as an afterthought, "I know that Captain Strange is a Latin scholar. Perhaps he could honor us with a heroic Latin motto for my command. What about it, John?"

Strange looked pensive for a few minutes, them smiling broadly he said, "How about this: 'Nunquam Animus Sed Ignis Via."

"That sounds good. What's it mean?" asked the puzzled Forrest.

Responding sheepishly, Strange answered, "Well, General, translated it means, 'Never mind but fire away.'"

At that moment spontaneous laughter broke out with Forrest pounding his fist on a table. When the General regained his composure, and relaxed by the merriment, he said, "John, that's not exactly what I had in mind, but I'll consider it."

24 • Discipline

General Joseph E. Johnston, after replacing General Bragg following the defeat of the Army of Tennessee at the Battle of Chattanooga in November 1863, was ordered to rebuild the army quickly, then take the offensive against General Sherman's Union forces moving south into Georgia. But when Johnston's army was driven back to the outskirts of Atlanta, Johnston was dismissed on July 17, 1864. President Davis made the decision despite Johnston's victory three weeks earlier at the Battle of Kennesaw Mountain.

Davis' choice to succeed Johnston was the 33-year old Kentucky native, John Bell Hood (West Point, 1853). Hood was a rising star in the Confederate command. He had fought in the Second Battle of Bull Run in 1862, and at Antietam in Maryland that same year. At Gettysburg in 1863 he commanded a division under General James Longstreet. Most recently, he served under Johnston in the Atlanta Campaign as an infantry corps commander.

Stephen Lee, newly promoted to lieutenant general, was ordered to Atlanta on July 20, 1864 to assume command of Hood's Corps. He saw his first action on July 28th, less than two weeks after leading the Confederates in the fierce and indecisive battle with Union General A. J. Smith's army near Tupelo, Mississippi.

On August 15, 1864, a non-West Pointer, the 38-year old General Richard Taylor (Yale University, 1845) was appointed to replace Stephen Lee as commander of the Department of Alabama, Mississippi and East Louisiana. Taylor, a pre-war sugar planter in Louisiana was the son of the former President of the United States, General Zachary "Old Rough and Ready" Taylor, hero of the Mexican War. Richard Taylor's sister was Sarah Taylor, first wife of Jefferson Davis.

Meridian, Mississippi, September 5, 1864

General Forrest met his new commander, General

Taylor, at the latter's headquarters to receive his instructions.

"I liked General Taylor instantly," Forrest later told Matt Gallaway. "I am impressed with his straightforward manner and his charm. I was convinced after that initial meeting that the Department would now have better direction. Lee treated me fine. We never had a harsh word. But he wasn't aggressive enough for me, and this bothered me terribly."

At the initial meeting, Forrest briefed Taylor on his cavalry's performance against General Smith's Union force of 14,000 at the Battle of Tupelo. Forrest was second-in-command behind Lee.

"General Taylor, we didn't do well there despite trying to hit the enemy with everything we had. Charge after charge was driven back. We couldn't penetrate the Federal's defenses no matter how many soldiers we ran at them. That was on July 14th. Things died down late in the afternoon. It was hot as Hell there; and the troops were dropping from exhaustion.

"We hit 'em again the next morning; but then all of a sudden the Federals started withdrawing. I think they ran out of ammunition. We were beat up good, too. The Federals probably won if you consider casualties. We had 210 killed and over 1100 wounded. They didn't have anywhere near that number put out of action."

"But Forrest, at least Lee and you kept Smith from linking up with Sherman. And you protected once again the Mobile & Ohio Railroad."

"I hate to lose, General Taylor. I hate it something awful. Ever since that disaster at Fort Donelson, I get upset if we don't win."

"Well, Forrest, you've had your share of successes. That recent raid on Memphis was a daring move. I bet that quick strike into the center of that city shook up General Washburn. Your strategy was a good one. The Union army is less likely to move their Memphis forces elsewhere if they fear an attack there."

"Did you experience any losses?"

"No, sir, not really — just a hand full of casualties."

"We've got some tough assignments coming up, Forrest," said Taylor with a look of deep concern. "This Department is no longer considered a backwater, secondary fighting force. We're going to be asked to provide a support to General Hood's planned offensive into Tennessee to try to close Sherman's back door to Georgia.

"I'm happy to keep this Department intact, but don't be surprised is your unit, or someone else's, is ordered on detached duty to plug up a hole in Hood's army."

"Forrest, what is the present status of your cavalry?"

"Sir, we are on leave until September 15th. The soldiers need a rest."

"I know that, Forrest. Your cavalry has been among the most active forces in the Confederate army this year.

"You are reassembling at Verona, near Tupelo, Forrest?"

"Yes, sir, I'll be there in a few days to work with my staff."

"Fine, all communications from my headquarters shall be directed there. Good luck, Forrest."

Verona, Mississippi, September 14, 1864

At 7:00 p.m. General Forrest and Matt Gallaway walked to the train depot after officers' mess. There was mass confusion on the streets. Arriving soldiers were shouting greetings to their friends, or standing in groups swapping stories and laughing.

But there was rowdiness also. Some had obviously been drinking heavily, and were boisterous and unruly.

Forrest grabbed one by the collar, and said, "Soldier, you're drunk. You had better watch yourself."

Immediately the skinny, freckled face young private stared at Forrest. Then he said, slurring his words, "May you go to Hell, sir. Yes, sir, that's right. You and your friend can go to Hell."

"Private, you are about to get into a lot of trouble. What's your name?"

"It's Simon Peters, sir. I was named after one of the twelve apostles. You can look it up in the Bible — Mark 3:16."

"Well, my biblical friend, what would they think about your drinking whiskey?"

"If they were in my situation, they'd be drinking too. It gets my mind off minié balls whizzing past my ears. That's a fact!"

"Soldier, are you aware of *Article 9*? It states that any soldier who disobeys any lawful command of his superior officer shall suffer death, or such other punishment as shall according to the nature of the offense be imposed on him by court-martial."

"I know that, sir! But begging your pardon, sir, no one ordered me not to drink. I am doing it on my own, yes, sir! If one of the officers, or my sergeant, told me not to drink, I wouldn't have. And I'm going to keep drinking till someone orders me not to drink."

"Now I'm telling you Private Simon Peters you better be sober when we move out of here on Sunday."

"Don't worry. I'll be ready to go if my goddamn body comes on time."

"Private, you've got guts — maybe no sense — but you do have guts. You better sleep it off. I don't want you to get hurt," Forrest said half-smiling to the amused Gallaway. "Now get back to your camp."

Then Forrest said to Gallaway, "Hell, Matt, if I were his age, that's what I'd be doing."

Gallaway replied, "Me too."

September 15, 1864

At 8:00 a.m. Forrest summoned Major Anderson to his quarters.

"Anderson, you've been working on that leadership efficiency report for three months. Can you tell me briefly what you found out?"

"General, as you know I worked with General Chalmers and General Buford on this review. We have a generally favorable report.

"The efficiency of our officers in our success at Brice's Cross Roads was meritorious. With few exceptions, all of our senior and junior officers performed quickly and precisely. We found no instances of cowardice or insubordination.

"All-in-all, morale during and immediately after Brice's was exceptionally high.

"We found great pride throughout the enlisted ranks too. We believe that pride will minimize desertions in the future.

"The negative findings relate to the excessive drinking of certain officers while in camp, and instances of inefficiency and neglect in their administrative duties.

"We have three names of officers, and the evidence necessary to act on these cases."

"Who are they, Anderson?"

"Major Abner Howell, Captain Harold Shults, and Lieutenant Henry Pennington."

"Captain Strange, get in here quick," yelled Forrest in a highly agitated voice.

"Yes, sir," responded Strange who was working nearby.

"I'm going to make examples of these three officers. Major Anderson, give Strange the names," said Forrest. "Find them by this afternoon, and have Captain Goodwin's men bring them here under arrest."

"I'll take care of it, sir," answered Strange.

By 3:00 p.m. Captain Goodwin appeared at Forrest's quarters. "General Forrest, I have the three officers you requested."

As soon as the bewildered looking miscreants stood at attention Forrest shouted, "You are under arrest for insubordination and drunkenness. You have failed to secure and inventory equipment; you have failed to reprimand your soldiers found abusing their horses; you have failed to maintain discipline; and you have disgraced yourselves in front of your men by excessive use of alcohol.

"You are relieved of your commands.

"Captain Goodwin! These men are to be put under arrest and remanded to your custody for transportation under guard to the Department's military court in Meridian. You are to leave first thing in the morning.

"A copy of my charges will be made available to you at the time of your arrival at the Judge Advocate's Office.

"You officers are a disgrace to the Confederate army. I will not tolerate such conduct. You are dismissed!"

Major Anderson was called outside as Captain Goodwin and his provost staff were preparing to escort the prisoners to a make-shift temporary jail. Colonel Gallaway, who was standing next to a civilian, signaled Anderson to come over.

"Major, this is Sheriff Herman Barksdale from over in Lafayette County. He is here to arrest Lieutenant Eli Broadhurst on a charge of rape. Do you think General Forrest will see him?"

Anderson turned ashen. "Oh my, wait until the General hears this! He's already in a terrible mood with what just happened in there. Now this.

"Matt, will you do me a favor? Will you escort Sheriff Barksdale in there. He won't jump all over you. You're his best friend."

Gallaway, sympathizing with the apprehensive Anderson, nodded yes, he would do it.

As they entered, Forrest was washing his face in a metal basin as if he were trying to remove his look of intense anger, He looked up and said, "I know you. You're Barksdale from Oxford, aren't you?"

"Yes, sir, we used to do a little business together over in Lafayette County before the war. I did a little cotton brokering before I became sheriff."

"Yes, I remember," nodded Forrest. "Well, maybe I'm glad to see you; and maybe not. What brings you to Verona?"

"Bad news, General. I have a warrant for the arrest of one Lieutenant Eli Broadhurst, who I understand is one of your company commanders."

"Yes, I know Broadhurst. Good soldier. What's he done?"

"Well, sir, he is charged with raping a 13-year old farm girl on Saturday, August 13th while he was supposed to be on duty in charge of a perimeter patrol near Oxford. The girl's father, a disabled veteran, and all the folks around Oxford are up in arms about this. We have witnesses to the act."

"Barksdale, that's a serious charge. I'm shocked. My officers know I won't tolerate misconduct toward civilians. And if what you tell me is true, I will personally hang Broadhurst if he raped that child. That is outrageous conduct. There is no more despicable crime than the rape of an innocent woman or child."

Then Forrest, shaking from anger for the second time in half an hour turned to Gallaway, "Matt, what do we do about this? Do we arrest Broadhurst and ship him to Meridian for trial? Or do we give him to the Sheriff here, and let the Mississippi state courts decide Broadhurst's fate?"

Gallaway hesitated for a few seconds, then said, "Common sense tells me to let the Sheriff have him. But maybe we should await an opinion from the Judge Advocate's Office."

"No," replied Forrest. "That will complicate matters. I think we can trust the civilian courts over in the Oxford area to serve justice. Doesn't *Article 33* require that we turn him over to the civil magistrate?"

Barksdale, a friendly-looking man with large, expressive eyes, said softly, "He'll get a fair trial, General Forrest. He'll be judged on the evidence fair and square."

"I believe you, Sheriff. As much as I'd like to hang him in front of the troops, I'll respect the wishes of the people of Lafayette County. He's yours!"

Stammering again, Forrest said to Gallaway, "Don't

Anderson and you bring me any more aggravation today. Gee...zus, what's happening to my army all of a sudden. Discipline is nonexistent despite Anderson's glowing report to the contrary. We've got to do something quick.

"Matt, get together with Strange, Anderson and Colonel Kelley to organize an assembly of all troops on Saturday. We're going to straighten this out fast.

"Now, if you will excuse me, my head's splitting. Don't disturb me for two hours. I'm going to try to forget any of this happened."

September 16, 1864

Captain John Morton was standing about 30 feet from General Forrest's tent waiting for his friend, Captain Strange, to emerge from the General's tent. Both Morton and Strange had been invited to a cotillion to be held that night in Tupelo at the home of Miss Mary Lou Pettigrew, the 19-year old daughter of Senator Hiram Pettigrew.

Morton was acquainted with friends of Miss Pettigrew; and it was one of them who had instigated the invitation. Miss Pettigrew had a note delivered to Morton inviting him and a friend — "preferably an eligible bachelor," it read. Morton asked John Strange, who was a widower and who had made it known he would like to remarry, to go with him.

Strange exited Forrest's tent shaking his head in a negative manner.

"What did he say, John?"

"He said that he knew I was anxious for the company of females, and he also knew I wanted them for something other than improving my dancing steps. But he said I was needed here. There's work to be done to get ready for breaking camp on Sunday."

"Do you think I should ask?"

"Go ahead, all he can say is no."

Morton entered Forrest's tent apprehensively. Before he could say anything, the General said, "I know why you're here. You want an overnight pass to Tupelo.

"Sit down, Morton, I want to talk with you.

"John, you think you're a man of the world now after three years touring Tennessee, Alabama, Mississippi and Kentucky. Heh-heh-heh!

"But you only know fighting, marching and sleeping on hard ground. You better wait till this war is over, then you'll get to know what ordinary folks are like. There's going to be plenty of women around, mark my words."

"General, you think I'm going to try to get married, don't you?"

"Yup! Not a doubt in my mind! You're a gone goose. I know you have your eye on one of those girls that's going to be at Senator Pettigrew's house tonight."

"Well, you're dead wrong, General Forrest. I just need to talk with young people other than soldiers."

"John, if you're telling me the truth, I definitely must deny your request. And I'm not saying that if you were going to get married, I'd let you go."

"Sir, I am disappointed, but I guess I appreciate your advice."

"John, you joined the Confederate army when you were just 18. You were a small boy just out of school, weren't you? And when you joined me, just after you were released from prison at Johnson's Island, you remember how I couldn't believe you were just 19? I believe I said, 'You couldn't be more than 15.' Well, not to offend you, but you don't look much older now.

"Tell me what you've learned about women slogging around dirt roads pulling cannons. Probably all you've heard are lies told you by other officers about all the women they fornicated in Corinth, or maybe some of those mangy whores with crab lice in Nashville when we were there a couple of years ago. Don't believe them. They have wild imaginations.

"My advice to you is to wait a few years before you take any girl seriously.

"Now go back to your battery and relax. We've got a lot of miles to cover in the next couple of weeks."

September 17, 1864, 10:00 a.m.

Verona was alive with military activity. Preparations were underway to get equipment and supplies ready for the train ride Sunday morning north to Cherokee Station, Alabama. Some 4500 troops had been alerted to clean their weapons, groom their horses and bathe themselves.

Orders were issued to each unit to marshall their soldiers promptly at 3:00 p.m. in a hurriedly prepared, makeshift parade ground for an address by General Forrest and for religious services to be conducted by Colonel Kelley.

Forrest called his staff and key field commanders to his headquarters to go over the nature of the mission.

"Gentlemen, detailed orders arrived last evening from General Dick Taylor," said Forrest. "We are to move north into northern Alabama and Middle Tennessee with the prime objective of destroying Union army communication and supply lines to General Sherman's army over in Georgia.

"We're going to be raiding a lot of small outposts and blockhouses. And if possible, we're ordered to tear up the Nashville & Decatur Railroad tracks.

"Colonel McCulloch's regiment down in Meridian won't be joining us. General Taylor has ordered 'Black Bob's' soldiers to Mobile to help defend that city. It's temporary, detached service.

"Some big things are going to be happening soon. Dick Taylor says that Sherman is going to move into North Alabama and Tennessee to eliminate us if he can. We'll have something to say about that, won't we?"

"How's the war going, General?" asked Colonel Bell.

"General Taylor told me that Jubal Early and Sheridan are having it out in the Shenandoah Valley in Virginia, and the siege of Petersburg, Virginia by Meade's Army of the Potomac continues. Our boys there in the Eastern Theater simply won't give up."

"We've certainly upheld our end of the war here in the Western Theater."

"How long will we be out this time, General?" asked General Buford.

"I don't know, Abe. We'll be doing some hard riding for quite awhile. We should prepare for the worst."

At 3:00 p.m. all units had assembled on the temporary parade ground. Soldiers were packed together tightly in front of a small platform. General Forrest was grim faced as he ascended the steps. There was dead silence. Most knew that he was disturbed about flagging discipline, and that he had dealt harshly with several of his officers. They were apprehensive.

Forrest, immaculate in his uniform as always, had some prepared remarks, but he promptly tore them up as he started to speak.

> *Soldiers!*
> *If you were civilians, indecent conduct would get you two months on the chain gang and 20 lashes in the public square. Just because you are soldiers doesn't excuse you from common courtesy and respect for women and children. I will not tolerate any misconduct toward innocent civilians.*
> *If you are found guilty of rape or similar brutality toward women and children, then God help you. Trust me, I will not interfere with the civilian authorities if they decide you shall hang. I will applaud their decision. I shall volunteer to assist the hangman to see that low curs get what they deserve.*

Then, after going into the details of the Lieutenant Broadhurst incident, he continued on another subject.

> *If any officer, noncommissioned officer or private is found drunk while on duty in any capacity, he shall be court-martialed, reduced in rank, and subjected to hard labor. And he will lead all suicide squads I may appoint. Whiskey is banned from Forrest's Cavalry as of this moment.*
> *You took an oath to be soldiers. I intend to hold you to*

> the discipline necessary to be good soldiers.
> All company commanders will go over the Articles of War with your soldiers tonight. I want them chiseled on your brains.
> Now, soldiers, I have high regard for most of you. Our recent victories at Okolona, Union City, Fort Pillow and Brice's Cross Roads are the result of your great courage in the face of overwhelming odds. I expect no less courage in the battles ahead of us.
> But, soldiers, amid this pride do not forget our gallant dead. Honor the sacrifice they have made to the Confederacy.
> Good luck in the campaign ahead.

The soldiers were so sobered by Forrest's tempestuous and incisive remarks they did not cheer or applaud. They knew instinctively this was not appropriate.

Forrest left the platform quickly, and headed off the field to return to his headquarters.

Then, immediately, Chaplain Cotton Mather Sims and his assistant, Corporal Ronald Papanek jumped on the stage.

"Before Colonel Kelley begins his sermon, I want to announce that we have received a fresh supply of *Bibles* and many pamphlets from the Evangelical Tract Society," announced Chaplain Sims proudly.

"Corporal Papanek and I will be here at the platform later to distribute the Bibles and the reading material. The Bibles are pocket-sized; and they'll fit easily into your pockets. Don't rush. There are enough *Bibles* for all who want them. Thank you."

Colonel Kelley, who had waited patiently during General Forrest's address, then took the platform. With his head slightly cocked to the left, he scanned the crowd for a few moments, then began to speak slowly:

> *Blasphemy, drunkenness and whoredom! Cursing, saloons, grog shops, and brothels! Our gathering here in this open field shall be called a temporary house of*

prayer. Some of you, however, have made it a den of sinners.

Questions you all need to consider individually are: 'Where will I spend Eternity?' and 'Can I atone for the sins I have committed?'

Lying and cheating are rampant sins. And you have heard my admonitions on these subjects many times. Today, however, I choose as my subjects some immediate concerns.

Blasphemy! The reviling of God by brazen mouths. Why do you swear? Blasphemous oaths are not the measure of a person's manhood. Mocking God or calling down evil upon your superiors or comrades is injurious to your character. It's an injury to your self-respect. Would you say profane words in front of your mother, your wife and children, or your sweetheart? No, I think not. And why is that? Isn't it because you respect them? Of course it is. Think about that!

Then there is the curse of whiskey overhanging on ranks. There are soldiers amongst us sotted with alcohol, brawling and mocking authority in their crazed blindness.

Awake drunkards! Be sober and be free. Christ cries out for your return from your wanderings into intemperance. You are endangering your minds and your bodies. You may also be endangering comrades in battle action by your abuse of spirits.

And whoredom! What wickedness has permeated our army! Let not these wayward wretches offer their evil bodies as fuel for your sensuous desires.

Whoredom and alcohol blunt your moral senses.

And again, what would your loved ones think if they knew you were consorting with these disease ridden outcasts of society?

Colonel Kelley continued his sermon in the same general manner on the subject of gambling. He concluded this subject by saying:

Beware of those vultures who rob you of your money and your moral fabric. Your idle time can be better spent in more wholesome activity.

Then Kelley concluded his sermon:

Soldiers! Recognize our Savior in your daily actions. Cut loose from the grip of Satan. Avoid those who wallow in sin. Keep your Christianity. Repent now so you can be brought into the glorious light of God.

Soldiers! Now let us sing together that wonderful old hymn, *Rock of Ages*." Then, I shall ask Chaplain Sims to give the benediction to conclude our service.

25 • Franklin and Nashville

General John Bell Hood's Army of Tennessee continued disrupting General Sherman's supply lines northwest of Atlanta even after losing that city in early September 1864 to the Union army. But in October 1864 Hood was ordered to alter his plans, and to disengage from fighting Sherman in Georgia.

Hood's army was repositioned in Tuscumbia, Alabama in the northwest corner of the state. This would become the base camp for a major Confederate offensive drive on Nashville, some 100 miles north. The latter city had been a principal Union military and supply center since captured in February 1862. The Confederate strategy was to dislodge the Federals from Nashville, then drive north to the Ohio River.

The Confederate War Department believed such an expedition would force Sherman's army to pursue Hood, and thus reduce the Union's military pressure in Georgia and the Carolinas. But the Confederates erred. Rather than follow Hood's army into Tennessee, Sherman was ordered back to Atlanta. The task of handling Hood was assigned to General George B. Thomas, the Union's hero at Chickamauga. Thomas was ordered to Nashville to mobilize Union forces and to ready the city's defense network for the anticipated attack by Hood.

General Forrest, whose cavalry from October through mid-November 1864, had soundly defeateded a number of small Union detachments protecting Sherman's communication and supply lines in Middle Tennessee, was ordered to join Hood's army.

During the height of his success in October Forrest requested a leave of absence. "I am in poor health and suffering from fatigue," he wrote General Richard Taylor, his immediate superior. "I am totally worn out. I need rest and recovery time if I am to be effective in the future."

Forrest's request was denied. Hood decided that Forrest's Cavalry would be less effective without its daring leader.

Tuscumbia, Alabama, November 17, 1864

"Matt, I've just come from General Hood's headquarters," said Forrest matter-of-factly. "I've been put in charge of all cavalry for this expedition north to Nashville."

"Well, wonderful General, at last you're getting the recognition you deserve."

"No, Matt, Hood's doing me no favor. I'm in much too poor physical condition to be responsible for 6000 to 7000 troops. I hurt all over. It's not only the boils. It's the wear-and-tear of being on the move for the past two months. Sometimes I feel like I'm going to fall off the saddle. And that damn diarrhea has weakened me. Don't I look thin, Matt?"

"Yes, you've probably lost 15 to 20 pounds since we left Verona. What's Dr. Cowan say?"

"Matt, he tells me to demand a leave, and not to take 'No' for an answer. He says I won't make it through the winter.

"But Hood says I'm crucial to his plan of attack, and that my cavalry is experienced for the type of fighting he expects. And, Matt, after seeing Hood's physical condition, I can't feel sorry for myself. General Hood is only 33, but he looks 53 or older. He's taller than I am, but he's all stooped over. The poor devil lost his right leg at Chickamauga and before that the use of his left arm in the fighting at Gettysburg.

"They tell me he directed the fighting around Atlanta strapped in his saddle. We have two things in common. He loves to fight and so do I. And we both hurt all over. So if he can do it, I can do it too."

"General, you don't want to end up a martyr, do you?"

"If the weather cooperates, maybe I'll manage for another month or so. If not, will Fannie and you look out for Mary?" he said semi-seriously.

"Ask Strange and Anderson to come in. We've been ordered to cross the Tennessee River tomorrow, and to leave Florence on Saturday. That gives us two days to get ready."

On Sunday, November 20th, the first day after entering Tennessee, it rained. The following day it was a light snow. Then on Tuesday it was a cold, sharp wind which caused the heavily-grooved dirt roads to freeze. These were just the type of weather conditions Forrest hoped to avoid.

By Saturday, November 26th Hood's main force reached Columbia, Tennessee — the town where Forrest had maintained his headquarters in the Spring of 1863. The Army of Tennessee had travelled a distance of 75 miles in one week. Some resistance had occurred enroute. These skirmishes removed any doubt on Hood's part that General Thomas in Nashville was well aware that Hood's army of 40,000 troops was well on its way.

Thomas had assigned Major General John M. Schofield with two corps of infantry and Brigadier General James H. Wilson (West Point, 1860) and his cavalry to thwart Hood's drive. Their combined force was 34,000 soldiers.

Fighting broke out on Tuesday, November 29th near

Spring Hill, Tennessee. This hamlet was 12 miles northeast of Columbia on a road leading to Nashville. Here, late in the afternoon, it appeared a Confederate victory was possible. Schofield's troops were in retreat. Hood's army had two hours of daylight left to attempt to administer a stunning defeat on the Union army. But Hood's forces lacked coordination. They weren't able to organize themselves in time to try to rout Schofield before darkness.

The Confederate forces bivouacked for the night. Schofield was well aware of a possible entrapment. That night while the Confederates rested, he ordered his army to retreat toward Franklin, Tennessee. The failure of General Hood, General Cheatham and other principal commanders to communicate effectively among themselves permitted Schofield's forces to march unmolested out of a seeming trap, and to move up 15 miles to Franklin, Tennessee.

General Hood blamed General Cheatham and other commanders including Forrest for the blunder. But many officers blamed Hood. They claimed he was exhausted from lack of sleep, and that he was ranting and raving about "*God* being on our side," and "It was *God*'s will." He had asked his immediate staff to pray with him during the long night while Schofield's army was slipping away from danger.

Forrest's Cavalry took off in pursuit of Schofield's army in a futile attempt to keep it from reaching the safety of Franklin. Forrest was distressed about what had happened. He said to General Abe Buford, "You can see the results of too many cooks, can't you, Buford? When I ran my own command without interference from November 1863 to September 1864, we performed miracles. Now, in this tangled chain-of-command, exercising one's initiative is prohibited. Hood doesn't know what is going on; and everyone is afraid to tell him the facts. *God* help us, Buford!"

Schofield reached Franklin just after 1:00 p.m., Wednesday, November 30th. He ordered his soldiers to begin strengthening the city's defenses already in place. These crudely-constructed earthworks, fences and log piles encircled the south and western sides of the town. The Tennessee & Alabama Railroad tracks were on the east side and the Harpeth River bounded the north side.

Hood's main Confederate force reached the southern outskirts of Franklin early that afternoon. Immediately he positioned the army on a line extending nearly three miles right to left. The line was from one to one-half miles more or less distance from the Union's defense. To attack head-on would require Hood's soldiers to charge across a largely unobstructed open field to reach the Union entrenchments.

Hood called a meeting of commanders at 2:30 p.m. to announce his plan. He ordered General Chalmers' Cavalry to position themselves on the extreme left end of the line, and Forrest's, on the extreme right end. All infantry units were positioned in-between.

"We're going to make an all-out frontal assault," said the highly agitated and physically haggard Hood. "We've got 38,000 soldiers to overrun the enemy. With only a few hours of daylight left we cannot delay the attack. Any questions?"

"Yes, sir," shouted Forrest.

"What do you have to say, Forrest?"

"General Hood, in my opinion it's a senseless plan. We'll be slaughtered in the large open field. Our men have to go on foot for over a mile. The Federals are behind their works ready to fire away with artillery and small arms."

"Then what's you plan?"

"We should go around them, and cut them off from Nashville."

"Well, Forrest, my plan for your cavalry is to do just that. Circle around on the right of Franklin."

"No, General Hood, I mean all of us should go around."

"That's out of the question! We've got the enemy directly in front of us. My orders are to charge them out. The bugle sounds at 2:45 p.m. for a full frontal assault. It's settled. I'll stand for no backbiting on my decision. We are at *Armageddon*. This is that battle between the forces of good and evil before the *Day of Judgment*."

The bugler was ordered to sound, "Charge!" Thousands of Confederate soldiers rushed forward across the open field directly into a thunderous volley of artillery and rifle fire from Schofield's troops behind the Union entrenchments. Dead and wounded soon lay everywhere on that broad field before the town of Franklin. Thirteen times the Confederates charged, only to be repulsed. Smoke from the gun fire at first masked the landscape covered with dead and wounded. Few Confederates reached the Union breastworks. There were no breakthroughs.

On the north side of Franklin Forrest's cavalry force of 2,535 troops met in combat General James Wilson's full cavalry. The latter far outnumbered Forrest's force, and successfully pushed the Confederates back across the Harpeth River. Without Forrest's cavalry in his path, Schofield's army was able to withdraw safely from Franklin toward Nashville. Forrest rationalized later that he would have defeated Wilson if Chalmers' brigade of cavalry had been with him.

At dawn on Thursday, December 1st survivors of bloody Franklin witnessed one of the greatest scenes of slaughter in the Civil War. Dead bodies, strewn about the battlefield in grotesque positions, shocked the survivors. The hair and eyebrows of many of the dead were flaked with white crystals — the result of a heavy overnight frost. One of the more horrifying spectacles was a dead Confederate private whose upper lip had been shot off. With his head facing the morning sun, he appeared to be grinning. Some bodies were in the shape of a ball. They had been shot in the stomach and had brought their knees to their chests before they died trying to stop the bleeding.

The dazed, walking Confederate wounded directed their wrath against General Hood. "We never had a chance!" shouted one in anguish. Another said gleefully, "I'm glad a lot of officers got it." And a third was mumbling, "Where was Hood? — where was Hood?"

Some 5550 Confederates had been killed or wounded. The Union casualties were 1200. Among the Confederates killed were five brigadier generals and a dozen brigade commanders. Overnight Schofield's Union army had abandoned Franklin. It quickly moved on to Nashville where General Thomas was continuing to strengthen an already formidable military bastion. Hood's army, now seriously crippled, followed Schofield to the edge of Nashville. There Hood prepared for a siege of the city.

In a surprising tactical move Hood ordered Forrest, and two cavalry brigades and two infantry divisions to operate against isolated Union forces garrisoned in and around Murfreesboro, a town some 30 miles or more southeast of Nashville. Forrest's assignment was to disrupt train movements on the Nashville & Chattanooga Railroad. Hood's decision to detach Forrest and the others seriously weakened his fighting strength in front of Nashville. He left his army with only limited cavalry support. General Chalmers commanded one of these units in front of Nashville.

Forrest commented to Captain Strange, "I think Hood wants me out of his sight. My presence reminds him of his blundering at Spring Hill and Franklin. But I'm not objecting."

"General, there's an old saying that the best way to convince a fool he is wrong is to let him have his own way."

"That's very good, Strange. I'll have to remember that. "Now, old Bragg's got company. Hood joins him in the conspiracy against Bedford Forrest. Heh-heh-heh!"

Detached service proved troublesome to Forrest. His combined cavalry-infantry force enjoyed some early success in overrunning isolated Union garrisons and destroying some railroad trackage, but in a pitched-battle at Murfreesboro on December 7th he suffered a humiliating defeat. His infantry troops panicked and fled the field despite Forrest's attempt to stop them.

Despite Forrest's lack of a major contribution in the Murfreesboro area Hood did not order him to rejoin the main force at Nashville.

Thomas had been expected to attack the Confederates almost from the moment of Hood's arrival on the outskirts of Nashville. But the attack didn't come right away. Hood left his troops on alert. He told his commanders on December 10th, "I believe General Thomas will attack, and we should be prepared for it any time now."

President Lincoln and his War Department were outraged that Thomas delayed in attacking with his large and well-supplied army. Demands were made on Thomas to take the initiative or face discipline. Upset with Thomas' inertia General Grant ordered Thomas replaced with General Schofield. But Thomas pleaded for more time. "The weather is not right for an attack," he replied to Grant. "When the ice melts, we'll go." Grant then rescinded the order for Thomas to step down. But he kept the pressure on Thomas to attack.

On December 14th Thomas informed Grant that the attack would come the next day. Fifty thousand Union troops had been mobilized in Nashville for the fight.

At 4:00 a.m. Thursday, December 15th the first of the Union units moved forward, but at a slow pace. But by 10:00 a.m. the bulk of the Union infantry and cavalry were moving in an encircling arc against the left side of the Confederate line. Initially, Thomas attacked the Confederate right with a smaller force to draw Hood's troops to this side of the battle line while his larger force struck the opposite side of the Confederate line. The pressure on Hood's forces was intense. In manpower he was far outnumbered. He had 23,000 soldiers to face Thomas's 50,000. And Hood, with Forrest's cavalry units near Murfreesboro, had only limited cavalry. Without an effective cavalry, Hood lost mobility and the opportunity for sudden lightning-like strikes.

Hood's army gave up considerable ground during the first day of intense fighting. It had been pushed to the south side of Nashville's outskirts. But, as night fell, Hood's army, now in a more compact formation, had not been routed. Understandably it was disorganized.

At dawn on Friday, December 16th Thomas struck Hood again using the same basic attack plan of the previous day. The Union struck against the Confederate left line into the bulk of Hood's forces. The objective was to turn Hood's left flank. The Union artillery kept up a barrage against the Confederate positions throughout the morning and early afternoon. Tremendous pressure was inflicted on the rear of the Confederate troops by General Wilson's Cavalry fighting dismounted. With heavy artillery fire directed to the front of the Confederate line, and Wilson's Union troops behind them, General Cheatham's Corps, positioned in the center, withdrew in a scene of wild disorder.

General Stephen Lee's troops were positioned to keep the Franklin-Columbia Pike open as an escape route for Confederate units fighting on the southern periphery of Nashville. General Chalmers was ordered to do the same on Granny Smith Pike, a road running parallel to the Franklin-Columbia Pike, two miles west. The out-manned Chalmers delayed successfully the aggressive Union forces who had moved forward quickly in pursuit of the fleeing Confederates.

That night Chalmers' Cavalry was assigned to protect the rear of Hood's retreating army. Fortunately for the Confederates, General Wilson chose to rest his cavalry overnight before resuming the chase the next morning, Saturday, December 17th.

Forrest was ordered to rejoin Hood's main force in Columbia. Hood had reached there on Sunday, December 18th. Forrest arrived that night. He was delayed by his drive of several hundred head of cattle and hogs captured near Murfreesboro.

Within one hour of his arrival, Forrest was summoned to Hood's headquarters. He found Hood visibly distressed and quivering and muttering to himself over and over, "Why is *God* penalizing me? What have I done to displease Him? I know *God* is on the Confederate side in this war." Several of his inner circle of senior officers assured Hood that he had done no wrong and that his life was exemplary.

Forrest was amused by Hood's rantings. He thought to himself, "Hood has lost his sanity. A good night's sleep will calm him down."

Hood, however, had no intention of forgetting the war, or his bewilderment with *God Almighty* for even a few hours.

"Forrest, I am assigning you to protect the rear of our withdrawal back to Alabama. You'll have Chalmers and Buford with you. And I'm ordering General Walthall to consolidate some scattered divisions of infantry to join you in the rear guard.

"We must move south quickly despite this terrible weather. I fear that Federal gunboats on the Tennessee River between Decatur and Florence, Alabama may get to our main river crossing points first. If that happens, we'll all be prisoners of war. I realize we should rest until the weather improves. There are soldiers out there who are barefooted and sick. Most lack heavy clothing. It's best to get them back to Alabama as fast as possible.

"Can you do the job, Forrest?"

"General Hood, we'll attack; we'll counterattack. I'll do everything I can to protect the rear."

"May *God* protect you, Forrest."

"Thank you, sir!"

Waiting for Forrest were General Buford, Matt Gallaway and Dr. Cowan.

"What are our orders, General?" inquired Buford anxiously.

"I think *God* told Hood that he wants us to protect the rear as we move south to the Tennessee River. General Walthall is joining us with some infantry. Hood's asked that we hold Columbia for as long as possible. Let's try to stay here until December 22nd; then we'll dash south. The Duck River here should protect us for a couple of days."

Dr. Cowan, who had listened intently as Forrest described the raving of General Hood and his extreme nervousness, said, "General, I think we've got a problem with General Hood that's serious."

"What's that, James?"

"I can't prove it, but he appears heavily under the influence of opium, or maybe its laudanum — a mixture of opium and alcohol. He's probably using it to kill pain. His nerves are frazzled.

"Did you notice him sweating or itching?"

"Well, yes I did now that I think about it," answered Forrest.

"What about his eyes, General? Did they look dilated, or pupils unequal?"

"How in-the-hell do I know, James. I didn't put my face up against his."

"General, he's got all the symptoms of drug addiction. No wonder he can't sleep and is talking about his *Maker*. He should be relieved of command."

"Too late now, James! He's already done about as much damage as possible on this expedition.

"Well, let's not worry about Hood. We've got our own troubles," concluded Forrest.

Major General Edward C. Walthall reported to Forrest the next morning.

"How many effectives do you have, General Walthall?" asked Forrest.

"General, I've got 1900 fighting Mississippians — but one serious problem. Some 300 or so are barefooted."

"Goddamn, what good are they? Hell, General, there's ice and snow, and frozen ruts in the road, they'll have to walk over. They'll hold us back."

"We have wagons, General Forrest. And let me assure you, when the time comes to fight, they'll fight. They're Mississippians!"

"All right, but if they become a yoke to us, be prepared to abandon them," said the perplexed Forrest as he shook Walthall's hand.

On Thursday, December 22nd Forrest's and Walthall's troops withdrew from Columbia to retreat to Pulaski, some 30 miles south.

The weather was gray overcast with a chilly wind blowing from the west. The landscape through which they passed was desolate and depressing. Burned out farmhouses and barns were everywhere. Most of the picket fences around the fields were no longer standing. Fields hadn't been cultivated in several years. Fragments of dried up cotton plants were a reminder of what once had been a productive field.

Forrest, who was riding next to Matt Gallaway, remarked, "Matt, this sight is almost as bad as a battlefield full of dead soldiers. Look over there! There's nothing left, is there? Have we lost the war, Matt? Do you think it's like this all over the South?"

"You ask about the war, General. I'd say that after what happened at Franklin and Nashville, we can't go too much further. We're pretty well spent. But you and I can't see the whole picture of the war right now. From our vantage point, however, it doesn't look good.

"Sherman's Union army is at the gates of Savannah preparing to encircle the city. One of Hood's staff told me that General Lee couldn't spare any troops from Virginia because of the Union's siege of Petersburg. The Federals have pinned Lee's forces down for almost six months. I believe, General, when we get back to Alabama, some of our units will be sent to Savannah to try to contain Sherman.

"Morale is a serious problem, General. The desertion rate is mind-boggling. Since we left Columbia, several hundred of our troops have run off."

"Yes, Matt, I've gotten reports this morning that some of our soldiers left in the middle of the night. The countryside is full of those goddamn cowards. If we catch any of them, you know my orders. Shoot 'em!"

At that moment they passed some civilians — mostly women, children and old men struggling with their horses and wagons in the mud trying to escape south. As they passed there was no cheering, no words of encouragement — just blank stares straight ahead.

When it started raining that afternoon, Forrest said to Matt Gallaway, "When I was a boy in Tippah County, Mississippi they used to say it'll be a bad winter if squirrels' tails grow bushier and fur on the bottom of rabbits' feet is thicker. Next time you shoot a squirrel or a rabbit, take a look, will you Matt?

"This cold rain makes me feel all those old wounds. I guess that crazy Hood is right, *God* may not be on my side either."

"General, if it's any consolation, I believe we are better off than Napoleon's retreating army back in the winter of 1812. The French reached the gates of Moscow only to be driven off with the Russians in pursuit. They had no food for the soldiers and the horses. It was 17° below zero. Can you imagine that?

"Marshall Ney became a hero. He was in command of Napoleon's rear guard, fighting off Kutusov's attacks to permit the French to get to Smolensk. But all the French found in Smolensk was a destroyed city — no food, no supplies, no shelter — nothing.

"Napoleon's army lost thousands. Some killed by the Russians, but most froze to death. But Marshall Ney, cut off at times, always reappeared to protect the retreat as best he could. He was one resourceful fellow."

"How old was this Marshall Ney, Matt?"

"I think he was 43. Your age, General."

"Matt, are you making up that story?"

"No, it's absolutely the truth."

At night, Forrest's soldiers huddled around campfires wrapped in blankets trying to keep warm. Most of the wood was damp from the snow and rain, and it didn't give off much heat. Forrest, sympathetic to their plight, spent an hour each night visiting campsites.

At Lynnville on the night of December 23rd he saw a familiar face huddled close to a fire. It was Walter X. Jester, his friend.

"Private Jester, we meet again. How are you?"

"Fine, sir, but it's now Sergeant Jester."

"When did you get promoted, Jester?"

"Right after I recovered from my wounds at Brice's Cross Roads. I guess it was a reward, sir."

"Well, I'm pleased. You and I have come a long way, haven't we?"

"Yes, sir, it seems like 25 years ago when you signed me up in Memphis."

"How are you doing tonight, Jester?"

"Well, sir, that damn wood is wet. I guess I'll just have to curl up like a cat to stay warm."

Then Forrest said, "I recognize your buddy there from somewhere. What's your name, soldier?"

"It's Sergeant Bozarth, formerly Corporal Bozarth of the Forrest Minstrels."

Forrest laughing said, "Oh yes, the fellow dressed up like a Southern belle. That was damn funny. Have you been doing any singing lately, Bozarth?"

"No, sir, that was a one-time performance. And besides I don't know what happened to Captain Wilbourne who produced that show."

"Oh, you mean, 'Frozen Eye.' He's with Colonel McCulloch down in Mobile. He'll scare hell out of those Yankees if General Canby attempts to take that city from us. "Well, men, I'll see both of you when we get back to Alabama. Good night."

"Good night, General Forrest," they both said in unison as Forrest disappeared into the dark.

On Christmas Eve day Forrest, sensing an opportunity to catch the enemy by surprise, ordered a counterattack. "Let's push them back toward Columbia," he said to his commanders Buford, Armstrong, Chalmers and Ross. At Richmond Creek, after a bitter two-hour fight, Forrest's troops inflicted heavy damage on the Federals. But General Buford was wounded during the height of the fighting. Chalmers assumed command of Buford's troops. Sensing nothing more could be accomplished that day, Chalmers and the other commanders withdrew. They reached Pulaski that night.

On Christmas morning Forrest ordered General William Jackson to destroy all the ammunition that could not be removed from Pulaski, them remain in defense of the town for a few hours before destroying the bridge over Richland Creek.

Another skirmish took place later that day south of Pulaski. Many Union soldiers were killed, and many taken prisoner.

The two forces skirmished again on December 26th with the same results. That night Forrest's army camped at Sugar Creek just north of the Tennessee River.

On December 27th, Forrest's troops safely made their way during the day to the north bank of the Tennessee River, and that night crossed the river without incident. No Union gunboats had arrived to prevent their crossing.

Sixteen hundred Union prisoners taken during the retreat were turned over to the Provost Marshall's department.

Forrest thanked his commanders for their efforts in successfully protecting Hood's retreating army. He gave special thanks to General Walthall and his Mississippians who performed heroically.

When Forrest reached Tuscumbia, Alabama, he requested that Dr. Cowan visit with him immediately. But Cowan had not yet arrived in Tuscumbia; so Forrest gave orders that he was going to bed and did not wish to be disturbed. Miraculously, despite his weakened physical condition at the start of the campaign north with Hood's army, he had made it back to Alabama alive.

26 • Surrender

The Civil War was winding down in the first weeks of April 1865. There were several major setbacks for the Confederacy. Forrest's loss at Selma, Alabama to Union forces under General James H. Wilson's Cavalry did not affect the war's outcome.

On April 2, 1865, the same day Selma fell, General Grant's Federal troops finally broke the last of General Robert E. Lee's defenses at Petersburg, Virginia in the Eastern Theater of the war. The Army of Virginia went into a mass retreat. On that very day, recognizing that Richmond was about to fall, Jefferson Davis and his cabinet decided the time had come to evacuate, and to head south into the Carolinas and Georgia to escape capture.

When the Federals arrived in Richmond on April 3rd the city was in flames.

On April 9th General Lee surrendered his Army of Virginia to Grant in a solemn, dignified ceremony at Appomattox Courthouse in Virginia. But the news verifying this surrender did not reach the Western Theater until later in April.

Mobile fell on April 12th. General Edward Canby's Union force of 45,000 captured what had once been a strategic port city in the Confederacy after months of trying to oust the entrenched Confederates, and after a loss of nearly 1600 soldiers.

General Sherman's army was near Raleigh, North Carolina pushing General Joseph E. Johnston's retreating Confederate army farther and farther north. On April 14th Johnston contacted Sherman requesting a temporary halt in the fighting to permit peace discussions. On April 18th Sherman and Johnston concluded a peace agreement.

On the night of April 14th at Ford's Theater in Washington, President Lincoln was shot. He died at 7:22 a.m. the next morning at age 56.

Andrew Johnson of Tennessee, Lincoln's Vice President, was sworn in as the 17th President of the United States at 11:00 a.m. that day, April 15, 1865.

General Forrest, his Escort Company, and several small detachments arrived in Gainesville, Alabama on April 12th — ten days after fleeing Selma.

This small hamlet in Greene County had been untouched physically by the war. The general area was tranquil. The surrounding fields were abundant with clover and Spring wild flowers. Gainesville, located on high ground above the navigable Tombigbee River, was an active river port for flatboat and barge traffic hauling primarily cotton between Columbus, Mississippi and Mobile. Most directly of benefit to Forrest was the short rail line which connected Gainesville with the Mobile & Ohio Railroad located 25 miles west in Mississippi.

Not until April 25th did the last of Forrest's scattered command reassemble. This 13-day gap gave Forrest much needed recovery time from his painful wounds.

But nothing slowed the frenetic leader. He emersed himself in administrative details as if they were an elixir to get his mind off his pain and off thoughts that the war might be lost.

"Major Strange, get in here. We've got work to do," barked the hyperactive Forrest. "The work is piling up. There are letters I need you to write. We've got to take inventory. General Taylor expects us to reorganize quickly."

"Sir, we could use more help in your headquarters."

"Well, goddamnit, get me some scribes from General Taylor's command, and do it quick," said Forrest in his characteristically high pitched voice when he was agitated.

"I'll take care of it, General!"

On April 14th at mid-morning Major Strange entered Forrest's headquarters with a small, thin young private who appeared to be very nervous at the sight of General Forrest.

Pvt. George W. Cable

Forrest looked up and said, "You! — are you a scribe? — You don't look like one to me."

"I am sir. I'm Private George Washington Cable from General Taylor's staff."

"Scribe! How old are you? You look like a small kid who has been starved to death. No wonder we're losing the war."

"I'm 20, sir. I weigh about 115 pounds, I guess. But I eat as much as any two soldiers you've got. I can do any job as long as it doesn't require heavy lifting."

"Have you seen any fighting, or have you just been toting a quill?"

"Sir, I've been wounded twice in fighting. While recovering they use me as a clerk."

"All right, I will tell you what to do. But let me warn you. I've got one rule around here. There's to be no whistling. I hate that. It gets on my nerves. Do you understand?

"Now, prepare a note to Dr. Cowan and Dr. Jones, our two staff doctors. Tell them I want a complete inventory of our medical supplies by this afternoon.

"Then get a message to Colonel Kelley. Tell the Parson I'd appreciate a fine sermon this Sunday. But be sure to say that I don't want to hear any 'Hell and Brimstone.' The boys are in no mood for that.

"Next, get me those blacksmiths, Bowlegs Teet and the Bemis twins, in here quick. I need to get my new mount shod."

Private Cable was writing as fast as he could wondering when General Forrest would pause to take a deep breath. But that didn't happen for another ten minutes.

"Clerk, do you know what manumission papers are?"

"Yes, sir, that's a legal document for freeing slaves."

"That's right. Tomorrow morning I'm going to issue papers for all my boys. I promised them I'd let them go last year, but I never got around to it."

"That's a wonderful thing to do, sir. My family down in New Orleans granted their slaves manumission. My mother came from New England puritan stock, and she's always been against slavery."

"Well, enough of that Clerk, I'm just glad most folks down South didn't think that way."

Early Saturday, April 15th, Forrest's slaves who had served him faithfully as teamsters and as cooks and body servants were lined up outside headquarters waiting their turn to enter. Forrest was in his usual state of nervous, high energy. Over and over he explained to Private Cable the same instructions.

"Now, Clerk, here's the legal form for you to follow. The niggers will come to you one by one as you want them.

"Here, Tom, you be the first!

"Now, Tom, tell me square! Ain't I always been a good master to you?"

"Yas, suh, Gen'ril."

"Tom, the clerk here will take care of you."

Then Forrest opened the door and hollered outside, "Sam, you're next; then Jeremiah."

By 1:00 p.m. Private Cable had prepared papers for all 44 of Forrest's slaves.

"Clerk, Major Strange says you are on loan to me only through Monday. So get something to eat, then get back here quick. I've prepared a list of tasks I want you to complete today."

Major Strange entered as Cable exited to go to the cook's tent.

"How is Private Cable doing, General?"

"That puny kid is good. Ask General Taylor's adjutant if we can have him permanently."

"I'll try, but Cable's well-liked over at General Taylor's command.

"General, may I ask if you think it appropriate we have some camp entertainment. We can probably get 'Frozen Eye' Wilbourne to organize another show just like Oxford last year. Wilbourne's back from Mobile."

"Oh no, not again. He's comical and talented to be sure, but I don't think the soldiers are in a mood for a big show. Maybe later. I have no idea where we might be in a week or so. Better wait."

Most of Forrest's staff relaxed that warm Saturday afternoon. Some were fishing in the Tombigbee River. Others, like Colonel Kelley, were sleeping.

Forrest, accompanied by Rambaut, Morton and Strange, looked in Kelley's tent and heard snoring.

"Look at him," said the grinning, mischievous Rambaut. "Let's play a trick on him."

"Like what?" asked the inquisitive Forrest.

"Well, gentlemen, there's a dead rat in that barrel over there. Let's put it down his pants."

Kelley had loosened his pants before going to sleep. so it was easy slipping the dead rat down his pants. Rambaut and Morton quietly crept into the tent, gently lifted Kelley's trousers at the belt line, dropped in the rat, then went outside and waited.

Within minutes Kelley bolted out of the tent hollering, "Goddamnit to hell, I'm going to kick somebody in the ass for doing this!"

As Kelley ran top speed toward the Tombigbee River, trying at the same time to get his pants off hollering, "Rambaut, you'll pay for this!"

Everyone in the vicinity ran down to the riverbank, slapping their thighs, laughing uncontrollably, and yelling, "Parson, shame on you for taking the *Lord*'s name in vain."

Forrest, laughing convulsively for several minutes, said to Major Strange, "I forgot for a few minutes that I still hurt all over. I hope the Parson is forgiving. But Gilbert Rambaut better be prepared for retaliation."

Then Forrest asked Strange to accompany him on a visit with some of the privates in camp.

"Hello soldier, what's your name?" inquired Forrest.

"It's Private Harry Threat, sir."

"What's your friend's name over there?"

"That's Private Carlos Hendree, sir. We're both from Aberdeen, Mississippi.

"General, do you think we'll have to surrender? We're not beat. There's a lot of fight left in us."

"Well, Threat, it's not what I want, but our troops up in Virginia and over in Carolina are all beat up. And things don't look too good here in Alabama either. We've done better than anyone thought we'd do. And so far, we can be thankful we made it out alive."

Private Hendree asked, "General, sir! What should we do if the war stops? There isn't much to go home to. Everything is ruined."

"How old are you two?" asked Forrest.

Threat said, "I'm 18."

And Hendree said, "I'm 20 next birthday."

"If I were your ages, I'd go to Texas. There's a big future down there in all kinds of businesses. You don't have to go back to farming, you know!

"Tonight, get together with your comrades. Talk about all you've been through together. I think you'll be proud of yourselves."

"General, may I ask what you plan tonight?" asked Private Hendree.

"Well, boys, as you may know I hurt all over. Sometime tomorrow morning I'm going to stop drinking. So in the meantime pick me up if I fall on the ground. Heh-heh-heh!"

As Forrest and Strange returned to the former's headquarters, the General commented, "Isn't it remarkable the courage and the spirit of those boys. Let's hope they all make it through the war if it continues."

Sunday, April 16th was quiet in camp. Rumors

circulated that Lee had surrendered. The question everyone asked: "Is it true, or isn't it?" Huddles of soldiers discussed the latest rumor brought into camp from General Taylor's headquarters in Meridian.

Monday morning, April 17th, General Forrest had Private Cable in tow at 7:30 a.m.

"This is your last day here, Clerk. Let's make the most of it.

"I want to dictate this special order to all company commanders. Are you ready?"

"Yes, sir," snapped the efficient Cable.

"All right, here it is:

Anyone caught with head lice or body lice tomorrow will be dunked 25 times in the Tombigbee River and placed in isolation for one week. All company commanders will conduct an inspection of their soldiers at 7:30 a.m. They shall be lined up single file and naked. No exceptions. I want a full report by noon. Dr. Cowan and his staff will coordinate this inspection.

"Have you got that, Clerk? Now get it done and have Major Strange's aides distribute copies throughout the camp. Report to me by 1:00 p.m. today. Now, Clerk, don't fail me."

Cable finished the assignment; and as requested by Forrest, reported to him that all commanders had been notified.

"What time do you leave today, Clerk?"

"At 4:00 p.m., sir."

"All right then, let's get to work. I want to get my money's worth out of you."

General Taylor notified Forrest on April 30th that he had entered into an agreement with Union General Edward R. Canby (West Point, 1839) for the cessation of fighting for 48 hours. Taylor and Canby had met in a cordial meeting in Citronelle, Alabama, about 25 miles north of Mobile, to discuss surrender terms.

On May 4th Taylor formally surrendered to General Canby. He was aware that Robert E. Lee and Joseph E. Johnston had previously surrendered. Taylor asked for and received the same terms as Lee and Johnston.

Forrest went immediately to General Taylor's headquarters in Meridian to discuss the procedure of surrender. Colonel Don Marshall of Forrest's staff accompanied him. Taylor and Forrest spoke at length about the reasons for surrender. After Taylor convinced Forrest that it was futile to continue, the latter didn't protest. He accepted it all matter-of-factly.

As Forrest prepared to leave, Taylor in an apologetic way asked Forrest if he had seen a copy of *The New York Times*, issue of March 19, 1865.

Forrest answered, "No, I haven't."

"Here Forrest, read it while I get some coffee. You'll find it interesting."

Ten minutes later Taylor returned with coffee for both of them.

"You are quite a star attraction up North, Forrest. I should think you would be honored to be singled out with General Robert E. Lee as outstanding Confederate military leaders."

"General Taylor, do you think of me as a barbarian — a wild frontiersman like Jim Bowie? I read that article with great interest. There's some truth to what it says. I have fought with my wits, not with a West Point manual telling me step-by-step what action to take in a given circumstance. What those people don't understand is that most of us fought undermanned, and without proper or enough equipment.

"My hell-bent style has been necessary to counteract Federal superiority in numbers and supplies. Because some of my tactics resembled Indian attacks, they accuse me of not fighting fair-and-square. Hell, General Taylor, I've always fought to win, and to do what was necessary to win.

"I've been an outsider in the Confederate high command since Fort Donelson back in early 1862. Because I didn't have much schooling and little military training to become an officer, I have borne my share of persecution and pettiness from all the Braggs and Pillows of our army. Except for old Beauregard, you and a few others, I've been classified as a misfit.

"But I'll put my case in the hands of the common folks of Tennessee, Mississippi, Alabama and Kentucky to judge me. They're more aware of what my cavalry has done to try to win this war. They judge a soldier by what he's done, not his social manners and his spit-and-polish on the parade grounds, or his West Point diploma.

"No, sir, General, I'm not offended by *The New York Times*.

"I do not know Robert E. Lee, or know much about him. Fighting exclusively in the Western Theater of the war has prevented me from learning much about the fighting styles and courage of those fellow in the Army of Virginia. I hope General Lee is not offended by the label *The New York Times* pinned on him, 'the Southern Gentleman.' Heh-heh-heh!"

"General Forrest, I know you must return to Gainesville and prepare for a formal surrender ceremony. Keep me informed of the plans. We'll coordinate them with General Canby's staff.

"Goodbye Forrest, and thank you for your outstanding leadership. I trust we shall meet again."

"I hope so, General Taylor. I am honored to have served with you."

Gainesville, Alabama, Saturday, May 6, 1865

Forrest's camp was active during the morning and afternoon. Equipment and supplies were being sorted, and detailed inventories being prepared by a battery of commissioned and noncommissioned officers.

"I want every last item accounted for," ordered Forrest. "When General Canby's men arrive here on

Tuesday for the formal surrender ceremony I want them to see how Forrest's Cavalry does things. Soldiers will be permitted to take only their horses, rifles and personal possessions. Nothing else. All military equipment and supplies now belong to the Federals."

Of primary concern that morning was the preparation of General Forrest's final address to his soldiers. Forrest met with Major Anderson and Matt Gallaway to discuss what should be covered in Tuesday's farewell address.

"I've got some ideas which I've already discussed with you. Let me see what you write by tomorrow. Just be sure to point out that the war is over, and that the men must make the best of it."

That night Forrest invited his staff to join him for a farewell dinner. Sergeant Flaxy Berry, in charge of officers' mess since just after Shiloh, was asked by Forrest, "Perform your culinary magic one more time. This is our last meal together."

At 6:00 p.m. Forrest and his staff sat down to eat. Colonel Kelley, still trying to think of a way to get even with Major Rambaut for the rat incident, gave his standard blessing — but with one addendum, "May *God* bring his wrath down on ex-Memphis innkeeper, Gilbert Vincent Rambaut, and condemn him to life in a snake pit."

Laughter prevailed for a minute or more. Kelley's humor set the tone for what was to be a night of camaraderie. During dinner most talked about returning to civilian life. Some expressed an eagerness to return; others were apprehensive because of the devastation and great uncertainty of postwar life. And a few said they were considering the idea of going to Texas to continue the fight.

Invariably in these informal conversations the topic changed to discussing women in their lives or the type of woman they would like to meet. On the latter subject, Morton, Strange and young Willie Forrest took the brunt of the kidding from their comrades.

"Tell the women in Columbus, Mississippi to lock their doors. That infamous Lothario and ex-cannoneer of Forrest's Cavalry, John Morton, is coming to town," shouted Dr. Cowan gleefully.

"And all you rich widdy women in Memphis, watch out for that rake, John Strange," added Matt Gallaway. "He's about to separate you from your inheritance."

When dinner was finished, Forrest's staff eagerly awaited some final comments from their leader. Forrest stood up and apologized for not having any prepared remarks. He said, "Why don't some of you ask me questions? Preferably about the war, not women. Heh-heh-heh!"

"Sir, you served with a lot of generals during the war. Do you have any favorites? And ones you weren't too fond of?" asked Major Anderson.

"Well, if you all promise me that what I say stays under this canopy, I'll make a few remarks.

"I like Dick Taylor a lot. He's one of the few that understands my style of fighting. And he's a fine gentleman.

"General Stephen Lee is a good fellow too. But I think I made him nervous. Heh-heh-heh! There were no problems between us, but as you know I disagreed with his battle plan at Tupelo last July. He ran us straight at the Federals, and we took an awful licking in casualties. Lee was almost the same kind of soldier as Wheeler. He's part of that West Point crowd. They love those almighty manuals.

"And speaking of 'Little Joe' Wheeler, I had my differences with him as you know. He's a courageous fellow for sure. But he's so deadly serious. And he has zero sense of humor. I bet he would have court-martialed our friends here, Dr. Cowan and Gilbert Rambaut, if they had told their jokes to him.

"Of course, Wheeler and I were bound to clash. You all know my feelings about orders from above. I have regarded them purely as suggestions.

"Now one fellow I really like is Beauregard. He didn't consider me some lower form of life because I didn't go to West Point, or because I wasn't a so-called, 'Southern Gentleman.' Did you know he was a hero at Bull Run? That took place before most of us joined up. After Shiloh, President Davis never gave him much responsibility. There were jealousies going back to their Mexican War days, I believe. Davis needed a scapegoat for what happened at Shiloh."

Then Anderson interrupted, "What about General Polk?"

"Oh, you mean the Bishop? That poor devil got himself killed over near Atlanta after he left our Department last April. The old Bishop was a tricky fellow. I could never figure out if he felt more like a preacher than a soldier; or more like a soldier than a preacher. He was a friendly fellow with a broad smile on his face. But to tell you the truth about him. I worried that he wasn't going to support me on that Fort Pillow business. The Bishop played politics. He always stuck his fingers up to see which way the wind was blowing. If I were 25 feet in the Tombigbee River and drowning, he'd throw me a 20 foot rope and brag he went more than half way.

"Now, something about Hood! I've felt sorry for him. I really do. I think about that day last November, before Franklin, and seeing this tall, gawky, heavily-bearded officer with a wooden leg and a dead arm, raving about what *God* had done to him. Like the rest of us he was worn out from the hard riding, the terrible weather, and the awful pain of his injuries.

"At the time I was very upset with him. I guess if he hadn't been exhausted, he would have been thinking clearer. But you know how Richmond takes care of those fellows who run a monkey show. They're sent into the backwaters and kept out of sight."

"What about General Joe Johnston, sir?" inquired Strange.

"I only met Johnston briefly, John. He's probably the exception to what I just said. Johnston is like an old tom cat. He's got nine lives. Davis has put him down several times, but he keeps bouncing back. I hear he's a very proud fellow — a lot like Beauregard. They're both banty-rooster-sized fellows who like to strut around.

"I don't want to carry this subject much further. I'd just like to say that I regret never having met any of those Confederate officers in the Eastern Theater of the war. The fighting in Virginia was like a million miles away from us. I really know very little about Robert E. Lee, Jubal Early and those folks.

"It seems to me like there have been two totally separate wars. It amazes me how Davis and his friends in Richmond could keep it all straight. Of course, if someone asks old porcupine-faced Bragg how it was all held together, he'd tell you point blank that he really ran things. Heh-heh-heh!

"Now, gentlemen, our time is growing short. In less than three days we'll all go our separate ways. It's really hard to believe it's over. I know we'll all have our problems of adjusting. But we can be thankful we all got out of it alive by some stroke of luck. Each of us came close to dying at one time or another.

"I have wondered for the past 47 months what I would like inscribed on my tombstone. Do any of you have any suggestions?"

"Yes," said Matt Gallaway. "How about this:

Here Lies General Nathan Bedford Forrest, CSA
He Was Born; He Fought Yankees; and He Died.

"That's kind of simple, isn't it Matt?"

"Well, General, it's better than the one I have for General Bragg."

"What's that, Matt?"

"All right, here it is:

Here Lies Braxton Bragg
He Meant Well; Tried a Little; Failed Much.

"That's kind of cruel, Matt; but I guess it fits. Have any of you written your own?" inquired Forrest.

"No, sir, not me," said Major Strange. "But I've written one for Gilbert Rambaut."

"Let's hear it."

"All right, sir:

Here Lies Gilbert Vincent Rambaut, from Misery
Freed, Who Long Was an Innkeeper Hack.
He Led Such a Damnable Life in This World
I Don't Think He'll Ever Come Back.

"I've got one for Matt Gallaway, General," shouted Morton. "Here it is:

Dear Friends and Companions All
Pray Warning Take From Me;
Don't Venture Into Nathan Bedford's War
As 'Twas the Death of Me'.

"Here's one for George Dashiell, our beloved paymaster and Memphis shopkeeper," said Dr. Cowan.

His Disconsolate Widow
Continues to Carry on
His Dry Goods Business
At the Same Old Stand on Front Street.
Cheapest and Best Prices in Town!

"All right! All right! This has gotten out of hand," Forrest said laughing. "Some of these epithets are getting too personal.

"Now Flaxy Berry brought some spirits to the party. And I authorized the use of our brandy supply from the surgeon's medicinal stock. James, you won't be needing the brandy for treatment after Tuesday. If we don't drink it, those Union boys sure will. So you fellows can have some refreshments for the worms."

Sunday, May 7, 1865

"Major Strange, come in here," yelled Forrest to his adjutant who was outside talking with friends.
"John, I'd like you to do a few things for me."
"Yes, sir."
"I want you to prepare a letter for me to send to John Morton's father. You know how much I've admired that young fellow. He's been like a son to me, and I'm going to miss seeing him. Put in the letter some remarks about what a fine officer he has been. Would you do that this afternoon?"
"Yes, sir, I'll take care of it."
"And also, John, I'm curious. Who is our oldest soldier? I'd like to visit with him if he's here in camp."
"Sir, that's no problem at all. You're talking about Corporal David Hummer, that Yankee-born fellow from Michigan. Yes, I've got his records right here. Let me look to make sure he's the oldest.
"Yes, sir, here it is. Corporal Hummer is 52. He enlisted in Memphis in October 1861. It says here that he was turned down at first because of age, but he appealed the rejection, and we enrolled him."
"Now John, that is something. It's a miracle a soldier his age has survived three and one-half years of this war. Hell, I'm 43 and just barely making it. Send somebody out to find him, and ask him to come see me, will you?"
"Yes, sir, old Hummer will be surprised."

One hour later, Major Strange announced that Corporal Hummer was outside.
"Good, ask him to come in."
"Sir, I'm David P. Hummer, a corporal in General Frank Armstrong's Cavalry."
"Well, Hummer, it's good to see you. Have we met before?"

"We haven't met, but I used to see you in Hannigan's Saloon on Main Street in Memphis."

"Oh my God, Hummer, that seems a long time ago. I hope you didn't see me in those scuffles I used to get into with those crazy Irishmen."

"I saw you lay out the Rafferty brothers one night, sir. That was something to behold. One of them had a club, but you rammed it into his stomach. After that night the Rafferty brothers would peek in the windows to see if you were in Hannigan's. If you were there, they'd go over to Paddy Ryan's place."

Forrest, smiling broadly, said, "Hummer, I hope you haven't told too many people about me. I'm now a respectable General in the Confederate States of America army. Heh-heh-heh!

"Hummer, are you happy it's over? You and I have been at it a long time."

"Yes, sir, I'm 52 now, but with my rheumatism I feel like I'm 75. Too many nights on the cold ground or traipsing through the mud and snow. A warm bed in Memphis looks mighty inviting."

"Did you know that you are my oldest soldier, Hummer?"

"No, sir, I didn't know that. Some of the boys look older than me. I guess they look that way 'cause they're worn out, or haven't been around women in a long time. That can put an old look on your face for sure."

"I know exactly what you mean, Hummer.

"Before you go, I've got a present for you. Wait here a minute."

Then Forrest asked Major Strange to step inside.

"Major Strange, I want my friend Hummer here promoted to sergeant right now. Take care of the paperwork immediately. And get somebody to sew on his new stripes before he returns to his unit."

"Well, thank you, sir. Now you have my word I won't tell anybody about Hannigan's Saloon."

Forrest howled in delight, and said, "It's no bribe,

Hummer. You deserve it.

"Promise me you'll look me up in Memphis, will you?"

"Yes, sir, I will," said the surprised new sergeant.

Tuesday, May 9, 1865

The entire camp was active at dawn. Normally sleepy soldiers were quite alert, and busy getting their belongings. Some went to check their horses, and to make certain they had been fed.

Major Anderson and Matt Gallaway went to headquarters to check once more with General Forrest on the content of the "Farewell Address."

"Is it all right, General," inquired Gallaway.

"Yes, Matt, its a fine speech. I particularly liked the remarks about reconciliation. Sad as it is, we all need to accept it."

Major Strange came in and announced, "General Canby's officers are here to oversee the ceremonies, General."

"Good, everything is set for 11:00 a.m. I'll give my address; then the paroles will be issued.

"I want no firing of cannons, or noise of any kind from this moment. Warn the soldiers I would appreciate total respect for General Canby's officers. Let it be said by them that Forrest's Cavalry is an organization of pride and honor."

At 11:00 a.m. all soldiers were in formation. Forrest's staff stood together at one end of the platform; General Canby's at the other end,

Forrest greeted personally each of the Union officers; then he huddled with them for a few minutes discussing final arrangements. Forrest was given assurance that he too would be paroled; and that General Canby had received no orders to place him under arrest.

As General Forrest moved to the center of the platform, there was total silence. Most of his soldiers removed their hats as a sign of respect. Forrest stood ramrod straight, looked from right to left over the assembled troops, then pulled his prepared remarks from his pocket.

"Soldiers!" he said shrilly. Then he began reading slowly:

> By an agreement between Lieutenant General Richard Taylor, commanding the Department of Alabama, Mississippi and East Louisiana; and Major General Edward Canby, commanding the United States forces, the troops of this Department have been surrendered.

A voice came from the back ranks, "No, General, never!"

Forrest continued reading his statement for the next five minutes. He reminded his troops of their new responsibilities as they returned to being citizens of the United States. He complimented them for their bravery and devotion to duty.

Then he folded his address, put it back in his pocket and ad-libbed the remainder:

> I have never on the field of battle sent you where I was unwilling to go myself; nor would I now advise you to a course which I felt myself unwilling to pursue. You have been good soldiers; you can be good citizens. Obey the laws, preserve your honor, and the Government to which you have surrendered can afford to be, and will be, magnanimous.

Silence prevailed when Forrest finished. No one moved for at least two minutes. Then Colonel Kelley broke the silence.

"Soldiers, prepare for the issuance of your paroles. May God be with you," he said in a clear, confident manner.

By 2:30 p.m. the majority of soldiers had passed through the tents where officers were issuing paroles. A special group of officers were outside to advise the men to go home immediately and to avoid trouble. Many soldiers embraced one another; and most shook hands with their officers before departing. A large number gathered around Colonel Kelley and Dr. Cowan — two of the most popular individuals. General Forrest did not make an appearance.

One hour later the camp was almost deserted except for Forrest's staff and some noncommissioned officers who were transferring supplies and equipment to General Canby's party.

Early Wednesday morning, May 10th, Forrest left for Meridian with Dr. Cowan and a few others from his staff. When asked what he intended to do, Forrest replied, "Gentlemen, I want solitude for awhile. I'll be going to Sunflower Landing over on the Mississippi River in Coahoma County. I think I still have a plantation there."

Jefferson Davis was captured by Union Cavalry early in the morning of May 10, 1865 near Irwinville, Georgia. He was taken to General James Wilson's headquarters in Macon, Georgia, then transported to Savannah, Georgia. There he joined fellow captives, General Joseph Wheeler, Confederate Vice President Alexander H. Stephens, and Postmaster- General J.H. Reagan for the ocean journey on the steamer, Clyde, to Fort Monroe, Virginia. Here, Davis was imprisoned. The others were imprisoned elsewhere.

Principal Battle Sites of Forrest's Cavalry • 1861-1865

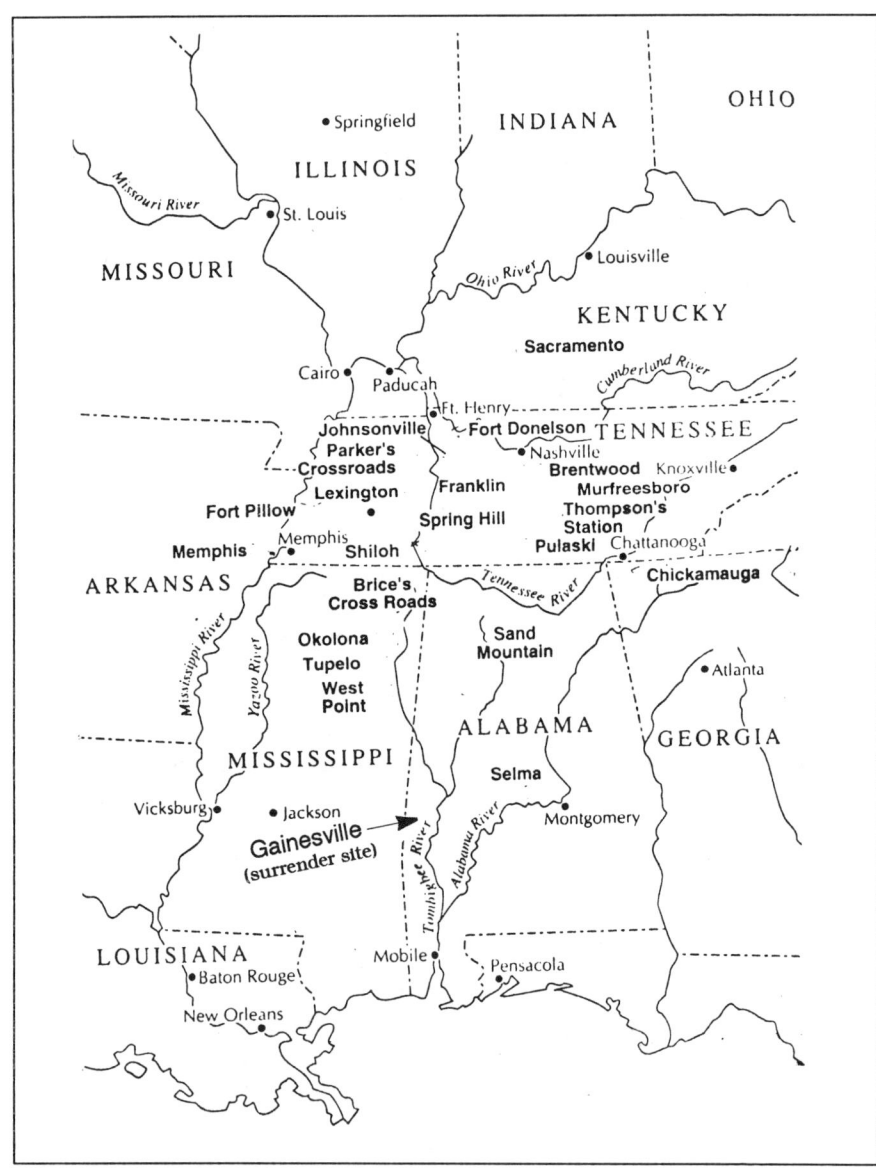

27 • Reconstruction

The Civil War's aftermath in the South was chaotic. Defeat was total. An agrarian economy and a social structure based on slavery and a caste system were destroyed. And its political leaders and military heroes so prominent for the four years, 1861-1865, were banished.

President Jefferson Davis was charged with treason. His vice president, Alexander H. Stephens, and military hero General Joseph Wheeler, were held briefly in military prisons.

General John C. Breckinridge, the one-time Vice President of the United States, and the Confederacy's last Secretary of War, fled to Europe. Judah P. Benjamin, first Secretary of War, then later Secretary of State in Davis' cabinet, escaped to the West Indies, then to England.

Pre-war Tennessee Governor Isham Harris had a $5000 bounty placed on him by the vengeful Reconstruction legislature in Tennessee. Harris moved to England after a brief stay in Mexico.

Beauregard and Jubal Early fled to Mexico where they joined many other Confederate leaders including the distinguished commander of the Confederate Navy, Matthew Fontaine Maury.

Those not pursued, or arrested, returned to an uncertain civilian life. Many were so demoralized that they were incapable of achieving even the semblance of a normal life. Forrest, like others who had pre-war wealth, worried about how to restart their businesses and professions in a devastated environment.

The deep pessimism concerning the political rule of the South, however, overrode almost every other concern of the ex-Confederates.

Recruiters sent by Mexico, Brazil, Cuba and British Honduras roamed the South offering the inducements of free land and political freedom to planters and their families. Those looking for fresh starts, and a means of escaping poverty, physical desolation of the South, and the yoke of Reconstruction laws left by the thousands in the immediate post war years. A conservative estimate was 10,000 in that initial emigration.

Foreign military powers sought Confederate officers to lead, or to advise, their armies. Many ex-Confederates were tempted, but few actually accepted positions.

Forrest discussed relocation to Mexico with friends, and once even described to them a plan he had to conquer that country with an army of 25,000 to 30,000 ex-Confederate volunteers. But he really wasn't too interested in leaving the United States despite the indictment for treason that was still outstanding. Along with Bill and Jesse Forrest, General Forrest, General Pillow and former Governor Isham Harris were among the prominent names on the indictment list issued in mid 1864 by the Federal District Court in Memphis. At the time all of those named were out of the jurisdiction, and warrants could not be served.

United States marshals finally served Forrest on March 13, 1866. He posted a $10,000 bond guaranteeing his appearance for trial.

If Forrest was concerned about the indictment, he didn't show it. He made no effort to leave the country. He told reporters, "I am endeavoring to make an honest living. I am not bound for Mexico like a lot of them. I did all in my power for the Confederacy, I admit. But it was a useless undertaking. I have resolved to stand by the Federal government as earnestly as when I fought it."

Forrest's case never came to trial. President Andrew Johnson's full pardon of Forrest on July 18, 1868 closed the matter.

Forrest and several influential friends had complained to President Johnson since mid-1865 about the partiality of the investigation of the Fort Pillow incident by the Wade-Gooch Congressional committee. Forrest's pardon was among the last granted to a Confederate officer. Most had been pardoned by 1866. But to President Johnson, the Forrest case was a particularly sensitive one. The mere mention of Forrest's name dredged up the memory of Fort Pillow. President Johnson feared public opinion, and he waited for over three years before granting Forrest his pardon.

Forrest's stay at his Mississippi plantation was temporary. He did get one cotton crop planted before he returned permanently to Memphis. His friends were in Memphis; and he sensed that he would have his best chance there of succeeding in new business ventures.

The first years back Forrest spent considerable time with Matt Gallaway, Minor Meriwether, and Meriwether's vocal and socially-liberated wife, Elizabeth. Politics was the chief topic at the frequent evening meetings at the Meriwether house on Union Street.

Matt Gallaway had reemerged as editor of the *Memphis Avalanche*, and was back with his inflammatory editorials attacking all his perceived demons of contemporary life. Day after day he railed against the Reconstruction laws being imposed on the South by Congress. And he denounced the Tennessee State Legislature and Radical Republican Governor, William Brownlow. He considered their actions pure vengeance against ex-Confederates.

Gallaway charged massive corruption on the part of those outsiders who came to Memphis to administer Reconstruction programs. "Those Northern carpetbaggers and traitorous Southern white scalawags who control this city are the scum of the Earth," he told anyone who would listen. The Meriwethers held similar views, but they were far less animated in expressing their concerns.

Forrest found the arguments of his friends persuasive. He considered them the best informed people in Memphis.

Congress established the Freedmen's Bureau at war's end. This agency was established to assist ex-slaves to enter the free labor system, and to protect them from overt discrimination. The Bureau's presence in Memphis was an extremely sensitive issue with ex-Confederates.

Gallaway seized on this subject. "The Radicals believe that 'all men are born free and equal,' and just now the nigger is their equal. This we will not question. We only insist that the Radicals are not the equal of Southern men."

At the Meriwethers' house one evening the discussion turned to the subject of the growing in-migration of ex-slaves into Memphis. Since 1861 the black population had increased from 4000 to 15,000. The streets were crowded with these newcomers as well as black Federal soldiers garrisoned in Memphis to maintain order.

Elizabeth Meriwether was indignant. "They shoved me in the gutter today as one of them said to me, 'We's all ekal now, white woman. You gotta get into da gutter an let us pass.'"

"Yes, the tension is mounting, Elizabeth," added Gallaway. "Something must be done to protect the good citizens of this city. We'll get no help from the white trash coming in here and stirring up trouble. Mark my words, a blood bath may occur."

"What shall we do about it, Matt," asked Forrest.

"Well, Bedford, we're going to have to defend ourselves. Congress has just passed the Civil Rights Act. That means every slave is not only a citizen, but he's got access to the courts, he can make contracts, and he can own property."

"Matt, of what help is that law to the Negroes? They don't have any money or property," questioned Elizabeth Meriwether.

"That's what is going to set them off," answered Gallaway. "They'll want property. They'll kill for it."

"I agree, Matt. They've been promised a lot of things that the Reconstruction people can't deliver. It's one thing to turn them loose, but without the prospect of jobs or anything else, they're going to cause trouble," added Forrest.

Within weeks of this conversation a riot broke out in Memphis that attracted nationwide attention. During the first week of May 1866, white mobs aroused to anger by the constant harangues of local demagogues including Matt Gallaway, attacked the Negro quarter in the city killing unarmed people, wounding many more, and torching their houses and shanties in a wild meleé that continued unabated for hours. When it finally ended, 48 ex-slaves had been killed, 75 wounded, five women raped, and 91 houses and shanties burned.

Congress, alarmed that this might be an emerging pattern in the South, sent an investigation team to Memphis later that month to conduct hearings.

Matt Gallaway, editor of the *Avalanche*, and editors of two competing anti-Reconstruction newspapers were singled out for engendering feelings of hatred and revenge toward ex-slaves. Influenced by these newspaper editorials, it was concluded that the mob— largely composed of the city's poor Irish population — acted violently.

When interrogated by the Congressional Committee, Gallaway admitted he was approached to join the mob, and that he was lifted on their shoulders for a short time, but that he took no part in the riots. And he said he couldn't recall the names of any of the rioters.

Throughout the summer of 1866 tensions grew even greater. On September 17, 1866 a public rally was held at the city's Court Square. The subject was Reconstruction and what to do about it. Forrest, Gallaway and General Chalmers were among the more prominent participants. A resolution was proposed and unanimously approved which stated: "Our sympathies are with the restoration of the South and that we are opposed to the policies of the Radical Republicans."

Gallaway's slashing editorials continued well into 1867. If anything, he became more extreme. One read:

The dirty, fanatical, nigger-loving Radicals of this City, who hate the gentlemen of the South because they hold no intercourse with them, and whose equals and companions are the negroes, have been

uttering their howls since the riot. They have been socializing with negroes, educating negroes, and ruining negroes...while they have been slandering and defaming the white men around them who would shun them as they would the plague.
We will not suffer Radicals to squat down here among us, fatten on the patronage of our citizens and then offer political insults as odious as they are degrading.

"Radical Republicans" was the name given the pro-Union Reconstruction governments installed in the South after the Civil War. In Tennessee the party was controlled by the crafty, idiosyncratic Governor William G. Brownlow. The six-foot, 62-year old former newspaperman and Methodist preacher was called "Parson" Brownlow by most Tennesseans.

Brownlow detested ex-Confederates. They, in turn, showed mutual contempt for him. The Brownlow-controlled state legislature passed the Negro Suffrage Act in February 1867. Tennessee became the first ex-Confederate state to permit blacks the right to vote.

Ex-Confederates, however, were denied the right to vote. Without this power they feared the vengeful Brownlow would manipulate the black population of Tennessee to serve his ends.

These fears were the impetus to the formation of the Ku Klux Klan. the Pale Faces, the White Camellias and several other secret societies. These organizations spread quickly throughout the South. Members claimed it was necessary to bond together for self-preservation. Such personalities as General John Gordon of Georgia, General William Hardee of Alabama, General Albert Pike of Memphis and General Forrest were said to be prime movers of the Klan.

The question was raised: "Is Forrest the Grand Wizard of the Klan?" He publicly denied membership, but it was widely known that he had met with the Meriwethers where such an organization was discussed.

He had met in Nashville with his former chief of artillery, Captain John Morton, where the Klan was discussed. And Forrest traveled beyond Tennessee to meet with Klan leaders of other states. This activity was in 1867.

When Brownlow organized a military force he called the State Militia purportedly to protect Negro voting rights in Middle and West Tennessee, ex-Confederates were outraged. "Brownlow is out to destroy us," Matt Gallaway, the Meriwethers, and Forrest agreed. "He must be dealt with, and quickly. To deny ex-Confederates the right to vote is a vengeful, dastardly act."

Throughout 1867, time permitting, Forrest met with many Confederate friends to discuss strategies dealing with the zealous Brownlow and his Radical Republicans in control of state government in Tennessee.

Forrest was destitute at war's end. On his return to Memphis he began playing poker again to try to raise funds to support his family. For a brief period he was a nightly player in Memphis card rooms.

Never one to be idle, Forrest reestablished himself as an enterprising businessman. He had initiative and organizational skills. His first project in Memphis was as a street paving contractor. This lead to other construction projects including a $400,000 contract from railroad promoter and friend, Sam Tate, to complete a section of the Memphis & Little Rock Railroad in Arkansas.

Confederate veterans idolized Forrest. Daily he received letters or personal visits from dispossessed individuals seeking his counsel. He received them cordially, and encouraged all to make the best of their desperate situations.

Local leaders in the Democratic Party, aware of Forrest's popularity among ordinary white citizens, saw value in recruiting him to represent them in attempts to regain political control of state government in Tennessee. Forrest accepted their invitation to be a delegate at the June 1868 Democratic Party state convention in Nashville. The main accomplishment of the Convention was a call for just rights for the states and a formal declaration protesting the Reconstruction policies of Congress.

Forrest, always a star attraction among ex-Confederates, was called on to speak. He was brief. "I am not an outcast," he explained. "When I gave my parole of honor, I meant it; and I have kept it; and I mean to keep it."

Impressed with his forthrightness, Forrest was elected to be a delegate-at-large to the National Democratic Party presidential convention in New York in July. At first, he declined. "I have no desire to enter politics," he protested. But he didn't want to disappoint his friends; so he accepted. As to the possibility of a hostile reception, he said, "I don't believe there is a brave reasonable Union soldier who dislikes or doubts me as a man. I'm not concerned."

On Saturday, June 20th — five days before leaving for New York — Forrest had lunch with Matt Gallaway at the Peabody Hotel in Memphis.

"Bedford, we need your voice to tell those Northern newspaper rascals what the Radicals are doing to us here in the South. Those political carpetbaggers that hibernate here make me hold my nose. The plundering and outraging they're doing is an abomination. Now they're fighting over the spoils like beasts over a dead carcass. Burglars and pickpockets after a successful night's operation never quarreled more over their spoils than those carpetbag cur dogs do over their plunder for which they are scrambling."

"Matt, that sounds like one of your better editorials," responded Forrest laughing. "You have a way of dramatizing a situation. Why don't you write something for me to tell the Democrats in New York if I'm called on to speak."

"Well, Bedford, you're taking enough of a chance just going to New York. What are you trying to do, get yourself lynched right there in Tammany Hall before 4000 delegates?"

"No danger of that! Politicians are like you, Matt. They're too busy listening to their own oratory to pay any attention to some obscure, retired Confederate general."

"Don't deceive yourself! You're going to be a star attraction — the Wild Man of Borneo — right there in New York. Why I'd pay to see it."

"It sounds like something I ought to avoid, Matt."

"Hell, Bedford, you'll love the attention," said Gallaway with a conspiratorial grin on his face.

Thursday, June 25, 1868

Forrest boarded the train at 4:00 p.m., bound for Louisville. General Chalmers was on board along with several delegates from West Tennessee, Mississippi and Arkansas.

The first stop was at Brownsville, Tennessee just after 6:00 p.m. Local citizens boarded the train looking for General Forrest to shake his hand and to wish him well. Several were old military comrades in Forrest's Cavalry.

Noticing a crowd of about 200 people at the station, Forrest disembarked to greet them. He jumped up on a baggage wagon to give a few remarks.

"Fellow citizens and old friends, what a pleasant surprise to see all of you. I see faces of old comrades in the Late War. It gives me a warm feeling to think of the gallant efforts you all made on behalf of the cause to protect our rights and way of life. I celebrate all of you.

"I'm going to New York to the Democratic Convention. Now, I guess you can call me a politician. Heh-heh-heh! But I'm not. I'm a retired soldier, a retired planter and a worried businessman struggling like most of you.

"I am going to New York for one reason only. It is my desire that we Southerners regain our rights as citizens, and to restore to Confederate veterans the right to vote. [Huge applause].

"I do not know exactly how I will be received up North. As you know, Yankee newspapers and most of the Republican politicians have done their best to discredit me. There have been vicious lies written about me. I'm called a renegade and a butcher. Let me ask you: 'Do you think I'm that awful person?'"

"No, no, no, it's a lie," rang through the crowd.

"I appreciate that response. I will defend myself to the day I die that I fought by the normal rules of war. I showed compassion to the enemy when victory was at hand. Those of you who served with me know that."

"Yes, General, that's right," several yelled out.

"Now, good citizens of Brownsville, those train engineers are waiting for me to get back on board. If I keep talking the Convention will be over before I get there.

"Thank you for your kindness. Goodbye."

Forrest received similar receptions at McKenzie, Paris and Clarksville, Tennessee.

The train arrived in Louisville, Kentucky at 7:00 a.m. There to greet Forrest and the other delegates was the politically-ambitious, 30-year old General Basil W. Duke, former Confederate cavalryman and brother-in-law of the fallen Confederate raider, General John H. Morgan.

Duke, a strong pre-war secessionist, was now practicing law in Louisville. He aspired to be a rising star in the Democratic Party, and wished to make the most of his opportunities in New York to become better known by party leaders.

The following afternoon Forrest and the rest of the delegates traveled up the Ohio River by boat to Cincinnati. There, they were invited to attend a large reception hosted by consummate politician, the 42-year old former U.S. Congressman from Ohio, George H. Pendleton.

Pendleton, called "Gentleman George" because of his impeccable good manners, had been the Democratic Party's vice-presidential candidate in the 1864 election when General George McClelland opposed Lincoln for the presidency. Now in 1868, he was seeking to become the Party's nominee for the presidency.

During the Sunday afternoon reception at Pendleton's home, he made it a point to speak with Forrest.

"General, it is an honor to have you active in the Democratic Party. Your presence is an indication that our country's wounds are healing, and in not too many years the United States will be totally united and prosperous. It is my hope that our party will lead the way."

"I wouldn't be here if I didn't think the Southern states would be helped by fair-minded Democrats. We don't expect any consideration from the Republicans. Our only hope is with your party, Mr. Pendleton," commented Forrest. "Well, General, if I am the candidate, rest assured, I will make every effort to meet your expectations. I think I have as good a chance as anybody to win the Party's nomination next week. With Tennessee's votes, and those of other Southern delegates coming to New York, I can win."

The delegates entrained for New York on Monday, June 29th. The Tennessee delegates liked George Pendleton, but their allegiance appeared to be with President Andrew Johnson, their native son.

28 • New York

July 1, 1868

"Welcome to New York City and the Democratic National Convention, General Forrest," said Jack Schwandt of the Host Committee waiting at the terminal when Forrest arrived in the early evening. "We have arranged quarters for you at the Fifth Avenue Hotel. I hope that is acceptable, General. Many of the other prominent delegates are headquartered there."

"That will be fine, sir," answered Forrest to the affable, portly, cigar smoking Schwandt. "May I ask who made this arrangement for me?"

"Yes, of course, General. It was Mr. George Pendleton. The Fifth Avenue Hotel is Pendleton headquarters. You'll like it. It's noted for its luxury and its impressive architecture, General. It has a great white marble facade, elegant ballrooms and dining rooms, and the most comfortable guest rooms in New York." Then Schwandt laughed as he added a further comment, "General, wouldn't you know with all that luxury this hotel is a year-round gathering place for wealthy Republicans."

When Forrest arrived at the hotel, the lobby was full of familiar faces. It became obvious that Pendleton was making an all-out effort to court the Southern delegates votes at the Convention. There, huddled in conversation near the reception desk were General Duke, General Wade Hampton of South Carolina and General John Gordon of Georgia. All came forward to greet Forrest.

July 2, 1868

General Duke invited General Gordon and Forrest to have breakfast with him in the hotel's elegant, high ceiling, chandeliered dining room. As they were sitting down Duke was laughing about the derogatory remarks being made about the Democratic Party delegates in the New York newspapers.

"Listen to this, gentlemen, it's in today's *New York Tribune*. It says, 'The Democrats are a common sewer into which is emptied every element of treason North and South, and every element of inhumanity and barbarism which has dishonored the age.'

"And listen to this! Here's another. 'Smart country lawyers are as thick as blackberries in a patch. They have a preference for barrooms appropriately located near Tammany Hall, the convention site.'

"Here's another one, 'Tammany Hall is now ready for the reception of the motley crowd which is to fill it on Saturday.'"

Forrest said laughing, "It sort of sounds like they don't exactly like us. They think we're animals in a zoo."

The discussion of the three turned to Pendleton's chances for the nomination. "Pendleton's got a lot of support going into the convention," said Duke, "but I don't think he has anywhere near the 211-1/2 votes he needs to win."

"It depends on those of us from the South. President Andrew Johnson has a lot of support in Georgia, and we'll stay with him if he looks like he's got a chance," added General Gordon.

"Tennessee is for Johnson," said Forrest. "And I think Alabama and Louisiana are for him, too."

"But do you think he has any chance, Forrest?" inquired Duke.

"No, I don't He's not popular in the North even though he was for the Union in the war. He's had an impossible job trying to tie up all the loose ends resulting from the war."

"Well, if Johnson doesn't make it, do you have a preference?" continued Duke.

"I think I could vote for General Winfield Hancock. He's a Union man, I know, but he was a good soldier, and I think he would treat us right. But I have no strong convictions one way or the other."

"Look who is coming in the dining room," said Duke. "Do you know who that is, gentlemen?"

"No, but he's a big, fat old boy, isn't he?" said General Gordon.

"That's the one-and-only William Marcy Tweed — otherwise known as 'Boss Tweed', replied Duke. " He rules the Democratic Party in New York with an iron hand."

"I bet he weighs 300 pounds. Look at him in that dark suit with the white cravat. I'd call him the bloated Mr. Tweed," said the amazed Forrest.

"He obviously loves to eat. Pendleton told me he's a tip-top dancer too. Can you believe that?" added Duke.

"Do you know his motto? It's 'Something for Everyone.' And his tactical plan is, 'Do it now!'"

"I guess I can identify with that," said Forrest. "Old Tweed and I might make a good team."

"Well, Forrest, Tammany Hall where the convention is being held is a monument Tweed built to honor himself. He's a mighty force around here," concluded Duke.

"Who is he promoting for President?" asked Gordon.

"I hear he plays it behind the scenes. He loves to make a deal. I doubt anyone knows who he is for," answered Duke.

Then Duke asked his guests if they would like to visit Tammany Hall. "We are invited to tour the brand new building today. It was completed yesterday. I hear it's a splendid place. It's to be the new headquarters of the St. Tammany Society, the political organization for Democrats."

"Can we walk there?" asked Forrest.

"Yes, it's on 15th Street between Third Avenue and Irving Place, about ten blocks or so."

"After that long train ride, walking would be good," said Forrest.

A large crowd had gathered in front of the huge red brick, Victorian building with marble trimmings. Workmen were hanging colorful red, white and blue window banners on the outside. Most eyes were focused on the top of the building where adjustments were being made to the 12-foot statute of legendary Chief Tammany, the 17th century leader of the Delaware Indians known for his friendliness to white people.

Spanning 15th Street in front of Tammany Hall was an arch 50 feet high, decorated with evergreens. At the apex was a huge portrait of Thomas Jefferson.

Forrest, Duke and Gordon were met by a guide who escorted them inside the Hall. The ground floor was nondescript. It looked like an ordinary office building. The second floor, however, was the big attraction. Here was Boss Tweed's "Great Hall." The ceiling was 51 feet above the floor. The guide, when asked the seating capacity, said, "Officially it's 2500, but Tweed wants 4000 in here when the Convention starts."

Then the guide laughed in a guarded manner, "Gentlemen, there's a real problem facing us. Mr. Tweed has distributed over 7000 tickets. Do you see that bunting hanging over the windows? That's going to shut off air circulation. It's going to be awful if they let them all in here."

Then the guide continued, "Each state has its coat-of-arms on the walls."

"Where's Tennessee's?" asked Forrest.

"Just to the right of the stage, General."

Several friends of Forrest were milling around the Hall, and they all came forward to greet him.

"How are you enjoying New York, General?" most asked politely.

"So far, it's been enjoyable; but I haven't seen much. The local people at the hotel are friendly and courteous. Nobody has brought up the subject of the war, thank goodness."

Tammany Hall, July 4 - July 9, 1868

On the Fourth of July at 12:15 p.m. the Convention was called to order in the sweltering heat of the Great Hall. The Democratic Party had given credentials to 634 delegates. Among the delegates were people from the North and South. There were many former Union and Confederate officers, Congressmen, perennial political candidates and political bosses like Tweed.

The New York Tribune reported sarcastically that among the opening days' activities was the entrance to the convention hall of "General Napoleon Bonaparte Forrest."

No substantive business took place on opening day except the welcoming address.

On Sunday, July 5th there was no session. The pro-Republican New York press reported gleefully that the saloons had ordered additional stock and hired more bartenders to help quench the thirst of the motley delegates. And thanks to Boss Tweed, saloons operated on the Sabbath with impunity.

On Monday, Horatio Seymour, the 58-year old several term Governor of New York, was elected president of the Convention. Candidates for the Presidential and Vice Presidential nominations worked furiously throughout the day soliciting support.

A minor furor broke out on the Convention floor on Monday, July 6th when a written request submitted by Susan B. Anthony to address the Convention was considered. The request was written on letterhead of the Women's Suffrage Association. "I wish to urge the Convention to support 'Universal Amnesty and Universal Suffrage' as steps toward a peaceful and permanent Reconstruction, I represent the interests of American women," she wrote.

Miss Anthony's remarks, read by the Convention's Clerk, were greeted with derision and widespread laughter by the otherwise bored delegates. When he finished the South Carolina delegation announced defiantly it would bolt the Convention if the Democratic Platform included a declaration for universal suffrage.

On July 9th the balloting began to select a presidential candidate to oppose the Republicans' candidate, General Ulysses S. Grant. The latter had been selected by his party on the first ballot in Chicago in May.

To receive the Democratic nomination a candidate needed 211-1/2 votes of the total 317 votes to be cast. Each delegate had one-half of a vote. On the first ballot taken George Pendleton got 105; Andrew Johnson, 65; and Winfield Hancock, 33-1/2 Pendleton's vote total climbed steadily to a high of 145-1/2 on the 12th ballot; then his vote total drifted downward quickly from the 13th to the 19th ballot, when he received no votes. General Hancock then had his turn. He started gaining after the 14th ballot; reached a high of 144-1/2 on the 18th; then started falling back. It was obvious to the delegates that Hancock was also finished.

After hours of voting without a result, pressure from behind the scenes was being exerted by Boss Tweed and his inner circle to sway the delegates in favor of New York Governor, Horatio Seymour. Tweed had packed the Great Hall with his Tammany Hall members to yell support for Seymour. Pendleton's forces, who hours earlier realized their candidate couldn't win, threw their support to Seymour hoping this would bring support from New York delegates should Pendleton decide to make another run for the nomination in 1872. A compromise was reached among the delegates. Seymour would be the candidate. In the final vote Seymour received every vote.

Southern delegates were compensated for their support of Seymour. They were permitted to incorporate into the Democratic Party Platform the statement: "Reconstruction laws are unconstitutional, revolutionary, and void."

Forrest played no real role in the nomination of Governor Seymour. He had been lukewarm about Pendleton as a candidate. But he became more active in the selecting of the vice presidential nominee. He agreed to help General Frank P. Blair, Jr., the 47-year old Missouri lawyer and politician who had served in the Union army under Sherman.

Northern newspapers described Blair as a crude racist who had been advocating the colonization of freed slaves outside the country. Forrest felt a special obligation to Blair. Two years earlier Blair had made an appeal to President Johnson to grant Forrest a pardon.

On the final day of the convention, July 9th, during the balloting for the vice presidential candidate, Forrest was introduced to the convention to cast the vote of the Tennessee delegates. Rising to enthusiastic applause, Forrest, smiling broadly, waved to the crowd, then said, "I have the pleasure, sir, to cast the vote of Tennessee for General Blair."

Forrest paused for a few seconds; then continued, "And I wish to take this occasion to thank the delegates for the kind and uniformly courteous treatment that the Southern delegates have received at this convention."

Cheering for Forrest rang out through the Great Hall when he finished. He waved again, then sat down smiling once again. Many of the Southern delegates surrounded him to shake his hand.

When Forrest returned to the Fifth Avenue Hotel that evening with General Duke, the desk clerk handed him two messages. The first was from General Joseph E. Johnston; the second from Publisher and Editor of *The New York Tribune*, Horace Greeley.

Forrest looked surprised. He said to Duke, "I didn't know General Johnston was in New York. Do you know why he is here? Doesn't he now live in Savannah?"

"I don't know why he is here, General. He could be here selling insurance. That's his new business, you know. I would guess he is trying to meet as many prominent Union and Confederate officers as he can. But he may be here to talk with publishers. Rumor has it that he wants desperately to publish his memoirs."

"Have you met General Johnston?"

"Just once — briefly," answered Forrest. "It was just after Davis transferred me to Mississippi after Chickamauga. We had a pleasant meeting. I was impressed with his military bearing. Damn!, he looked like a high ranking general should — ramrod straight, clear-eyed, jutting chin and a spotless uniform that fit perfectly. I was somewhat in awe of him, but he put me at ease. He's a serious fellow. No nonsense. No small talk. He had no concern about anybody's personal life."

"What do you think he wants to talk to me about?"

"It may have something to do with his proposed book, General Forrest."

"What are your plans tomorrow, Duke?"

"Several of us from the South have been invited to meet with Governor Seymour at the Astor Hotel. He wants to solidify the Party; and probably he wants to assure us that he is sympathetic to our position on Reconstruction."

"Good, please let me know what he has to say. When I get back to Tennessee I may have to reassure folks about Seymour. But, Hell! What difference does it really make. None of us can vote for him.

"Now, what am I to do about this invitation from that Greeley fellow? He wants me to meet him at Delmonico's Restaurant at 1:00 p.m. tomorrow. His paper, *The New York Tribune*, just like *The New York Times* and *The New York Herald*, has accused me of about every sin imaginable. Why in-the-hell should I sit down with those snakes?"

"Oh, Greeley's not a bad sort. Pendleton told me how helpful Greeley has been in getting Jefferson Davis released from prison. He even put up part of the cash for Davis' bond. And did you know, he opposed Lincoln's nomination for a second term?"

"Well, Duke, curiosity compels me to accept. And I have heard Delmonico's is the best dining room in New York."

Central Park, Friday, July 10, 1868

General Johnston's invitation suggested that Forrest meet him at 7:30 a.m. at the stables in Central Park. "Wear your riding clothes," the note read.

Johnston greeted Forrrest warmly and they chatted briefly as the grooms prepared the horses.

"General Johnston, I want to say how pleased I am that you received a full pardon from President Johnson last week. It must make you very happy."

"It does indeed, Forrest. My wish now is that the President will soon issue you a pardon."

"Thank you, sir."

The bridle path was a three-mile course through Central Park. Johnston and Forrest rode around the course twice at a leisurely pace as they conversed.

Johnston, although he may not have realized it, did

most of the talking. The subjects were mostly related to the war, and to various military personalities with whom Johnston had served. Forrest found what Johnston had to say interesting. Being an outsider in the command structure of the Confederate Army, Forrest had not been privy to most of the inner politics and a witness to the jealousies among the highest ranking Confederate leaders. It became obvious to Forrest that Johnston had not put the war behind him.

"The war left me very frustrated, Forrest. And now I want to set the record straight. Much has been made of my relations with Jefferson Davis during the war. We had our difficulties in 1863 during the Vicksburg campaign, and again on a much larger scale in late Spring 1864 in front of Atlanta when Sherman was moving against us. The true story has never been told. And I want to get the record straight so war historians in the future will judge me correctly."

"What did happen at Vicksburg, General?" asked Forrest who had been listening patiently to the animated dialogue of Johnston.

"Davis felt I should have taken personal charge of General John Pemberton's army in the Vicksburg area. He claimed we shouldn't have been caught in the siege. But what he failed to mention was that I pleaded with him to send me the 55,000 troops he had sitting idle in Little Rock. I could have rescued Pemberton.

"Davis vilified me for not fighting there and for not fighting in Georgia. Davis's problem was he couldn't delegate anything, and he meddled into all details of a military operation. He thought he was still leading a charge in the Mexican War in 1847.

"I know Davis says I was undiplomatic in dealing with him, and insulted his intelligence. That's probably quite true. But what's wrong with expressing your views? That's not being insubordinate, is it?" Johnston said apologetically.

Without giving Forrest a chance to answer, Johnston

continued, "My greatest complaint about Davis is the manner in which he dismissed me during the Atlanta Campaign. I asked repeatedly for cavalry to cut Sherman's supply lines, and he refused.

"Forrest, I requested your cavalry. Did you know that?"

"I had heard you did, but I never received any direct information verifying it."

"Well, Forrest, if I would have had your cavalry against Sherman's railroad communications, I could have fought Sherman on my terms.

"The final insult was the way Davis relieved me of command, and put Hood in charge of the Army of Tennessee. He sent Braxton Bragg down to Georgia. That two-faced Bragg said his visit was casual, and that there was no problem he was investigating. He said nothing to me to indicate that Davis had decided to get rid of me. But the truth is Davis had already selected Hood. Any man of honor would have communicated directly with me. That lying Hood accused me falsely in his report on the Atlanta Campaign. They used that false information against me.

"The ironic thing is that when Hood took over and started to attack a much larger and better equipped Union army, he got whipped good.

"Forrest, if it's the last thing I do in life, it's to get this story told. You can understand my position, can't you?"

"Yes, sir, I have similar feelings about Bragg, and his treatment of me. About Davis, I don't know. He listened to Bragg too much. And I'm afraid Davis viewed me through Bragg's eyes."

"Thank you for listening, Forrest. Defending my honor is important to me. I was trained to be a professional soldier. I still carry the values instilled in me at West Point."

For one brief moment Forrest did manage to divert Johnston from the latter's defense of his war record. Forrest, who had nurtured an interest in railroads for over ten years, wanted Johnston's opinion on the potential for future railroad ventures in the South. Johnston had been president of the Selma-based Alabama & Tennessee River Railroad in 1866 and 1867, but left after it failed financially.

"Forrest, railroads in the South are a risky business. You need lots of money. Despite all my efforts I found it impossible to raise capital for construction of additional trackage. Of course, 1866 and 1867 were horrible years in the South as you know, Forrest. When I saw an opportunity to become a general agent for several insurance companies, I left Selma. So far, operating out of Savannah, business has been fair. At least I have a little time to undertake research in preparation to writing a book to clear the record on my differences with Davis. If it is the last thing I ever do, it is to get the truth out."

Johnston and Forrest dismounted at the stables. Johnston said, "Forrest, I feel better after talking with you. I get the feeling you understand why I wish to bring these subjects to the public's attention."

They shook hands and wished each other well.

Forrest hurried back to the Fifth Avenue Hotel to rest briefly before proceeding to Delmonico's to meet with Horace Greeley.

Promptly at 1:00 p.m. Forrest arrived at the restaurant which was then located at Fifth Avenue and 14th Street near Tammany Hall. Waiting in the reception room was Greeley and the *Tribune*'s chief political reporter, John D. Stockton.

"Forrest!...Forrest!...over here," signaled Greeley with his shrill, abrasive voice.

"Why General Forrest, you look exactly like I thought you would."

"How's that, Mr. Greeley?"

"Oh, tall, broad-shouldered, distinguished and resolute looking like a warrior.

"Please meet John Stockton. He's requested to join us. Stockton here is my ace reporter — or should I say, political analyst."

"Hello, Stockton! Are you the one who called me General Napoleon Bonaparte Forrest in the paper the other day? Heh-heh-heh!"

"No, General, we've got some boys at the paper who write that kind of thing."

"I thought it was flattering, Stockton. To be compared with Napoleon is quite an honor for a poor ex-citizen soldier."

"Forrest, have you been to Delmonico's before?" inquired the 57-year old, odd-looking Greeley.

"No, sir, this is my first visit to New York. The Convention kept me busy; and so far, I haven't seen much."

"Ah, yes, the Convention, Forrest. That must have been some experience for you. What do you think of that boisterous, unruly band of politicians?"

"They looked like ordinary folks to me. They do business like we do down in Memphis. They mix it up good, but they accomplish what they set out to do."

"Let's enter the dining room, gentlemen," said Greeley. "We may see some other famous people in there. General Grant often dines here. And General Winfield Scott, before he died, was a fixture in here every day. He liked the food. He weighed over 300 pounds.

"I recently had the honor of introducing Charles Dickens at a banquet in his honor held here. He was awfully sick on his visit to America, but continued to give his readings up and down the East Coast. Are you familiar with Dicken's work, General?"

"I'm not too familiar, but I had a fellow on my staff who enjoyed reading Dickens."

"Do you like lobster, Forrest? The lobster salad here is a specialty."

"I'll try it. I often ate lobster in my New Orleans days. We don't see much of it in Memphis."

Forrest then asked Greeley, "I'm curious, sir. Why did you want to meet me?"

Horace Greeley

"Forrest, I'll tell you the truth. You are the only interesting person other than that rogue, Boss Tweed, who attended the Democratic Convention. You're a folk hero down South, and you probably represent current public opinion down there."

"Mr. Greeley, I think perhaps you look upon me as some sort of freak. That damn Fort Pillow incident has been so damn exaggerated. What happened there was pure and simple, warfare. Good or bad, that type of close fighting happened everywhere.

"That Wade investigation was a gross distortion of the truth. As we say in the army, 'Wade put on a monkey show to whip up emotions up North.' Lincoln and Congress used it to revive lagging Yankee interest in the war. I've given so many interviews on the matter that I'm sick of it. I chose to learn from the Fort Pillow crisis rather than let it overwhelm me. There isn't anything to add. I hope you will forgive me if I don't go over old ground like Fort Pillow, my slave trading days, or my difficulties with General Bragg."

A waiter approached the table and asked if anyone cared for a drink. Greeley, a blunt man, peered from behind his round wire-rimmed eyeglasses and said, "I am an unrelenting foe of liquor, tobacco, gambling, prostitution, capital punishment, divorce and women's suffrage."

"But, Mr. Greeley," interrupted the smiling John Stockton," General Forrest may want a drink. You commented in the paper last week that Democrats attending the Convention drink heavily, and that all Democrats are saloonkeepers."

"Goddamnit, Stockton, I only said that all saloonkeepers are Democrats! If you keep irritating me, you'll find yourself begging for a job from that little villain, Henry Raymond of *The New York Times*, or that viper James Bennett of *The New York Herald*."

Stockton, who was used to the irascible Greeley, looked at Forrest and winked in amusement.

Forrest added, "Mr. Greeley, I'm glad I don't work for you. Heh-heh-heh! I couldn't meet your standards of moral conduct. Now, my wife Mary, she would meet them 100 percent."

"Good, Forrest, there may be hope for you after all. I'll pray for you on Sunday."

"Thank you, sir!" said Forrest laughing.

Then, proprietor Lorenzo Delmonico approached the table with his head waiter.

"Mr. Greeley, good to see you again. And you too Mr. Stockton. I understand your guest here is General Nathan Bedford Forrest."

"Yes, that is correct. Please meet the distinguished General."

"General Forrest, we have had many Union officers as our guests, but very few Confederates. We are honored," said Delmonico with great dignity and ceremony.

"Thank you, sir. I can tell you why so few of us have been here. We were out there fighting a war, and we never made it to New York. Heh-heh-heh!"

Even the typically somber Greeley laughed.

"General, I'd be delighted to fix your favorite foods if you wish," said Proprietor Delmonico with a ready smile.

"Mr. Delmonico, anything other than salt pork and hard tack would be fine. I will have your lobster salad."

"Fine choice, General."

"And Mr. Greeley, do you wish your usual vegetarian dishes?"

"Yes, you know damn well I abhor meat," Greeley snapped. "And I strongly oppose the killing of animals to provide nourishment for man."

John Stockton with a mischievous grin said, "General Forrest, Mr. Greeley has no vices he'll admit to except swearing."

The conversation among the three continued.

"Forrest, how is your health?" inquired the undiplomatic Greeley. "We had a report some time back that your physician didn't expect you to live — that your injuries had taken their toll."

"Oh, I guess I'm all right. My right arm is almost useless, and I have some internal problems. To be honest with you, I didn't think I'd live beyond 1866, but here I am."

John Stockton then asked, "General, in 1861 what was your personal view on secession?"

"I voted to stay in the Union, but public opinion in Tennessee was for secession. I have to admit I went reluctantly in the war. I really loved the old United States, but I also believed strongly in states' rights. That's what pushed me in the Confederacy. We were all frightened to death about what Lincoln might do.

"I fought my best and have nothing to regret or repent. My duty now is to assist in the practical restoration of the governments down South, I do not wish to isolate myself from public affairs or ignore the past. That's why I chose to be a delegate to the Democratic Party's Convention.

"Let me ask you a question, Mr. Greeley. You worked hard on behalf of Jefferson Davis to get him released from prison and pardoned. Isn't that rather an odd thing for a publisher of a Radical Republican newspaper? Didn't your position on Davis go against public opinion in the North?"

"Yes, circulation dropped, and some of those sonafabiches over at the Union League Club tried to expel me. When Cornelius Vanderbilt, James Lyons and a dozen other prominent fellows agreed to post a $100,000 bond guaranteeing Davis' appearance in court all hell broke loose," answered Greeley as he nervously twisted a red handkerchief with his left hand. "We did get Davis out last year in May, but there hasn't been a trial yet.

"He's in England now. Did you know that Forrest?"

"Yes, and if I know Davis, I imagine he's trying to be a special advisor to Queen Victoria. Heh-heh-heh!"

"Do I detect some sarcasm there, Forrest?"

"Oh, no, not at all. It just fits Davis' personality. He meddles in everything. At least that's what he did with the Confederate army," answered Forrest assertively.

Forrest was captivated with the blunt Greeley. His odd physical appearance and his shrill voice masked an intense and intelligent person. Greeley's head was as round as a ball except for his bulging forehead. His extremely white face was encircled by thin, silky hair, and his small, round glasses gave him an owl-like experience. Forrest enjoyed the company of this unique personality. He also liked the good-natured Stockton.

Greeley continued, "Did you know I was against the war? I advised the authorities in Washington in November 1860 to let the Cotton States go in peace. And since the war I have opposed all punitive measures against the South.

"I'm supporting Grant in this year's presidential election. I believe he will take a conciliatory position toward the South. We've got to put all the hatred and emotion behind us."

Forrest shook his head in agreement. Then he said to Greeley and Stockton, "I have been thinking about a plan to rebuild the South. All anyone talks about in the North and South is what to do with the Negroes. It's politics — everyone is tugging and pulling at them to get power. My idea is to get the Negroes back into agriculture on a free labor basis. They are wonderful workers."

But questioned Greeley, "Are there enough Negroes interested in returning to the land?"

"Probably not from the existing Negro population. We'll probably have to repopulate with Africans. Bring them here as free laborers. They have tremendous initiative. We'll put them in squads of ten with a leader for each squad. They would soon revive our country.

"I'd like Northerners to come down South. And Europeans too. But they won't come. When prejudice dies down our government will see the merit of this scheme. The whole country will prosper."

Then Stockton intervened, "General Forrest, I must say I'm shocked at what you just said."

"Why is that?"

"Well, sir, you have been labeled 'the Grand Wizard of the Ku Klux Klan,' a secret group to keep Negroes from gaining their rights."

Forrest laughed, "Oh you mean old Forrest wants to boil Negroes' heads to make soup!

"No, people have got that all wrong. The only secret organization I belong to is the Odd Fellows Lodge. We've got 83 lodges in Tennessee and 3300 members. Our mission is to work for the betterment of the human race. The only secrecy concerns our passwords, signs and grips.

"I've been identified with the Pale Faces. They're like the Odd Fellows and the Masons. I'm not a member, but I agree with their program of self-preservation.

"My personal view is that I oppose giving the right to vote to the Negroes while ex-Confederates are excluded. Governor Brownlow down in Tennessee is using the Klan as a whipping boy to keep all of us ex-Confederates from having any say in how the state is governed. He wants to destroy us.

"Mr. Greeley and Mr. Stockton, I invite you to come down to Memphis and see first hand what Reconstruction policies are doing to us. You seem like fair-minded gentlemen. You may also want to interview Parson Brownlow and his people to round out your story. I think your readers would appreciate learning more about what is happening in the South."

When they finished coffee and dessert, Horace Greeley thanked General Forrest for joining John Stockton and him.

"You are a fascinating man, Forrest. Fascinating! Perhaps unique in these troubled times. I wish you well.

"What are your plans for your remaining stay in New York, Forrest?"

"Oh, Mr. Greeley, the most important thing is to visit the famous A.T. Stewart's Retail Store on Broadway. I can't return to Memphis without buying Mary a present or two."

"That's just a short walk from here. Go down to Tenth Street, then turn right to get to Broadway. Watch out for pickpockets," said Greeley as he got up to leave.

Dedication of Tammany Hall, July 4th, 1868
at the National Democratic Party Convention

29 • Radical Republicans

Forrest returned to Memphis elated over his reception in New York. He was flattered by the attention. But he told Matt Gallaway that he felt embarrassed that perhaps he had been singled out as a rising political voice in the South. "I did nothing to promote myself for such a role, Matt. I do not crave a politician's life. I only want to see justice done."

"Whether you like it or not, Bedford, you are a celebrity. A lot of ordinary people in the old Confederacy are looking to you for guidance. They're dependent on you. What you do and say gets passed around throughout the countryside. You're stuck with this leadership mantle."

"But Matt, I've got to look out for myself first. That fire insurance business I've gotten myself into is going nowhere. Those Planters Insurance Company people are just using me as a figure head. It's a dead end. I've got a lot of thinking to do."

On July 17, 1868, one day after arriving home in Memphis, Forrest was notified that President Johnson had granted him amnesty. "I am truly grateful," he told friends who came to congratulate him. But he added as an afterthought, "What good is it if I cannot vote. As long as Confederate soldiers are denied the vote, we aren't citizens of this country. I cannot be for anybody who will deny us our vote."

Forrest moved about West Tennessee attacking Governor Brownlow and Reconstruction policies. Despite a lingering cold and sore throat he kept speaking before citizens' groups. At Brownsville, Tennessee on August 10th he was so sick he could hardly talk. But he spoke at length despite being ill.

"I apologize for the raspy throat, folks. I just couldn't let you down by not appearing today. Honestly, it must have been that Yankee food I ate. It may have been too much for an old soldier used to salt pork and greens." [Laughter].

Then he started speaking with intensity. "Parson Brownlow's actions with his State Militia will cause a civil war in Tennessee. I don't want another war and more bloodshed. And I don't want to see Negroes armed to shoot down white men.

"I wish to state that I am not against the colored man. I never have been against the colored man. I carried 45 with me during the war, and all but one remained with me during the war. The last time I saw the one who deserted me he was in the hands of the Memphis police for stealing. [Cheers and laughter].

"Now I promise you if things get any worse, I will get as many of my old soldiers as possible to go with me. If Brownlow sends the black men to hunt those Confederate soldiers they call Ku Klux, then I say to you, 'Go out and shoot the Radicals.' If they want to inaugurate civil war, the sooner it comes the better. We'll know what to do," he told the enthusiastic crowd.

A similar emotional speech was given in Memphis with Forrest concluding, "I like peace, but if any of us is shot down, I will toot my horn. My old troops will answer as they have always done. Arm yourselves and be ready! We don't need any drilling. I'm in favor of giving no quarter."

Soon thereafter, Brownlow became less of a threat. Dissention first appeared within Brownlow's Radical Republican Party in late 1868. The controversial and peevish Brownlow chose to bow out as Governor in early 1869. He got the Brownlow controlled Tennessee State Senate to elect him as the United States Senator from Tennessee. He took office on March 4, 1869.

The black vote counted on heavily by Brownlow's forces to sustain their control of Tennessee was disappointing. Intimidation by the Klan to discourage Negroes from voting in many counties was a factor. Several Radical Republican candidates for state offices withdrew from the election when threatened by the Klan. They also faced a backlash from many supporters of the old pre-war Whig Republican Party. That group of citizens largely from the middle and upper income classes recognized the gross injustice of disenfranchising ex-Confederates.

In 1870 Tennessee repealed the punitive Disenfranchisement Act.

Whatever direct association Forrest had with the Klan in Tennessee or other Southern states ended.

HARPER'S WEEKLY September 5, 1868
"This is a White Man's Government."

"We regard the Reconstruction Acts (so called) of Congress as usurpations, and unconstitutional, revolutionary, and void." 1868 Democratic Party Platform.

30 • The Convert

The nation changed rapidly in the final years of General Forrest's life — at least in the North, the Midwest and the newly-opened American West.

On July 4, 1876 the United States celebrated its centennial. Rutherford B. Hayes, a Union army major-general, succeeded Union hero Ulysses S. Grant as President. That year the telephone was patented by Alexander Graham Bell, and Mark Twain wrote *Tom Sawyer*.

A tragedy occurred in the emerging West. On June 25, 1876 General George Armstrong Custer and 265 soldiers of the 7th Cavalry were killed in the Battle of the Little Big Horn in Montana. Custer, then 36, was operating under orders to search out and destroy the local Sioux. Instead, the 7th Cavalry was destroyed by 3500 Sioux and Cheyenne braves led by Sitting Bull and Crazy Horse.

The Reconstruction era ended on April 10, 1877 when the last of the Federal occupation troops withdrew from the South. The Civil War was officially over.

The emergence of new political leaders and public personalities, new inventions, industries, and transportation systems, settlement of the American West, and rapid population growth helped dim the memory of the Civil War in the North.

In the South recovery and noticeable change were far less apparent. Without adequate investment capital, entrepreneurs like Forrest had less opportunity to rebuild their regions. State and local governments had bankrupted themselves, and barely functioned. A pall of pessimism covered the South.

On a personal level death claimed Forrest's friend and trusted wartime adjutant, Major John P. Strange in 1875; and two of his old enemies, General Braxton Bragg in 1876, and Reconstruction-era Governor of Tennessee, William "Parson" Brownlow, in April 1877.

Forrest's railroad career ended abruptly in early

Spring, 1874. Discouraged and in poor health he once again returned to planting cotton after doctors advised him to adopt a less rigorous work schedule. He planted a crop that season on holdings east of Memphis.

In 1875 Forrest expanded his commitment to farming. Shelby County, Tennessee solicited bids for the leasing of its prisoners. Its jail in downtown Memphis was badly overcrowded, and it needed a quick solution to its housing problem. With a source of cheap labor at hand Forrest seized the opportunity to submit a bid. He had utilized convict labor successfully in his railroad venture.

At the same time Forrest was asked by the owners of Presidents Island — a 6000-acre undeveloped island in the Mississippi River just south of Memphis — if he was interested in leasing it. "I am very interested if I can acquire cheap labor," he told both the Island's owners and Shelby County officials overseeing the bidding process. "But the Island has to be cleared first before any planting can occur."

At the court hearing on his bid, his experienced business mind was at work in making his case. "Gentlemen, as I understand it, persons sentenced to work out fines are sent to jail, and it costs you 40 cents a day to house and feed them," said Forrest. "My proposition is that for each and every jailbird you place at my disposal, I shall pay Shelby County 10 cents a day for each one of them. And I will be responsible for housing them, clothing them and feeding them. Yes, 10 cents per head plus taking care of all overhead on these jailbirds." The County quickly accepted Forrest's bid. The lease was effective July 9, 1875.

His 28-year old son, William, joined him in the management of this prison plantation. The so-called "jailbirds" were not hardened criminals in the true sense. Most were petty thieves, town drunks and bigamists. Sentences ranged from one to six months. And most were black males.

Forrest, the experienced organizer and disciplinarian,

quickly implemented a hard, no-nonsense penal farm system. Work schedules were set with military precision. Prisoners worked from dawn to dark. The lash was Forrest's symbol of authority. Punishment was meted out if a prisoner was judged not to have done a full day's work.

The so-called "jailbirds" led a harsh, austere life. They were quartered in crude, wooden huts with no amenities.

The first year prisoners spent their time clearing trees and brush to prepare the land for cultivation. Forrest realized no income. But by 1876 he had 1200 acres ready for a cotton and a corn crop.

That summer Forrest's health declined rapidly. Few of his friends knew how sick he was. He seldom ventured into Memphis, and none came out to the Island to visit him. He was almost a recluse.

But as weak as he was, Forrest accepted an invitation to attend the reunion of the 7th Tennessee Cavalry — the original unit — at Covington, Tennessee on September 21, 1876.

Seated on horseback before the veterans and their families, the haggard, gray-haired hero of the 7th Tennessee Cavalry spoke to a hushed crowd in a surprisingly firm voice:

Soldiers, I was afraid that I could not be with you today, but I could not bear the thought of not meeting with you, and I will always try to meet with you in the future.

He continued his prepared remarks by recalling the hardships they had endured and praising them for their bravery in fighting for a cause they thought right. He paid special honor to those who died in battle.

Then he concluded his remarks with a plea for reconciliation. He paused for a few seconds while looking out over the crowd and mustering up his strength to finish, he said softly:

I love the old flag of the United States, and I hope that you do too despite the circumstances of the late War. God bless you all, friends.

A huge cheer rang out and the band played *Dixie* as the proud Forrest feebly dismounted, embraced Mary who was standing nearby, then entered the carriage for the 35 mile trip back to Presidents Island.

Forrest, exhausted by the ordeal of speaking while mounted on a horse, didn't speak until they have traveled several miles. Then, looking at Mary wistfully he said, "I've been rejuvenated by the reception I received from my soldiers. I've got to be truthful, Mary. I loved that war...the excitement and danger...and the comradeship. Today I realized all of that."

He stared at Mary for a moment and noticed a certain sadness on her face. Realizing that she may have had her feelings hurt, he said laughing, "Of course, Mary, I've always loved you more than that old war." She squeezed his hand in appreciation.

Dr. James Cowan, his wartime friend and physician as well as being Mary's cousin, often wrote to the Forrests after the war. He had practiced briefly in Memphis in 1865 and 1866; then moved his practice to Nashville, before relocating to Tullahoma, Tennessee in 1873 — a town 70 miles southeast of Nashville. Realizing that Forrest's health was declining rapidly, he begged him to spend some time at Hurricane Springs, a health spa and resort near Tullahoma. "The sulphur and freestone waters will do you a world of good. Why, you can drink it, soak in it and inhale the vapors. It will restore your entire system to a healthier state," wrote Dr. Cowan. "And besides that, Bedford, it will give me an opportunity to visit with my cousin Mary."

Memphis doctors advised Forrest to get off Presidents Island. "It's a haven of miasma," he was told. "The marsh vapor from the decaying animal and vegetable matter causes malaria. The air is poisoning your system."

Forrest's health declined further in the early summer of 1877. Finally, he decided to accept Dr. Cowan's invitation to Hurricane Springs. In late August Mary and he left for Tullahoma. Forrest knew he was dying, and this decision was a last desperate attempt to cleanse his system. He urinated constantly. He ate and drank liquids continually throughout the day. He was fatigued and nauseated, and breathed deeply.

Dr. Cowan was at Hurricane Springs to greet the Forrests when they arrived on August 25th. Forrest was familiar with the area. He was born in nearby Chapel Hill.

After settling in, Dr. Cowan and Forrest discussed the latter's symptoms. Cowan advised, "Bedford, you need rest and you need to cleanse your system of impurities. This sulphur vapor and this clean mountain air will do wonders. I am prescribing an herbal tea as an enema to cleanse your system immediately. And, Bedford, you're going to love the waters. The sulphur looks like bourbon and water mixed."

Every day, while Forrest soaked in the sulphur waters, he talked with Dr. Cowan. Mostly, Forrest wanted to talk about his war experiences and his frustrations dealing with the Confederate hierarchy. He said very little about the failure of his Selma, Marion & Memphis Railroad.

"James, one of my greatest disappointments was not meeting Robert E. Lee," said Forrest. "I had no opportunity to go to Virginia before Lee's death in 1870. I was never summoned to Richmond during the war. They thought I was a goddamn freak and an embarrassment because I hadn't been in the pre-war U.S. Army. Those goddamn West Pointers hung together like Mississippi clay, and they made damn sure no goddamn slave trader was going to penetrate that tight circle.

"Lee, I understand, was a good fellow. If nothing else, he believed in preserving the traditions of the South at the cost of his distinguished career in the regular army and possibly high political office. Of course we all gave up something to fight, but we probably didn't have as much to lose as he did."

"Bedford, when you think of Robert E. Lee, you wonder how officers like Bragg could have risen so high and had so much influence."

"Don't get me started on Bragg. I'm sick enough without getting worked up about that grizzled fool. About the only good thing he ever did was to pick Wheeler for cavalry command. What's that old saying? Even a blind pig occasionally finds an acorn. Maybe I didn't think so at the time, but looking back he picked a good soldier. Wheeler was as tough as boiled owls. That little fellow didn't back away from anything. He was as fine an officer as the Confederate army had in the field. Yes, I was upset the way he handled the fight at Dover, but he was man enough to admit his mistakes. He was all book learning at the time. That book he wrote on cavalry tactics affected his judgment. All that stuff about parade ground formations, wheeling around dozens of horses at one time, and sabre charges didn't make sense to me. Hell, most of the time we were dismounted when we fought. The only fancy maneuvers were by the horseholders back of the lines feeding the animals oats or corn. Heh-heh-heh.

"I saw Wheeler shortly after the war. He was a merchant in New Orleans at the time. Now I hear he's a lawyer in Alabama. Remind me to write him a letter when I get back to Memphis."

"That's a good idea, Bedford. If that's what you think of Wheeler, let him know. He'll appreciate it."

"James, another fellow I didn't give enough credit to was Chalmers. He was so proud. He resented me something awful. I frankly didn't think he'd fit in with the rest of the officers."

"Don't you think he was resentful because Richmond didn't promote him to a higher command in 1863? Chalmers had a remarkable field record beginning with Shiloh."

"Maybe I should have tried to do more for him when he was with us. The truth is we needed him. He was bold and he had a quick mind. Anyway, if I would have interceded for him that jug-eared Bragg would have thrown my recommendation into the latrine."

"You're probably right, Bedford."

Two days later Forrest received a visit from his former aide, Major Charles Anderson. He had come down from Murfreesboro for an overnight visit. Dr. Cowan had notified him that Forrest was at Hurricane Springs.

"Anderson, it's good to see you. How are you getting along?"

The quiet, pleasant Anderson, although terribly distressed at seeing Forrest's emaciated body, smiled broadly. "I'm fine, General. Farming agrees with me."

"Yes, I hear you are a prominent citizen in Rutherford County. How is your good wife, Mattie?"

"Fine, sir. We're celebrating our silver wedding anniversary this year."

"Twenty-five years. That's good. Mary and I are celebrating 32. We're lucky fellows."

"Yes, sir."

"Anderson, something has bothered me for years and I mean to rectify it right now."

"What's that, sir?"

"Well, I never thanked you properly for all you did for me in the war. You fought bravely; you preformed valuable staff assistance; and you wrote all those letters and orders for me. And you were always agreeable and never got upset with my wicked temper and my cussing. I know what a good Baptist you are! I guest Baptists are a forgiving flock, judging from your patience."

"I was honored to serve with you, General Forrest. If there is anything I can do for you, just ask."

"That's very kind of you, Anderson. You can say a prayer for me. Does that request surprise you? Well, don't look so shocked! Mary and her parson in Memphis, Reverend Stainback, have shown me the correct path to follow. Sometimes I can't believe what a sinful life I have led. But getting sick has given me concern that I better get right with the *Lord.*

"I shall pray indeed, General. I shall pray for a speedy recovery and many more years of personal peace."

"Thank you, Major."

Forrest and Mary returned to Presidents Island on Saturday, September 15th. They had enjoyed the visit to Hurricane Springs, and during their short stay at the spa, the General felt better temporarily as a result of the sulphur waters and the rest.

But the severe hunger and thirst, and the need to urinate frequently, returned almost immediately. His new prescribed diet was meat and limewater, but no carbohydrates. The result was slow starvation.

Matt Gallaway, who continued to monitor his friend's condition, was told by doctors that the General was ailing from either miasma or amoebic dysentery. But they did admit that little was known about internal disorders. The remedies they were prescribing were on a trial-and-error basis.

Mary was constantly at her husband's bedside. They spent his waking hours talking about their marriage and his conversion to religion. Mary asked if he wished her to write letters to any of his friends.

"Please write to General Wheeler for me, Mary. You know what to say. You overheard my conversation about Wheeler with your cousin at Hurricane Springs."

"All right. Is there anyone else? How about General Taylor? You admired him greatly."

"Yes, write him and tell him how much I have valued his friendship. Mention that I am not feeling well, but that I expect to be active shortly.

"Also, write to General Johnston. Tell him how much I appreciated his remarks about my wartime performance. As you know, Mary, compliments were scarce from those West Pointers running the war."

"Bedford," said Mary with a mischievous twinkle in her eyes. " It's too bad General Bragg isn't alive so you could have a nice letter written to him."

"Oh, he was a thorn in my side. No, no, no. I wouldn't be that forgiving."

"I knew that would rouse you and rekindle your fighting spirit."

"We better get you dressed, Bedford. Remember, Reverend Stainback is coming about 2:00 p.m. today. I know how you are enjoying his visits."

"Yes, I like him, Mary. I truly believe he's the only person on this earth other than you that I can discuss my feelings with. He listens and he understands."

Thursday, October 25, 1877, the day of Reverend Stainback's visit, was a warm autumn day. Forrest was sitting in a chair on the front porch of his small frame house when Stainback arrived.

"Hello, General. I'm pleased to see you," said the affable clergyman. "The *Lord* has provided us with a glorious autumn afternoon."

"I'm about the same, Reverend. The weather may be warm, but I need this blanket on me just the same. How are things in Memphis?"

"Oh, just average, I guess. We still have our sinners, but I have high hopes for them."

"Well, Reverend, with what you've done for me, I'd say Memphis now has one less sinner."

"I'm happy to hear you say that, General. In our business we use the expression, 'It's never too late.'"

"I've got some things to discuss with you, Reverend. I hope you don't mind."

"Of course not. That's why I came to visit you."

"Reverend, I am embarrassed about my financial status. Since the collapse of the railroad I have almost killed myself laboring to pay off my creditors. I want to live long enough to pay each and every dollar I owe. My honor is at stake.

"I accept the possibility of death, but I don't like the

thought of leaving this life not having squared accounts. I hate owing anyone. I've been a sinner and I may have to pay for it. I may be headed for Purgatory. In my life — or at least before I got sick — when someone was trying to whip me, I could handle myself. But death is a cruel joke. I do want to be able to hang on long enough for the world to say, 'Nathan Bedford Forrest was an honorable man. He squared his debts.'"

"The Lord will forgive you, General. He is understanding. And I dare say your creditors will not doubt for a moment your honesty and integrity as a man. But what is really important is that you have given your heart to the *Lord Jesus*. That is what really matters."

"Reverend, you have given me peace with what you have said today. I have put my trust in my *Lord and Savior*."

Forrest extended his emaciated hand to Reverend Stainback and thanked him for his counsel.

"General, I shall be back again in a few days. We shall talk some more."

On Saturday, October 27th Forrest was visited by Reverend Suratt, pastor of the First Methodist Church of Memphis. He prayed with Forrest briefly, then holding the General's hand he sang softly, *Nearer My God To Thee*. The once powerful and fearless Forrest wept when Reverend Suratt finished singing.

Early Sunday Forrest's physical condition worsened. Jesse, his brother, was there at the time. He suggested to Mary that the General might be better off in Memphis where it would be easier for doctors to look in on him. Jesse suggested his house on Union Street. "I have my carriage here and we can leave immediately," said Jesse. Mary agreed it was a good idea.

By 11:00 a.m. Forrest was safely in the guest bedroom of Jesse's house, a modest, two-story frame structure close to the street. The General was conscious but barely able to speak.

Jefferson Davis had been in Memphis for a few days

visiting his wife, Varina, and his daughter. The latter were living in Memphis. Davis had moved from Memphis shortly after he failed in his insurance business as agent for the Carolina Insurance Company. He was living in Beauvoir, the plantation on the Mississippi Gulf Coast owned by a friend of the Davises, Sarah Anne Dorsey.

Davis was visiting at the Peabody Hotel when he heard the news that General Forrest had just been brought to Jesse Forrest's house, a few blocks from the Hotel.

At noon Davis sent a messenger to Jesse Forrest's house with a note to Mary Forrest asking permission to visit her husband that afternoon. Mary responded, "Your visit will cheer him. Please come by."

At 2:00 p.m., the 69-year old, tall, ramrod-straight ex President of the Confederacy arrived alone. Upon learning from Mary Forrest that the General's doctors were expected soon, Davis promised his visit would be brief.

Davis walked into the semi-dark, partially-furnished bedroom. He noticed the walls were bare except for a faded portrait of George Washington.

"Hello, General, I'm pleased to see you," said Davis in a soft voice.

Forrest looked up, surprised to see Davis there in his bedroom. "Mr. President...Mr. President," Forrest stammered. "I hate for you to see me this way. I'm completely broke up. I am broke in fortune, broke in health and broke in spirit."

Davis was shocked at Forrest's appearance. There, lying in front of him was a living skeleton of a man barely alive. "Is this the same person I remember seeing for the first time at the Exchange Hotel in Montgomery 14 years ago?" he thought to himself. Davis remembered the energetic and volatile six-foot, 185 pound Forrest of 1863 whose powerful personality frightened many in his presence.

Forrest extended his spidery hand a few inches along the mattress. Davis reached out to grasp it realizing that

Forrest couldn't lift it off the bed.

Not much was said during the 15 minute visit. Forrest stared at Davis as if pleading desperately for help. All Davis could do was to gently squeeze Forrest's hand and stare into his deep-sunk eyes.

Davis, by nature not a sentimental man, was visibly shaken. He felt uncomfortable and totally helpless. He rose from his chair, looked at Forrest one last time, then said, "Goodbye." Forrest probably didn't hear Davis. He appeared to be sleeping as Davis bid farewell and left the room.

In the parlor Davis spoke briefly with Mary Forrest. "I shall be back in a few days, Mary," said Davis.

"Do you think he will get better, Mr. Davis?"

"Yes, Ma'am," replied Davis politely although he thought to himself that there wasn't any hope of recovery. "He is very sick, but your husband has never been known to give up."

"I know Bedford appreciates your visit. You help bring back memories of the days he was gallantly fighting in the war. Thank you so much!"

Late that afternoon Forrest fell into a deep sleep. Undoubtedly the carriage ride from Presidents Island, the visit of Jefferson Davis, and the prolonged examination by a team of doctors exhausted him.

Mary, as she had done the previous six weeks, kept a vigil at his bedside. Jesse was out in front of the house answering questions from the General's friends and many curious local citizens who knew him only by reputation.

On Monday, October 29th, Forrest faded in and out of comas all day. His bedroom had a mixture of odors. The combination of herbal teas, medicines and urine emitted a powerful aroma within the small bedroom. The windows were closed to prevent Forrest from getting chills.

At 6:30 p.m. Minor Meriwether, along with his young son, Lee, came to visit Forrest.

"I shouldn't let you in, Minor," explained Mary. "He is barely able to speak. And he may not recognize you. But you are one of his oldest friends, and he would be disappointed to learn I had turned you away. Please go upstairs."

Forrest recognized Meriwether as he entered the bedroom with his son. " Is that your son, Minor? Have him come over here," said Forrest in a whisper. "Come here. Don't be afraid."

Young Lee Meriwether approached Forrest hesitantly. He had never seen anyone dying, and he was frightened. He withdrew from the bedside when Forrest went into a coma.

The Meriwethers sat for a few minutes just staring at Forrest. He didn't appear to be breathing. Minor Meriwether reached out and placed his hand over Forrest's heart. He turned to his son. "Lee, it's still. The General is dead. He just went to sleep."

The time of death was approximately 7:15 p.m. General Forrest was 56 years old.

Minor Meriwether notified Jesse Forrest first. "I'm not surprised, Minor. It's a miracle he hung on so long. It hurt us all to see him so helpless, "said Jesse Forrest. "I'll break the news to Mary, and his son. They're downstairs visiting with Matt and Fannie Gallaway."

Minor and Lee Meriwether walked out of Jesse Forrest's house at 7:30 p.m. The temperature was a mild 61 degrees. Across the street were a group of reporters and a few Memphis policemen huddled in small groups. Local editors had anticipated that General Forrest's death was imminent and had assigned their reporters to stand vigil. A big story was in their grasp. General Forrest was still a national figure twelve and one-half years after the war had ended.

Pondering Forrest's death as he walked away from the house, Minor Meriwether shook his head resignedly. Then he looked at his son. "Lee, who would have believed that General Nathan Bedford Forrest, the ferocious Confederate cavalry leader, would die peacefully in his sleep?"

31 • Funeral

At 7:00 a.m. in Memphis on Wednesday, October 31, 1877, the day of General Forrest's funeral, bells at the Court Street Cumberland Presbyterian, the First Presbyterian, the First Baptist and 12 other churches, started ringing. Each of the bells rang for 56 strokes — Forrest's age at death — then a pause of 15 seconds before repeating the 56 strokes again and again until 12:00 noon. Some bells made harsh, discordant, deep-based sounds; others made clear, higher-pitched melodious sounds. The bells rang incessantly in staccato fashion.

By 8:00 a.m. a line of some 200 people, including many black citizens, lined up on Union Street for admittance into Jesse Forrest's house to view the General's body. Lafcadio Hearn, the *Cincinnati Commercial* reporter who had disembarked from the packet A.C. Donnally just the day before was also there hoping for a few more interviews.

Undertaker G.H. Holst, who had just emerged from Jesse Forrest's house, was approached by Hearn. "Mr Holst, do you know the cause of death of General Forrest? I'm Hearn, a reporter from Cincinnati, and I'm covering the story."

"Mr. Hearn, it could have been any number of things. His body was badly wasted. He was little more than a skeleton at death. Frankly, I'm surprised he survived as long as he did.

"What's your impression of this crowd? Surprising, isn't it? Look at all the Negroes in line. Old Forrest made his living before the war buying and selling them like livestock."

"Mr. Holst, why do you think they are here? Did they come voluntarily, or do you think someone paid them to put on a little show? My impression is that the Negroes feared him. Forrest was the symbol of the evil white master."

"Well, Hearn, to insinuate somebody paid them is a little cynical, isn't it?" Holst looked at Hearn with a slight whimsical smile, and then carefully choosing his words, replied, "They may have come to confirm the fact that he is dead."

Holst wished Hearn good luck, and headed toward his mortuary on Main Street to check last minute funeral details with his staff.

About 9:30 a.m. Hearn saw Jefferson Davis step out of a carriage near the Forrest house.

"President Davis!...President Davis!...May I have a word with you. I'm Hearn with the *Cincinnati Commercial.*"

"Yes, of course, but you'll have to be brief."

"Sir, what is your assessment of General Forrest?"

"Military or business or personal? What?"

"Military, sir."

"Mr. Hearn, Forrest was a formidable cavalry commander. He was a resourceful, ingenious leader who demonstrated resolve and courage at all times," answered Davis as if he had pre-prepared the statement.

"Why didn't recognition come from Confederate leadership in Richmond, Mr. Davis?"

"Several reasons, I suppose. He didn't have a military background. Most of our commanders had been in the regular army before the war. Many fought in the Mexican War or against the Seminoles down in Florida. All these officers know each other. Forrest was completely unknown to them. He was an outsider with nothing in common with them. And, of course, he was unpolished and the butt of much malicious humor because of that.

"Then, of course, Forrest never had a command in the Eastern Theater — primarily Virginia. That's where major newspapers had their correspondents. So Forrest never got much publicity other than what he got from the Fort Pillow incident. And that was mostly negative, and left a deep mark on him.

"I myself misjudged his contributions. Largely, my opinions were formed from information fed me by my immediate staff and some old line field generals. They characterized Forrest as a reckless raider and a misfit. I deeply regret he never received full recognition for his contributions.

"I cannot talk with you any longer, Mr. Hearn. They're signaling me to come inside with the other pallbearers. Perhaps we shall meet again."

"Thank you, Mr. President."

Pallbearers met with Chief Marshall Butler P. Anderson at 9:45 a.m. to receive their instructions. The most prominent of the 12 selected were Jefferson Davis; Tennessee Governor James D. Porter; and Jacob Thompson, Southern financier and controversial Confederate agent who operated in England and Canada during the war. Also in the group were Forrest's long-time friends and wartime aides, Matt Gallaway and Gilbert Rambaut. The Odd Fellows Lodge in which Forrest was active had six representatives.

Six pallbearers walked on each side of the horse-drawn hearse on its one-quarter mile route to the Court Street Cumberland Presbyterian Church. Jefferson Davis led on one side; Jacob Thompson, on the other.

All businesses, government offices and schools closed from 10:00 a.m. to 2:00 p.m. to give the public an opportunity to bid farewell to General Forrest. Many shopkeepers, and all of the hotels and restaurants along the route of the funeral procession, draped their buildings in black.

The streets were jammed with people straining for a glimpse at the casket and Forrest's widow, Mary, whose face was hidden behind a black crepe veil. Forrest's son, William, rode in a carriage behind the hearse with his mother.

Police had difficulty clearing a path to the church. There were 7000 people crowded in the street near the entrance. None expected to be admitted inside since the few hundred seats available had been assigned to special guests and friends of the Forrest family.

At 11:45 a.m. Forrest's body was carried in the church. The casket was opened, and guests were invited to pass in single file to view the General for the last time. Most were shocked at the appearance of Forrest. The ravages of his illness made some gasp. His flesh was drawn tightly over his face. His skull was quite visible. The once robust six foot, 185 pound warrior had been reduced to an emaciated skeleton of a man weighing no more than 100 pounds. The body seemed too tiny for the Confederate officer's uniform with which it had been dressed. And those who had not seen Forrest for several years were surprised that his hair and beard were snow white. "How could this man have been only 56 years old?" some wondered. "I wish they had kept the casket closed," others said sadly shaking their heads.

Exactly at 12:00 noon the pallbearers moved the rosewood casket richly trimmed with silver to a bier near the pulpit where Reverend George P. Stainback, pastor of the Court Street Cumberland Presbyterian Church; Reverend David Walk; Reverend S.B. Suratt and Reverend Eugene Daniels were waiting.

Reverend Walk read the *Nineteenth Psalm*, and also selections from the *Fifteenth Chapter of Paul's First Epistle to the Corinthians*. Reverend Daniels sang, *Rock of Ages*. Reverend Suratt and Reverend Daniels then gave brief eulogies.

Reverend Stainback, a Confederate war veteran, approached the pulpit to give the principal tribute. For the first five minutes he described the hardships of Forrest's early life on the frontier. He praised his resolve to overcome all obstacles in his path to become not only a war hero, but an outstanding citizen. "No one can deny his dedication to the South and his unflinching patriotism," said the pastor emphatically.

Then, Reverend Stainback changed direction in his remarks. "One November evening in 1875 General Forrest, not previously known as a religious person and church man, attended the service here with his beloved wife, Mary. After the service the General and Mary approached me in the vestibule. He said to me, 'Sir, your sermon tonight has moved the last prop from me. I am the fool who has built his house upon the sand. I am the miserable lost sinner you described.' And General Forrest stood there trembling while great tears ran down his cheeks. And I said, General Forrest, thank *God* for this. When a man realizes the fact that he has been building his house on sand he is clearing the way to get it on the rock.

"Six days ago, as he lay dying, he confessed to me that he had said many things not like a Christian and done many things he should not have done, and that no man ever felt this more keenly than he did. And then he said, 'But *God* has forgiven me. All is peace here. I want you to know that between me and my *God* there is no cloud. Tell my brethren and sisters that for the past six weeks I have lain in my bed and communed with my *God*. Tell them to take up their cross and follow their *Savior*. Tell my old comrades in sin to give their hearts to *God* and seek a higher and holier life.'"

Reverend Stainback concluded the service by leading those assembled in the church in *The Lord's Prayer*.

The pallbearers proceeded to carry the casket out to Court Street to the hearse parked directly in front of the entrance. Chief Marshall Anderson was mounted on his horse. He had just completed conferring with his assistant marshalls who assured him all units were in line, and that as soon as the carriages transporting Forrest's family and relatives, the clergymen, and the pallbearers were loaded, the procession to Elmwood Cemetery — some three and one-half miles distant — could proceed.

Again the huge crowd on Court Street delayed the departure. Many pushed their way forward to try to touch the hearse. The police, who had tried to form a cordon around the hearse, good-naturedly gave up. Captain Leonard Halderman frantically pleaded with the crowd to back away. "You may panic the horses. Someone may get hurt. Please back away," he pleaded. Halderman said to his fellow officer, Captain Hoke, "Why don't these people show some respect?" Hoke answered, "They mean well. Let's wait two or three minutes, then form a wedge so the hearse can move forward."

The crowd slowly dispersed. Most raced over to Main Street to try to find a place to view the procession. Some 20,000 persons — many who had come from miles around — lined the long route to the cemetery. People were on roof tops, on balconies, on ladders and boxes or packed tightly along the sidewalk to witness the most spectacular procession in the city's history. Many war veterans wore their medals on their coats.

The cortege moved north on Second Street to Poplar; then west on Poplar one block to Main Street; then south on Main Street — the city's principal street — to Vance Street; then another one and one-half miles to Elmwood Cemetery.

Chief Marshall Anderson and his staff wore gray top

hats and dark gray coats and trousers. Each was adorned with a light blue sash and a colorful maroon rosette attached to his coat lapel. Anderson was an imposing figure. He was tall, robust, with sandy-colored sideburns and a jutting jaw. He was the perfect physical symbol of authority. Immediately behind the marshals, creating eddies of dust and a rumbling noise, was a contingent of 200 ex-Confederates on horseback. Many had ridden into Memphis that morning from nearby northern Mississippi and from West Tennessee counties to pay final honor to General Forrest. The majority were dressed in everyday work clothes. Most wore soft, wool slouch hats typical of those worn during the war. A few wore kepi — the gray cap with the flat, round top and stiff black visor. None were in full uniform at the request of the funeral committee. A few, however, wore their old, gray tunics with their medals prominently displayed on chests. There was also a smattering of Confederate *Stars and Bars* flags and military standards representing some of Forrest's old battalions.

Because of the dust and litter from the horses, Professor Herman Arnold's Brass Band of cornets, trombones, tenor and baritone horns and tubas maintained a respectful distance to give the city's street cleaners time to sweep. The tall, distinguished-looking, mustachioed Professor was dressed in solid white except for gold buttons and braid. His 30 bandsmen were in dark blue uniforms and white caps. No public ceremony in Memphis was complete without Arnold's Brass Band led by the 40-year old musician known throughout the South for being the first to arrange the score for *Dixie*.

As the procession moved slowly south on Main Street the band played again-and-again Chopin's *Dead March*. Only when halted temporarily at the main entrance to the Peabody Hotel did it break this routine. Assembled in front of the hotel were many of General Forrest's field officers and personal staff. First, Professor Arnold ordered the band to face the Hotel, then he directed his band in a rousing version of *Dixie*. Next, the band played *Auld Lang Syne*. The crowd did not applaud, but Hearn observed as he scanned the crowd that most were deeply moved, and a few were crying unabashedly following the Band's inspiring tribute to their Confederate war hero and comrade.

Professor Arnold ordered, "Left face;" and the bandsmen in unison made a 90° turn, and moved south on Main Street once again playing the slow, mournful *Dead March*.

Cannons had been positioned on the nearby Mississippi River bluff near Front Street; and they were being fired at one minute intervals as a salute to General Forrest. A local military group, the Memphis Artillery, was in charge of firing the 12-pounder Napoleons and the 10-pounder Parrot guns.

Lafcadio Hearn mingled freely in the crowd near the Peabody to talk with a cross-section of citizens gathered there. "What do you think of this procession?" he asked several bystanders. Most answered somberly, "The General was a hero to us who lived through the war. Times were terrible for us Confederates here in West Tennessee after the Federals moved in here in 1862, and General Forrest and his cavalry gave us hope we'd win. It's only right we honor him." Others said, "Forrest was one of us. There is no bigger hero in the South than the General."

Several admitted Forrest was controversial. "He had his faults. He could be a fearsome adversary in war or in business. He was unique, I'll say that," said a tall, distinguished looking man about Forrest's age who admitted he had served in the Union Army in West Tennessee.

Another spectator, who was standing nearby offered this unsolicited comment to Hearn, "I heard he got religion just before he died. Isn't that something? He's a fellow who killed people without remorse; swore oaths against the *Lord*; and spent much of his life gambling and associating with scoundrels and vermin up and down the river. If *God* forgives him, He is indeed a merciful, although slightly confused, *Maker*. Confessing his sins may have made the General feel better, but it does nothing to make up for all the pain and fear he caused hundreds of people during his life. Sir, he wasn't what I would call an exemplary citizen."

Hearn, slightly taken aback by the blunt spectator, asked, "Do you think General Forrest was a hero? What about his war record? Doesn't that tend to compensate for all of what you just said?"

"No, it doesn't. Forrest enjoyed the war whereas most of us who served did so out of loyalty to the South. Forrest saw it as a license to kill people. He had no real convictions."

Directly in front of Hearn was a Memphis policeman trying to control the crowd. Hearn asked, "What do you think of this funeral procession?"

"Sir, General Forrest would have enjoyed his own funeral. It's well-organized. Like Forrest, those old friends of his who planned this left no stone unturned. There's been attention to detail. No doubt about it, he taught most of them how to organize something like this."

Following behind Professor Arnold's Brass Band were three local military organizations: the Chickasaw Guards, the Bluff City Grays, and the Memphis Light Guards. Members came largely from Memphis' elite families. Their primary function was ceremonial. They competed against each other in drilling contests, and carried on the traditions of predecessor militia groups that went off to war in 1861.

The Chickasaw Guards, with some 40 members dressed in blue uniforms with red piping and black helmets with red plumes, carried their rifles in a reversed arms position as was the custom at military funerals.

The Bluff City Grays, in gray uniforms with gold collars and braid, carried sabers. And the third group, the Memphis Light Guards, wore dark suits and white gloves. They carried no weapons.

Next in line were the colorful, elaborately-costumed delegation from the Odd Fellows Lodge. They were there to honor their long-time member. The 150 lodge members were adorned with yellow and red sashes, braid on their black coats and hats with ostrich plumes. All had scabbard and blade attached to their left sides. Their marching precision rivaled that of the preceding military companies.

The crowd applauded softly as the carriages bearing Jefferson Davis and the other pallbearers, and the clergymen led by Reverend Stainback, moved by.

Then, a stillness fell over the crowd as the hearse bearing Forrest's body, arrived in line. It was a black vehicle trimmed with black plumes set in urns positioned on top at the corners. Heavy plate glass windows on each side permitted the crowd to view the rosewood coffin. The four jet black horses pulling the hearse were draped with veils of netting. The driver was dressed in livery. His coat was single-breasted, buttoned up to his neck. He wore black kid gloves and a black top hat.

The only noise came from the cannon fire on the river bluffs. Hearn recorded in his notebook crowd reactions as the hearse passed by. He wrote, "Many were in tears, particularly the women; others waved their handkerchiefs tentatively as a silent gesture of farewell. Children were lifted by their fathers to give them a look at the hearse bearing the fallen Confederate hero."

The carriage behind the hearse transporting Forrest's widow, Mary, and their son, William, was enclosed. Only the silhouette of Mrs. Forrest could be seen. As they had done when the hearse passed, men in the crowd removed their hats as a sign of respect to Forrest's widow and son.

Hearn listening intently to crowd reaction overheard one woman say to a friend. "The Forrests were married 32 years. One wonders what it was like living with the General. She is such a quiet, religious lady." The other woman just shook her head indicating she didn't know.

Mayor Flippen and the city council followed the Forrest family carriage. Hearn noted some unfavorable comments about the city officials. "What are they doing here? Politicians have no business trying to capitalize on this funeral," said one cynical observer to a group of his friends. The latter nodded in agreement.

The crowd's spirits were lifted at least momentarily when a large company of Memphis firemen paraded by. They were dressed with blue trousers, and bright red shirts and suspenders and black fire hats.

As Hearn moved among the crowd hoping to get one last interview before the funeral procession ended, he noticed a stooped, elderly-looking man with a long flowing white beard who was wearing a worn Confederate gray jacket and holding a brown felt hat across his chest as the Confederate veterans passed by. He thought it odd that a man this old was wearing part of a Confederate uniform. Approaching him Hearn asked, "Sir, were you in the Confederate service? I am curious why you are wearing the uniform. What was your relationship with General Forrest?"

"Mister, what business is it of yours? Who in-the-hell are you anyhow?"

"My name's Hearn. I'm a reporter covering the funeral. I'm trying to capture the opinions of ordinary people about the General."

"All right, I did serve with the General. It's probably hard for you to believe an old reprobate like me could have been in his cavalry. Cris' sakes, it was a goddamn honor. He's the best warrior the Confederates ever had. He wasn't afraid of nobody or nothin.' He was in the thick of every charge like the rest of us."

"May I ask your name, sir?"

It's Sergeant David P. Hummer, Forrest's Cavalry, August 10, 1861 to May 9, 1865. Are you going to put my name in the newspaper, Mister? I'd like to send a copy to my kinfolk up in Michigan."

"I'm a correspondent for the *Cincinnati Commercial*. Maybe the article will be reprinted in the *Memphis Daily Appeal*. Your papers here often carry items about Memphis that appear in out-of-town newspapers. Ask Editor Gallaway over at his office on Second Street."

"I will, Mister. Make damn sure you say good things about General Forrest. You Yankees have damned him ever since Fort Pillow for no good reason."

Hearn smiled and wished the old veteran well.

By the time the final group of veterans on foot passed the Peabody Hotel, Hearn noted that the procession had taken one hour and fifteen minutes to pass. Quickly, he introduced himself to one of the Memphis Police commanders, and asked if he could ride with his party to Elmwood Cemetery.

"Jump on board, young man. We'll get you out there before the procession shows up. We'll take an alternate route to get around the procession," said the hospitable police commander, Terrance Keenan.

Within half an hour Hearn was at the cemetery. "Mr. Hearn, come with me," said Keenan. "I'll get you close to the grave. It's over there beneath those towering oaks. If anyone questions you, tell them Captain Keenan gave you permission."

"Thank you, Captain. You have been very helpful."

"That's quite all right, Mr. Hearn. I want the world to get the full account of this magnificent farewell."

By 3:00 p.m. the pallbearers had unloaded the coffin and transported it graveside. Police formed a large square cordon around the grave to permit privacy for Forrest's family and close friends who had gathered for one last look at the body before the Odd Fellows Lodge and its chaplain, Reverend Landrum, conducted the solemn fraternal burial ceremony.

It took 15 minutes for the Lodge officers to perform its ritual for their departed lodge brother. Then, the Chickasaw Guards moved into position some 15 yards from the grave. On the signal from Captain Carrie, the Guards fired three volleys high over the grave. Officially, the funeral was over. Some 44 hours after his death, General Nathan Bedford Forrest, CSA, was laid to rest in the tranquil Elmwood Cemetery.

After the crowd dispersed a group of students from the nearby State Female College were led to the grave. The young women carried armloads of flowers to be placed on the grave when the Negro gravediggers finished covering it up.

Hearn, who was kneeling on one knee as he wrote the last of his notes on his pad, was hailed by Minor Meriwether, who had been graveside with his wife, Elizabeth. "Well, Hearn, did you get a story for your paper?"

"Yes, sir. It's a much bigger story than I could have imagined when I first heard the news of General Forrest's death on the deck of the A.C. Donnally. Mr. Meriwether, I have one last question, "How is it possible that General Forrest packed all of that adventure into just 56 years of life?"

"Amazing, isn't it?" replied Meriwether shaking his

head. "I can assure you of one thing; the general will be restless in his grave."

Meriwether went into deep thought for a few moments, then asked, "Do you know Shakespeare, Mr. Hearn? Of course you do; you are European-educated.

"In *The Two Gentlemen of Verona* there is a statement apropos to the general's present state. Do you recall this line:'I reckon this always, that a man is never undone until he be hanged.' Ponder that Hearn."

Appendix:
Final Roll Call

Most of the major characters in this book led normal lives after the Civil War. Some distinguished themselves in business, the professions, politics, military service or as literary figures. A few experienced violent death.

I.

Major Charles W. Anderson, CSA. After the war he became a prominent citizen and farmer in Williamson County, Tennessee. He died in 1908 at 82.

William G. Brownlow. After resigning as Governor of Tennessee in 1869, he served one term in the United States Senate; then resumed editorship of *The Knoxville Whig*. Brownlow died in 1877 at 71.

General Abraham Buford, CSA. Returned to Kentucky to become one of the state's most prominent horsebreeders. The death of his wife and son, and financial reverses, led to suicide in 1884 at 64.

General James R. Chalmers, CSA. Resumed his law practice in Mississippi, and served in the United States Congress from 1877 to 1881, and again in 1884. Moved to Memphis in 1888 to practice law. Chalmers died in 1898 at 67.

Dr. James B. Cowan, CSA. Practiced medicine in Memphis briefly after the war; then moved his practice to Nashville, then to Selma, Alabama, and finally located permanently in Tullahoma, Tennessee in 1873. Cowan died in 1909 at 77.

Mary Montgomery Forrest. After General Forrest's death she lived quietly in Memphis, spending her time with son, William, and her grandchildren. Mrs. Forrest died in 1893 at 65.

Captain William Montgomery Forrest, CSA. Enrolled in the University of Mississippi to study law, then joined his father, General Forrest, first in the construction of the Selma, Marion & Memphis Railroad, then in the management of the Shelby County, Tennessee Penal Farm. Later worked as an engineer constructing levees. Forrest died in 1908 at 61.

Continued

Colonel Matthew C. Gallaway, CSA. Resumed editorship of *The Memphis Avalanche*. Then in 1870 became co-editor of the *Memphis Appeal*. Retired in 1887. Gallaway died in 1898 at 77.

Governor Isham G. Harris. Following the Confederate surrender he fled first to Mexico, then to England. Returned to Memphis in 1867 to enter a law partnership with General Gideon Pillow. Served in the United States Senate from 1877 until his death in 1897 at 79.

Colonel David C. Kelley, CSA. Returned to the ministry in late 1865 to become pastor of the largest Methodist Church in Nashville. Became a leader in the prohibitionist movement in the 1880s and 1890s. He authored religious tracts. Instrumental in the development of Vanderbilt University. Kelley died in 1909 at 76.

Colonel Minor Meriwether, CSA. During the initial years of of the Ku Klux Klan, he served as Supreme Counsellor. Moved to St. Louis in 1880 where he practiced law. Date of death unknown.

Captain John W. Morton, Jr., CSA. After the war he studied medicine at the University of Tennessee, then practiced medicine for 15 years before going into farming and politics. Served as Secretary of State of Tennessee for eight years. Morton died in 1914 at 71.

General Gideon J. Pillow, CSA. Returned to Memphis to resume his law practice. His partner was former Governor Isham G. Harris. Pillow died in 1879 at 72.

Major Gilbert V. Rambaut, CSA. After the war he was employed by a wholesale grocery and cotton factor firm in Memphis. He died in 1896 at 60.

Colonel Robert V. Richardson, CSA. Moved to New York to become vice president of the United States Cotton Co. Returned to Memphis in 1868 to oversee his cotton plantation interests. Murdered behind a tavern in Dunklin County, Missouri in 1870. Richardson was 49.

Major John P. Strange, CSA. Returned to the retailing business in Memphis. Strange died in 1875 at 51.

Samuel Tate. Continued his career of developing railroads in the South after the war, acquiring considerable wealth. Tate died in 1892 at 74.

Continued

II.

General Pierre G. T. Beauregard, CSA. At war's end he became president of the New Orleans, Jackson & Mississippi Railroad; then manager of the Louisiana Lottery. Beauregard died in New Orleans in 1893 at 74.

General Braxton Bragg, CSA. He served as superintendent of the New Orleans waterworks; chief engineer for harbor improvements at Mobile; then in 1874 he became chief engineer of the Gulf, Colorado & Sante Fe Railroad. He dropped dead on a street in Galveston, Texas in 1876 at age 59.

General John C. Breckinridge, CSA. He fled the United States at war's end. Returned in 1868 after being pardoned by President Andrew Johnson. Resumed his law practice in Kentucky, and was involved in railroad development in his home state. Breckinridge died in 1875 at 54.

Jefferson Davis, CSA. He was released from prison in Virginia in 1867, and went to England for a brief time. Settled in Memphis in 1870 to serve as agent for the Carolina Insurance Co. His investment in this firm, and his other entrepreneurial ventures, all ended in failure, leaving him destitute. He supported himself from lecture fees, and from a publisher's advance on his memoirs, *The Rise and Fall of the Confederate Government*, completed in 1881. Davis died in New Orleans in 1889 at 82.

General Basil W. Duke, CSA. Practiced law in Louisville; and was editor of *Southern Bivouac*, a veterans' magazine. He also authored several books on the Civil War. Duke died in 1916 at 78.

General John Bell Hood, CSA. After the war he settled in New Orleans where he worked in the commission business, and served also as president of the Louisiana branch of an insurance company. He wrote the book *Advance and Retreat: Personal Experiences in the United States and Confederate Armies*, published after his death. Hood died in the 1879 yellow fever epidemic in New Orleans at 48.

General Joseph E. Johnston, CSA. Engaged first in railroading in Alabama, then operated an insurance business in Savannah, Georgia. Johnston served one term in Congress as a representative from Virginia in 1879. In 1885 he was appointed to the U.S. Railroad Commission by

Continued

President Grover Cleveland. His book, *Narrative of Military Operations During the Late War Between the States*, was published in 1874. Johnston died in 1891 at age 84, one month after attending General Sherman's funeral in New York City.

General Stephen D. Lee, CSA. He returned from the war to engage in farming in Mississippi. In 1880 he became the first president of Mississippi Agricultural and Mechanical College [now Mississippi State University]. Lee died in 1908 at age 74.

General Leonidas Polk, CSA. He was killed on June 14, 1864 by an artillery shell while reconnoitering the Union army positions atop Pine Mountain, Georgia. Polk was 57.

Colonel Abel D. Streight, USA. Escaped from Libby Prison in February 1864, and rejoined Union Army. Served in the Nashville Campaign of December 1864 with General George Thomas' forces. Returned to Indianapolis after the war, and started a furniture factory, then built a wholesale lumber business. Defeated as a candidate for Governor of Indiana in 1880. Streight died in 1892 at 63.

General Richard Taylor, CSA. Spent considerable effort advocating Southern rights during the Reconstruction era. Interceded with President Andrew Johnson on behalf of Jefferson Davis. Taylor authored *Destruction and Reconstruction* in 1879. He died in New York later that year at 53.

General Joseph Wheeler, CSA. Released from prison after one month and returned to Alabama where he studied law and began practicing law. Wheeler was elected to Congress in 1880; defeated in 1882, but regained his seat in 1884 and served continually in that position until the Spanish-American War. He volunteered and commanded a cavalry unit in Cuba fighting at Santiago in July 1898. Wheeler published later that year the book, *Santiago Campaign*. He was reelected to Congress upon his return from Cuba. Wheeler died in 1906 in Brooklyn, New York at 69.

Continued

III.

Private George Washington Cable, CSA. After discharge in 1865, Cable became a reporter for the *New Orleans Picayune*. Thereafter he became a successful author, writing about life in Louisiana. He found much of his material in New Orleans' French Quarter. He remained a prominent literary figure for half a century. Cable died in 1925 at 81.

Horace Greeley. Retired as editor of the *New York Tribune* to make the run for the presidency as the candidate of the Democrat-Liberal Republican Party in 1872 against the Republican Party's candidate, President Grant. The popular vote was 3,597,000 for Grant, and 2,834,000 for Greeley. But the electoral vote was a landslide for Grant — 286 to 80. The combination of the death of his wife days before the election and his humiliating defeat by Grant probably contributed to his death at 61 just one month after the 1872 election.

Lafcadio Hearn. After leaving Memphis, he remained in New Orleans writing for several newspapers and launching his literary career. Hearn took assignments in Japan from American magazines and newspapers writing about life there. He married a Japanese woman and remained in Japan to become a professor of English at the Imperial University of Tokyo. From 1890 until his death in 1904 he authored many books using as background the customs, religion and literature of Japan. Hearn was 54 at death.

About the Author

Robert A. Sigafoos, born in 1923, is a native of Doylestown, Pennsylvania. He is Professor Emeritus from the University of Memphis where he served in the Fogelman College of Business and Economics until his retirement in 1985. Previously, he was an economic consultant to major U.S. corporations and government agencies.

His initial interest in the Civil War began on July 4th, 1938 when he visited the final encampment of Union and Confederate veterans held at Gettysburg celebrating the 75th anniversary of the battle. Strong interest in Confederate war history developed after moving to Memphis from California in 1973.

He is author of *Absolutely, Postively Overnight: The Story of Federal Express*, *Cotton Row to Beale Street*, *Corporate Real Estate Development: The Pursuit of America's Leading Corporations for Profit in Housing and Land Use*, and several other business books.

Sigafoos holds B.A. and M.A. degrees from Penn State and a Ph.D. in economics from Indiana University. During World War II, he was a medical first aid man in the 111th Infantry Regiment.

He lives in retirement in the Ozark Mountains of Arkansas with his wife, Katherine, and their long-haired, calico cat, Gremlin.

Dedication
This book is dedicated to my classmates of Doylestown (Pa.) High School, Class of 1941. Many of these wonderful people served honorably in World War II. Close friend, Don Chubb, never returned from the War.